Also by Emily Barr

Backpack
Baggage
Cuban Heels

Atlantic Shift

Emily Barr

review

This edition published in 2005 by REVIEW
First published in Great Britain in 2004
by REVIEW

An imprint of Headline Book Publishing

10 9 8 7 6 5 4 3 2 1

Cataloguing in Publication Data is available from the British Library

ISBN 0 7553 0194 3 (B Format)
ISBN 0 7553 2566 4 (A Format)

Typeset in Garamond Light by Palimpsest Book Production Limited,
Polmont, Stirlingshire

Printed and bound in Great Britain by
Mackays of Chatham plc, Chatham, Kent

Headline's policy is to use papers that are natural, renewable and recyclable
products and made from wood grown in sustainable forests. The logging and
manufacturing processes are expected to conform to the environmental regu-
lations of the country of origin.

HEADLINE BOOK PUBLISHING
A division of Hodder Headline
338 Euston Road
London NW1 3BH

www.reviewbooks.co.uk
www.hodderheadline.com

For my boys: James, Gabe and Sebastien

Thanks are due to the following people: Nadine Thompson, Sarah Howard and Providence Music in Bristol for helping out with details. Jonny Geller for being the best agent in town. Jane Morpeth and everyone else at Headline for making it such a pleasure. Tammy Gallacher: thanks for looking after Gabe while I wrote – he will miss you terribly. Thank you to all my friends for understanding that writing a book while pregnant, and in charge of a toddler, edged everything else out of my life for a while and meant that no one heard from me for months on end. Finally, thanks to James and Gabe for providing such gorgeous distractions, and for putting up with me, sick, tired, and busy for the past nine months. This is for you, with all my love.

chapter one

November 14th

I am halfway through a solo cello performance on stage at the London Palladium when I decide to leave my husband. I have been considering the idea for the past two years, half hoping that he would take action before I did. Now I realise that if I want to be free from Jack I must fashion my own freedom; and there will never be a perfect time to tell him. Tonight is an imperfect time for many reasons: it will do.

I have played this suite a hundred thousand times, so I let my mind wander, confident that the notes will keep coming. I want to turn my head, to evaluate the way Jack is watching me from the wings, but this would be unprofessional. Two thousand pairs of eyes are focused on me alone. It would have been less scary if I'd asked to play something that needs at least a piano accompaniment, but no one wants to hear me playing Brahms. They demand the prelude to the Bach Solo Suite No. 1 in G major. The reason they want to hear that, and that alone, is because I played it on a mobile phone advertisement.

I have desecrated Bach's memory by playing his music on an advertisement, which in turn led to a surprising number of people downloading the opening bars as a ring tone. I might not do the music justice, but mobile phones slaughter it.

I tilt my chin, instead, towards the Royal Box, wondering whether His Highness is enjoying my performance, or whether he's picking his nose. Although famously cultured, I can't imagine that this could really be his favourite way of spending his birthday. Then I force myself to refocus my attention on the music. I am coasting. I am always coasting, and so far I have got away with it. In a concert like this, in a hall which has been sold out for months, I know that I can give an acceptable perform-ance on adrenalin alone. The hot lights keep me going, along with the prospect of dismal failure. I force myself not to go completely on to automatic pilot: that would be too dangerous. One day I will make a complacent misjudgement and the result will be a disaster. I must play with some degree of musicality. The trouble is, I can clone my performance of this Bach suite from the advert, and I can do it without really thinking. I, like everyone else in this hall, have heard it countless times, and I can play with exactly the same nuances as I did then. That's what these people want. That's why the organisers were so keen to make me play the Solo Suite No. 1, rather than anything else I might have wanted to offer them. I didn't even try to change the programme. I like an easy life.

These suites are deceptively simple. It's very hard to play them properly, I tell myself, as I dip from A string to

D string. It is all in the phrasing, and I copy my phrasing from a recording by Rostropovich. It seemed the safest way to do it. I do not try to convince myself that I play this anything other than adequately. But I give my adequate performance with an enormous confidence, and since I play it like I do on the telly, everyone is happy.

I am confident because I know I look like a professional cellist. I am a professional cellist. I make my living this way. Every day, I expect to be found out. Real musicians don't take me seriously; neither do music critics. Everyone else thinks I'm fabulous. Jack knows I'm not. He has always let me know that, although he is far from a musician himself, he sees through me. He knows I'm not brilliant, and he uses this fact to keep me in my place. He would call it encouragement – 'If you do this well, Evie, when you're not really trying, think how fantastic you would be if you put your heart into it' – but I know that he's playing with my mind. He would love me to fail, in the way he failed as an artist. He wears me down, and I don't need him any more.

This stage is vast, and I am lit, mercilessly, by the spotlight, so I can't make out anything in the audience beyond the glint of glasses, and the exit signs, far back in the darkness. The sound of my bow across the strings fills every corner of the concert hall. I rarely play for live audiences – my preferred venue is a small recording studio, with a few men in black moving dials and knobs behind a sheet of thick glass. I was almost sick with nerves before I came on to play my mercifully short part in this enormous classical-lite charity concert. I prefer to play wearing jeans and a T-shirt, with my hair scraped back and no make-up

3

on. This evening I am dolled up so my own mother must barely recognise me from her seat in the stalls. I'm wearing a dusty-pink long dress by Maria Grachvogel, designed for me personally, because the cello does not lend itself to the wearing of clingy scraps of skirt, and because I am, in my own way, famous enough to have my own dress. My hair is shining blonde, freshly bobbed, with a diamond clip in it, and absurdly over-styled. My make-up is frighteningly garish, but the make-up woman assured me that it wouldn't look that way to the audience.

Jack laughed when he saw me. He said I looked like Barbie's mother. This was not what I needed to hear.

With relief, I note that I am on the homeward stretch. It doesn't take long to get to the homeward stretch of a piece that is less than three minutes long. I know I'm nearly there when the high notes start coming in. I am tempted to rush the last few bars, to get this over with, to move on to the thing I have to do, to make myself free. I know the audience is loving my performance, and that they're loving it for the wrong reasons. I am now reprising the very passage from the advert, and the two thousand two hundred and eighty-six people who have paid £150 a ticket to see me, among many others, are humming along collectively. I can hear a breathy rush coming towards me from them, a random mass hum-along. It has the same out-of-time, tuneless quality as hymn-singing in church.

I hold myself back, and pace my performance, not wanting to make it obvious how desperate I am to be off the stage and attending to my personal life. I will tell him. Things have been going wrong for far too long. I am certain that I'm strong enough to get by without him, at last.

When I come to the end of the piece, relief swamps me, and I allow myself to smile a wholehearted smile. I love this moment. It makes everything worthwhile. Every person in the auditorium is applauding me. Even, I note after a quick glance, my husband. All eyes are on me. I have played my part, played my cello, and these people have paid very good money to hear me, and now they are clapping. I love them, because they love me.

I stand up and bow, and the applause grows slightly stronger. My smile goes up a notch, and I look out into the audience, genuinely grateful to every single one of them. A light shines on Prince Charles, and I see him clapping for me.

At moments like this, I always have the same thought: I hope Louise is watching me now. The thought lasts a fraction of a second. I bow twice more to the audience and once to the Royal Box, not caring, for once, about the obsequiousness. Although the television cameras are here, I ignore them like a professional. I stiffen my resolve not to play an encore, and accept a bouquet of pastel roses from a little girl who stumbles on to the stage wearing a shiny pink dress. I kiss her, and hear an 'Ahhhh!' from my fans. She curtseys to me, as if I were the Queen, and walks backwards off the stage, to her waiting, beaming mother. I smile again, at everyone, and depart from the stage as my applause starts to die away. It is my applause. I wish I could keep it, and bring it out when I need to hear it.

'Well done, Evie,' says Penny, the stage manager, giving

me a pat on the shoulder. 'Good stuff.' Then she is off, attending to the next performer, an eleven-year-old male pianist who has been fingered by the press as a rising star. What they mean is that he, like me, is photogenic. Little Billy, as he is known in print, has blond hair that flops across his eyes, an angelic face, and, unless he's exceptionally lucky, an incipient drug or alcohol problem. He will be delighting the audience with Rachmaninov's Prelude in C sharp minor. God help him when he reaches puberty.

I am the perfect candidate for a concert like this. I am classical-lite through and through. My musicianship would be put to best use in one of the London orchestras, or playing solos on the second rung of the semi-professional ladder. My talent has been promoted far beyond its value because, apparently, everyone loves a blonde girl in lipstick who can do interesting things between her thighs. I always have a CD out at the beginning of December, and it has always sold hundreds of thousands of copies by Christmas Eve. I make most of my income playing for adverts, and I seem to be increasingly filmed, as well as recorded, as my profile has risen. I have played for the President of the United States, and for a reception at Downing Street, and I have been invited to the Kremlin. My agents say I should branch out into pop music – 'That is where the money is' – but I have resisted, so far. When I try to picture myself playing the cello on *Top of the Pops*, all that comes to mind is a vision of Dexy's Midnight Runners. Unless I put my foot down, however, my next CD will contain several tracks played over a techno beat.

The press like me, and I like them, too. I'm often

pictured in the tabloids, and I enjoy it. If I suspect some-one is waiting for me, outside the house or anywhere else that I'm going, I make a particular effort with my hair and make-up, and they appreciate that. I appreciate it, too. Every time my picture is printed, hundreds more CDs vanish from the shelves. My personal life has never been interesting enough for them, so I've had to wear out-rageous dresses and high heels to sustain attention.

Now I'm going to leave Jack. They will adore that, when they hear about it. My profile will soar. Briefly, I wonder whether I should call a friendly hack in the morning. There are several in my address book who would leap upon my news.

My cynicism is disgusting: I haven't told my husband yet, and I'm already contemplating telling the readers of the *Mail*. I look around among the dusty stage lights and random clutter, and catch sight of him chatting to a stage hand. I pause for a moment and look at him. He looks cheerful. He hasn't dressed up for the evening, because he knew he would stay backstage with me. When I met Jack, he looked like what he was: an art student. I loved that look. Now he looks like what he is: a computer tech-nician. I walk towards him purposefully, holding my cello like a shield. I have no doubt at all that I am doing the right thing.

'Evie,' says Jack, throwing a companionable arm around my shoulders. I look up at his face. He is rosy-cheeked, and he looks pleased. 'Well done, gorgeous. You were great.'

'Yeah,' says the stage hand, with a shy smile. 'You were.'

I smile at him. 'Thanks.'

Jack ignores him. 'Shall we grab some dinner?'

I shake him off, irritated, and shift my cello to the other hand, so it is between us.

The boy produces a biro from behind his ear. 'Could I possibly have an autograph?' he asks nervously. 'I'm your biggest fan, Miss Silverman.'

'No,' I tell him, and stare pointedly until he shuffles away. I know I'm supposed to be charming to the fans, but that was an intrusion.

'Jack,' I say to my husband, 'I have to stay here till the end. You know that. I told you before. They need me back on stage for the finale.'

Little Billy's three chords ring out, confident and arresting. I want to stand exactly where I am and listen to him. He is good. Jack takes no notice.

'But you don't have to play again. No one will notice.'

'I *do*. They will. We're all playing "Happy Birthday" to Prince Charles. Cringeworthy, yes, sure, but I have to do it. They will notice if I'm not there – how could they fail to in a dress like this? And don't tell me I didn't tell you about it, because I know I did.'

'Then let's just say, if you told me, it slipped my mind. Bugger it, Evie, I don't want to spend my whole evening hanging out backstage at some pageant of arselicking sycophants. I have a lot else on, you know, and of course I wanted to come and support you here, but unfortunately there are other things I need to get on with.'

'Then go home.'

'Sure you won't come with me?'

'Why don't you get us a takeaway and we can have it in my dressing room? You know I can't leave.'

Jack shrugs. He looks annoyed. 'Whatever.'

We have reached my door. I go in, and look around the tiny room. It is meticulously tidy. The only time I cannot bear to have an item out of place is when I am about to perform. I feel like a fraud anyway, and I know that if I wasn't prepared mentally for a performance – if I let the chaos creep in – then I would no longer get away with it. My serious reviews would go from mediocre to scathing. I only get good reviews from *Heat* and *Smash Hits*, and that's because they hardly ever review anything classical. Never, in fact, but they make an exception for Evie Silverman because they like my hair and they like my clothes. They would love it if I shifted my focus to pop.

One mag did a feature a couple of weeks ago, based on a photo of me, advising people how to 'steal her style'. I was wearing jeans and a cardigan. Not a difficult look, I wouldn't have thought. It included phrases such as 'Evie swears by John Frieda Sheer Blonde Spun Gold Balm'. Which was news to me, but I might try it out, to see why it is that I love it so much.

I put the cello away, and leave the door of its case swinging open. Then I turn back to my husband.

'I still think you could sneak out now,' he says, grumpily. 'You can play the diva, can't you? It's your right. You do it with me all the time.'

I hold up a hand. 'Jack,' I say, my heart suddenly thumping, 'sit down a minute.'

He takes an apple from my fruit bowl and paces round the room. 'Why? I'm starving. Got anything to drink that isn't water?'

'No. Actually, there might be some wine in the fridge,

I think. But sit down a sec. There's something I've got to talk to you about.'

He sighs. 'What?'

I don't reply, and he lowers himself, with a show of reluctance, on to the sofa.

'Jack,' I tell him, terrified by what I am about to do, and still elated by the post-performance adrenalin. 'It's about us. You and me. Our marriage. I don't think it's working any more.' I hear myself speaking, wondering why it's not possible to say words like these, words which change the course of two people's lives, without sounding as if you're in a bad soap opera.

He freezes, the apple almost at his lips. I watch him intently. Jack has always been good-looking, but age and confidence have not served him well, and now, at thirty, his pores are blocked and his chin and cheekbones have lost their old definition. Nonetheless, I know he is handsome. I just don't want him anywhere near me.

'What are you talking about?' he demands. 'That's bollocks.'

'It's not.' I am still terrified, but now that I have begun this, I am going to finish it. My emotions are heightened anyway, and this is not a moment for backtracking. 'I know you know I'm right, really. I don't want us to be together any more. I'm not happy. I don't think you're happy either – I think you're happy in most of your life, but not with me. It would be best if we tried living apart for a while. I'd like you to move out. Go and stay with Ian and Kate, maybe.'

He pretends to splutter. 'Evie, this is completely out of the blue. Are you having a laugh?'

I shake my head. 'Of course not.'

He looks around the room. 'And you tell me this now? Backstage at the London fucking Palladium?'

'I'd been wanting to talk about it for ages,' I tell him, trying to be soft and sympathetic, 'but it never seemed the right time. Then I realised there was never going to be a right time, and that I just had to do it when I had a moment. When we were alone together. I know you must have noticed it too.'

He stares at me. 'You are a hard bitch, do you know that?'

I'm stung. 'I'm not! I'm right, and you know it. You've had your head in the sand for the past three years or more.'

'Oh, have I? It's all my fault?'

'No! It's not all your fault. It's no one's fault. We've just changed a lot since we were twenty-two, that's all.'

'And in five minutes you're going to go back out on to that stage and play "Happy Birthday" to Prince bloody Charles?'

'Yes,' I tell him. 'Even divorce won't get me out of that.'

I sit, he stands, and we look at each other in silence while the word echoes between us. Jack looks at the apple in his hand, then tosses it into the bin. His arms hang by his sides and he doesn't seem to know what to do with himself. I look at our reflections in the big mirror above my dressing table. We present a strange tableau: a computer technician in his jeans and a shirt, with an over-grown Barbie doll.

'All right,' he says, after a while.

I look at him. 'Thanks, Jack.'

11

He avoids my eyes as he picks up his coat from the back of a chair. 'I'll go home now. Pack up some stuff and get out. We can sort out the rest of it later. You're going to regret this, Evie, I promise you. Let me know when you come to your senses.'

He leaves the room, the theatre, and my life without looking at me. As I watch him leave, I force myself not to smile. The moment the door shuts behind him, I look at myself in the mirror and grin. I am still high from the performance, and I am certain I have done the right thing. Finally, I am capable of being on my own. I don't need my mother to look after me, and I don't need my husband. Fifteen years after the event, I can stand on my own two feet.

I reapply my lipstick and wait to be called back to the stage.

chapter two

A week later

I'm sitting at home in the early evening, watching our wedding video forwards and backwards, and waiting for Kate to arrive. She said she'd be over after work, and it's now half past six. The trouble with living in Greenwich is that it sometimes takes people hours to reach you. I think I should move somewhere more central. I need to get away from the remnants of my married life.

I haven't really worked today. I practised for two hours in the morning, packaged up the proof of my past three months' earnings and a blank VAT return for my accountant, and sat down to watch daytime television. I tell myself that I am doing fine. I didn't miss Jack today: how could I have missed him at a time when he would never have been home, anyway? After *Neighbours* and *Doctors* I had a little nap, then walked to the corner shop, as an experiment, to see how I felt leaving the house. I thought that, perhaps, the boring, unchanging real world would make me feel superior, as it normally does. I walked along the

13

familiar pavements to the shop where they almost know my name, after five years of daily patronage. The wind was evil, and I wished I'd worn a proper coat, rather than my flimsy denim jacket. Denim jackets are for summer, not for November. I passed a few people as I went. Two mothers with pushchairs ambled along side by side, blocking the pavement. As I loitered impatiently behind them, with no reason in the world for my impatience, nowhere to go except the shop, I heard one of them say to the other: 'Oh! I know what I was going to tell you!' in a tone of great excitement. I walked on her heels to hear what it was. 'Bernie did a wee in the potty yesterday!' the woman continued, and my heart sank. 'He's such a clever boy, aren't you, darling?'

The other mother was enthralled. 'Really?' she gushed. 'A wee in the potty? That's so clever. Well done, mister.'

I rolled my eyes, sighed as audibly as I could, and stepped into the road to pass them, nearly finding myself mown down by a speeding motorbike as I did so. Slim chance, then, of distractions from mothers. I turned to look at the children. Clever Bernie had a snotty nose and looked old enough to use a loo like any civilised human being, and the other child was red-faced and asleep. I have to be scathing about children I see out with their mothers. It's the only thing that works.

The mothers were plump. Their hair was messy and they were both in need of some foundation. Women have babies, and let themselves go. I would never be like that.

I passed a couple of kids who should have been at school, and a few old people. They all looked normal. None of them looked as if their world had fallen apart lately.

Mine hasn't either. I am absolutely fine. In fact, I am rather enjoying the excuse to lounge around. If you can't watch bad television and eat junk food when your husband has just moved out, when can you? It is the novelty of it all that is confusing me. Jack and I were so settled for so long that I'm simply not used to rattling around on my own. I felt like Superwoman when I dumped him, but now that the high has worn off, I'm not finding it easy to be alone.

I've cancelled several work engagements, which I've only ever done before when I've been too ill to get out of bed. Even then, I've sometimes forced myself. I've been citing personal circumstances, and told my agent to let people know, subtly, that my marriage has broken down. I may as well use it. It's now only a matter of time before it appears in the tabloids.

I am, perversely, looking forward to that day. Once the press start taking an interest, the decision will be made for me. Events will be taken out of my hands. I'll have to get on with my life. I will have to get my hair done, think about what I'm wearing, choose a bright lipstick and go to a party or premiere one evening, to prove that I'm emerging stronger and wiser from my ordeal. If they catch me moping about in tracksuit bottoms and a big T-shirt I will be in trouble. Image is everything. In a few months I could judiciously allow myself to be caught with an aspiring pop star or someone similar. I can see myself on the front pages entwined with someone young and fresh-faced. Some boy from a band.

My trip to the shop was a resounding failure, and it took all my strength not to cry until I got home. South-east

London can be unremittingly grim. I came back with a thin plastic bag, the handles already stretched almost to breaking point, which contained a pint of milk (no need for large quantities any more, now that Jack no longer gulps it straight from the carton every day), two bottles of red wine, and an enormous bar of Dairy Milk. Having never been in this situation before, I am turning for comfort to the sort of props recommended by women's magazines. I can't think of anything else to do. I put it down in the hall, next to three cardboard boxes of Jack's things, leaned back on the front door, and took deep, gulping breaths. I feel that he's died. But that is good.

Our house has always been my sanctuary. Jack, if it had been up to him, would have lived in a bachelor pad with no ornamentation or decoration whatsoever. All he needs is a Gameboy and a duvet. Left to his own devices, he would be a prime candidate for buying a 'men's' duvet cover, a black one with thin grey and orange stripes on it. Perhaps he will get one, now, to see him through until the next woman comes along. There will be a next woman. I know there will. Jack will replace me, just as I will replace him. I hope I replace him, with a fanfare of publicity, first.

I moulded this place, over the years, into the home I wanted. On the outside it's a grey-brick terrace with a red front door and a tiny front garden. The most striking thing about it is its location, with the Thames at the bottom of the street. Indoors, it is open plan, light and airy. The walls are all white, the floors all stripped and varnished, with rugs here and there. The sofa is large and welcoming and cream, with heaps of cushions hiding various red wine and curry stains. There are paintings on the walls, a few of them done by people we know from Jack's art school days. A few years ago I had the fake fireplace removed and a woodburner installed, which we light on cold evenings. There's a pile of kindling next to it. I have been lighting it, all alone, lately. I'm good at doing that. I always lit it for Jack and me too. I love the ritual of the kindling and the scrunched-up newspaper.

The coffee table is cluttered with books and papers and pens and letters, and the shelves are overflowing with books. This is not an immaculate house, by any means: it is a friendly house. People who come here comment on the welcoming atmosphere, and sometimes I find it unlikely that I have created such a home, while I have relatively few close friends.

I keep finding Jack's bits and pieces in among the clutter. Every time I come across a book or a CD or a magazine that belongs to him I force myself to throw it into one of the boxes in the hall. I love our house, and I would never have imagined that I was capable of feeling lonely here. Yet here I am, alone and, perhaps, not as happy as I would like to be.

I watch our wedding over and over again. When I watch it forwards I stare at myself, younger and skinnier, barely a size eight in those days. I walk slowly up the aisle in my dream dress, with its tight bodice and full net skirt, smiling beatifically, pretending to be Grace Kelly, and adoring the attention. My hair was long then, loose down my back, with rosebuds tied into it at the crown. I am holding a small, tasteful bouquet of roses. As I watch myself, again, pledging myself to Jack for as long as we both shall live, I remember exactly how I felt.

I was deliriously happy. I was twenty-two; and I was happy because I was the first of my friends to get married. I was happy because I knew I looked adorable, and because there were a hundred and fifty people in the church and every single one of them was staring at me. I thought I loved Jack, but now I suspect that a large component of that love was the fact that he reflected my view of myself. In those days, when he, too, was twenty-two, Jack was struggling as a professional artist. I already had a recording contract and was in the process of being launched into the classical stratosphere as a scantily clad cello babe. I felt we were superior in every way to people with proper jobs, and anyone who had to ask why we were better than they were was a philistine and would never understand. I knew nothing, back then. I was obsessed with the surface. As I told *OK!* magazine the other day, I am much deeper and more spiritual now.

Above all, I was making a stable life for myself. I gambled on my instinct that Jack would never leave me. It never occurred to me, back then, that I might, one day, leave him. I didn't want to be on my own, so I got married. If it hadn't been Jack, it would have been someone else.

I remember, as I walked up the aisle, half wishing that I'd asked Louise to the wedding. I wanted her to see how gorgeous and happy I was, to show her that, despite her best efforts, I had won.

I see Kate, in the second row of pews. She wipes a tear away as I glide past her. Ian is standing with Jack, as his best man. I wish we'd captured Kate and Ian exchanging glances on tape. I think they dance together later on the video. They met at our wedding and have been together and, as far as I can see, properly happy, in a way that I can barely imagine, ever since. That happiness has been tested, but it hasn't faltered. Three years have passed, now, since Kate breezily announced that they were trying for a baby.

'Fingers crossed,' she said, unable to sit still with excitement, 'it'll be a late summer baby. If I'm pregnant this month, it'll be due on August the twenty-fourth. I wonder if I'll have morning sickness? I won't care if I do, you know. I'm sure it'll be worth it. I won't mind at all if it's a boy or a girl.'

Such concerns long ago began to seem like a luxury. Kate and Ian have 'unexplained infertility', and no amount of tests, diets and, lately, fertility drugs and IVF seem to be able to do the trick. I'm immensely thankful that Jack and I never decided to have a child; not just for the child's sake, but also for Kate's. When we got married, I thought I would like to be a mother before I was twenty-five, but when it came to it I didn't want that at all. We never even discussed it. I might have a child with my next husband. The magazines would love it.

I mouth the words in perfect synchronisation with my twenty-two-year-old self.

'I, Evelyn Rose,' we say, 'take you, Jack Matthew, to be my lawful wedded husband. To have and to hold, from this day forward . . .' I wonder whether we should have a divorce ceremony, if we do reach that point. We could dress up again, get all the same people back to the same church and retract our vows. 'I, Evelyn Rose,' I could say, 'demote you, Jack Matthew, to be my lawfully divorced ex-husband. To snipe and to argue, from this day forward, for as long as we both shall bother to see each other.' I think Jack would like the idea.

At the moment when Jack and I kiss, I pause the video. This is the happiest moment of my life: from here, it went downhill. I press rewind, and watch myself eating my words, and rushing off, backwards, down the aisle.

The doorbell rings, and I freeze the screen. When I try to get up, I discover that I have been sitting on my leg, that it's numb and alien to me. I punch it a few times, and as the feeling comes back it seizes up in an agony of pins and needles.

Kate is on the doorstep.

'Hello!' she says, with forced jollity. She jigs up and down in the cold. Kate is beautiful, with long corkscrew curls and a creamy complexion. She's holding a bag which smells of chips.

'Come in!' I tell her, forcing a breezy smile. ''Specially if you've brought food.'

She hands me the bag. 'Fish and chips. Thought you probably weren't eating, so you can get a whole day's calories out of this.'

'I've got wine and chocolate.'

'Perfect. Pour us the wine and I'll get this on some plates.' She steps into the hall, and looks round the ground floor. 'Evie! I don't believe you. You're watching your wedding video. That is *so* unhealthy.'

'I know. I've been torturing myself. Wishing I could step back in time and run away at the last minute. You know' – I pick it up and fast forward, then pause it again – 'if you rewind it from exactly this point, we're divorced.'

I press the rewind button, and we both watch Jack and

me, in turn, swallowing our words. Then I rush backwards down the aisle, for the ninth time today. The tear flows upwards into Kate's eye and melts away.

'You don't really wish you'd never done it. Not really,' she says, quietly, staring at the screen. 'You and Jack have had great times together. You were good. You were perfect, actually. You two have always looked perfect from the outside. You were an inspiration to us all. I'm sure Ian and I wouldn't have got married as soon as we did if you hadn't already done it.'

I think about it. 'Really? You're my inspiration now. I want what you and Ian have got, not me and Jack. Unfortunately, though, I don't think I'm ever going to find it. I'm too selfish. I'm no good at relationships. I've got too much else going on.' I can't explain exactly what I mean, but I know this is the truth. I am not cut out for long-term relationships, for fidelity.

'You're not. And don't romanticise us. It's impossible to know what goes on in other people's marriages. We were gobsmacked when Jack told us about you two splitting up. You know that. I would never have predicted it in a million years. And you of all people know what Ian and I have been through. It does put a strain on your relationship. A horrible strain. It's not all roses at our house, Evie.' She looks away. 'Far from it, in fact.'

I crumple up yesterday's paper and arrange it in the woodburner. I'll need another bag of kindling tomorrow.

'But you're so solid together,' I tell her. 'I just don't know about Jack and me. I didn't think I'd miss him. I felt great when he moved out. And now I think I might be missing him a little bit. Part of me can't help thinking that we'll give it another go and maybe get it right this time, and that this is just a blip.' I place the last piece of kindling in the stove and light a match. 'It's the strangest thing, Kate, it really is. I remember times, so many times, when Jack was away, with work or with the boys, and I adored having the house to myself. I used to secretly hope that he'd stay away longer because I enjoyed being my own boss so much. And you're the only one who knows that I wasn't always exactly impeccably behaved when he wasn't around. So I should be getting on with it, getting out and meeting new people. But I just can't quite seem to shake myself into action. I wait for the sound of his key in the door. If he came back now and asked if we could give it another go, I might even say yes.' I can't look at her. No one else knows that I'm feeling like this. Most of the time I don't know it myself. All my family think I'm fine and strong and happy.

I feel Kate looking at me. I can't look back, so she turns away. She takes the food into the kitchen, and I follow and start hunting for the corkscrew.

'It's easy for me to say this,' she says carefully, 'but I don't think that missing him is necessarily the same thing as wanting him back. I think that missing a relationship that's been at the centre of your life for years is completely normal. If you were really completely lost without him you wouldn't have dumped him in the first place. It was your choice, remember?' She looks up and smiles, her face framed by her light brown hair. Kate doesn't realise it, but she is saying exactly what I wanted her to say. 'You're just not used to being on your own. It's a different issue. You're going to be absolutely fine, whether you take him back or not.'

I smile at her. 'Promise?'

She puts a plate of fish and chips in front of me. 'Promise,' she says.

I open the first bottle of wine, and take the huge wine glasses – for special occasions only – from the top shelf of the cupboard. I hand her a glass as she puts the salt, vinegar and ketchup on the table.

'Cheers,' she says. 'To you coming through this and enjoying being single.'

The fire is beginning to warm the kitchen. It is cosier with company. I shudder at the idea of a future where I am on my own, and clink my glass with hers. 'I quite like the idea of being single, most of the time,' I tell her. 'Cheers.' I try to think of something to toast other than my seducing a young boy from a manufactured band. 'To something happening, anyway,' I say lamely. 'To your and Ian's baby.'

'We've got some news on that front, actually,' she says with a grin.

I put down my glass and grip the edge of the table. 'You're not!' I shout.

She holds up a cautioning hand. 'No, no, no, hold your horses. Just another avenue to explore. Eat up and I'll tell you.'

With the first hot salty chip, I realise exactly how hungry I am.

chapter three

Early December

After four weeks of separation, I go to meet Jack in a café we used to go to, years ago. He has been begging me to meet him. It has been quite embarrassing. I'm fine on my own now. I don't particularly want to see him, except to discuss putting our house on the market and the terms of our divorce. If he gets difficult about that, I'll tell him to divorce me for adultery. That will shock him.

However, a small part of me is interested in being wooed back. I have a slightly open mind. If Jack surprises me and impresses me, I might give him another chance. It would be good, at least, to leave him believing he might have another chance. I like knowing that he is there, waiting for me, desperate for me. I will probably not mention the adultery, today, to keep my options open.

When I see him pretending he hasn't seen me walk in, I pause and try to judge my reaction. I wait for my heart to leap, for my stomach to constrict, for every fibre of my being to tell me that I have made an enormous mistake, but it doesn't happen. Jack looks bad. He seems to have made very little effort for our meeting. His hair is shaggier than normal, he's pale, and he doesn't look as if he has been sleeping. He looks as if he's been drinking, instead. He is wearing a thick green jumper that I bought him four Christmases ago.

Our eyes meet for a fraction of a second, before he looks away. I see his face light up, briefly. Then he picks up his coffee and cradles it between both hands. He flicks a page of the magazine in front of him. He is pretending not to have seen me, trying to keep his composure.

'Jack,' I say, warmly, pulling out the seat opposite him. He looks up, pretends to be surprised to see me, and jumps to his feet. He lunges to kiss me, and for a moment I panic. There is no etiquette for situations like this. I don't want to kiss him on the mouth, which seems to be his plan. A kiss on the cheek would be a slap in the face. I give him a firm hug, and deflect his snog. Jack smells nice, unfamiliar and slightly perfumed. He must have been using Kate's shower gel.

I sit down gracefully, aware of the way he is watching me and knowing that I look good. The tabloids and magazines caught up with me a couple of weeks ago, after I got fed up of waiting and made my agent tip them off. I was delighted, the following day, to see a solitary photographer from the bedroom window, so I washed and dried my hair, plastered myself in make-up and changed from tracksuit bottoms to a micro skirt and knee-high boots.

The paparazzo beamed when he saw me. 'Evie, love,' he said. 'Give us a smile, darling.' I obliged. I played the game, simpered winningly, and stood in a flattering pose, peeping back at him over my shoulder. I paused to decline to comment, then strode confidently all the way to the DLR. I made sure I strutted, putting one foot directly in front of the other as if walking on an imaginary tightrope. Someone once told me that this is what models do. If you do it right, you bounce gracefully as you walk. I led him down the alley and past the Trafalgar pub, then along the riverfront. Maze Hill station is closer to our house – to my house – than the DLR, but I wanted to take him along the scenic route. When I reached the station I stopped by a ticket machine to check he wasn't still following me, and skulked around till I thought it was probably safe to go home via the main road, in case he was lurking or, more likely, having a pint in the Trafalgar. As soon as I got in, I took off my make-up.

The photos turned out well. 'Evie riding high,' said the headline, in reference, I assume, to my hemline. I know Jack will have seen it, because his colleagues have always shown him anything they could find about me in the papers. They love the fact that he has a famous wife, and I'm sure there is a hint of hostility in their scouring of the tabloids. I've never got on with Jack's colleagues. I don't know how to behave with them, and I have never had the patience to make an effort. Normally I can make people like me by smiling at them, but these men demanded more. They wanted to interact with me, to make me their mate, and I lacked both the inclination and the ability. It doesn't matter any more.

I have always happily accepted demi-celebrity as part of my job. This is the life I have chosen for myself. People ask if I find it annoying, being in the tabloids, and I find it hard not to laugh. I find it annoying when I'm not in the tabloids. I enjoy the publicity more than I enjoy the music. I relish it, and I have to hold myself back from offering everything I have to the media. I know that people who serve themselves up to the press end up mauled by them. That will not happen to me, because I force myself to be elusive. I know that my slight obscurity makes me appear classier. The attention validates me. I love the knowledge that people out there whom I will never meet, millions of them, know who I am. I hope that Louise and the other girls see me and regret everything they did, everything they said.

I am meticulous about the way I appear in front of a lens. I almost wish I could walk in front of a photographer wearing my tracksuit bottoms and Jack's old T-shirt, with my hair in its morning bird's nest, and three-year-old espadrilles on my feet. I should make myself do that one day. But I know I am incapable. I couldn't do it. I care too much about what people think of me. The current version of Evie Silverman was created to be looked at: she is an object. She exists to be photographed, packaged, bought, played on a stereo, and written about. I have no idea whether the old me still lurks beneath my brittle exterior. I suspect she does, and I will make sure she stays hidden, for ever. Being shallow works best for me.

The café is busy, and no one takes any notice of us.

'How've you been?' says Jack. He leans back and tries to catch the waitress's attention, without success.

'Oh,' I tell him, 'you know.' I shrug and smile. It is one of my professional smiles, which gives nothing away. 'I'm getting by.' I assume an expression that I hope appears wry.

'You *look* great.'

I toss my hair. 'Thanks.' I changed outfits six times before I came out to meet him, finally settling on jeans and a red top, with my hair swinging jauntily, and red lipstick.

I look at my husband's face, at the short stubble that means he didn't shave this morning, at his black hair, barely tamed, today, by his Brylcreem. He is as familiar to me as my own reflection, and that is *extremely* familiar. I have declined interview requests, so far, because I wasn't sure whether to say that I am being strong and moving on from my failed marriage, or whether to hint that we are giving it another go. Now I know.

'That's fine,' he says. 'You know you look good.'

'How are you?'

'I'm all right. Getting by too. Feeling quite positive, actually.'

'Good.'

We both look up, relieved, as the waitress arrives. She is toned and blonde, and looks like an LA rollerblader.

'Latte, please,' I tell her, trying not to feel threatened. I prefer it when pretty women are dark-haired and short, so they don't intrude on my territory. I hate anyone else to be blonder than I am.

'I'll have another cappuccino,' adds Jack.

'Lots of chocolate,' I add, and we smile at each other. I want to leave, now. I should never have come to meet him. Now that I'm with him, I feel nothing. All those nights and days I've spent at home on my own, forcing myself to play my cello, making myself get dressed and look decent and leave the house from time to time, I've half hoped that the moment I saw Jack again I would heave a sigh of relief and book an exotic holiday to put the excitement back into our marriage. That's what the magazines tell you to do. Instead, I'm accepting that being married to this man left me feeling half dead. Of course I made the right decision.

'How's life at Kate and Ian's?' I ask, when the waitress has gone.

'Fine, if you like sofa beds,' he tells me. 'And baby obsessions.' He's looking at me with a strange expression on his face. Mentally, I beg him not to say whatever it is that he's thinking. 'Are you sure,' he adds, sadly, 'about giving me back the house?'

'Until it's sold, yes.' I am as brisk as possible. 'It makes sense. To be honest, I'd like to be somewhere else and see what it's like.' I regret my briskness at once, so I look at the table. 'I miss you when I'm there,' I tell him sadly.

To my slight horror, Jack reaches across the table and takes my hand. 'I miss you too, Evie,' he says quietly. He is staring at me with a horrible sincerity. 'I really do. I know you think we're finished and I can see why you say that, now that I look back on it. I guess things were pretty stale for a while there. When I saw you in the paper looking fucking fantastic, I knew you missed me. Well, I kind of thought you did. I hoped you did. You looked to me like you were trying just that little bit too hard.'

I glare at him. 'Cheers.'

'Only because I know you so well, babe.'

'I'm not a *babe*.'

'You looked like one on the front of the paper. And you knew it.'

29

'You know what I'm saying. You know I hate it when you call me babe.'

Jack looks at me. His nostrils flare slightly, and his full-ish lips form a self-satisfied smirk. 'I do know that. Sorry. But that's my point: we know each other inside out, you and me. I'm not sure if we should be throwing it all away because it went a bit stale. I think we should be trying to jazz things up before we give up on it. Let's go to Venice for a weekend. Hire a car and drive to a grand hotel in Scotland. Anything. We can do anything together.'

I look at Jack. I am imagining Venice, and it is seductive. Jack and me walking together across St Mark's Square, as we did on our honeymoon, avoiding the pigeons and laughing at the tourists drinking seven-pound cups of coffee. Riding water buses without tickets. Stepping into the darkness of a church and waiting for our eyes to adjust before we saw the frescoes. Throwing coins at buskers. If I took him back, I wouldn't have to be alone any more. It won't be long, I know, before I find out whether I am as strong as I imagined I was, in the post-performance euphoria at the Palladium. I was confident that, now I'm thirty, I would be able to cope on my own. I didn't think the cracks I've papered over could be ripped open, after all this time. I am terrified. If I took him back, I could make myself safe again. It would be a trade-off, but a sensible one. Everyone has to make compromises. I don't have to tell him anything he doesn't already know about me.

Jack is looking back at me intently. 'You read enough magazines to know what I'm talking about,' he adds, fixing me with his dark eyes and staring. 'They're packed with articles about putting the passion back in, and regaining the old magic. I used to read them all the time on the loo.'

I sigh. 'I know.' Jack would shut himself in the bathroom with a mug of coffee and a stack of magazines, and I wouldn't see him for hours. Occasionally he would shout to me to bring him the phone. I found the whole ritual entirely unsavoury, but he said he went there to relax.

'So how about it?' He lets go of my hand and I remove it immediately. I pick up my coffee and take a large slurp.

I study his face. This is the man I married for many reasons that seemed good at the time, but which don't add up to a recipe for long-term happiness or stability. I longed for security, to be able to say 'my husband' in a casual, tender way. I wanted someone to look after me.

I needed somebody. I couldn't bear to be on my own. I had to consolidate my reinvention of myself, and Jack, without realising it, let me do it. Whether I loved him or not was irrelevant.

Jack and I did love each other, I think. We have had happy times together. But we are adults now; we are more than adults. We're thirty. And what we have is no longer enough. I always feared there would come a time when I had to stand alone, to jump from a cliff and hope I could fly. In recent years, I have sometimes longed for that test.

'The past four weeks haven't been easy,' I begin, slowly, knowing exactly what I want to tell him, but not how to phrase it. I don't want him to hate me. 'I have thought about us a lot, and I've watched our wedding video far too often.'

Jack interrupts. 'Crazy woman!' He is laughing, pleased with what he is hearing. He is about to crash to earth.

'But,' I continue, looking into his eyes, 'I don't feel that I've made a mistake. I truly believe that our relationship has run its course. I just don't think we can make each other happy any more. I'm sorry, Jack, but we need to accept that this is permanent. And we both need to move on.' I wait for a response, but he is just gazing at me, so I keep talking. 'You say we could go to Venice or Scotland, but we've had the opportunity to do those things for years and we never did them. Every winter we'd talk about trekking in Nepal, or skiing, but we never even looked up the prices of flights. We don't do each other any good. We both need to see what else is out there for us. It would be so easy, sweetheart, *so* easy to say OK, let's give it another go. But it would be the wrong thing to do and I'm not going to. That's why I want to leave our house and find a flatshare.'

I try to make eye contact. Jack looks at my right shoulder. There are tears in his eyes.

'So this is it?'

'Yes,' I say firmly, reminding myself not to smile. 'This is, indeed, it.'

Jack puts his head down on to the table. I watch him, interested. He leaves it there for a while, then pulls himself up and rests his chin on his hands.

'You have to give me one more chance,' he says, suddenly. 'You have to, Evie. I love you. I've always loved you and I always will. I know you love me a little bit. I'll do anything.' He is crying now. I am embarrassed. 'Anything at all. Whatever it takes, just tell me and I'll do it.'

'Jack.' God, this is awful. 'Stop it. I'm not saying it's over for ever, all right?'

He sits up, smiling warily. 'It sounds like you are.'

'I can't say what'll happen between us in the future.' I spread my hands. 'I have no idea. Maybe we will come together again and maybe it'll be fantastic. We were young when we got married. We need to reassess things.'

'We don't! We don't. I don't. I know how I feel about you and I know that I can't manage without you. I can barely make it through the days.'

When I look at him, I believe him. He looks dreadful.

'Jack,' I say, sharply this time. 'You have to make it through the days. You have to be strong. You're better than this.'

'I don't think I am. I'm useless. I can see why you don't want me around any more.'

'Don't talk like that,' I tell him. 'Go away for a break or something. Go to a Buddhist temple and get yourself together.'

He nods. 'OK.'

'But first of all, get our house sold. We'll pay off the rest of the mortgage and split the rest fifty-fifty. All right?'

'But you've paid for more of the mortgage. You should have more of the money.'

'I don't care. I don't need it.'

By the time I leave the café, I am beginning to despise him.

Kate and Ian are waiting for me outside WHSmith by Notting Hill tube, as arranged. I'm late, because the train stopped for fifteen minutes in a tunnel, with no explanation. The staff don't bother to apologise any more, if the delay's less than half an hour.

I am on my own. I am free. Jack is in reserve, just in case I need him, but I am ready to move on. I am thin and thirty, stylish and celebrated, and I plan to begin having a very good time indeed.

I pause for a moment, before they see me. Kate is tall and slender, and is dressed beautifully, as ever. She wears a long camel coat and black suede boots, and her hair is over her shoulders. She and Ian are deep in animated conversation. They wouldn't have spotted me if I was standing between them. I remember talking like that to Jack when we first met, before we married. I was besotted with him for six months, and obsessed with the idea that he was my passport to being someone else. The old Evie would never have landed a handsome, sensitive art student. Today's Evie would never put up with one. I have outgrown him.

We used to sit up in our student bedrooms and talk, and drink cheap wine or vile instant coffee through the night. I can't think what we used to talk about, but I remember the sun coming up and the thrill of having stayed up till morning with my lover. Often he would ask me to play my cello for him, and with the blatant selfishness of youth, and no regard whatsoever for our neighbours, I would perform. I loved the way he watched me while I did it. I kept up my practising regime just for him.

At college I used to make sure I dropped my relationship into conversations at every opportunity. I'd yawn ostentatiously, and apologise in as clear a voice as I could muster. 'Sorry,' I'd say. 'I didn't get to bed till six.' Many of my classmates didn't know Jack, but they all knew all about him. I made sure of that. I had reinvented myself –

losing weight, dyeing my hair, and paying close attention to fashion – before I went to college. A handsome boyfriend was the perfect finishing touch to the new Evie S.

I can't believe Kate and Ian are still wrapped up in each other like that. Neither of them has an ulterior motive. They have been together for years, yet they'd still be blissfully happy marooned on a desert island for the rest of their lives. Despite their fertility problems, they are the luckiest, most innocent people I know.

'Hey, lovebirds,' I say, walking right up to them before they notice me. 'Room for a gooseberry?'

Ian grins broadly. As Jack's cousin, he looks disturbingly like my husband, but he is completely different. I like Ian. He is straightforward, and he dotes on Kate.

Jack and I never discussed babies. I avoided the subject, and, when his mother asked him hopefully if we were planning to give her any grandchildren soon, Jack always shook his head and said there was plenty of time. I had the feeling that he would have loved one, but that he was waiting for me to suggest it. I was the one with the exciting career, after all.

If we had found ourselves in Kate and Ian's situation, if I had been as desperate to conceive as Kate is, I suspect that Jack's patience would have worn thin long before three years were up. He would probably have left me. But Ian wants a child as much as Kate does. He supports her totally. I am slightly jealous of what they have, now that I'm on my own. I should be looking forward to meeting someone like Ian, but I know that it will never happen to me. I don't deserve it. I can't keep up my façade. Kate does. For her, it isn't a façade.

'Sorry, Evie,' she says, with a laugh. 'We didn't see you coming. How did it go?'

I grin. 'It went great, thanks.'

She catches her breath. 'So you're getting back together?'

'That's what Jack wanted, but I said no. I feel fantastic.'

'You said no?' She looks pained as my words sink in. '*No?*'

Ian chuckles. 'Kate promised him you'd say yes.'

She glances at him in annoyance. 'Sorry,' she says to me. 'He asked whether I thought he had a chance and I told him he probably did. I didn't want to get involved but it's hard work not to when he's living with us. Every time I see you he wants to know everything you said. And you said you wanted to give it another go. It's a bloody nightmare, actually.'

'I didn't know what I was going to say when I went in there,' I say carefully, knowing that Jack is Ian's cousin and friend and their lodger, 'but when I saw him I knew it wasn't the moment to be going back to the relationship. So I told him so. There's no point not telling the truth.'

'So,' Ian says, with a small sigh, 'you left him crumpled on the floor, despairing of everything. He's either drunk by now or he's slashing his wrists.'

'Don't say that! He's fine. I've seen him happier, but he's fine. Let's find my new home. Then you can have your sofa bed back. Four weeks is a long time to have a lodger.'

'Oh,' says Kate, taking a band from her slender wrist and tying her hair back, 'it's only Jack. It's not like we have to be polite to him or feed him or anything. He's hardly my mother-in-law.'

We run across the road to the central reservation, and climb over the railings. Kate manages it elegantly, despite her long coat.

'Any news on the American guy?' I ask them, as we wait for a gap in the traffic. It's a sunny day with an improbably blue sky. This is proper winter. My heart leaps as I realise that I love it. It has been weeks since I last noticed the weather, or anything outside my internal world.

Ian answers. 'We were just talking about that. There is news, actually. We've got an appointment with Ron Thomas, and we've just booked some flights. So we're going to see him on January the fifteenth.'

Kate is glowing, and so excited that she almost steps into the path of a passing Porsche. She jumps back as the driver blasts his horn at her and speeds past. 'He said in his email that he could guarantee us a baby,' she says, unruffled. 'No get-out clauses. That's what's so great. We pay upfront and he carries on treating us for as long as it takes. This is it, you know? This is the big one. It's *going* to happen.'

Ian puts an arm around her shoulders. 'Normally at times like this it's my role to counsel caution. But this time I can't do it. I'm just as bloody excited as she is. This guy is very impressive. He has an amazing success rate.'

'How much do you have to pay?' I ask, as we scuttle to the other side of the road. 'If you don't mind my asking.'

'It might sound like quite a lot,' says Ian, cautiously. 'And that's because it is. We've had to do all kinds of begging and borrowing and scraping to get it. An IVF cycle is the equivalent of ten thousand pounds.'

'Ten grand? And flights and everything on top?'

Kate touches my arm. 'The great thing is, when you're paying that much for treatment, the money for flights and hotels pales into insignificance. We were even thinking of flying business class, just because we can't afford any of it.'

'But we came to our senses quick enough.'

I look from him to her, and laugh. 'You two are such Pollyannas. Not that you shouldn't be optimistic about the treatment, but to wave all the other expenses aside as insignificant is very cool.' I stop for a moment and think of the times they have been wild with excitement because they were embarking on IVF, or Kate was starting her first cycle of Clomid, or when they got Ian's sperm analysis back and found it was fine, and when a laparoscopy revealed that Kate had no obvious problems either. I think of the number of times they've been disappointed over the past three years. Then I think of the money sitting in my bank account.

'I'll get your flights,' I tell them firmly. 'And your hotel. You're not arguing. I want this to work as much as you do and it's the least I can do, with all that money sitting around doing nothing.'

We turn down Kensington Church Street. I see them looking at each other.

'Thanks, Evie,' says Kate, after a pause. 'I'd love to say no, of course you can't help us out, but we're not in a position to turn help down, so thank you very much indeed.'

'Yes,' says Ian. 'Thank you. That's extremely kind.'

I am feeling satisfied with my own benevolence, pleased

with my place in the world, by the time we arrive at Bedford Gardens to look at the first of today's flats. When I see the mansion block, my spirits are lifted further. It is a red-brick and grey-stone building which towers above the neighbouring townhouses, and within a few seconds I have mentally reinvented myself again. I can live here. I could be a happy west Londoner, living in my 1930s apartment, strolling down to Kensington High Street to shop, and popping to the extremely smart restaurant round the corner for dinner with various new, glamorous male admirers.

Helping Kate and Ian with the money has given me a surge of optimism. I can afford it. I will fly them business class, and find them a gorgeous New England hotel with hand-stitched bedspreads. I consider offering to help with the cost of their treatment too. Once the house is sold I'd be able to do that. I open my mouth to extend the offer, then close it again.

One of the traits I most despise in myself is my rash propensity to make offers I haven't thought through. I say things to people because they make me feel good about myself. This is not a noble trait, and I wish I felt secure enough not to do it. It doesn't matter when it involves money, but over the past couple of years I have frequently found myself on the verge of offering my services to Kate and Ian as a surrogate mother. The offer has sprung to my lips again and again. It is laughable. Each time I have forced myself, just in time, to realise what a grotesquely inappropriate offer I am about to make. I force myself to consider the reality of pregnancy, of bearing a child only to give it up. It is funny, really, that I even think about it.

I, of all people, should never contemplate it. My friendship with Kate, one of the things that grounds me and keeps me going whenever I feel like running away, would deteriorate. It would be the worst thing I could possibly do. The papers would notice the pregnancy, and then they would realise that I wasn't keeping my baby. I know I would let my music become worse and worse until my career evaporated. I cannot believe I allow myself to be tortured by thoughts like that. It is an impossible idea. And yet I still find myself opening my mouth to make the offer. A year ago, I even began to suggest that Jack and I could have a baby and give it to them. Or that we would have twins, and keep one. I am insane.

The flat is on the top floor. Its ceilings are low, its windows small and square. The walls are painted in light colours, and although the spare bedroom – my room? – is barely wide enough for its single bed, I like the atmosphere, and I can imagine myself living here. My cello would fit behind the door, and I could sit on the bed to play it, unless it was all right for me to play in the large living room.

When I see the only flatmate, Megan, I am shocked by her youth. She has flawless skin and very long brown hair, and is dressed unseasonably in a blue cotton dress, with bare feet. She looks like Alice in Wonderland. I size her up instantly. She is not a threat.

'Hello!' she exclaims, with a giggle.

'Hello,' I tell her. 'I'm Evelyn. These are my friends, Kate and Ian.'

'Hi, Evelyn!' she says, turning a delicate pink. 'Hi, Kate! Hi, Ian! Come in.'

Megan giggles constantly. After a few minutes I decide she is not, after all, eighteen, but probably in her mid twenties. She has a strange manner, and I am unsure whether she is nervous or simply irritating. I want to look round her bedroom door, to see whether her room contains an elaborate doll's house, or stuffed toys enjoying a tea party.

Megan announces, with a little laugh, that her flatmate, Andrea, moved out last week because of family problems, but that she's agreed to keep paying rent until someone else moves in. She twirls her hair around her finger and explains that, while she had sixty-three responses to her advert in the *Guardian*, 'almost all of them were so clearly unsuitable! I can tell immediately on the phone. I've only let eight people come and see the flat. So you are honoured.'

'Thank you,' I tell her, catching Kate's eye and smiling.

The living room is bright and spacious. All the furniture is perfectly tasteful, which I believe to be a rarity in a rented flat, and the rooms at the front of the building, which don't include my prospective bedroom, have views over the rooftops and aerials of west London. There are some birds on the sitting room windowsill, looking in. I would love to practise in here, every day.

I look at the CD collection, which spreads over two shelves of the bookcase. 'Are these yours?' I ask Megan.

She twists her hair around her little finger. 'Yes,' she says, once again turning pink, and appearing to execute a little ballet step on the spot. 'Some of them are my parents'. It's actually their flat. But mostly they're mine. I love classical. I know it's a bit uncool of me.'

Ian and Kate burst out laughing. Megan's flush deepens, and she looks at them both, confused and suspicious. She seems on the verge of tears.

'Evie's a cellist,' Kate explains. Megan laughs, relieved.

'Oh, right,' she says. 'Sorry, I thought you were laughing at me, for some reason. I didn't know why.' She turns to me. 'A cellist in the house would be glorious. Do you play much?'

'Yes,' I tell her. 'I do it for a living.' I savour this moment. I know Megan has heard of me, and I am fairly certain she won't say anything cutting. If she does, I will be cutting back and will leave. I take a CD from her collection. 'This is one of mine,' I say, casually. I have seen my CDs all over the place for years, but I am still wary of anyone saying offhandedly that they are overrated, overpriced rubbish. While I know that they're not brilliant, I want everyone else to adore me. I want the rest of the world to be blind to my faults.

'Yours?' asks Megan, confused. 'But this is . . .' She looks at me, then down at the CD case, which bears a picture of me, draped in a tiny piece of pink chiffon, and holding a pink rose. 'Christ, sorry,' she says, smiling tightly. 'You must think I'm stupid. I knew you were called Evelyn too, and it's an unusual name, but I didn't even recognise you. If you'd said you were Evie I might have got there in the end. But I don't expect to have famous people turning up at my flat!' She giggles again, and looks down.

I look sideways at Ian, raising my eyebrows as an instruction to him to say something to lift the excruciating atmosphere that seems to have descended.

'Evie loves not being recognised,' he says cheerfully.

'Pretend you've never heard of her. What do you do, Megan?'

I smile at Kate. Ian can always be relied upon.

Megan turns to him with a shy smile. 'I work for a bank. Would anyone like a cup of tea?'

We all nod, and mutter about how lovely that would be, and follow her into the large kitchen, where she motions for us to sit at the table. I watch her graceful, precise movements as she puts an old-fashioned kettle to boil on a gas ring, and takes a bright red teapot from a pine-fronted cupboard. I think living here would be like living in a doll's house.

'I only do that to pay the rent,' she says, over her shoulder. 'It is deeply boring. Even though this place belongs to Mummy and Daddy they still say I have to pay them, because they think it's important that I live in "the real world".' She forms quotes in the air with her fingers. 'But what I would love to do is photography. These are my pictures.' She indicates some prints on the wall. I look at a shot of three dirty children staring at the camera. The closest one is grinning happily. The middle one appears shy but curious, and the girl on the end is looking suspicious. It is an intriguing image. 'I guess we can't all be good enough at what we love to be paid to do it, like Evie,' she adds. 'Is it OK if I call you Evie, rather than Evelyn?'

'Of course,' I tell her, sensing that this adorable flat is about to become mine. 'And these are truly gorgeous pictures. Is this in India?'

She smiles. 'Cambodia. Near Angkhor Wat. As you can see, there is a somewhat ambivalent attitude to camera-wielding tourists. Does everyone take milk? Anyone for sugar?'

Ian is looking at the other framed prints. 'One, thanks, Megan. These are great. You've done a lot of travelling, then?'

Megan nods. 'Not enough.' She hands us big comforting mugs of tea, and sits at the table. 'I love it. I'll go away again when I've saved up. Maybe to Central America.'

'You don't seem like a travelling type,' I say, without thinking. It is hard to reconcile her outward appearance with her obviously adventurous nature. 'I mean, you must have hidden depths.' I try to decide how rude I have just been, but Megan changes the subject.

'Evie,' she says, 'I thought you were married? Sorry to be blunt. I'm just beginning to remember things I've read about you. I'm not sure the bedroom would be big enough for a couple. You were brilliant at that Royal Gala performance, by the way. Gracious, if you live here I might get my own private performance of the Bach! I'll make a confession: I used it as my ring tone for about two days until I realised everyone else was doing the same.'

I smile at her. 'You'll be as sick of it as I am. And, Megan, I am happy to see that you're obviously not a reader of the tabloids or the gossip magazines. I left my husband nearly a month ago, on the night of that gala, actually.' She composes her face into an *oh, I'm sorry* expression. 'It's OK,' I say, quickly, holding my hands up. 'Nothing nasty. No one else involved.' No one that I'll admit to, anyway. 'Just one of those things. You know. Lovely cup of tea. Is it Darjeeling?'

She nods sagely. 'English breakfast. Well, I'm single too. We'll have to go out together and see who we meet. Oh, crumbs, sorry. That's assuming you do want to move in.

I am totally jumping the gun here. I hardly need say, the room is yours if you want it. Sorry it's so small.'

She's not like anyone I've ever met before. I'm not convinced that her sweetness is genuine, and wonder how she manages when she's travelling around Asia, but I think she might be rather entertaining. I have no intention of going out with her to meet men, but her flat is spectacular.

'I'd love to, Megan,' I tell her. 'Thank you very much.'

chapter four

December 18th

I pick up my letters from the kitchen table, put the kettle on the stove, take my Sultana Bran out of the cupboard, and drop the last tea bag into one of Megan's big mugs. Every morning I lurk in bed until I hear Megan leave the flat. It is very rare, at the moment, for me to have something to get up for. It is extremely rare for me not to have a hangover. Christmas, I have discovered, is the best possible time to be single.

I yawn, make my tea, and rub my eyes. I think about taking the tea back to bed and dozing off for another hour. Then I will have to get up and do some practice. I have been having too much fun, and my career will slip before I know it.

I try to remember how I got home last night. It is encouraging that I woke up alone, in my own bed. I went to a party on my own, and held my head up and waited for someone to come and talk to me. Most people recognised me, so it didn't take long. I was wearing a clingy white dress which, I hoped, looked classic as well as sexy. I had a fake tan treatment yesterday afternoon, so I glowed. I felt wonderful, and I scouted the guests for likely young men. A toyboy was what I wanted.

I drank, ate nibbles, had shouted conversations, and revelled in the fact that I was at an exclusive party and that I looked fantastic. I tried to spot any women who looked better than I did, but there weren't any. I spoke to journalists from gossip columns and assured them, with a wry smile, that I was doing my best to get over my heartache.

I found an eighteen-year-old boy, the runner-up in a television talent competition and thus a mega-celebrity for the next couple of months. He had chocolate button eyes and clear rosy skin, and he smiled shyly when I strode up to him and introduced myself.

'I'm Evie,' I told him with a dazzling smile.

'I know,' he said. 'I'm Dan.'

'I know.'

I took him by the hand and sat him down in the corner. He looked bewildered and flattered by the attention, and we drank, shouted to each other, and snogged for the next couple of hours. I know we had our photo taken. I think I gave him my numbers and left him sitting there, smiling a dazed smile as I departed.

I have done what I wanted to do. It was satisfying to kiss someone new and I imagine Dan and I will be meeting again. I know we will be in the magazines and papers. Jack will be heartbroken when he sees the photos.

I had too many vodkas. Everything is looking bleary, and I sit down at the table to eat my cereal and drink my tea. I look through my post. There are four envelopes, three of which are Christmas cards. Christmas is a week away, and I still haven't bought any cards or presents. I have been too busy enjoying myself to think of anyone else. I will hit Kensington High Street, and do it all today. I will also confront the question of Jack. Do I buy him a present, and if so, how much should I spend? Should I make it something I know he will love, or a token, an acknowledgement of the fact that we are still married? Can I give my estranged husband nothing for Christmas? Would a book or a CD be an insult? What will he buy me? Every time I consider doing my shopping, I hit these barriers, and procrastinate.

Two of the cards are corporate ones, one from my record label and the other from my agents. They are each signed by about thirty people. The third is from Dominic. Jack has forwarded it without opening it. I knew I would hear from him eventually, and although I fantasised about him constantly before that night in Paris, I am not at all pleased to see his name on the card. He's written a couple of words – *How's things?* – and signed *Dom* with a lavish row of kisses. Dom is a pianist I have worked with several times, and the most recent beneficiary of my adulterous tendencies. He is tall and rugged and nearly forty, a Londoner who has lived in Paris for years and years. I'm glad he's stayed away since our last recording, three months ago. He didn't show much respect for my marriage when he was cajoling me into bed with the words 'One night won't matter, and he'll never find out anyway,' but at least he's shown some sensitivity since then. Either that, or he has been too busy with the other women in his life.

I liked Dom at the time, but I don't want to see him again. I have moved on. I am going to be seen with innocent young boys from now on.

I put Dominic's card on the mantelpiece and wonder whether to send one back to him, whether it would even reach Paris by Christmas.

The other letter is in a small white envelope, printed on a computer. The address is incomplete, but full enough for it to reach me. It's probably a charity letter. They usually are. As I pull it out, I'm wondering whether to go shopping or to practise first.

Bitch, it says. Nothing else. Just that one word. I turn the page over. There is nothing on the back, nothing on the envelope. Naturally, it must be from Jack, and I suppose he is quite justified. I wouldn't have thought anonymous notes were his style, but I don't blame him. I am well aware, objectively, that I'm not being particularly nice, and I know that he will have seen pictures of me at parties in the past week. If he felt bitter enough to send this yesterday, I wonder how he will feel when he sees me and Dan in the tabloids tomorrow.

Briskly I tear the note in half, in quarters, in eighths, and set light to the pieces in a blue Le Creuset saucepan. I eat my breakfast quickly, and decide to force myself to forget my hangover, and to play my cello all morning, to restore my calm.

Megan and I share a takeaway, late in the evening. We sit at the kitchen table and spoon biriani and jalfrezi on to our plates, and rip naan bread apart with our bare hands. Jack and I used to have Indian takeaways every couple of weeks, and by suggesting it to Megan, I was making an effort to reclaim every part of my life. I will not let curries belong to Jack. We are on our second bottle of wine. I have been drunk every night this week.

I shouldn't drink this much. I have always made a point of keeping my alcohol consumption under control, and I've never told anyone why. It is no secret that my father, Howard, is an alcoholic. My secret is that I know how easily I could go the same way. I haven't lived with him since I was two, and I can't remember anything about him, in those days, but I feel the pull of oblivion in the same way that I know he did. I drain my glass and put it firmly to one side. Then I stand up and fetch myself a pint of water.

If this morning's pithy letter is from Jack, I must make sure it's brought into our divorce. Of course, we have no reason not to have the most amicable divorce ever undertaken: we have no children, not even so much as a goldfish to split between us. We should not need to blacken each other's name. Jack might divorce me for adultery after he sees the photos of me and Dan, and I wouldn't mind that. I can see myself portrayed as a glamorous scarlet woman. I should arrange to be photographed with a glass of red wine in one hand, perhaps a small cigar in the other, and a pair of killer heels on my feet.

If it's not from Jack, it must be from a nutter who reads the tabloids. A woman called Jane turned up here last Monday, from the *Mail*, wanting to know how I was getting on. I felt obliged to ask her, through a wide smile, to tell me how she knew my new address, but, through her own sympathetic simper, she steadfastly refused to enlighten me. It doesn't take them long to track anyone down. I was glad to see her. She wants to do a big feature interview about the way I am coping with the realities of separation. I said she could do it in the new year, and gave her my mobile number. When she left, I was elated. I adore that sort of attention, and I know exactly what kind of interview it will be. I will be strong and brave and independent. They will print a picture of me and Dan. I will drop in the 'fact' that my playing is improving with my new confidence. I will talk up my career, lay a foundation for next year's recording and my upcoming New York trip, and gain something material from this fiasco. I need my sales to carry on increasing, and the *Daily Mail* is a perfect forum through which to reach my fan base.

The day after Jane's visit, a photographer appeared, and the *Evening Standard*, which shares office space with the *Mail*, ran a photograph of me coming home, lugging my cello. Luckily I was wearing a new sheepskin coat and knee-high boots, and, objectively speaking, I looked fabulous. I'd had an inkling that something like that might happen. The words 'Bedford House' were clearly visible above the front door. They mentioned that it was off Kensington Church Street. It wouldn't take much for anyone in possession of an A to Z to realise that Bedford House might be in Bedford Gardens.

This morning's letter came without an apartment number on it. If it's not from Jack, it *must* be a nutter.

'Sorry, Meg,' I tell her, noticing that she's trying to pass me the rice. Megan has changed out of her work clothes, and looks as doll-like as ever in a pink sweatshirt and a pair of jeans. She's even wearing a pink Alice band. 'I'm a bit preoccupied today. I've got so much work on after the new year, I'm just trying to get my head round it.'

She smiles prettily. 'Evie,' she says, 'your life must be so glamorous. You have the dream job, and you're always out and about.'

'Mmmm,' I concede, enjoying the fact that she is so impressed with me. 'Christmas is a good time. You should come out with me tomorrow night. Things are a bit quiet workwise, though. It comes in bursts. I'll have months of practising, doing groundwork, signing contracts, getting things set up. Then it all happens at once and my feet don't touch the ground. I might not be around at all in February, for instance. There's an ad I'm doing in New York, and with any luck that might lead to more work out there, maybe even a big concert. Fingers crossed. Then I'll be back in Paris in the summer.' I will be working with Dominic once more. It is good to have my options open, I suppose, and I might be interested in him again by then.

'Goodness. I can't believe my flatmate is famous! Mummy and Daddy are such fans, you know. I think they would have let you live here for free! Daddy told me last week that I should have let you have the big bedroom.'

I smile. 'That's ridiculous.' I would love the big bedroom, but I would need Megan to be insistent before I could accept it. 'This is a wonderful place to live,' I add. 'Maybe I'll meet your parents at Christmas?'

'They would love that.'

My family – my mother, stepfather, stepbrother and half-sister – live in Bristol. Megan's smaller and more conventional family – her mother and father – live in the countryside nearby, in Somerset. We will be catching the train west together the day after tomorrow.

'This biriani is gorgeous,' I tell her.

'Isn't it just? This is the best Indian delivery in London, I swear. I wish they'd deliver men as well.'

'The guy who brought it was OK-looking, wasn't he?'

'He was about fifteen!'

'Meg, you look twelve yourself.'

She mops up some curry with her bread. 'That's probably why I'm always single. I only attract paedophiles.'

'Don't say that! You're so pretty. You could have anyone you wanted.' I really mean that. Men love waifs like Megan.

She looks sceptical. 'The men I want don't seem to know that. Not that there are many of them about. I'll tell you who I like. Older men, particularly if they're French. Gracious, when I went to Paris I was in heaven. All those sensitive-looking guys in their forties with hair down to their collars and lovely coats! They look like intellectuals and artists. I positively adore them. I was swooning.'

I laugh at her rapture. 'There must be men like that in Notting Hill.'

'A couple. And I've been out with them. What about you, Evie? What's your type?'

'Right now,' I tell her, 'boys. Only as a reaction to marriage. I've been an old married woman for so long, and completely off the market.' Best, I think, not to mention the affairs to innocent little Meg. 'So now that I'm out and about I'm finding the greatest novelty is the fresh-faced young boy. Dan Donovan, that sort of lad.'

She laughs. 'Dan Donovan? Are you joking? What's he, seventeen? His single's playing in every shop I go into.

That's his, isn't it? "If you want me" . . . It's awful. Do you fancy him?'

'He's a surprisingly good kisser,' I tell her laconically.

'No *way*!'

'Though not such a good conversationalist. And he's eighteen.'

'You've kissed him?'

'Last night. I couldn't help myself. He's so adorably young and rosy. Like a little puppy.'

'Wow.'

'But I do realise that I won't always be vamping after little lads who've just got famous. What is my type? You haven't met Jack. And he's not my type any more anyway. Brad Pitt, if he was available. When I met Jack, I went for skinny artistic types like Leonardo DiCaprio used to be, with floppy hair and girlish skin. That's how Jack was when I met him. Him and Leo have gone to seed in exactly the same way. Thinking about it, I suppose Dan's in the same mould as the young Jack. So I haven't moved on after all.'

'Will you bring Dan Donovan home to meet me?'

'If you want.' I picture it. A photo of a dishevelled Dan emerging into Bedford Gardens would be excellent. 'Depends if he calls me.'

She fills both our glasses with red wine, and we clink. 'Cheers,' she says. I realise that Meg might be able to become my friend after all, now that she's relaxing with me. She is a rewarding audience.

As we are washing our plates and throwing away copious quantities of leftovers, the buzzer sounds. We look at each other in bafflement, since nobody ever drops in, least of all after eleven, and Meg goes to the intercom. 'Hello?' she asks, warily. Then she smiles.

'No I'm not,' she says with a giggle. 'I'm not, because I'm not her. But come on up!' Then she turns to me. 'Hope you don't mind. You did just say I hadn't met him, and here he is. He says he's come to tell you that you're the love of his life.'

I rinse my hands under the cold tap with a shiver of foreboding. 'Jack or Dan?'

My husband is drunk. I haven't seen him since our strained parting in the café. It is quarter past eleven, and he is almost paralytic. I know he will be mortified in the morning.

He has shaved since I last saw him, and had his hair cut. He still looks terrible, with white skin and bags under his eyes. He beams when he sees me.

'Evie!' he says, lunging at me in the hall for a kiss. I peck him on the cheek and hurry to the kitchen to retrieve my wine. I need it to get me through this encounter. Jack smells of smoke and alcohol. Other people's dirt is clinging to his clothes.

'Jack, this is Megan,' I say reluctantly, motioning from one of them to the other. 'Meg, my estranged husband, Jack.'

Megan is smiling coquettishly. 'Hello, Jack. I've heard a lot about you.'

'Nice place you've got here, Megan. Are you looking after my wife?'

She nods, amused. 'I do my best.'

I push him into the sitting room, where he slumps on to the sofa.

'Jack,' I say firmly. 'What are you doing here? If you wanted to come over you should have called first. Megan and I might have been in bed.' Instantly, I wish I could retract the accidental innuendo.

His eyes widen. 'Oh! Oh, I see. Did I lose my wife to the world of lesbianism? That's cool. Go ahead. Can I watch? You dirty little vixens.'

I hold my head in my hands. 'Jack, you are so drunk. Sorry, Megan. Feel free to go to bed. I'll get rid of him as quickly as I can.'

She giggles. 'I'll fetch a glass of water.'

'Good idea.'

'I was in the area,' he says expansively, leaning forward and shocking me with his alcoholic breath. 'At the pub. Knew you were just round the corner so I thought it would be rude to be right here and not to pop by and say hello to my darling wife. Remember me? I wanted to say Happy Christmas.'

'Happy Christmas, Jack. Shall I call you a cab?'

'I'm a cab! There, I did it for you.'

'Fuck off.'

He looks at me. His eyes aren't focusing properly, but he's trying to look plaintive and appealing. 'Evie,' he says, 'that's not very kind. We are married. I didn't want the next time I spoke to you to be via a solicitor.'

'Jack, we speak to each other at least once a week.'

'Only because we're selling a fucking house together.'

'But we don't just talk about the house. I think we're doing well. We were, anyway, till tonight. This isn't easy for either of us, and I think we've both been very adult about it. You're going to be mortified in the morning.'

'I won't be if I wake up next to you.'

I can't help laughing. 'Jack. You reek of beer and fags. You can't stand up without swaying. I'm terrified you're going to throw up on Meg's carpet or her sofa. You are not seductive.'

'I keep seeing you in the paper, out at parties. You never used to go out that much.'

'I like going out.'

'You should be home with me. You look desperate. Come out with me, Evie. You know you want to. OK, it's a bit late tonight, but we could go to the all-night Greek place in Stoke Newington. How about it? You could get bladdered too. It would be cool. Way better than those poncey parties.'

'No. N-O. Absolutely no way. I'm going to sleep.' I catch his eye. 'Alone. Not with you. Not with Megan. Not with anyone else. All by myself, like I do every night. I live in a single bed now.'

'Tomorrow night then.' He puts his hand on top of mine, and I am suddenly afraid he is about to cry. 'Come on,' he continues. 'Please, Evie. You have to give me something. I'm dying here.'

'Sorry about that.'

'I've got to tell you something. That's why I came round. I'm doing what you said. After Christmas I'm going to Scotland. I'm going to stay at a Buddhist monastery to find myself. It's all booked.'

He looks at me, expectantly, waiting for my approval. Although it is pathetic that he's following a throwaway comment of mine as if it were gospel, I can't help feeling relieved.

'That's wonderful, Jack. Well done. I'm very pleased for you.'

'Are you? Are you pleased?'

'Of course I am.'

'I'll stay about a month, I think. When I come back I'll be calm and collected and we can give it another go. Our marriage, I mean. If you want to.'

'You might not want to.'

'I will. I love you. *Love is not love which alters when it alteration finds*. That means I won't stop loving you just because you stop loving me.'

He reaches out to me. I look at his hand. It is large and familiar. I know the squat shape of his nails, and the patterns of the hair on the bottom sections of his fingers.

My heart sinks. The familiarity of his strong hands gives me a moment of regret, then, at once, I am glad to be rid of him.

'Go to Scotland,' I tell him, 'then we'll see.'

I look up gratefully as Megan comes in with a glass of iced water and a cup of coffee. She has used one of her best cups, in rose-patterned china on a matching saucer. Jack looks at her, astonished, and takes one in each hand. The cup rattles loudly against the saucer.

'I didn't know if you took sugar or not,' she says, smiling.

'He takes one.'

'I put some in the spoon, just in case.'

'Thanks, Meg. I'll stir it in. Don't want him scalding himself.'

'I'm fine!'

'Of course you are.' I make sure he's looking at me.

'Jack, I'm going to call a cab for you, OK? I'm going to give the driver our address and make sure he takes you to the door. Have you got your keys?'

'Course I have, but I'm not ready to go home. I have lots more things to say to you. There's a speech in here.' He taps his head. 'It's foolproof. No woman who heard it could possibly turn me down. The boys said so.'

'I'll call,' trills Megan, and she picks up the phone. While she speaks to the minicab operator, I sit close to Jack.

I want to ask him if he knows anything about the letters that keep turning up, but I'll get no sense out of him tonight, and if he *has* been sending them, we need to have a serious discussion.

Meg puts the phone down. 'Twenty minutes,' she says. 'Better drink that coffee.'

Jack obediently slurps it. 'What have you got,' he asks Megan, 'that I haven't?' He stares, waiting for an answer. She shrugs.

'My wife!' he says loudly. 'You've got my wife!'

'Bloody hell, Jack.' I have my head in my hands, and my hair flops over my face. 'You are wasted.'

'Remember something you used to say to me? No one ever says something drunk that they don't mean. They lose their inhibitions, but they don't make stuff up. So here's something for you: I love you. I want us to have a baby. I really, really mean that, Evie, and I've never dared to say it to you before. A baby. Yours and mine. Please.'

There is a stunned pause. Megan stands up and yawns.

'On that note,' she says, 'I think I'll go to bed.'

* * *

59

As I climb under my lavender duvet, wearing my thick pyjamas, I realise how glad I am that Jack turned up in the state he did. If he'd dropped by on any pretext, sober and charming, I would probably have slept with him. He did us both an enormous favour by being drunk and obnoxious.

I see his Christmas present, still in its plastic bag, on my small table. I should have given it to him. I can't post it, so I'll have to give it to Kate next time I see her. In the end, I got him what I knew he wanted: an Xbox. He will not have much use for it in a Scottish temple.

I snuggle down, enjoying my haven. My room is clean and tidy and smells of moisturiser and hair products. It is a girl's room. My cello stands guard behind the door. Jack is going away, but he still loves me. He will always be there if I need him. I drift off to sleep happy with the way I have handled him.

chapter five

December 20th

We have reserved seats on the train, which never solves the problem of how to travel in the week before Christmas with a cello. We got round it this time by arriving early and shoving it under the table before the people opposite arrived. They were not amused, but did not ask us to move it. Instead, they have demonstrated with rolled eyes, exaggerated huffs, and, for the woman nearest the aisle, legs ostentatiously stretched out into the gangway that they are displeased. This is easy to ignore. They look like a pair of middle-aged lesbians, and they also look as if they hate us.

I'm glad to be leaving London for a while. Dan called yesterday, and we giggled over the photographs of us together which were in all the red-top tabloids. He told me that his management rang him as soon as the papers were out, and told him to stay away from me.

'They said I shouldn't have a girlfriend,' he told me. 'If I have to be seen with a girl, it's got to be someone young and sweet.'

'I'm sweet,' I told him, 'and I'm not that old.' I am, of course, in his eyes. He is still in his teens. Thirty must seem ancient to him. 'Are you going to let them run your life, or do you want to meet up in the new year?'

'Yes,' he said at once, and we wished each other a Merry Christmas. I am still delighted with myself.

Megan and I drink enormous coffees that we bought on Paddington station, and share out sections of the paper.

'Go on then,' I say, looking up from the *Guardian* as we are pulling out of Paddington. *Guardian* readers are sadly unaware of my most recent conquest. 'I've barely seen you since the other night. Tell me exactly what you thought of my disgraceful estranged husband.'

I glance at the women opposite, checking that they're not undercover tabloid reporters or opportunistic celebrity-spotters who will secretly record this conversation. One is absorbed in a book called *Learn To Do the Cryptic Crossword*, while the other is writing a pile of Christmas cards, occasionally muttering under her breath when the motion of the train jolts her arm. I see, upside down, that she's signing them 'from Aggie and Maggie'.

Megan smiles into her coffee. 'I can't believe he's your husband,' she says tentatively.

'Me neither. I look forward to the day I can call him my ex-husband.'

'I mean, it's so grown up to have a husband anyway. I can't imagine that. And Jack and you. You're so different.' She laughs. 'So very, *very* different. Almost as different as you and Dan Donovan.'

I look round. 'Shhh. Jack's not normally that bad,' I tell her. 'I wish I could have seen his face yesterday morning, when it all began to come flooding back to him.'

'And when he saw those photos. I can see he could be quite cute though. If you caught him at a better moment. But I thought your husband would be a conductor or an artist or something.' She nudges me in the ribs. 'He wants you to have his baby!'

I sigh. 'That's the first time we've ever talked about children. When he's roaring drunk and we've split up. Talk about a functional relationship.'

'But Evie,' she says, suddenly serious, 'look at it this way. The way Jack behaved the other night. OK, it was annoying for you. It was hilarious for me but that's beside the point. What I mean is, it shows he really cares about you. He's cut up about you. And that means a lot. The kind of men I go out with, when we finish they sometimes don't recognise me on the street. They just go from one little slip of a girl to the next. I suppose I'm trying to say that it proves you and Jack really have had something special, and that counts for something. It *was* a functional relationship. Like he says, he wouldn't say he loves you if he didn't mean it. However misguided he is, you have to appreciate that. Do you know what I mean?'

I might be imagining it, but I think I see the lesbians catching each other's eyes. I don't care if they're listening.

'I suppose I do, in a way,' I tell Megan, trying to speak a little more quietly. 'But I don't feel anything for him any more. I suppose I had many motives for marrying him and none of them was true love. I was only twenty-two. I was very unhappy at the time and I thought marriage would make everything all right.'

Megan smiles. 'And now you're thirty and you know that it doesn't work like that. That's fine. All part of the process.'

I look at her. 'You're surprisingly wise for one so young. How old are you, anyway?'

'Older than you think. Twenty-seven.'

'Twenty-seven. That's a nice age. I wish I was single and twenty-seven. Much better than being single and thirty. Still old enough for record companies to warn young boys off you, though.'

The train bumps to an abrupt halt, and Megan's coffee spills on to her lap. 'Flip!' she exclaims, outraged. I glance across the table and see that Aggie or Maggie has inadvertently drawn a blue line across a card. I dread to think what fate has befallen the cryptic crossword.

'Can I ask you something?' I say, turning back to Megan. 'Why do you never swear? Everyone else I know would have said *shit* then, or *Oh, God* at the very least.'

She looks at me. 'Got a tissue?' I hand one to her, and she dabs at her black trousers. 'At least these won't stain. I'm a convent girl. You clearly are not one yourself. I went to an evil school, and much as I don't believe in any of it, and much as I never go to Mass, I just can't do it. I can't make myself swear. It was drummed into me too forcefully. Once a Catholic, always a Catholic.'

'Really? Even though you don't believe in God, you can't swear?'

'Nope. I can't even say that, what you just said about God. I can only call myself an agnostic. I missed a family wedding last year because I would have had to have gone to confession beforehand so I could take Communion.

I couldn't bear that, so I pretended I was ill.'

'You couldn't just have had Communion without confession? No one would have known.'

'No I couldn't! God would have known, whether or not I believe in him. It's pathetic. They really got my soul. My parents sold me to the nuns, except that they had to pay them to take me.'

The woman opposite, the one with the crossword book, looks up and gives Megan a warm smile. 'Sounds extremely familiar,' she says drily. 'There's a lot of us about. We must have a support group somewhere.'

I am longing to follow this conversation, but my phone rings, and when I see that it's Kate I answer it. I turn to the window, because I don't necessarily want Aggie and Maggie to hear me. The sky is overcast. The trees loom out of the greyness. There are fields and a few clusters of houses. The English winter is strangely atmospheric.

'Hi, Kate!' I say, chirpily. I can hear Megan and the woman chatting animatedly, swapping stories of evil nuns.

'Hey,' says Kate. 'Where are you?'

'Oh,' I groan, 'don't make me say it. Please.'

'What? Where?'

'OK, you win. I'm on the train.' I say it in an exaggerated whisper. We always laugh at people making this particular announcement loudly in crowded carriages. Kate giggles.

'So, Jack was out with Ian two nights ago,' she says. 'I was well pissed off with them because we're both supposed to be as healthy and organic as possible before our appointment, like when we were doing Natural

Solutions, you remember, and it's going to be hard enough over Christmas anyway without your husband dragging mine to the pub.'

'My soon-to-be-ex-husband,' I remind her. 'Hello? Not responsible for his behaviour any more?'

'Neither is he, by the sound of it. He is a very upset and embarrassed little boy. I gather he made quite a spectacle of himself. Was it as bad as he fears?'

'Worse.'

'He's standing next to me now. I have a message for you, which is that he says he's never going to be able to face you ever again.'

I brighten. 'Is he really going to Scotland?'

'He certainly is.'

'Cool.'

Kate lowers her voice. 'He was a bit upset to see you and that singer draped all over each other in the papers, Evie. The guys at his work showed them to him.'

'That was nice of them.'

'Yeah, well. It's not your problem any more. What are you doing for New Year? Snogging Prince William? Or is he too old for you? Seducing Harry?'

'I wish. Staying in Bristol. Haven't seen the folks for ages. Do you two want to come down?'

'Mmm. Just a sec.' She goes off to confer, and as she picks the phone back up I hear Jack's voice saying 'Me too?' forlornly.

'No,' Kate tells him. 'That would be good, actually,' she says to me. 'I need a way to save Ian from excessive boozing. So we have to get out of London. Bristol would be great.'

The train plunges into a tunnel, and I am abruptly cut off.

'Flip,' I say experimentally. I see Meg and Aggie or Maggie looking at me, and laughing.

Megan's parents are waiting on the platform. Her mother is tiny, with Meg's waif-like figure but without her height. Her hair is sandy and flyaway. Megan was lucky to inherit her father's dark, sleek locks. Meg's mum looks at me shyly, a wary, feline smile playing around her lips. Her father is tall and slim and imposing. He has some high-powered job in business, and looks exactly like the sort of man who would own a beautiful flat in Notting Hill and live in a stately home in Somerset. His bearing is upright and he has an air of entitlement. He was born in the wrong era: he would have been perfect as, say, the Viceroy of India.

'You're Evie,' he booms, with an arm on my shoulder. 'It's the cello. It gives you away.'

'Yes,' I tell him, 'I am.'

'Oliver Sinclair,' he says. 'My wife, Josie. Are you being met, Evie, or may we offer you a lift?'

I look at Megan, and back to her father. 'I normally get a taxi,' I tell him. 'My mum's so busy I don't tell her what time I get in so she doesn't feel she has to come and get me. I just turn up.'

'Then you can turn up under the escort of Sinclair Cabs Inc. Firm established many years ago, at about the time this one started demanding to be taken into town to see her friends every Saturday morning. Specialists in ballet, tap, piano lessons. Cellos and extensive luggage no extra charge.' He rolls his eyes conspiratorially.

I would rather take a real cab, but I don't see how I could turn him down. 'Have you got room for me and my bags and the cello?' I ask, doubtfully.

'We could fit all that in five times over. Come on then. Where to?'

Bristol is swarming with last-minute shoppers. Now that I have completed my shopping, I look at them condescendingly. I see Megan's mother wincing as her father refuses to slow down for anybody. He drives a people carrier – he wasn't joking about the space – and uses his superior horsepower to barge through clusters of pedestrians waiting for a gap in the traffic, or groups of girls stranded in the middle of the road, laden with bags from HMV and WHSmith. People scream as he almost clips them in passing, and jump out of his way, and he doesn't seem to notice.

Josie is a different matter. She is nervous and quiet, and I keep catching her looking at me. When our eyes meet she looks away quickly. If I'd known I was to be scrutinised by my landlords I would have worn a skirt, not jeans.

'Your parents must find it very busy, living in the middle of town,' she says hesitantly, as we charge up Park Street.

'Yes,' I tell her. 'Well, not really. What's worse for them is being surrounded by students. Hardly any of the houses on their street are whole houses. After closing time, and then again at about two in the morning, it's like Piccadilly Circus.'

'They're very close to the university, then?'

'Yes,' I say, 'the Union's almost behind their house.' I wonder what else to say to her. I'm not sure how close Megan is to her parents, so I don't know whether Josie knows about Jack, whether she's sitting there desperate to ask me about him. I doubt they read the tabloids, so she probably doesn't know much about my love life. 'Left up here,' I say to Oliver, leaning forward, 'then follow the road up. It's the blue house here, with the tree outside.'

'Evie,' he says as he opens the car door and gives a small bow, 'it's been a pleasure to meet you. We are delighted to have you as a tenant. My wife has been dining out on the reflected glory.'

'Dad!' says Megan. 'Shut up!'

'It's delightful to be there,' I tell him. 'I really mean that. Thanks for the lift. Meg, I'll see you on Boxing Day, if that's going to be OK?'

'Sure. That's all right, isn't it?' she asks her parents. 'Evie's parents are having a party.'

'They always do. It's a tradition. You are all welcome, of course. The more the merrier. Mum and Phil would love to meet you.'

Oliver and Josie exchange glances. 'Thank you very much,' says Oliver, as he places my cello reverently on the pavement. 'We would be honoured.'

After I ring the doorbell, I look back and see the black people carrier still sitting by the kerb, with all three members of the Sinclair family staring at me. I suppose they're making sure I get in safely. It freaks me out a little. I am thirty years old, and it is not, apparently, enough for them to deposit me on my mother's doorstep. They have to make sure I'm not abducted before I make it through the door as well.

I hear footsteps and shouts from indoors and turn to give them a dismissive wave.

69

'I hope that's Evie!' I hear Mum shouting. 'Tess, let her in, would you?'

'Yeah!' shouts my half-sister, and her footsteps pound closer. 'It is you, isn't it?' she calls.

'It is me,' I confirm.

She flings the door open, and I hear the car crunching into gear behind me. 'Cool,' she says.

I reach out for a hug, and she snuggles in close to me. Tessa is twelve, and generally looks younger, although today she is dressed like a sixteen-year-old prostitute, in a minuscule pink skirt, pink fishnet tights and a tight pink top with the word 'Bitch' written in glitter across where her breasts might one day grow.

'What are you *wearing*?' I ask, shocked. I hold her at arm's length and look at her. 'Did Mum buy you this stuff?' It makes me think of my anonymous letter, and I shudder.

'Do you like it? I tell you what I did, I got Mum to get me some clothes from Top Shop with my birthday money, then when I went to Broadmead with Cassie, we took them back and changed them. Mum went mental.'

'I bet she did.' Tessa looks angelic, with a slight wave in her dark hair, and enormous grey eyes with long lashes. In these clothes she looks as if she has stepped out of an illegal website. 'Let's go in, then,' I say, nonplussed.

I have been looking forward to coming home ever since I split up with Jack. I could have come sooner. Mum wanted me to. Yet I wanted to see how much I could enjoy myself, single in London. I have had a wonderful time, and now I am back, ready to be cosseted.

I intend to make the most of this week. I will watch TV,

go for walks, and enjoy the lack of responsibilities. I will eat what is put in front of me, and raid the cupboards between meals. I will have endless slices of toast and peanut butter for breakfast. I will practise my cello for three hours every day, fuelled by mince pies and cups of tea, and make sure I'm on good musical form for the advert. Apart from at the party, I will wear jeans and jumpers and sensible boots. I will keep make-up to a minimum – just foundation and a smear of lip gloss, so I seem to be wearing none at all. Tess loves me to look glamorous. She will be disappointed.

'Hello?' I shout, standing in the hallway. Mum appears at once, smearing her hands on an apron. I can smell baking.

Behind her, my stepbrother Taylor appears. He looks at me shyly, and grins.

'All right?' he asks gruffly.

'Darling!' says Mum. She is deputy head of a local school – Tessa's school, to both of their chagrin – but over Christmas she reverts to a fifties housewife, cooking constantly, cleaning, delighting in providing food and drink for anyone who walks through the door. She has had a haircut, and put lipstick on. She always does that for the holidays. I, on the other hand, relish the rare chance to leave my hair to its own devices. 'Come in. Sit down. Have a drink. Are you hungry? Let's have lunch. There's soup, and I've just taken the rolls out of the oven. And the mince pies will be ready in a minute.'

I smile. 'Lead me to it.'

Taylor is taller and broader than he was last time I saw him. His skin is better, and, at twenty, he now looks like an adult rather than an adolescent. As I walk over to him, he reaches forward reluctantly and hugs me, and I smell beer on his breath. He has had his hair shaved in a number two cut since I last saw him, and I am unable to resist reaching out and stroking his fluffy head. He rolls his eyes and retreats.

I sit at the table in the large kitchen, and look around. The room is decorated with cards and holly and mistletoe. There is evidence of cooking all around the worktops. Washing is drying in front of the radiators. The rolls smell delicious. This is the Christmas I have wanted for years. I am the spoilt child, the famous daughter, the one they hardly ever see. I am single again, and I have a new energy. I pull my legs up and cross them on the chair in front of me.

Tessa takes the chair next to mine, and pulls it closer to me. She rests her elbows on the table, puts her chin in her hands, and gazes at me. I smile back at her. Taylor looks up from his task of pouring gin and tonics for four.

'Tess,' he says witheringly, 'you're tragic.'

'I am not,' she retorts. 'You're a tosser.'

Mum looks up. 'Tessa!'

'Well, he is.'

'You don't even know what it means,' says Taylor dismissively.

'I do,' she says. 'It means wanker.'

I burst out laughing. After a few seconds, so does Mum. She shrugs.

'Little girls have changed since you were young,' she tells me.

'Because that was the long-ago days,' explains Tessa.

I take the drink Taylor is holding out to me. 'Tell me about it. What's going on with you, Taylor?'

He shrugs. 'Nothing.' Taylor is still self-conscious about everything, according to my mother, and refuses to tell them anything about his life. I know that he's working to save up to go travelling in the spring, and that he lives with his mother on the other side of Bristol.

'How's work?' I ask.

'Boring.'

'Are you still at the pub?'

'Mmmm. I hate it. I might leave.'

'You must have saved some money?'

'Not enough.'

'I shouldn't say you've grown,' I tell him, 'but you have. You look great. Very handsome. Is that patronising?' I realise, suddenly, that the boy I kissed a couple of nights ago, the boy I will be seducing early next year whether his management like it or not, is two years younger than Taylor.

'No,' he says, swallowing his gin in two gulps. 'It's fine. You haven't grown. You've shrunk since last year. Do you have an Xbox?'

'No,' I tell him, and add proudly, 'but I bought one the other day. I got it for Jack.'

'Wasted on him. You should have kept it. Come up and play after if you want. Sega GT. I'll show you.'

'OK.'

Mum sits opposite me, her hands wiped clean of dough, her gin and tonic sparkling before her. She leans across conspiratorially.

'You seem all right, darling,' she says, a look of concern

73

on her face and a question in her voice. Taylor holds his hands up and leaves the room. Tessa leans forward too.

'I'm fine,' I say, looking at each of them. 'Really, I'm great. I'm better than I've been for ages. You'll like Megan. Oh, sorry, but I accidentally invited her parents to the party as well.'

Mum laughs. 'Good. I always worry no one's going to come.'

'The flat's gorgeous, right on the top floor, with views for miles. Maybe not miles and miles, but very good views for London. It's all light and airy too. I love it. It couldn't be more different from south-east London.'

'I always loved Greenwich,' says Mum. 'Don't you miss it?'

I smile. 'Not really. I miss our house and the river and the pubs, but I'm glad to be moving on. I think I have more of a west London personality.'

'So you're happy?'

My smile gets broader. 'Very.'

'And do you think there's any chance of patching things up with Jack?'

'Oh, you'll love this. I told him to get away and sort himself out, so he's booked himself a little cell in a Buddhist monastery in Scotland. He's going next month.'

'Poor Jack,' says Mum, looking at me.

'I know. He turned up in a state the other night and said he wanted us to have a baby.' I watch Mum's reaction. She is taken aback. 'I don't need him any more. I don't want to go back and try to force myself to be content in a relationship I don't enjoy. If we already had kids together, sure, I'd do my best to make it work, but for now I want to aim a little higher. I've written off my twenties, so the first half of my thirties is going to have to be good.'

'You and Jack were together a long time, Evie. He's allowed to be cut up about it. It takes time to get over a marriage. It can be hard to let go. I remember, with your father, even with all the . . .' She glances at Tessa.

'I know.' I know exactly what she was going to say. Even with all the drinking, even though his alcoholism made her life hell, she still found it hard to let go. I know, because we've spoken about it before. I stand up and get out bowls and plates for lunch. 'But it should be so *simple* for me and Jack. We got together too young, it's been eight years, we're clearly not right for each other any more, and we ought to be able to have the textbook amicable separation.' I look at Tessa. 'You shouldn't be listening to this,' I tell her. She smiles and flutters her eyelashes at me, as charmingly as she can.

'S'OK,' she says. 'I know about boyfriends.'

'No you do not, young lady,' says Mum. 'Go and get Taylor off his Xbox.'

'If you ask me,' Mum says quietly, when we are alone, 'the textbook amicable separation is a myth. It never happens. At least, like you say, you and Jack haven't got any children together.'

On Christmas Day I wake with a start to find someone next to me in my old single bed. I sit up, shocked. For a moment I think Jack has broken into the house and climbed in next to me. I would not be in the least surprised.

75

My heart is pounding. When I look down and see Tessa, I force myself to breathe deeply. Of course it's Tessa. It could not have been anyone else. Tessa's dark eyelashes curl away from her face. Her cheeks are pink, and her breathing is even. She senses me looking at her, and opens her eyes. Then she remembers what day it is, and smiles broadly.

'Happy Christmas!' she shrieks, reaching both arms around my neck and pulling me back down. Tessa's dark hair is tangled and she is warm and soft. She smells of little girls. The smell gives me a familiar pang. 'Has Father Christmas been?'

'I'm sure he has.' I snuggle back down with her. 'Happy Christmas to you too. How long have you been here?'

'Oh, I woke reeeeeeely early, like at five or something, and that's like when *kids* get up on Christmas, so I thought I'd better not wake Mum and Dad since I'm not exactly a kid any more. So I came in, so so quietly, to see you. And then I came into your bed and it was lovely and warm so I fell asleep.'

I check the clock.

'It's half past eight! I remember a couple of Christmases ago when you were waking me and Jack at quarter to six. Well done, sweetheart. Where's your stocking?'

'I brought it through with me. It's on the floor. I only looked at the things in the very top. Does Father Christmas come to you?'

I smile and run my fingers through my tangled hair. 'He asked if I wanted a visit this year, and I said no.'

Tessa looks conspiratorial. 'Evie, I actually know that Father Christmas isn't real. I actually knew that when I was seven. But Mum and Dad think I don't know so I haven't told them. You see, I have to pretend. Even though I'm twelve.'

'If I were you, Tess . . . .' I stop, not sure whether I'm right.

'What?'

'Well, I think you could tell them that you know. They won't mind. They'll probably be pleased that they don't have to pretend any more.'

Tessa looks crestfallen. 'You mean he really isn't real?' she says in a small voice.

I am horrified. 'Were you testing me?' I hastily try to work out if there's a way to backtrack.

Tessa bursts out laughing. 'Of course I knew! I'm only teasing. Evie, it's so nice to have my sister home. Will you stay living with us now that you're divorced?'

I sit up in bed and hug my knees. 'I'd love to. But I have to go back to London because of work, and soon I have to go to America. I'm not quite divorced yet, either. But now that I don't have to think about Jack, I'll come and stay much more often. And when you're maybe thirteen, you can come to London and stay with me.'

'Can I really?'

'Of course you can. I'll meet you from the train. Stay with me and Megan. I love your pyjamas.'

'I love yours.'

'Shall we go downstairs?'

Christmas lunch is late and large. I sit between Tessa and Taylor, and eat an enormous amount. I feel my stomach constricted by the waist of my trousers, and consider undoing a button. Taylor and I drain a bottle of wine between us before Phil finishes carving the main course.

'May as well get rid of the last few drops,' says Taylor jovially, filling my glass so full that the meniscus rises above the rim. I lean down to slurp the excess from the top.

'Cheers,' I say, picking up the glass.

'Cheers,' he says. 'It's nice to have Evie on her own, isn't it?'

No one replies, but I know they all agree. Phil changes the subject. 'Much work coming up?' he asks. Phil has been my stepfather for seventeen years. He has black hair and a black beard and olive skin, all of which come from his Spanish father. He is gentle and kind, and a good complement to my father, Howard, whom I rarely see because he lives in America. Howard has been sober for years and years, and Phil is the best thing that could have happened to my mother. For a dysfunctional family, we have got off lightly.

'Yes, actually,' I say casually. I used to be wildly overexcited by professional engagements, but at the moment I can't see how I'm going to muster the energy to get through them, particularly in America where I have to be exhaustingly nice to everyone all the time. I should be grateful for the opportunities I am given, I know, but right now I can't help feeling cynical. Like a Hollywood actress, I know that once I begin to lose my looks, the work will dry up. This is understandable for a film star, and less so for a musician. If I was stupendously talented, my age and looks wouldn't matter. But I am not; and they do. It bothers me that I am deemed unsuitable for Dan Donovan. 'I've got to play "The Swan", on an advert,' I tell him, and

I hum a few bars to remind them all which popular classic that is. 'Saint-Saëns. And I have to go to New York for it. They actually want to film me playing it sitting in the middle of a crowded street, at a junction, all dressed in white with my hair flowing like the Timotei ad but a bit funkier.' I shrug. 'The money's good, and this is my chance to make some inroads in America.'

Tessa squirms. 'I love it when you're on telly! When's it going to be on?'

'Not for a while yet, sweetheart, and then only on satellite. We don't film till February.'

Phil looks amused. 'What will you be advertising, sitting in the middle of this junction dressed in white?'

I laugh. 'Iced tea. Can you believe it? It's the launch of a new brand made by one of the big drinks companies, and they're going to be plastering the ads everywhere. Apparently its name was going to be Nice Tea but they decided if you say it quickly it sounds like Nasty. So now it's just called Calm. An oasis of peace in a crazy world, that kind of thing. All the traffic will be suddenly silenced by my playing. Like it always is. In real life. Particularly when I've had a synthetic sugary drink.'

Taylor nods to my glass. 'Drink up then.'

I scrutinise the bottle. 'Wrong sort of drink entirely, but never mind. A nice Bordeaux Cabernet. Not the bringer of sudden calm at all. Much more likely to make me obnoxious and tearful. I'll have to treat this as research into contrasts. This is what I am *not* recommending.'

Phil chuckles. 'Essential that you have a thorough awareness of the full spectrum of the beverage market, I imagine.'

Mum looks happy. 'And are there other things coming up, darling?' I nod, my mouth full of turkey and gravy.

'Apparently this Calm thing is going to launch me in the States. They're putting out my most recent album, you remember, the one that came out here a little while ago.'

Taylor interrupts. 'You mean the one with your kit off on the front?'

'I've always got my kit off on the front, except for the strategically placed gauze or cello. Anyway, they're releasing it there to coincide with the ads, so there'll be lots to do out there, and I'll hang around for as long as I'm welcome, really.'

'That's wonderful.'

'Do you get to fly first class?' asks Taylor, gulping a whole roast potato. I nod again.

'Business class,' I clarify, after swallowing. 'And I get to hang out in the first-class lounge at the airport. Honestly, it is the best. I turn up five hours early and get my hair and eyebrows done – for free. And all the food and drinks are free too, and there are people who keep appearing at your elbow asking ever so politely if they can fetch you anything. You can see the planes outside really clearly, and for some reason there's an enormous train set. It's free-bie paradise in there. The more money you have, the less you need to spend. It's terrible, really.'

'Yes,' says Phil. 'It sounds it.'

'What about hotels?' demands Taylor. 'Can you get free stuff on room service?'

'Mmm,' I tell him. 'Not free room service, unless I'm particularly lucky. They put me up in the most mediocre establishment they can get away with. But nice, obviously. The trouble with America, though, is that you have to tip everyone all the time. I always find myself in some position where I am so obviously supposed to hand someone a couple of dollars and I haven't got any change, or any money at all, and then the looks they shoot you. Pure hatred.'

I look around. I love being the centre of my family's attention, just for a few moments. They are all looking at me fondly. I know Taylor thinks my life is impossibly glamorous, and I am happy for him to believe in his enchanted stepsister for a few years, until he's wise enough to see through the trappings. I look down at Tessa, who is gazing at me with adoration.

'Hey,' I tell her. 'It's only me. I may get to go on planes for free sometimes, but I'm getting divorced as well. It's not all excitement and fun.'

Conversation turns to other subjects, to Phil's search for a new job and Taylor's working visa for Australia. I am pleasantly drunk. I will have a doze in front of the television this afternoon, followed by a walk. This is family life at its best. Everyone is flawed but everybody loves each other.

I can't quite shake the conviction, however, that someone is missing from the happy gathering. And it is not Jack.

chapter six

Boxing Day

I am forcing myself to do some practice when the door-bell rings. No one is due at the party for three hours, at least, so I ignore the interruption, and carry on with my scales.

I'm playing in my bedroom, which is, once again, something of a sanctuary for me. Lots has happened in this room, and it was long ago redecorated as a guest room, with neutral magnolia walls and pale green curtains, rather than the clashing reds and pinks of my day. That doesn't stop it being my little bedroom. I can still hide away here, when I need to. Today, for some reason, I need to.

This is the smallest bedroom in the house, tucked between Tessa's room and a little bathroom with views across to Clifton. I have been playing here, undisturbed, for an hour. Sometimes I love to sit and play, to let time stand still while I go over and over a cluster of notes. It is like meditation. I smell the house around me – the soothing scent of laundry, bubble bath and distant cooking

– and I go over E flat major again and again. Up the scale, from the C string through to the upper reaches of the A. Three octaves of E flat major, and I'm not hurrying it, not thinking about my marriage, my flat, my past, my future. I am simply playing. I wish I could always play like this. If I was this patient, this relaxed, every time, I might be the musician my press releases suggest. If I loved the music like I love the celebrity, I would lead an entirely different life.

I am finding the scale so soothing that I play more, concentrating on each note. I play scales fast and slowly. I play them with the accents on the first and fourth notes, and with no accents at all. I play minor and major scales, chromatic scales and arpeggios. For the first time in many months I am at ease with my cello. After the scales I play 'The Swan' from memory, and the first movement of the Elgar. Then I turn my attention to less flashy, more worthy pieces. I play groups of notes again and again and again. Then I return to the Elgar. There is a possibility that I might be playing this at a concert in New York in the spring, and the very thought petrifies me.

When, eventually, I descend the stairs to the first floor, and then the ground floor, I am serene. I have worked on parts of my repertoire that have been bothering me for years. The slow movement of the Elgar, for instance. I love it, but I've never carried it off very well. It looks simple on the page. A Grade 5 cellist could play the notes. But that is deceptive: it is one of the most demanding pieces there is, and I've never given a performance that has been more than adequate. If I do end up playing it in New York in a few months, I have vowed to surprise everyone. I know I'm going to be doing it in Paris in July. I am going to have to be able to give a confident, sustained performance, and at the moment I don't think I'm capable of it.

Mum, Phil and Guy are in the kitchen. The table is back against the wall, the double doors to the dining room are thrown open, and there are glasses arranged in rows. Bowls of snacks on every surface await the guests. I smell mulled wine.

'Hi, Guy,' I say, smiling at one of my parents' oldest friends. 'I didn't know you were here.'

He chuckles, and comes forward to kiss me. 'I knew you were. You play like an angel, my dear.'

I make a face. 'Thanks. I wish.'

Guy is my mother's age, and has been single for as long as I can remember. He was married, long ago, but his wife died, pregnant with his first, and only, child. I have never known exactly what happened, because according to my mother he was mad with grief and will not have either of them mentioned any more. Mum has been vague when I've asked her.

'Best not to dig all that up,' is all she says, and if I try to ask more she looks at me in a way that makes me feel tawdry and tabloid for wondering.

Guy is handsome, in a fifty-something way. His dark hair is slicked back, his skin creased with lines, and he wears well-cut shirts and trousers. He reminds me a little of Al Pacino. From time to time he brings a woman to the Christmas party, but it is never the same one two years running, and normally he comes alone.

'How's your love life, Guy?' I ask him, smiling.

'In a similar state to yours, from what I hear.'

Phil hands me a glass of steaming mulled wine. I clink glasses with Guy.

'Mine is great, actually. I've been out on the town with boys. It's wonderful.'

'Out on the town with boys? I don't think I'll try that strategy.' He gestures expansively. 'I don't care, you see, that's my problem. I can't be bothered with taking women out on dates. From time to time you meet someone, you decide to give it a go, make the requisite effort, and then it goes wrong and you start again. Or do you? Do you decide you're happy with your own company and leave it at that? Why embark on a doomed venture, and a costly one at that? A colleague of mine is going through his third divorce at the moment. Surgeons are notoriously bad husbands. He said the other day, that old cliché, "I'm not going to bother getting married again. I'm just going to find a woman I don't like, and give her a house." I've never wanted to get into all that.' He shrugs. 'I'm a doctor. There are always nurses.'

Mum interjects. 'That is extremely cynical, Guy.'

'Anna,' he says, 'I am fifty-five years old. It's a different matter entirely for me than it is for Evie. I'm not young, blonde, beautiful and famous with the best part of my life ahead of me. Not by any means. I possess the opposite of all your attributes, my dear. Old, grey, ugly and obscure. You will meet another tall, dark and handsome young man in the blink of an eye. I'll get by on my own.'

'I don't want to meet anyone just yet,' I say firmly. 'But Guy, I know you were married and that you were happy. I know that all ended terribly, but it can't really be the case that there was only one woman in the entire world for you. Don't you owe it to yourself to find someone to grow old with?'

I look at him warily, hoping I haven't gone too far.

Guy looks at his drink and smiles distantly, for a moment. Then he pulls himself together. 'Astonishingly, Evie,' he says, 'it seems there really was only one woman for me. So now I am destined to grow old disgracefully on my own. I intend to have as much fun as I can in the process.'

He looks around the room, at Mum, who is listening and taking a tray of vol-au-vents out of the oven at the same time, at Phil, leaning on the edge of the table with his head on one side, and at me, next to him. Through the back window I see Tessa tending her patch of bare garden, and Taylor and one of his friends having a cigarette next to the shed, where they think they can't be seen.

There is a pause. I watch Mum realising she needs to change the subject, and in a flash she says the first thing that comes into her mind.

'You remember Evie's friend Kate, Guy?' she asks, sliding the canapés on to big white plates. 'A Bristol girl? She and her husband are coming to stay with us over the new year. And after that they're off to the States for fertility treatment.'

Guy looks at me with raised eyebrows. 'Natural methods failed?'

I take a warm mushroom vol-au-vent. There is something deliciously seventies and uncool about it. It is creamy and flaky in my mouth. I take two more.

'Mmmm,' I agree, through the pastry. 'Been trying for

ever. They've found this guy near New York. Supposed to be the best. Though,' I add, swallowing a hefty mouthful, 'Kate and Ian were a bit hazy as to what he can do that all the others can't.'

Guy puts his head on one side. 'What's his name?' he asks. 'I might know of him.'

'You might well. He's British originally. Ron Thomas.'

Mum freezes for a moment. She gets over it almost instantly, and stirs the mulled wine. Then she looks at Guy.

I look at him too. He has gone quite white. When I turn to Phil, I see that his face is paralysed as well. He is gazing with concern at Guy.

'What?' I ask, looking at each of them in turn. 'Do you know him? What is it?'

Guy recovers himself. 'Used to,' he says. 'Many moons ago. He's practising in New York now, is he?'

'New York *State*,' I correct. 'Somewhere out of town, but near enough to bring IVF babies to the rich and in-fertile of Manhattan.'

'Ron Thomas and I trained together,' says Guy, lightly. 'Haven't heard anything from him for years. When are they off?'

'January the fifteenth,' I tell him. 'It's just an initial consultation. And a full medical. If he doesn't find anything new wrong with them, they're going to go back a few weeks after that, I think. On the right day of her cycle – she has to have done injections and stuff before they go. That's when he's going to take her eggs and Ian's sperm, and then they have to go back again to have them implanted.' I immediately feel I have given everyone too much information, but I needed to fill the silence.

'All right, troops,' says Mum, with a forced brightness. 'The guests are due in an hour. I suggest we all have a sandwich before they get here, so we lessen the chances of getting drunk and disgracing ourselves, and then I for one am going to get changed.'

Guy looks relieved. 'Shall I top up our glasses?' he asks. I watch him pour himself a glass of port from the table, and knock it back. I almost think his hand is trembling.

Megan and her parents turn up when the party is in full swing. There are about fifty people in the kitchen and dining room. Six of Taylor's friends appeared early on and disappeared upstairs with a bottle of vodka, while Tessa is holding court in a corner of the room with four other precocious pre-teens and several litres of Coca-Cola. I think I was the only adult who noticed her topping a bottle up with gin. Gin and Coke: a combination which only appeals to pre-teens and, perhaps, alcoholics. Mum and Phil's friends are people like them: the middle classes of Bristol and around. They are cheerful, friendly people, happily cocooned in a world where everyone has a disposable income and everybody reads books and goes to plays and concerts. I am periodically pulled into a conversation by someone I have known since childhood, and asked about my career.

'We always buy your recordings,' Mum's former colleague, Margaret, is telling me earnestly. 'We bought the Bach suites last year. Even though Nathan insisted we buy the Rostropovich version as well, and to be honest we do listen to that more often. Even though it hasn't been on TV!'

I despise comments like these. Whenever I meet a musician or a writer or an artist I make a point of telling them that I love their work. I think it's polite. I admire anyone who gets a recording released, or an exhibition put on. I know how vulnerable it makes you feel, and I consider it my obligation to reassure. I have no idea why normally pleasant people are so often unable to see that 'I like your work' is a basic courtesy. There is a particular mindset which forbids a person from enquiring after somebody else's relatively high-profile career without making a snide qualifying remark. Often I make a point of doing the same thing back.

'Are you still a financial adviser?' I snapped at Phil's friend Martin, this time last year. 'That's great. Though I do think that every financial adviser I've ever spoken to has been on the make. I mean, you can't trust a word they say, can you? It's all about commission. To be honest I'd much rather keep my money under the mattress, just so I could do without some jumped-up little prick trying to line his own pockets.' It was his fault for launching a conversation with the announcement that his mother, an amateur cellist, had been to see my recital, but that she'd been disappointed with various aspects of my perform-ance, which he went on to list. I knew that the night in question hadn't been my best performance, but he didn't need to spell it out at Christmas. He finished, smiling, by recounting, 'Mum said, though, "Of course, she gets away with it, being blonde." ' I could have punched him, and if Jack hadn't been by my side to lead me away to safety, I would have done.

Now Margaret is whistling at me through her teeth and

arranging her face into an expression which is supposed to denote sympathy, but which actually looks to me like wicked enjoyment.

'And I hear divorce may be on the cards?' she says with enormous pleasure. 'I'm so sorry, Evie.'

Megan taps me on the shoulder while I am smiling falsely and muttering about things just not working out. I turn to her with relief.

'Meg!' I cry, and kiss her cheeks. She looks like a china doll, in a white dress with a sticking-out skirt and a pink rose pattern. 'Margaret, this is Megan, my flatmate in London. Megan, Margaret used to teach with my mother. Who you haven't even met. Let's go and find her. Excuse us, Margaret.' As we walk off I say under my breath, 'Thank you so much for rescuing me! I hate that woman.'

'I could tell,' Megan replies, with a giggle, 'from your fixed grin. I've never seen you smiling like that before.'

'Happy Christmas,' I tell her. 'Did you have a good day? Let's introduce our parents to each other then mine can look after yours and we can disappear upstairs, away from all these people.'

We perform the introductions, and leave Megan's rosy-cheeked mother and her ebullient father making small talk with Mum and Phil. I take Meg up to the small sitting room, which is, surprisingly, empty of teenagers, and we sit on the sofa. The sunshine is pouring in through the back window, and I notice Taylor and a couple of his friends in the garden, starting a small fire. As I watch, one boy stamps on a cheap orange lighter and pours the fluid through the cracks on to the flames, which leap up.

'Had a good few days?' I ask her.

Megan shrugs, and pulls her legs up under her. 'Fine. Nice to see the family and the dogs. I got a car for Christmas, which won't be much use in London, but it's a nice thought. I can't even drive. This is Dad's latest hint that I should learn.' She looks at me and grins. 'Mum and Dad are excited that they got to give you a lift, and even more so that they're invited to your house. They've been telling everyone.'

I am almost embarrassed. 'I'm hardly the Queen. Surely the people of Somerset can't be that impressed. They must all have smarter houses than this, too.'

'We've had your music on a loop whenever anyone comes to the house so it gives them a conversational opening. It's mad. I've even been a little shy on your behalf at their effusiveness.'

'I can imagine your dad being effusive, but not so much your mum.'

'Oh,' says Megan dismissively, 'Mum's a funny one. It takes ages to get to know her.' She reaches over and taps me on the arm. 'Hey,' she says, 'there's a guy downstairs who's absolutely gorgeous. Who is he?'

I stare. 'There's a gorgeous guy downstairs? How come I didn't see him?'

'Not your type, certainly not a Dan Donovan. Mine. You must know who I mean. Exactly the kind of man I go for.'

Thus, five minutes later, I find myself, rather confused, saying, 'Guy, this is my flatmate, Megan. Megan, this is Guy.' Guy looks only vaguely interested at the sight of her, not least because she looks so young. And she is. She is almost exactly half his age.

'Delighted to meet you, Megan,' he says, but his heart

isn't in it. 'Can I get you lovely ladies a top-up?'

'I'll do it,' I say firmly, taking both their glasses. 'I need to talk to Mum anyway.'

Half an hour later, I look over and see that they have obtained new drinks for themselves without my help. They are deep in flirtatious conversation. I find myself hoping, surprisingly fervently, that Megan's father hasn't noticed.

chapter seven

Late January

'Thank Christ I'm out of the house,' I tell Kate with a sigh, as I sit down opposite her. 'Or thank heavens, as Megan would say, though I'm not sure why Christ is blasphemous and the heavens aren't. Anyway, tell me all about it. I want to hear everything.'

Kate is flushed. She has a new confidence. I am trying to remember whether I've seen her this positive before. I don't think I have.

'It was great,' she says, her cheeks flushed. 'I mean, I've been through these kind of appointments before, but it was different. It was all so posh, for a start. I can't believe you got us business-class tickets, and the hotel you booked us in was stunning. We pigged out on the breakfasts. And every other meal, come to that. Thanks so much.'

'That's fine. What about Ron Thomas?'

'Brilliant. His clinic is like a royal palace. It smells of polish and pot-pourri and stuff like that. The carpets are up to your ankles.'

'Even posher than the Whittington, you mean?'

'Ron would pass out if he saw the state of the Whittington. I suppose he wouldn't really, since he trained over here, but he was so cultured. He was really polite and friendly. Like he was our uncle or godfather or something. He says he's going to take what he needs when we go back, in two weeks, that's my eggs and Ian's sperm. So much easier for Ian, naturally. I know from last time that having your eggs extracted is agony, and I'm already on all sorts of hormone injections to make sure everything happens at the right time. In the bum. But who cares? He's going to implant three, and if nothing comes of that he's going to do it all over again until it works. He says there's loads more stuff he can try, and he says the success of IVF largely comes down to the skill of the embryologist. And he's the best.'

I put down the menu and look at her closely. 'Is he really or did he say that?'

'Both. Come on, Evie. We have to trust someone. Let's order breakfast.' She looks round, and a waitress duly appears at our side. Kate nods to me to order.

'I'll have the veggie breakfast, please,' I say with a smile. The waitress is petite and beautiful, with huge brown eyes, like a French actress. They are all like that, here in Notting Hill. 'And a latte, and a fresh orange juice. Thanks.'

Kate puts her menu down. 'The fruit salad for me, thanks, and a camomile tea, and I'll have a fresh orange juice too. Cheers.'

The waitress nods and drifts away cinematically, presumably to return to some opaque contemplation of a doomed love affair. 'Kate,' I say sternly. 'Is this in honour of the hormone treatment? Because I am going to sit here feeling like a fat pig now. Stuffing my face with beans and mushrooms and fried eggs while you nibble delicately on a slice of melon.'

She shrugs. 'Doctor's orders, miss. I feel bloated as it is, and I'm supposed to be being healthy.'

We both break off to watch a family arriving. It is ten thirty on Saturday morning, and the place is swarming with children. This, though, is a large family by anyone's standards. A couple in their mid thirties manage to settle at the table next to us, with a boy of about six, a girl around three, and twin babies in a double buggy that had to be collapsed to fit through the door. I see Kate's expression.

'That'll be you this time next year,' I tell her. I have said this hundreds of times over the past three years.

'I know,' she says, with a smile. 'It could be, couldn't it? If the three of them worked out, we'd have triplets by next Christmas. Imagine me, pregnant with triplets! I'd be massive. My body would probably never recover.' She is enthralled at the prospect.

'You'd wee every time you sneezed for ever more.'

'And I'd never wear a bikini again because of the stretch marks.'

'And you'd have to go for vaginal tightening.'

She looks horrified. 'Evie!'

Our food arrives. My plate is a foot in diameter. Kate's fruit comes in a white bowl, with a delicate serving of natural yogurt and honey on the side. I drink the coffee gratefully.

'I need this to wake me up,' I tell her. 'The bloody love-birds kept me up half the night, with their loud and passionate sex. They get worse every weekend. I looked at the clock at one point, when they started up again, and it was four o'clock in the sodding morning. I can't help imagining them. I would never, ever have asked her to that party if I'd had any idea that this would be the result. I suppose she had already told me about her "type", and Guy does embody it except that he's not French, but I never imagined . . . He's fifty-five!'

Kate winces. 'I can't believe you've got into that situation: The thing you dread about flatmates most of all. It's gross. I really wouldn't have thought Meg was the type. She looks so innocent.'

'I know! They do say convent girls are the worst. It freaks me out.' I look at my watch. 'The funniest thing is that I'm going out with an eighteen-year-old. Hope you don't mind, but Dan's going to pop in here in a minute. I wanted you to meet him.'

Kate covers her eyes with her hand. 'Do I have to? I'll only tell Ian and he'll tell Jack.'

'This has got nothing to do with Ian or Jack. Just say hi. He's so sweet. He is adorable. I'm taking him back to the flat. Do you want to come?'

'To witness the meeting between your toyboy and Megan's sugar daddy? No thanks, if it's all the same to you.'

'How's Jack getting on in Scotland anyway? He writes from time to time, but I know he's only trying to say the things he thinks I want to hear.'

'He's fine. It was a good idea of yours, even if you did think you were joking.'

Kate gets up to go to the loo, and as soon as she has

left the table I take the letter out of my handbag. I brought it with me to show her, to see what she thought. I haven't mentioned these letters to anyone yet, and they are starting to bother me. There was one waiting when I got back from Bristol two weeks ago, and another arrived this morning. The first was another one-worder – *Slag*, a strangely dated term – and this one is slightly more loquacious.

I smooth it out on my lap, and force myself to read it again.

See you soon, bitch. Like the others, it is printed on standard white photocopier paper. I can't decide whether it is a threat or a joke. I notice, with a strange objectivity, that my hand is shaking. It can't be from Jack, because it was posted in London W1. I will take it to the police, but I won't tell anyone else. Kate would be distressed and worried on my behalf, and she needs to be calm. If she can't eat a fried egg, she can't read hate mail either.

I am safe in the top-floor flat. No one can get in. I bolt the door and put the chain on every night, and Guy has promised to visit us every weekend. I correct myself. He will visit Megan. He has, so far, been rightly embarrassed by encountering me in my pyjamas outside the bathroom, or waiting for the kettle to boil in the kitchen. Guy is more reassuring a presence than Dan would be, if he ever stayed over.

Kate comes back, and at the same time, Dan comes through the door. I see her look at him and shudder.

I turn my electric smile on him, and stand up for a showy kiss. 'Hi!' I say, stroking the back of his neck and noting the glances we are getting from the other customers. He kisses me on the lips, and puts a hand on my waist. Dan's hair is shorter than it was last time we met, and it has been styled on top. In his wildly fashionable leather jacket, he looks every inch the young pop star.

'Dan,' I tell him, as he pulls out a chair. 'This is Kate.'

'Hello, Kate,' he says. He barely takes his eyes off me. I love being the object of this devotion.

She hides her distaste. 'Hi, Dan,' she says warmly. 'I hear your song everywhere.'

He smiles. 'I know! Me too! It's mad, isn't it?'

'It must be strange hearing your own voice singing when you go into a shop.'

'It is. I'm not stupid, Kate. I know this is just the start and I have to build on my success, but I just feel this is, like, such a great platform for me. Do you know what I mean? It's all my dreams come true.'

I look at him fondly. He is so young, so naive. In his half-unbuttoned shirt, he looks like he's trying too hard at the school disco. I want to look after him. This is not a line of thought I wish to pursue.

A teenage girl comes up from a nearby table, glares at Kate and me, and apologetically asks Dan whether she can have her photo taken with him. This, I realise, is real fame. That is something that never happens to me. I am famous, but I live my life in relative obscurity. I would love to be disturbed in restaurants. I am a classical musician. However hard I try – and I try extremely hard – I will never be an idol.

Dan's song comes over the sound system. I look round, and see the waitress smiling at us. At him. He looks at her too, and gives her a thumbs-up. She blows him a kiss. I look on, jealous.

The police station is a new building, and it smells of polish. I sit uncomfortably and wait to be seen, along with a strange assortment of other visitors. Some of them look positively scary, while others are clearly law-abiding citizens such as myself. Of course, I shouldn't make snap judgements based on idle prejudice. The middle-aged woman in the lavender twinset might be reporting in to have her electronic tag checked, while the scary man with the tattoos could be distressed over the theft of his shoulder bag. Who am I to judge?

I stare at the paper, trying to block out my surroundings, and wonder what I'm doing so far from my normal world. I almost convince myself that I am being stupid, and leave. I could ring Dan up, get him to come back over. I only made him go because the letters were niggling, and I thought I should do something about them. I didn't tell him that, and he didn't ask why I wanted him to leave. I think he likes being bossed about.

I study a poster that is trying to convince me to speak up about domestic violence, and another that reminds me to lock my car.

'Evelyn Silverman?' asks a young policewoman, walking up to me. 'Would you like to come with me?' She smiles and I follow her through a door, down a corridor carpeted with a scratchy blue matting, and into an interview room. She has blonde hair in a no-nonsense bun, and severely applied lipstick, and she looks like an actress from *The Bill*. This, of course, is because I have seen *The Bill* many more times than I have had dealings with the actual police. She flips the sign on the door to say the room is occupied. I am alarmed.

'It's OK,' she says when she sees my face. 'There's nothing official about this. It's just a place to chat. Have a seat.'

I sit on a hard chair and take the letter out of my bag.

'Right, Evelyn,' she says. 'I'm Eleanor. You've had a few nasty letters?' She takes the envelope I pass her. I watch her face as she reads it. She is completely inscrutable. 'This is to the point. How many of these have there been?' she asks, looking up.

'It's the third. I threw away the first one. It said "Bitch". The second one said "Slag". Am I being stupid coming here? The last thing I want to do is waste your time. I mean, people get *charged* with wasting police time, don't they?'

She smiles. 'Not in your case. Not unless you were writing these yourself.' I look at her, alarmed. She smiles. 'Which of course you are not. You did the right thing. If you get another one, try not to handle it any more than you can help. Put it straight into a plastic folder and bring it to me. It's best if you don't open it.'

'So can you do anything?'

She looks down at the letter again. 'Not easily, to be honest. It's printed from a computer, so that's going to make it hard to identify. If you have a good idea where they're coming from we can certainly check that out for you, although to be honest we are rushed off our feet at the moment. There's a possibility of DNA on the envelope, but I strongly suspect it was moistened with a sponge. People are wise to that one now, thanks to the TV.' She looks at me, with a friendly direct gaze. 'Do you have any ideas?'

I wriggle in my chair, trying to get comfortable. 'At first I thought they were from my husband. We split up a couple of months ago and he came over one night, the same day the first one arrived. He was in quite a state. But they're not his style, plus he's in Scotland. So . . .' I give her a dazzling smile. 'I don't imagine you've seen me,' I tell her modestly, 'but I'm in the papers from time to time. I'm a musician, and the tabloids take an interest occasionally. There was a photo of me in the *Standard* a while ago, before the first letter came, with the name of my apartment block in it. Then the same picture was in the *Sun*, and they said in the piece that it was off "swanky Kensington Church Street". I think it probably came from someone who reads one of those papers.'

'What kind of musician are you?'

I smile apologetically, wishing I could say I was, for instance, Radiohead's little-known female guitarist. 'Classical. I play the cello.'

She looks at me, eyes narrowed. 'Were you in that royal thing for Prince Charles's birthday?' I nod. 'I know you! You were on the mobile phone advert too.' I nod again. 'And,' she says triumphantly, 'you've been going out with Dan Donovan! Great! Well, like I said, we can't do a lot right now, and if it comes from a *Standard* or *Sun* reader, that doesn't exactly narrow the field. There are millions of them. If it was from someone who saw you in the *Standard*, that would suggest a Londoner, as do the post-marks. Do you live on your own?'

'No, I have a flatmate, but neither of us is exactly a black belt in karate.'

'Um, and I suppose I can assume that you have a boyfriend?'

'Dan? Yes, he's gorgeous, isn't he? Meg's going out with someone older. Dan comes over from time to time and Meg's boyfriend is only there at weekends, and not every weekend.'

Eleanor leans forward. 'Look, I don't want to worry you,' she says, 'and these things almost always come to nothing, but if she ever stays with him instead, or goes away anywhere, I suggest you go to Dan's, or to friends or family for the weekend. Just for your own peace of mind.'

I nod, scared.

'But like I said, ninety-nine per cent of the time there's nothing to worry about. It's just a precaution. Obviously don't open the door unless you're a hundred per cent certain that you know who it is, and that you believe them. You could consider a video entryphone if this continues. And maybe stop having takeaways delivered, that kind of thing. Avoid situations where you could be opening the door to strangers.'

'OK,' I tell her.

'But, Evelyn?' she says. 'Don't let this preoccupy you too much. I'm certain you're going to be fine and, like you said, that this is someone who saw you in the paper and has a twisted mind and is getting a kick out of the idea of scaring you. They'd be over the moon if they could see you now, talking to the police. They're very unlikely to come looking for you. I mean it. There is also a chance that this could be your husband, however out of character it might seem. So, if you feel that you can, it is worth confronting him about it and seeing what his reaction is.'

I smile wanly. 'Thanks,' I tell her. I hope she's right.

By the time I get home, looking over my shoulder all the way, I am not in the mood for seeing Guy and Megan again, and I am still less in the mood for an interview with the *Daily Mail*. Yet both of these things are on my agenda for the rest of the day.

'It's the famous cellist!' exclaims Guy, before I have even stepped through the door. 'Come back without her youthful consort. Come in, Miss du Pré.'

'Shut up, Guy,' I say, rather more curtly than I had intended.

He pulls an exaggerated 'oops' face at Megan. 'Sorry,' he says with fake contrition. Megan giggles. Guy is wearing a T-shirt and jeans, and Megan is in her dressing gown. I ignore them both, and head straight for my bedroom, where I shut the door firmly. There is a used condom on the table, from earlier, and I wonder what would happen if I impregnated myself with Dan's sperm. Then I drop it into the bin, and drop a magazine on top of it, just in case the journalist comes into my room.

I check my clock. In two and a half hours she will be coming round to write about what a survivor I am. I know I have to be shy about my relationship with Dan, and I'm glad she knows about it so I don't have to do anything so vulgar as saying his name. I take a clean towel from my cupboard, and decide I must start with a shower.

Megan taps on the door. 'Evie?' she says. 'Are you OK?'

'Hi, Meg,' I reply, as brightly as I can. 'Of course. Come in. Sorry if I was grumpy.'

'That's fine,' she says, slipping through the door. 'As long as you're all right?' She kicks her slippers off and sits cross-legged on the bed. 'Dan's sweet, isn't he? It's very odd to meet someone in real life who you've seen on telly a thousand times.'

'I know. He's lovely.'

'Though not your type, I wouldn't have thought.'

'He's just what I need right now. I'm very fond of him.'

'And he adores you.'

'His "people" are furious with him for being seen out with me all the time. So he must quite like me to carry on doing it anyway.'

'There was a call for you. Another admirer. A guy called Dominic? He said he's in London, wondered if you wanted to meet up. I wrote his number down for you next to the phone.'

I perk up a little. 'Dominic? Cool. Thanks, Meg.'

'Who's he?'

'Just a pianist I work with sometimes.' Just the man I spent a night with. The man with whom I had spectacular, guilty sex. The man who finally made me see that my marriage was over. 'But quite cute. I might get him to take me to dinner.'

'My word, Evie, you are in demand. He sounded flipping keen.'

The woman from the *Mail* has insane hair. It has been styled so that no trace of what it must have been like naturally remains. I try to imagine what it looks like in the morning, before she's blow-dried and styled it, and I wonder whether she's single, or whether only a married woman, whose husband is long since used to it, can maintain that sort of hairstyle. She is, I estimate, forty-two. Perhaps, if she's single, she sets her alarm for six on the mornings after she pulls, and leaps into the shower before her beau sees what she really looks like. Maybe she carries a hairdryer and an arsenal of products every time she goes out, just in case. I check the size of her handbag. It is capacious. Then again, her hair might be a wig.

'It's terribly kind of you to invite me to your home,' she says, again.

I simper. 'You're welcome. There's nothing to hide.' Except, I add to myself, for one used condom. 'Feel free to go through the bathroom cabinets!'

She laughs, a tinkling, fake laugh. 'Oh, that's not what we do at all, Evie. It's folklore.'

'Well, anything embarrassing belongs to my flatmate.'

She holds her head on one side and pretends to note this point in her notebook. I'm not sure which of us is sucking up to the other more keenly. I know she has the upper hand, that she could turn this interview into a slating of me if the fancy took her. I also know that the chances are strong that an offhand remark I make will end up as the headline, and that I have to select every word I say with enormous care.

'All right, Evie,' she says. 'If it's all right with you, I'll switch the tape recorder on now. Mmm, this tea is perfect.'

'Of course, Jane.'

'Now, I'd like to tackle the split between you and your husband first, if that's all right. I'm sorry we have to go over it, but you do understand, don't you? Let's get it over with.' I nod, and push my hair behind my ears. I have made myself, and our flat, into a fantasy version of real life. I am washed, made-up, moisturised and blow-dried, my nails filed and painted a sober neutral. I am wearing a long and demure black skirt with black tights, and a deep red cashmere jumper. My hair has been styled for half an hour to make it look artless. I'm wearing diamanté stud earrings and a simple silver necklace, and I've put my wedding ring back on. My make-up is subtle and, I hope, barely noticeable. I know some papers don't like divorced women, and particularly divorced career women, but I hope that I represent the acceptable face of Things Just Not Working Out.

'Was there a particular incident,' she asks delicately, pen poised, 'that made your separation inevitable?'

Yes, I want to say, I shagged a pianist. I committed adultery. It wasn't the first time by any means. My husband still has no idea. And then there's my past. Jane would adore that.

'No,' I tell her, 'there was no one else involved. Jack and I were very happy for most of our marriage, and I'm still extremely fond of him. But we both agreed that it wasn't working. Our lives were so diverse. My work takes me all over the world, and that caused problems in our domestic life. I'm very aware that I chose to have this career and I feel terrible . . .' I let my voice quaver for a moment. 'I really do. I feel awful that I made a decision to use the talent I have, if that doesn't sound too boastful, to do the thing I feel I was born to do. And that this choice has led to the end of our partnership. We are still very good friends, and I talk to him a lot.' I force a wan smile. 'Who knows, Jane? Who can tell what the future will hold?'

She smiles. 'Will Dan Donovan be a part of that future, do you think?'

I laugh. I try to make it a tinkling laugh, but I'm not sure whether I succeed. 'Since I've been on my own he has been a very good friend to me, Jane. I'm extremely fond of him. We seem to have a certain spiritual bond. I can't make any predictions.'

'But despite your high-profile romance, you say you remain good friends with Jack?'

Last time I spoke to him, I want to say, we were awkward and embarrassed with each other and couldn't think of much to say. And I've been getting these letters.

I nod. 'Oh yes, he really is a best friend to me. He's away in Scotland at the moment, but we are very much in touch. There are no secrets.' I almost guffaw as I say it. 'Any romances, as you call them, that either of us has are not for the long term. It's a shock when a marriage doesn't work, and I'm interested, right now, in sorting my priorities out. I've moved into this flat, which as you can see is very homely, and it's a great place for me to get my head together. I feel safe and secure here.'

Do I hell. This is a message to my anonymous correspondent, so he thinks I'm not bothered. I hope it doesn't inflame him. 'My flatmate, Megan, is a lovely girl,' I continue, safe in the knowledge that she and Guy have gone to the cinema at my insistence, and that Jane won't be treated to the spectacle of the two of them falling through the door together and tumbling straight to the bedroom. I don't think the sight of a young waif being felt up by a man who looks

107

old enough to be her grandfather would be edifying to Jane. Actually, I think she would relish it, but I don't intend to give her the chance. 'We sit and chat, drink tea, go shopping, and it's giving me time to get my life back on track. Although I know it's going to be a long road, whichever way things go. I'm under no illusions about that.'

Jane nods compassionately. 'About your husband,' she says, but stops as the phone rings. I am seized by indecision. If I let the machine pick it up, the message will be relayed to the *Daily Mail*. If I rush to answer it, I will look rude and flustered and like a girl with something to hide.

'Excuse me,' I say politely. 'I wouldn't normally, but I'm expecting a call about work.'

'I was hoping to hear about your work,' says Jane pleasantly. 'By all means.' She gestures to the phone. I snatch it up. Jane's head is cocked to one side.

'Hello?' I ask, as serenely as I can.

'Evie!'

'Yes?'

'It's me! Dominic. Hey, Evie, how're you doing? Long time no speak!'

'Hi, Dominic,' I say reluctantly. 'Look, can I call you back? I know you're in town and I know we've got a lot of rehearsing to do for Paris, and I'd love to talk it all through with you, but this isn't a good moment. I've got your numbers.'

He sounds confused. 'You sound really weird, sweetie. Are you OK? I was sorry to hear about your husband, but, you know, kind of glad. In a way. You're not too hooked up with this little boy, are you? I want to take you out, get you drunk again.'

I frown, hoping Jane can't hear him. 'Sure. Look, I'll ring you. Bye!'

'Are you—' I cut him off, turn the volume right down on the answer machine, and switch it on.

'Sorry,' I say with a big smile. 'An accompanist I work with in Paris. We've got a slot in a radio broadcast in July.'

Jane raises an eyebrow. 'Really? Tell me more. In a moment. First of all, I need to ask – a girl like you must receive a lot of attention and offers. Were there ever any moments during your marriage when you were tempted . . .?'

When she leaves, I breathe out, kick my shoes off, and text Megan to tell her it's OK to come home. Then I call Dominic back and explain. He laughs long and hard, and wishes he had been obscene. He sounds relieved that I wasn't being standoffish with him. I object to his familiarity. We have worked together for a year or so, but we've never been on friendly terms before. I used to admire his body and his haphazard dress sense from afar. He wouldn't be speaking to me like this were it not for the sex.

We arrange to go out on Friday. I know I have to play this skilfully, to keep his friendship without becoming his girlfriend. I don't particularly want to sleep with him, either.

I call Dan and tell him that I don't think anything I've said will get him into trouble.

'Don't worry about it,' he says. 'I'm in trouble anyway. I don't even care. I'd like to be in your interview.'

Then I call Jack. He answers his mobile on the first ring, sounding eager.

'It's me,' I tell him.

'Oh.' He sounds disappointed. 'How come your name didn't come up on my phone?'

'I went anonymous. Being a public figure and all that.'

'You wish.'

'Who were you hoping was ringing?'

He sounds guarded. 'What do you mean? I'm in a bloody monastery, Evie. It's exciting when my phone rings.'

'Cut the crap. You thought I was someone else and you were excited. Have you met a girl? Is that allowed, in a monastery?' I keep my voice light and teasing.

'Shut up,' he says abruptly. 'Why are you ringing me?'

'To warn you about the *Mail*. There'll be an interview in, probably next Thursday. I didn't slag you off.'

'Cheers. Look, I've got to go. Got some chanting to do.'

He cuts me off, leaving me staring at the receiver. My husband has a girlfriend, or at least a potential date. He is supposed to be hanging on for me. This might call for a change of strategy.

Dominic takes me to Soho House on Friday and gets me drunk. I lean on the table and stare into his eyes, as he tells me that I'm beautiful and sexy and that he wants to take me home and fuck me senseless. We are in a dark corner, and I gamble on the fact that no media people are sober enough, or observant enough, to spot me. To have two lovers and a husband could be regarded as immoral.

While I am there, I enjoy the attention and forget everything else, and I am happy to comply with his suggestion. For a few moments I feel carefree and sexy.

In the morning I look at him with horror. I feel nothing for him, and I can't wait to get him out of my bed, out of my flat. After he leaves I cry, although I'm not sure exactly what I am crying about.

chapter eight

February

The flight, or at least the business-class part of the plane, is almost empty. I study the menu with my legs stretched out, and smile to myself. I am getting good at this. Good at making sure things are the way I want them. Jack is putty in my hands, and it comforts me to fly to New York knowing that he would – he did – fly back from Scotland because I asked him to.

I would love to have an indulgent meal, and get drunk, but I know I can't. This is a working trip, and I'm only going to be working for the first three days, and I cannot possibly turn up the worse for wear and expect that no one will notice. I scrape by, professionally, as it is. Drinking at altitude will do nothing for my intonation and musicality when I get there. I have to be reliable or I won't get the work. Above all, this time, I have to look good, or I will be fired. This is the biggest advert I have done. It is my chance to break America. It is tragic that a soft-drink advertisement could do more for my career than any live performance ever would, but that is the way my life works. I chose that path with my eyes open and I love all the trappings. I have to stick to my side of the bargain.

I have slept with three men in the past three weeks. Although I don't want to shout about it, this fact pleases me. I am desirable to eighteen-, thirty- and forty-year-olds alike. I am a desirable woman, and I can use that fact. I feel powerful. Part of me feels sorry for Jack, but not very.

Books and magazines don't hold my attention. I look around the plane. I can't imagine travelling economy class any more. Even when we went on holiday I would always pay for Jack and me to fly in comfort. I am spoiled, but at least I am well aware that it won't last for ever. The fear is always there, nagging at the back of my mind. I know that one day, soon, someone is going to find me out, and I'm not going to get away with it any longer. I have to make the most of it while it lasts, and the moment I get complacent is the moment it stops. Everyone thinks I am grounded and happy. Nobody realises that I walk around with a constant expectation, at the back of my mind, of being unmasked.

The stewardess appears at my side, with the trolley.

'Something to drink, madam?' she enquires, with a smile. I'm sure the smiles are warmer in business class.

I sigh. 'Mineral water, please.'

'Sparkling or still?'

'Still, thanks.' How boring. How necessary. She hands me a snack to go with it. I look out of the window at the soft clouds, and straighten my legs. Even completely straight, they don't reach the back of the seat in front. I recline my seat and sip my water. I love travelling on my own. I adore long flights. I am flying trans-Atlantic with no one sitting next to me, or behind me, or in front of me. This should be heaven. I study the movie list, desperate for something to make me forget the other night, and decide to watch a random romantic comedy.

This jumbo is the best environment for me right now. I'm neither in one country nor another, and I'm completely alone, with, for these precious hours, no responsibilities to anyone.

When Jack called me, on the day Jane's reasonably friendly piece appeared in the *Mail*, I didn't expect an announcement. I thought he was just ringing to complain that I'd talked about Dan in the interview. Even though I only said a couple of words about him, it was the peg on which the entire piece was hung.

'I've met someone else too,' he said, abruptly. 'I may as well tell you. Since you're seeing someone so publicly. She's called Sophia.'

I was taken aback. 'Is she Scottish?' I asked, for some reason.

'No. She lives in London too. She's been up here for the same reason as me, to get a bit of perspective on her life.'

'Oh.'

'She's an actress.'

'That's great.'

I made a token effort to sound happy for him, but I was livid. Jack is supposed to be my reserve player. He said he loved me and he would always be there for me. And yet he has apparently managed to pull in a monastery.

I wonder if I have now sabotaged their relationship. I

can pretend to other people that I hope I haven't, that I hope Sophia will never find out, but I can't pretend to myself. Even if she doesn't find out what happened, Jack is now lying to her. They are no longer the perfect couple, and I am glad.

When the latest letter arrived, two days ago, I called Jack and cried down the phone. I started to tell him what was going on, then clammed up and sobbed and refused to say anything else. Much sooner than I had expected, he was telling me that he was on the way home. That afternoon, he rang the buzzer and took me out for some stiff drinks.

He looked good, I thought as I opened the front door. Life as a Scottish Buddhist clearly suited him.

'Evie,' he said. 'Come here.' He took me in his arms. 'You look gorgeous,' he added.

'You don't have to say things like that,' I told him with a smile. 'You're my husband.'

When I saw the way he looked at me then, I knew I could have him back.

Sometimes I wonder if I am a truly horrible person. I suppose I am, in many ways. I don't feel bad about it: if I felt bad, I would change. This is how I have been since I was sixteen. It's the way I have to be.

It could be worse. I could be an alcoholic. I could have fallen apart completely, but I haven't. I have a fabulous life. Everybody envies me. That is because hardly anybody actually knows me.

It is all Louise's fault. I told her my biggest secret. Mum said I should keep it from everyone at school, even from Louise, because my life would be hell if it was spread around. I told her that Louise was my best friend in the world and always would be, and so, before I left Bristol for America, I confided in her. I told her all about the thing that will consume me for the rest of my life, the thing that is beginning, once again, to keep me awake at night. For years I pushed it away and never articulated it in my thoughts, and now it is crowding back in.

Louise was my best friend from the age of twelve. We were inseparable for four years. She had short black hair, and freckles, and big brown eyes. I was skinny and mousy: I wanted to be like her in every way. She was more confident than me, more popular than me, and, I thought, nicer and more dependable than I was.

When I disappeared to America, only Louise knew the reason why. When I came back, she put her arm round me, comforted me, told me I'd get over it and that she would look after me. She said it would always be a secret and I could trust her for ever. I knew she was the best friend I would ever have, the only true friend I ever needed, and I told her every single detail of what had happened.

Two weeks after I got back to school, she changed her mind and started spreading the news. I came into the classroom one morning, at a quarter to nine, and saw her leaning into a huddle with two other girls. They were popular, gossipy girls, who usually ignored nobodies like Louise and me. My stomach tightened in fear, but I told myself I was being stupid. Louise was my friend. I had been away. She was bound to have made some new alliances. She was probably talking about the tickets she'd got us for the Nelson Mandela concert. I instructed myself not to be paranoid, and I sat at my desk, and looked back over to them.

Both girls were staring at me. When I caught their eyes they looked quickly back to Louise. She nodded, and their mouths gaped. I lip-read one saying, 'No *way*!' Louise nodded. 'Way,' said her mouth. She smiled, pleased with herself, and refused to look at me. She had decided to sacrifice my friendship on the altar of her own wider popularity.

I was still feeling weak, and my stitches were sore. I was empty and miserable, and school was the last place I wanted to be. The whole class knew by the end of the morning, and the whole school by the end of the day. I denied it when I got the opportunity, but most people gave me a wide berth, and talked about me as I passed. I ignored them as best I could, and devoted myself to my GCSEs. I ended up with As in all of them, because I had nothing to do but study.

I hate Louise. I hope she has died horribly from cancer or AIDS. If not, I hope she has noticed my career and been jealous of me, and regretted the fact that, if she'd stayed my friend, she could have enjoyed the reflected glory. It's exactly the kind of thing she would have loved. I hope she has a dead-end job cold-calling on behalf of an insurance company and that annoyed householders swear at her on the phone every day. I hope she earns a pittance and hasn't had sex for five years.

I went to sixth-form college and never spoke to anyone from our old school again. I knew that the only way I could have a future was by reinventing myself. It seemed to work. Before, I would never have had the courage to introduce myself to someone as pretty as Kate, but now I had nothing to lose, so while we were waiting for our music teacher for the first class of the A-level syllabus, I turned to her and made myself smile.

'Are you a musician, then?' I asked her, trying to talk like a happy, unconcerned person.

She turned back to me and grinned. 'I play the flute. I'm not brilliant, though. I think I'm going to find A level really tricky, but I want to have a bash at it. How about you?'

Kate and I were friends from the start. She'll never know how much her friendship did for me, in those early days. I never told her my secret. I never told anyone, after Louise. To this day, however, I sometimes pass women on the street in Bristol, and from the way they look at me, I know where they went to school, and when.

The repercussions of Louise's betrayal have been almost as bad as the legacy of the incident itself. I never confide in people any more. I only tell people things I would be happy to see passed on. I'm sure I could trust Kate, but I'm never going to test her. I have to get through this on my own. I've always got through things on my own before, and I will do it again now.

The stewardess reappears at my side, and I shake away the unwelcome introspection and ask for a vegetarian meal, in a half-hearted attempt to choose the healthy option. I would have been more virtuous ordering the fish, but the veggie option is linguine with creamy mushroom sauce, and that's what I fancy. It doesn't sound particularly slimming. I add that I'll have a white wine with it. I'm sure no one really expects me to cross the Atlantic without a drop of alcohol, and besides, now that Louise has re-entered my head, I need some support, and it's only going to come from the inside of a bottle.

She brings two bottles and I am grateful.

'It's a long flight,' she says, 'and I'm sure you need it. I would, if I was allowed. Can I just say, Miss Silverman, I read an article about you in the *Mail* a while ago and I was full of admiration. My husband and I are great fans of yours.'

I switch on the professional charm and hope she hasn't been watching me brooding. 'It's so kind of you to say so!' I gush. 'Really, I appreciate it so much. Please pass on my best wishes to your husband as well.' I attempt to give her a dazzling smile.

She reciprocates. I wonder who has the best professional faux-charm: an air hostess, or a minor celeb. 'Thank you. He's going to be so jealous that I met you. He'll kill me. I don't suppose I could ask you to sign something for him?'

It is becoming harder and harder to reconcile my public face with what's really going on. Several magazines followed up the *Mail*'s piece and I have been brave and self-deprecating, remorseful yet confident and positive on news stands everywhere for the past couple of months. The urge to be honest with them is almost overwhelming. As far as they are concerned, the most interesting facet of my life is the fact that I am sleeping with an eighteen-year-old who, three months ago, was completely unknown. Dan's charms are already wearing off. I need to get rid of him. We have nothing to talk about except the media.

Dominic is amused by my new persona, and threatens to sell his story and tell the world that I'm 'a great shag', and even though he's joking it terrifies me, because I don't know him particularly well, and he might do it. If I piss him off, he could do it.

I smile at the thought of Dominic. I doubt he would go to the papers with 'My Night with Evie'. He is too busy enjoying his life, and I don't think he's desperate for cash. Dan would never, ever talk to a journalist about me, because his minders wouldn't let him. I should be safe from kiss-and-tells, at least.

The food is astonishingly nice. I'm always surprised by the quality of airline food. I watch a bit of the film and eat every single thing on my tray. I drink one bottle of wine and the water, then let my new friend take the tray away, leaving me to drink the other bottle. Its contents disappear strangely quickly. I force myself not to ask for a third.

Jack told me about the couple who are buying our house in Greenwich. I couldn't have cared less, so I let it wash over me and waited for him to finish. They are expecting their first baby in a couple of months, he said, pointedly. The house will be perfect for them. It is an ideal house for a baby, not too big, not too small, and with the park a couple of minutes' walk away. Jack revealed he had even painted the walls to make it less tatty, more enticing to buyers. They won't need to change anything.

'Great,' I said, bored. 'Let's go for a drink.'

The pub was crowded and smoky. Jack found a table and bought me a glass of wine. I watched him while he was at the bar. He was dressed in new jeans and a jumper that I had never seen before. It suited him. I was alarmed to see him moving on. He wasn't my Jack any more. He was Sophia's Jack. He was no longer where I needed him.

Sophia and Jack. They even sound good together. And she is an actress. I imagine a twenty-year-old Juliette Binoche.

'Got you a large glass,' he said, smiling as he threw himself on to the stool. 'You sounded like you needed it this morning.'

'Thanks,' I told him, clinking glasses. 'Cheers.'

'So, what's up?'

He looked eager, and I made sure he reacted in exactly the way I wanted him to. It was almost too easy.

'Jack?' I asked. My voice came out small and vulnerable.

'Mmm?' He leaned forward.

'I have to ask you something. Don't be offended.'

'I can't imagine you could say much to offend me, Evie.'

'You haven't written me any letters, have you?'

He frowned. 'Letters? I did write some when we first split up, when things were a little raw. But I never sent them. Unless I did when I was drunk without remembering. Which is a possibility but I doubt it. What letters do you mean?'

'It's OK. I know they're not from you. Don't think that I'm even suggesting it. But the police said I had to ask you.'

He put down his pint. 'The *police*?'

'Mmm.' I took a letter out of my handbag. 'This is a photocopy of the latest one. It's the fifteenth, I think. Sixteenth, maybe.' I took a deep breath. 'They come all the time. Every week, now. Sometimes twice a week. And no one knows about them except the police and now you.' A tear slid down my nose and I blinked hard and wiped it away when I knew he was looking. Jack took the sheet of paper and stared at it.

'Evie!' he said, and moved his chair closer to mine. 'Evie, this is horrible. Bloody hell. It's disgusting.' He put a hand on my sleeve.

'I know.'

'And these are reaching you at home?'

'Yes. The address isn't quite right, but they get there.'

'And are they all like this? Threatening, I mean?'

'They're getting worse. This one is really quite specific, isn't it? They used to be a bit more vague than that. And much shorter.'

'Evie, this guy says he's going to come into your bedroom and rape you.'

I blinked harder. 'I know.' It came out as a whisper.

I told him how I'd hoped the first few were from him, even though I'd known, really, that they weren't. I told him that Megan doesn't know, despite the fact that she is as vulnerable as I am. I know I should tell her, because it affects her too. The policewoman always asks how Megan feels, and I always mutter something about being supportive. I can't admit that she doesn't know. The longer I leave it, the worse it gets. I can't tell her now that threatening, obscene, terrifying letters have been arriving at the flat since the week after I moved in.

'You have to tell her,' Jack said firmly. 'She has the right to know.'

'I know,' I said, looking down. 'But I feel terrible. It's her parents' flat. And I've brought it to the attention of a stalker.'

Jack sighed. 'Evie, he's not stalking the flat. He's stalking you. Talk to Megan. Get new locks on the doors, get a video entryphone. Get bars on the windows. Move out. Do whatever you have to do. You can't carry on living there under these circumstances.'

He looked at me, saw the tears, and put his arm round my shoulders.

'Come here,' he said, and pulled me towards him. I leant my head on his shoulder, and let him protect me for a moment.

'I'm sorry, Jack,' I murmured. 'I'm sorry to get you back from Scotland for this.'

It felt natural to turn my face up towards his, and he kissed me like he used to when we were first together. As our lips met, and then our tongues, I felt a surge of satisfaction. I had him back. I had used my letters to get him back where I wanted him. I knew I was cold and hard, and I didn't care.

When we pulled apart, I looked at him anxiously. I didn't want him to regret it. He smiled.

'Well, well,' he said. 'You're gorgeous. It's been too long. Do you want me to take you home?'

I nodded. 'Are you OK?' I asked. 'What about Sophia?'

He gave a small laugh. 'Hey, you're my wife. It's allowed.'

He stayed the night. We squashed together in my single bed, and I made sure I took the side next to the wall, exactly as I used to do when we were at university, so he couldn't push me off the edge in the night. Jack and I fit better in a single bed than Dominic and me.

He was with me almost all of yesterday. We walked around west London together, stopped in cafés and shops, talked about inconsequential matters, and acted in every way like a loving couple. I suppose a part of me does love him, in a way. Mostly, I love the fact that he loves me. We didn't talk about Sophia at all. Jack seemed happy to forget all about her, and when his phone rang, in the middle of the morning, he let it go to voicemail, then switched it off.

On the limo ride to the hotel, I try to muster some energy. I suddenly feel drained. It is the flight, I tell myself, though I know that, in fact, it's Louise. It's the fact that I let myself think about her again. Louise has officially been banned from my brain for fourteen years.

Being in America again also makes me edgy. I look through the tinted glass and try to enjoy the petrol stations and the rows of houses, and the sponsored highway litter collections. Everybody else loves arriving in New York, and I can see why, but for me there are too many complications. The traffic is fairly clear, and before long we are emerging from the Midtown tunnel into Manhattan. I look at the familiar lines and delicate curves of the Empire State Building, shrug my shoulders, and pour myself a drink from the well-stocked minibar. I don't have to pay for the drinks in the car, whereas I do if I raid the bar in the hotel room. May as well make the most of it. Besides, my body clock says it's nine in the evening, and everyone's allowed a drink at that time. I find some gin, because it's a depressant and I am wallowing, and add some tonic. Spirit and mixer mingle in roughly equal quantities. It numbs me, slightly.

I am back in America. Last time I was here was for Howard and Sonia's wedding. I went straight from the airport to their house in Queens, stayed one night, and avoided Manhattan altogether. The whole world loves Manhattan. It makes them feel that they're in a film, that they can be anyone they want to be. I love it, too, on a good day. I love the energy. I love the differences between this city and London. I adore the way it's so hard to get lost here, in the numbered streets and avenues. I love the fact that a park in a city can be so huge.

But New York can no longer work its special magic on me. I can only become one other person while I'm here: my teenage self.

All I can think of are those four terrible months when I was fifteen. I celebrated my sixteenth birthday in my father's apartment. I remember looking down on his street – East Fifty-fourth – and seeing a woman pushing a stroller down the road, with a baby asleep inside and a little girl holding the side of it, next to her. The girl had a woollen coat on, the sort the royal family used to dress their children in. The woman looked tired, and was wearing jeans and a tight white top and a leather jacket. She had long, light brown hair, like mine was back then. I watched them idling down the road, and before I knew what was happening, I was erupting in ugly sobs.

'What is it?' demanded Howard, rushing into the room. 'Evie, what is it?'

I pointed at them. 'A family.'

He looked. 'That's a nanny, darling.'

'You don't know that.'

'I do. You can spot them at fifty paces. A woman who dressed her kid like that wouldn't dress herself like *that*. She'd be in Gucci, head to toe. This woman's in the Gap.'

125

'It doesn't matter.'

He hugged me. 'I know. It'll be over soon.'

I remember looking at him. 'I don't want it to be over.'

'You'll be able to go home and get on with your life.'

'I don't want to go home and get on with my life.'

He sighed. 'Yes you do. You will. You'll look back on this in years to come and be thankful that you took the only choice that was available to you.'

'I wish I'd told someone earlier.'

He squeezed my shoulders. 'We all do, sweetie. But you didn't, and this is the only other option.'

The baby kicked. I felt sick. I hated it, and I loved it, and I wished I could wake up from the nightmare.

Don't think about the baby. Do not think about the baby. I refill my glass, this time with neat vodka, and knock it back. Out of the window, brownstone houses with fire escapes line the road, letting me know, casually, that I really am in Manhattan. I don't care. I never have to work out how old my child is. I always know it without thinking. Then I calculate it, and I am invariably right. She will be fifteen on June the second. I will be thirty-one on May the second. She was born exactly a month after my sixteenth birthday. I drink more vodka. I mustn't think about her. Nothing good can possibly come of it. I am over it now.

We have stopped. The driver says over his shoulder, 'Here we are, madam.' I swallow what remains in my glass, and step out of the open door, wondering why I didn't think to bring some dollar bills for tipping. I hardly ever let myself dwell on what happened. I never allow myself to articulate the words 'my' and 'baby' in conjunction with each other. Mum and Phil know about it. Howard obviously knows about it. The headmistress knew and so did some of my teachers. I have never told anyone else, not Kate, not Jack. But I did tell Louise, and so the whole school found out.

Once someone from Bristol told the *Sun* that I had an illegitimate child when I was a teenager and had it adopted, and they came round to ask me if it was true. I acted astonished and denied it, petrified because Jack was standing behind me at the door. They couldn't find any records of a birth, so they dropped it. I have always wondered whether it was Louise, or some bitchy opportunist looking to make a few hundred pounds. It chills me to know that, if Mum and Phil and Howard hadn't decided to hide me in America, my secret would be out by now. It doesn't bear thinking about.

The sun is shining in Manhattan, and I barely see my suitcase and cello as they are whisked away by a porter. The doorman ushers me into the foyer, and I look around. They have pushed the boat out this time. I thought a hotel in Times Square would be, at best, faceless and bland. This one is new and extremely trendy. The lobby is discreetly lit, with lamps, lots of wood, and a large abstract rug on the floor. This, I realise, is a 'boutique' hotel. It is not owned by a huge corporation.

I rummage in my purse and find a twenty-dollar bill.

'Before I check in,' I say brusquely to the tanned receptionist, 'could you change this for me?'

She beams as if my request has made her day. 'Hi there! *Sure!*'

I rush back through the hushed lobby, and tip the driver,

the doorman and the porter, all of whom immediately and enthusiastically like me again. Then I check in on autopilot, remembering to offer a false smile from time to time. If I run out of insincerity, I will be finished.

My room is large and airy, with blond-wood shutters surrounding a window which overlooks the Square from a reassuring height. Despite the flattering lighting, I can't help noticing that I look like death. I throw myself on the enormous bed, kick off my shoes, roll over and try to pull myself together. I am here to work, and it could take my career on to another stage. It is vital that I don't fall apart. If I turn up at the studio tomorrow wan and listless and hungover, they will fire me. They will do it in the most euphemistic way possible, and I might not even realise they're doing it, but I will suddenly find I am no longer welcome.

I am in New York. I had the baby in New York. She was adopted in New York. This is not a straightforward place. I study the ceiling, which is plain and white. No cracks. Nothing to watch up there. Then I pick up the remote control from the bedside and flick through some inane television channels. It seems to be mostly adverts, and I turn it off again. I am not in the mood for *Will and Grace* or home shopping. I consider calling Jack, but I can't be bothered to speak to anyone.

I wish my life had turned out differently. If I hadn't found myself pregnant at fifteen, I might have been shy and obscure for ever. I think I would have been happier, but I cannot wish that baby out of existence, even though I have played no part in her life. As it is, everything I have ever done has been a façade. I look like a success, but it's an illusion. Up close, I have no substance. I am a bitch, just because I can't feel safe being any other way. I don't know how you can be a failure when you have money and a career, friends and family, but I am living, walking, talking proof that it's possible.

The phone rings. I wait five rings before answering it.

'Hello?' I say, hoping for Howard, or for Kate.

'Evie! Hi there!' says an enthusiastic man. 'This is Alexis Stone! How are you *doing* there?'

Alexis Stone is the PR assigned to me by the label. His job is to launch me on to an unsuspecting New York. I sigh, take a deep breath, and step back behind the façade.

'Alexis!' I exclaim. 'Good to hear from you. I'm doing great. Just great.'

'Wonderful, Evie. Listen, I'm thinking dinner. We have reservations. How is the Gramercy Tavern at nine o'clock?'

I screw my eyes tight shut. 'Fabulous!' I tell him, in a sincere voice. He must not guess. 'That will be absolutely great. I've been *longing* to go there.'

chapter nine

The next day

'Evie, thank you so much,' says Roger, from behind a glass screen. 'That was wonderful.'

I smile winningly at everybody. 'Did you think so?' I ask, with mock self-deprecation. 'Thank you.'

'It was fabulous. But we need to do it again. Our fault. Sorry.'

Again, my fake smile. 'Not a problem, Roger. My pleasure.'

It won't take long before everybody is happy. It may be a hackneyed staple of the cellist's repertoire, playable by any Grade 4 kid with a reasonable vibrato, but I love 'The Swan'. I played it in a performance of the *Carnival of the Animals*, once, at a children's concert at the Royal Albert Hall. They had a huge screen with animal scenes on it, and I got to dress up in white – much as I will be doing tomorrow – to represent the bird in question. I was glad I wasn't on the double bass, portraying the elephant. Thank goodness my mother started me off on a graceful instrument, when I was six.

The studio is tiny, but high tech, and I'm quite impressed that they're recording me playing this afresh for their advert, rather than getting it from my second ever CD, *The Sensual Cello*. Or using someone else. I manage a far better performance today than I did when I was twenty-five. I have made a huge effort with my appearance, even though I am only here for the sound. I know that every single person involved in the process is scrutinising me and making judgements that will affect my future, so I have dressed judiciously in a pair of Armani jeans and a tight black T-shirt and cashmere cardigan, with boots that give just enough of a heel to make me look good, without letting me tower above the men. Owing to the fact that I've been awake since five, I have had ample time to wash, blow-dry and style my hair, so it's sleek but bouncy. I've also managed to conceal a worrying outbreak of spots and blotches, which I hope are a symptom of my stressful journey and jet lag, rather than an irreversible part of the ageing process. I can't age. I can't afford to. I'm wearing a little make-up. I am, in fact, wearing a lot of make-up, masquerading as a little, but I hope that no one else will realise this fact.

I am hiding behind my image. This strategy has worked for me so far, and it has got to carry on working for me now.

I know it was something of a gamble for them to cast a British cellist no American has heard of, and I suppose they have only done it because most people over here haven't heard of any living cellists at all. I am determined to be professional and impressive. They are treating me far better than I had expected – the hotel proves my worth in their eyes – and this really is my big break. Everything I do in America must be a performance.

I know Alexis is pleased, because every time I glance at the window he is looking at me and smiling to himself. He is an intense man in his late thirties, and I think I could warm to him. I am doing everything in my power to make him like me. He is, I discovered last night, a fanatically healthy eater; thus, while I am in the same room as he is, so am I. I don't know how I pulled myself together last night. As usual, the strength appeared from somewhere at the very moment I needed it. I sat in the Gramercy Tavern, ate salad, and chattered brightly about myself and my cello and where I saw myself in five years' time.

'I'd love to perhaps base myself in New York for a while,' I said on the spur of the moment, then realised that I had overstepped the mark when I saw the panic in his eyes. I should, I realised, have been far cooler. 'Perhaps for a couple of months,' I added quickly. 'My dad lives in Queens, and I haven't been in touch with this side of my heritage for years. You know, I lived here for a while as a teenager?' His relief was audible, in the guise of a contented sigh.

I asked Alexis about himself. Thus, I now know that he is a bachelor who takes 'dating' profoundly seriously, who has nothing but disdain for The Rules but appreciates it when a woman lets him know in advance that she is following them. The way he spoke about single life in New York disheartened me. I am single in New York, and while I heard about The Rules when the book came out, I never imagined the day would come when I would find myself in a position where I might have to follow them. If I met someone I liked out here, I would want to go out with them, a course of action which is, apparently, fraught with issues of etiquette. By the time I staggered back to the hotel, I was heavy with exhaustion and wine, and grateful that I wasn't expected to have a pudding because I knew that if I'd had to stay in the restaurant for thirty more seconds I would have collapsed, asleep, my head in the dregs of my organic mint infusion. But I knew I had risen to the occasion and done what was expected of me. It is almost more important for me to bond with Alexis than it is for me to play well today. It is vital that I do both; and so far, I am succeeding. I am getting through on terror and adrenalin.

They are impressed by me. I perform better than usual because I know I look good. Playing is bliss. I am alone in the recording booth, while about twenty people watch from the edit suite. While I am playing, it's just me and the music. This is a craft as much as it is an art. In my case, it's also a trade. I am so lucky, I think, as I ascend the A string to the high B, and make the note louder as I play it, to be able to do this – to have something like this which makes everything I was worrying about yesterday irrelevant. Everything else vanishes for a moment. I use the optimum amount of vibrato, and pause on the high B before descending back down the string. I pass into my own world, and am shocked when, as my last note dies away, a voice comes through the loudspeaker.

'Evie, sweetheart, that was great!' says Roger. 'As ever!'

I switch on the charm. 'Thanks,' I tell him. 'As ever!'

'Again, not your fault. Ours. One more time, OK? When you're ready.'

On the next attempt, my intonation is off on the high notes, and I stop. Fourth time I am holding off a cough all the way through, but succumb to it slightly too soon after I finish. Fifth time round they have a hitch again. Sixth time, miraculously, everyone is happy. I am sad that it's over. It's only two p.m. I love it when it's just me and the music. When I get home, I vow that practice won't be a chore any more. It will be my escape. That's the way it should be, and I've lost sight of that over the years.

I have a fashionably sparse late lunch with Alexis, who announces that 'Evie and I have to talk business, guys!' Because he's there, I remember to treat my body as a temple, and order grilled chicken and salad. I even send away the fries that come with it, although I promise myself that I will order some on room service this afternoon, and hope that Alexis won't see the itemised bill.

Alexis, who is a collage of shiny teeth and overstyled hair, nods knowingly.

'Atkins?' he asks. I realise, belatedly, what he means, and am about to shake my head when I realise that this man will be selling me to America, and instead I nod enthusiastically.

'It really works, don't you think?' I ask him, knowing that this is what one says about the Atkins diet. 'Refreshing to find one that does.'

His teeth glint at me. 'Oh, I should say so. If Jennifer Aniston wasn't already a good enough advert, we now have Evie Silverman! Actually, you've hit on another of my favourite subjects here, because a lot of people think Atkins is bad for the cholesterol and kidneys and so on, but in fact it's very healthy for your body to burn off the fat as you eat it. It's called ketosis and it makes sense.' He looks at me and laughs. 'I'm preaching to the converted. May I show you any sights this afternoon, Evie?'

I yawn. I can't face sightseeing.

'Alexis?' I say meekly. 'I'm sorry to be so boring. But I'm jet-lagged and also a bit knackered from this morning, and I know we've got an early start tomorrow. Would you mind if I went back to the hotel and slept for a while when we're done here?'

He pats my shoulder. 'Professional to the last. Anything you want, get it on room service. We'll pick it up for you. But, Evie? Knackered? I'm not familiar with *knackered*?'

'It just means very tired. Thanks, Alexis. But first, I think we have to talk business?'

'Right, Evie. Let's talk about you.' He takes a notebook and fountain pen out of his briefcase and lays them next to his plate. He consults a tightly hand-written list which I fail to read upside down. 'Evie. I'm hoping this ad will take off. I'm thinking we're going to make as much noise as we can about your album. Get you everywhere. Get you noticed. Marketing are doing a fabulous job already – you'll be in carefully targeted magazines and on billboards. *Elle* want to talk to you, which is just great.' I nod, trying hard to concentrate. He talks for a while.

'Do you have any traumas in your past?' he asks conversationally at one point, pen poised.

'Sorry?'

'Anything that Oprah would go for? Courageous Evie?

You know, abuse as a child, death of a loved one, that kind of thing?'

He looks up expectantly. I hesitate. He would be ecstatic if I told him about my teenage pregnancy, and for a moment I almost do, because I am so eager to please him.

'My parents split up when I was two,' I offer, lamely, instead. 'But it would be more unusual these days if they hadn't.'

'Mmm. Anything interesting? Gay dad in Queens, maybe?'

'No. He's married again now. So's my mum. They're both happy.'

'Right. I'm so happy for them, but it's hardly *Oprah* material, I'm afraid.'

I look at the table. 'Sorry.'

He gets more and more ambitious in his proposals, which culminate in a daydream that the advert might get the whole country talking about this ethereal cellist all dressed in white, at which point Alexis will book me on to the Letterman show.

'All from a TV advertisement for iced tea?' I ask dubiously.

'Stranger things have happened,' he smiles. 'Now, to this evening. We're going to meet some people, you and me. The great thing with you, Evie, is I don't need to coach you.' He smiles appraisingly and goes on to do just that. 'Be yourself,' he says earnestly. 'Be sparky. Look stunning – I know, hard for you to do otherwise! Wear great shoes. Everyone in this city adores girls in great shoes. Do you have a fabulous dress with you? You have to stand out in a room. Think SJP.'

I nod, relieved that I do, at least, know who SJP is. 'I did bring a couple of dresses, yes, just in case.'

'The girl's a professional!'

My heart is sinking. This is the kind of stuff I love in London, and suddenly, in New York, I don't want to do it. I don't want to go to a party and meet these people, whoever they may be. Kate has just had her eggs extracted. She and Ian are coming to town tonight, to see me. I had planned to take them both to a diner where we could all have eaten large platefuls of unsophisticated food, drunk beer from the bottle, and saved some space for pudding. Now I'll be forced to nibble on sashimi and drink half a glass of white wine and a litre of mineral water, and my face will ache from the insincere smiling.

'Alexis, tonight will be wonderful,' I tell him, meaning the exact opposite, 'but could you tell me where we're going? I have some friends from home who have been staying upstate, and they're in town tonight. Is it a party – could they come with us? – or shall I postpone seeing them?' I tilt my head to one side and look at him with a winsome quizzical look.

'Hey,' he says, all teeth and hair. 'Any friend of yours, Evie, is more than welcome. This is your party – you call the shots!'

It turns out that it really is my party. Alexis is the host and I am, essentially, the hostess. Kate, Ian and I have fortified ourselves at the hotel bar beforehand, and without two large vodka and tonics I would be lost. I nearly didn't bring my red Versace dress, on the grounds that it was over the top, but I'm glad I did. I spent all my scheduled nap and chips time shopping for a pair of strappy heels to go with it. I did manage to clear a window for a huge, greasy pizza slice which I crammed into my mouth as I walked. I may as well make the most of being a non-entity here while it lasts.

'How are you doing?' Kate asks, when we're in the cab.

'Fuck,' I tell her. 'Fucking terrible. I want to be anywhere but here, anywhere but a party. I haven't had a minute to myself. I wanted to slob out with you two tonight, not dress up like some high-class hooker. I'm still jet-lagged and that's the least of it.'

Ian looks at me, curious. 'What's the most of it?'

'Oh, nothing. Nothing compared to all this life-changing stuff you two are going through. I'm *so glad* it's going well so far.' I'm sitting between them, so I squeeze both of their hands. 'You must be more knackered than me.'

Kate smiles. 'I'm just glad that part of it's over, to be honest. It wasn't much fun, having a scanner up my fanny, and a needle taking out my eggs. And I'm going to be on tenterhooks waiting to hear what Ron reckons about the egg quality. But it wasn't as painful this time as it has been before. And he got twelve, which is way more than last time. Did you know, Ron's giving us a discount if we donate a couple of embryos for another couple to use, as long as the eggs and sperm are high enough quality? Which they might or might not be. But we've already talked about it so much, you must be bored stupid.' She looks at me shrewdly. 'Evie, you're really down, aren't you? I know you don't have the choice, but you really shouldn't be charging around like this. It worries me when you're hyper. You are going to get the chance to slow down after the filming, aren't you?'

I shrug. 'Yes? I hope so. God knows what new surprises Alexis has in store for me. They booked me into the hotel till the day after tomorrow, so I guess there'll be nothing after that. Then I'm going to stay with Howard for a couple of days.'

'Your dad!' Kate laughs. 'God, I've only met him once, Evie, and that was at your wedding.'

Ian joins in. 'Me too. Seemed like a nice bloke.'

'He is. He's great. And even though I haven't seen him that much in the past fifteen years—' I hurriedly correct myself. Kate and Ian have no idea that anything significant happened fifteen years ago. 'Twenty-nine years, rather, he's always been on the end of a phone or email. It'll be great to see him. A bit strange, maybe. It's been a long time since I last came to stay with him. He's not exactly a father figure, but he is a mate. You know he's an alcoholic?'

Kate nods.

'Reformed?' checks Ian, a little nervously. I smile.

'As reformed and presentable as can be.'

As we pull up outside the venue, I sit in the back of the cab and take some deep breaths. Then I check my lipstick, repin part of my hair, and attach a smile to my face.

'Ready for this?' I ask them, wondering how much of my exhaustion is visible in my eyes.

Kate rolls her eyes. She is wearing my spare evening dress, which is grey silk, and she looks lovely.

'I don't know how you do it,' she says.

'Neither do I,' I tell her.

My party is in the back room of a beautiful bar in the Village. The room has a remarkable glass ceiling, and a fountain in the centre. I spend three hours playing at being the next big thing. This is, in fact, what they are calling my album. *Evie Silverman: The Next Big Thing*. It makes me slightly uneasy that a recording of cello works is so blatantly about the artiste, and not the music.

'We have to,' Alexis explained, as if to an idiot, 'because no one buys classical otherwise. You have to have a personality. Classical is a small department for this label – otherwise we'd have gone under many years ago – and when we need to make a splash, it has to be personality-based. Otherwise there's no interest whatsoever. Zip. If we called your album *Bach Solo Suites and Other Cello Classics* we might as well melt the CDs down and remould them into earrings before they reach the shops.' He grinned dazzlingly. This is the world I move in. I have always known it, but it has never been spelt out to me so blatantly before. 'Your next release,' he added, casually, 'will be pop-classical hybrid, which will be much more marketable.'

I meet lots of people from the label. From the way Alexis grips my shoulder and pushes me into the centre of a group of them, I gather that marketing are the most important. I also meet a few journalists, mainly from classical music magazines, and therefore, I gather from their and Alexis's demeanour, they should consider themselves blessed to be at so glamorous a gathering. The president of the label, a terrifying woman in her early thirties called Mary O'Rourke, stands up and tells everyone in a New York tone that brooks no disagreement how wonderful I am – what a beautiful musician and how inspiring a human being. I exchanged a few insincere words with her, half an hour ago, and that is the sum of our interaction. She is wearing a cream suit with a skirt so short it barely exists, and her tiny, toned legs speak of many, many hours spent in the gym.

'Ladies and gentlemen,' she concludes, 'the woman herself. Evie Silverman: The Next Big Thing!'

Everyone applauds. I was half expecting this, so have rationed my champagne intake. I swap places with Mary, giving her a wide smile and wondering how she got so far, so young.

'Hi!' I say, looking round. I have done enough of these occasions, now, to know how to play it, so I go through the motions. 'I just want to thank you all. I can't get over this wonderful party, put on just for me. I feel so lucky, so blessed . . .' I am the wide-eyed innocent. It's the persona that people seem to like best at these occasions, when they are generally well disposed towards me anyway. I carefully name-check everyone from Alexis to Mary to Roger the sound engineer. 'And now,' I finish, 'I'm going to have to go back to my hotel for some much-needed beauty sleep, in advance of tomorrow's filming. I hope you will all excuse me. Thank you so much for coming, and good night.'

Alexis told me to leave early. He said it would impress them and leave them wanting more. I collect Kate and Ian, and rush outside before anyone can offer me a limo. I step into the Manhattan street, which is full of groups of noisy, well-dressed people, and jump into a cab as it is vacated by three beautiful transvestites.

chapter ten

A week later

I used to sleep well. It took me a while, after the Caesarean and its fall-out, to get back into my old pattern of eight hours' oblivion, but once I did, I have barely deviated from it. A particularly heavy evening can see me awake and thirsty at four in the morning, but I always drop off again easily, and sleep later in the morning to compensate.

After I'd faced the truth about my baby, I used to lie awake until I started to hear people going to work – the roars of car engines, the slamming of doors, the fast clicking of heels along the pavement. Then I would sleep for an hour or so. After the operation, I only slept under sedation for several months. Now I can feel the horrible insomnia returning.

Howard's study is not a bad place to be awake in the dark. The walls are lined with shelves of books. I can switch on a desk light and disturb nobody. My bed is a mattress on the floor, but it is a comfortable mattress, covered with a thick duvet and a multitude of pillows. I get out of bed, switch on the computer, and decide to see whether I can check my emails from here. Scrolling through spam mail offering Viagra and pornography has to be better than tossing, turning, and trying to think of anything other than the baby. The computer lights up the room with a sickly glow.

I never get emails. The last person I expected to hear from by this method was Megan. She doesn't even have a computer. She must have gone to considerable trouble to send it. I didn't even know that she knew my email address. Still, I am delighted to allow her to distract me from the night-time terrors.

As I wait for the contents to arrive on the screen, I am suddenly afraid. I left her in the flat, with those letters arriving thick and fast, and I gave her no inkling that it was happening. She might be writing because the stalker broke in. Perhaps, in my absence, he attacked her. Raped her. She didn't even know she had to double-lock the door and put the chain on every night. I am a terrible human being.

Darling Evie, *she writes*. How are you getting on in the Big Apple? I can imagine you there, now, the Queen of New York. Entrancing everyone with your glorious music. It has rained constantly since you left, which has been good for the window boxes, but otherwise dreary.

All is going well between Guy and me. He suggested I write you this email, because he has been asking many questions about you, Kate and Ian, and I have been unable to answer any of them. All answers

143

gratefully received to spice up the pillow talk! Have you made the advert yet? Are you with Kate and Ian? How did they get on with their fertility doctor? Do you have any idea when you will be back? The flat feels strangely empty without you. I call it strange because I never felt like this after Andrea left.

Apparently you should speak to your mother. Guy says you never tell her about the details of your glamorous career. Now, I have heard you on the phone to her and I know this isn't true, but Guy seems to feel he needs all the information he can gather about you so he can 'reassure Anna'. He is a law unto himself, my boyfriend.

I hope you get a chance to write back. I'm looking forward to your company again.

With lots of love,

Meg xxxxxxx

I sit in the semi darkness and write her a brief and jaunty reply, filling her in on my successful day's filming, my party, my fabulous hotel. I leave out the parts about forcing myself to keep going, about carrying myself through on coffee and alcohol, about being scared to stop and relax because of the fear that I would never be able to stand up again. I don't mention the strange feeling I have been having, the one I have been desperately holding at bay, the feeling that I might be heading for a breakdown. Megan has no idea that I have a secret, that I am not what I seem, and I would like to keep it that way. Very few people have any idea, and that is extremely good.

I don't tell her that, when I reached Howard's doorstep

in Queens, I fell into his arms in tears the moment I saw his grizzly beard, now entirely grey. He understood, even though the last time I saw him was four years ago, at his wedding.

'Little girl,' he kept saying. 'Evie, my sweetheart. Come. Come through. Sit down.'

Howard and I look the same. He is tall and skinny and his hair is light brown, as mine should be. Despite appearances, I don't really feel that he's my father. Phil is a far more conventional father figure. I do feel an easy friendship with him, and right now, that's probably better. I would be embarrassed to fall apart in front of Phil, but with Howard it is absolutely fine. I think this has something to do with the fact that, when I was fifteen, he told me all about his alcoholism. He hid nothing from me, and so it is easy to reciprocate.

He sat me down, and my stepmother, Sonia, who clearly knows exactly why I was here in my teens, brought me a hot coffee and stroked my hair and left the room. Sonia is exactly the right woman for Howard. He should have married her first time round. She's not a young trophy wife, but a rotund, dark-haired New Yorker of around his age, and, although this is only the second time I've met her, she is obviously deeply sensible. That is exactly what he needs. Sonia is also a recovering alcoholic. I can't imagine either of them drunk. If I have any subconscious memories of Howard on an alcoholic rampage when I was two, they are deeply buried. He and Sonia met at their AA meetings, which they still go to with a religious fervour at least once a week, and often once a day.

I will always love Howard for making those four months

as good as they could possibly have been. He was limit-lessly compassionate, and he never once demanded to know what irresponsible scumbag got his daughter into that sort of a mess in the first place. He must have been dying to ask. I would have been. He left plenty of open-ings for me to tell him, but I ignored them. Mark was never going to be a part of my life, and I wanted to forget that the whole ill-advised incident had ever happened.

I hadn't wanted to come to America, but no one could think of an alternative. It was a godsend that I had a parent in a country where I knew no one and no one knew me.

'You're sending me away?' I asked Mum, aghast. That terrible morning, she'd looked at my stomach under my baggiest school jumper, and I had watched something finally click into place in her head.

'Evie?' she'd said, staring. 'Are you all right?'

That was all it had taken. I dissolved, relieved that at last she had noticed, that I hadn't had to make the announcement I had practised every day since the dread-ful moment, five months before, when I'd seen the blue lines on the pregnancy test that I had bought, dull with shame, at an unknown chemist miles from home. I had opened my mouth to make the announcement countless times, and had always closed it again, hoping against hope that I might be imagining it.

'No,' I told her. Then I said it. 'I think I'm pregnant.'

I had been waiting for months for a miracle, a miscar-riage, but none had been forthcoming. Through Kate and Ian's ordeals, I have been eaten up with the unfairness of it all, the fact that my tenacious child hung in there against my best efforts with spirits and crash diets and hot baths, while theirs has failed to materialise at all. Mum made me put on her big coat and took me straight to see the doctor, who estimated that I was twenty-nine weeks, and more than a month too late for an abortion. An emergency rush to the hospital for a scan immediately confirmed it.

Mum called Phil home from work, and rang Howard.

'But I can't go to America!' I wailed. 'I don't even *know* my dad.'

'You'll get to know him. He's a good man, he swears he's sober now, and he's going to look after you. I know it's hard, and I'm going to fly over with you because I can't bear you to make that journey on your own, and I need to check that he really isn't drinking. There is no other option.' I looked at her face, and I knew I couldn't argue. 'You have got to have the baby, I'm afraid. Now, we've all discussed you keeping it,' I shook my head vehemently, 'and we know you're only fifteen, and although Phil and I could bring it up as our own . . .' I shook my head again and sobbed. 'So, you'll have the baby in America, and someone will take it away, and it will go to a good home where it'll be cared for, OK? It will have a wonderful start in life.'

I nodded weakly. It wasn't as if I had an alternative plan.

Straight away, I grew a huge bump. It was as if the moment that Mum noticed it, it leapt a foot out in front of me, delighted not to have to hide any more. I skulked indoors while they booked my flight. Mum went to Dorothy Perkins and bought me some maternity jeans and T-shirts, and a couple of big jumpers. I literally didn't leave the house until, at a quarter to six one April morning, I was bundled into the back of the car by Mum and Phil, and driven to Heathrow. Both Mum and I were paranoid about being spotted at the airport, or sitting next to someone we knew on the plane, but it didn't happen. People gave me funny looks – I was fifteen, but I was young and naive, and could have passed for two or three years younger – and Mum held my hand and whispered to me to ignore them.

Howard met us, with a huge hug, at the airport, and took us back to his apartment. I had never been out of Europe before. Mum stayed for two days, which must have been weird for them both, then flew home, checking again that I was sure I didn't want her to look after the baby for me. Now, when I look back, I don't know why she didn't insist. Every time I see Tessa, I wonder how I would feel if she was my secret daughter. It would be fine. It would be wonderful. I wish Mum had imposed that decision on me, so I could have followed my child's progress, influenced her, been a force in her life. Then I wouldn't have had to wonder, all the time, what she was like, and to know that she might find me one day, and to hope she doesn't hate me too much. I might not have to keep wondering whether my miscarriage strategies had harmed her.

I barely saw my baby. I had her at thirty-eight weeks. Dad booked me into a good hospital, where I had a Caesarean because I was terrified of going through labour only to see the child who had been kicking and hiccuping inside me snatched away. Everyone agreed a section would be better (America, happily for me, even then saw Caesarean deliveries almost as the norm), and I had it under a general anaesthetic because I didn't want to see,

148

or to feel, the baby being lifted out of me. I thought if I didn't see her emerge into the world, I wouldn't feel a connection with her.

I remember coming round after the operation, and forgetting, for a few blissful moments, where I was and why I was there. Then I remembered.

'It's a girl,' they told me, when I asked. 'Would you like to spend a few minutes with her?'

The second that I saw her, my breasts filled up with colostrum. She was tiny – just under six pounds – and red-faced, and for those brief moments, she was mine. She stared up into my eyes and I stared back. She had been inside me all those months, and I knew her. I recognised her. It was a homecoming.

'It's you,' I told her. She seemed to be saying the same to me. It was like meeting someone you've known for a lifetime. She was a stranger, yet I knew her better than anyone in the world.

She had a little bit of brown hair, and her eyes were light blue. Her hands were tiny, and I picked one up. She gripped my finger. Her nails were the most perfect things I have seen in my life.

Then they took her away. I shouted 'Sorry!' as they left the room. I cried and screamed and begged to be allowed five more minutes with her. They said a lovely couple were going to adopt her and that she would have a happy life. I never asked anything about the couple. I didn't want to know then. Howard handled that side of it for me.

My milk came in three days later, and my breasts were hard and enormous. I had to squeeze out the white liquid to stop the pain. I tasted it. It was warm and sweet. This was my daughter's milk. I was sorry she was being bottle-fed. I wanted to pull her back and give her everything I had. I knew, however, that the lovely couple was the best thing I could do for her.

I'd had some names in my head before she was born. Louise and I had discussed them, and she'd agreed with me that the best names were Poppy for a girl and William for a boy. In the event, though, I called her Elizabeth, because it suited her. I don't know what name her new parents gave her. I have a photo of her on the day she was born, the last day that she was mine. I have only ever shown it to my parents. She was my little girl, and I never fed her. I never got up to her in the night, never comforted her, never changed her nappy. I was never her mother. She has learned to walk and talk without me, has been potty-trained and started school. She has grown up without knowing anything about me.

Jack traced the scar with his fingertips when we first met, and asked me where it came from. I told him I'd had my appendix out. Then I prayed every day that I would never get appendicitis. I suppose it doesn't matter, any more, if I do.

One of my biggest setbacks came three years after I had her, when Mum told me, very gently and nervously, that she and Phil were expecting a baby. Throughout her pregnancy I was determined that she would have a boy, but as soon as Phil said those three terrible words – 'It's a girl' – I had to make an enormous effort to be nice. In fact, I had to get ragingly drunk. If I hadn't spent those months with Howard, talking to him about everything, this would have been the point at which I developed a problem with alcohol. Instead, I dyed my hair blonde, bought some sexy clothes, and reinvented myself as a femme fatale. I was unbelievably lucky that my elastic teenage skin didn't bear any stretch marks. I visited Bristol only rarely until Tessa was two, and not a baby any more. I always see, next to her, the spirit of Elizabeth, three years older, her unknown niece. And I have just about kept in control of alcohol, although sometimes my longing for a drink, at stressful moments, scares me to death.

So Howard knows exactly what is wrong with me, and he knows how to make me feel a little better. He and Sonia buy me wine, despite their teetotalism, and take me out to delis and diners for meals. They take me to parks and on the F train into Manhattan for some old-fashioned sightseeing. One night, we go to a diner called Googie's, that I liked when I was fifteen. I am as relaxed as I have been for days, and I order a burger with curly fries and a side salad and a glass of sauvignon.

'Evie,' says Howard, looking at Sonia, who nods.

'Mmm?' I say, cramming my mouth with fries. I am wearing jeans and a cream jumper, and I have scraped my hair back into a ponytail. I hope I don't run into Alexis. He would be horrified by the sight of me in no make-up at all, rather than a pretence of no make-up. He would be still more horrified to see the fries poking incriminatingly from the corner of my mouth. Alexis, luckily, would never come here. It is the sort of place that must have Dr Atkins spinning in his grave.

'I know we've talked about baby Elizabeth a bit since you've been here,' he says gently. 'And I know that being here is stirring up a lot of memories for you.'

I pause, mid chew, and stare at him. 'Mmmm,' I agree through the carbohydrates.

'But have you thought that in three and a half years, when Elizabeth will be eighteen, she might want to look for you? Have you thought about leaving your details on the Adoption Registry on that date?'

I execute a huge swallow. I was not expecting this. 'Of course I have,' I say, looking from Howard to Sonia and back again. 'And I will. I think about it all the time. In a way I hope she doesn't get in touch because I'm so scared she'll be angry with me. But at the same time, I'll be waiting to hear from her every day.'

'Have you considered, though,' says Sonia, softly, 'how it would impact on your life? None of your friends know about her. Your husband doesn't know. And Kate and Ian, for example. How will it affect your friendship with them if suddenly, out of the blue, you have a daughter you've never mentioned?'

'They should have their own child by then. Children.'

'They sure should,' she agrees, popping a dainty piece of cucumber into her mouth. 'Life doesn't always run to schedule. All of us round this table can testify to that. They might or they might not have their own children, and even if they have, it's going to impact pretty heavily on your relationship.'

I look at her. I've been trying not to think about this. 'I've always been scared that Kate would find out,' I tell her. 'Or Jack. Jack doesn't matter so much now, but Kate does.' I think about it for a moment. I have pushed it to the back of my mind, because I am uncomfortable knowing how much it would hurt her. 'I didn't tell her when

I met her because I'd vowed never to tell anyone again. Since then, it's built up into a huge secret. She's said loads of times how happy she is that Jack and I haven't got any kids. She always says that would make it worse for her than it already is. It's unfair, isn't it? There's me having a child completely by accident, and getting rid of it, and there's her . . .'

'Evie,' says Sonia, firmly, 'life isn't fair. You can't beat yourself up about what happened. Your fertility doesn't make you a bad person. Lots of people have trouble conceiving and if it does come out then Kate will get over it. She is a reasonable, compassionate human being. It will be no surprise to her to learn that other people have babies. It's you we're concerned about. Your daddy and I think you need to be prepared for Elizabeth, if and when she comes back into your life.'

I smile. 'Do you really think she will?'

Howard shakes his head. 'You can't make any assumptions, honey. She might. She might not. Who knows if they've even told her she's adopted?'

'Mmm.'

I can't think of anything else to say, and we all carry on eating in silence. I drink six glasses of wine, one by one, which is normally something I'd feel shy about doing in the company of two recovering alcoholics.

I sometimes wonder what Howard and Sonia would be like if they got drunk. Would they rampage around shouting? Become maudlin and self-pitying? Would a drop of wine passing their lips send them into a frenzy of brandy and tequila? Or would they just be like me, ordering drink after drink, kidding themselves that each one was the last?

In the middle of the night, I wake up abruptly. I haven't consciously been thinking about Megan's email, but suddenly all her talk of Guy and his questions about me and his false assertions that I don't tell anything to Mum and Phil point me to one, drunken conclusion.

Guy might be my stalker.

chapter eleven

March

'Mum?'

'Darling! How was New York?'

I look out of the window, across the rooftops of Kensington. It is a typical early March day. The cloud is so thick that it seems to be compressing London beneath it. All the fumes are trapped. Children are breathing foul air. Exhaust and effluent are circulating, in an ever-decreasing space, unable to disperse. London is filthy. Sometimes you have to leave your home to see it clearly, and now that I am back, I know where I want to be. I imagine the crisp blue spring of New York, and wonder how easy it would be, in fact, for me to move there.

'Great,' I tell her, listlessly. 'You know, New York, including the Boroughs, is probably the same size as London, ish, but because it's on the edge of a huge continent that's far less densely populated, it doesn't seem to have the pollution that we do here. Though LA does, because it's in a basin. But London's awful. I'm looking at it now, Mum. It's horrible.'

Mum sounds nonplussed. 'Right. And how was the advert? When can we see it?'

'It all went fine. They seemed to like me. At least they said they did. They'd never in a million years have said if they didn't. But I met lots of people, smiled a lot, played OK, I think. I didn't butcher "The Swan", at least.'

She sounds artificially bright. 'Great! Well done, darling. Will you get a video then? Can we watch it?'

'They're going to email it to me. I'll send it on to you. Taylor can download it for you and play it to you on the computer.'

'Really? Are you sure? So what about the rest of it?'

I sigh. There's no point pretending, with Mum. 'Bit hard, actually,' I tell her, sitting down on the floor and playing with the phone cord. 'You know I haven't been there in years. But I had a great time with Howard and Sonia, and I feel OK about it now.' I pause. I check again that Megan has not come home quietly. 'Actually,' I tell her, 'I'm trying not to obsess, but I can't stop wondering what would happen if she tracks me down. When she's eighteen. We talked about it quite a bit and now I can't stop imagining. What do you think she looks like, Mum?'

I hear Mum's hesitation. 'It's hard. It's easy for me to say this, but thinking like that isn't going to make life any more straightforward for you. We don't know what she looks like. Can you put those feelings on hold for a few more years?'

I laugh, but mirthlessly, and put my shield back up. 'Of course. I've lived with it for this long. I can do it a bit longer. You know, she's nearly as old now as I was when I had her.' I realise something. 'She could get pregnant! I could become a grandmother in a couple of years!'

Mum laughs warmly. 'Evie, don't be silly.'

'I know, I know. I wish I'd kept her.' I take a deep breath. 'Mum, did you ever tell anyone else what happened? Anyone at all?'

'No, darling. You know that. It was just Phil and me and your father, and, I assume, now Sonia. Nobody else. Of course your school had to know, and you told Louise . . .'

'Because I don't mind if you did.'

She is slightly aggrieved. 'But I didn't! I promise I didn't, Evie. I wouldn't have done that.'

I twirl the phone cord around my finger. 'It's just, I sometimes wonder if Guy knows. He gives me the creeps, lately, and I'm not sure why.'

Mum chuckles. She sounds relieved. 'He probably fancies you, old fool that he is. He certainly has no idea of what happened, don't worry about that. Honestly, though. He's making himself ridiculous with Megan. You must all laugh at him terribly. We're pleased to see him happy. He seems more animated than he has been for years. Perhaps a twenty-year-old girl is what he's been missing all this time.'

'Twenty-seven. And I wish they'd go to a hotel sometimes. It makes my skin crawl, the way they carry on. It's disgusting.'

The flat is empty. I came home two days ago, and haven't seen Megan yet. I've heard her, through my jet-lagged sleep, getting up early in the morning and going to work, but I haven't had the energy to get up and see

157

her. She was out all evening, yesterday and the day before, and stumbled home long after I was in bed. I did hear a loud orgasmic exclamation (male) at some point in the night, but decided not to get up to say hello. This morning, as it's Saturday, I thought we'd meet in the kitchen and finally manage to speak to each other, with Guy butting in every two seconds. I have been quite looking forward to the opportunity to size him up as a potential writer of threatening letters.

The letters are scaring me now. I came home to a pile of them. They have long since progressed from single words to explicit threats. I want them to be from Guy. I long for him to be messing around with me. He might hate me: the fact that I have known him all my life doesn't mean anything. I don't believe that Guy would ever really want to harm me, unlike the faceless reader of tabloid newspapers. So I want these letters to be his.

As it happened, though, I didn't wake up till eleven, and no one was home. The only company I have is my cello, and while I appreciate it, it isn't a great conversationalist. I stroke its curves, and consider taking over the living room for three hours. I would prefer to speak to a person.

Megan placed a pile of letters on my desk, very neatly, while I was away. Four of them were threats, one was a fan letter forwarded by Jane at the *Daily Mail*, with a compliments slip bearing a jaunty 'How's things? Lunch? J x'. The rest were bills from Vodafone, my accountant, and Visa. I took the dodgy letters to the police station yesterday, weary with it all. There were a couple of phone messages for me, but nothing from Jack. Dominic called, and so did *Heat* magazine. I rang *Heat* back, and ignored Dominic. I can't face his oafish charms at the moment. There was no word from Dan. I was glad. I have no desire, any more, to hang around with a boy on my arm.

I didn't tell the policeman that I had a new suspect for the letters. I tried to match their syntax to Guy's, but I failed. Sometimes the letters are misspelt, and sometimes they're not. Whoever is writing them is messing around, avoiding detection. This latest batch called me a bitch and a cunt. The writer said he knew I was waiting for him. He went into graphic detail about what he is going to do to me.

I can't think of anyone but Guy. Megan could be an unwitting accomplice. He could be using her to get to me. I used to feel secure on the nights when he was in the flat. Now I wonder where I can go tonight, to get away from him. I might even check into a hotel. All that is missing, for Guy, is a motive.

Guy might, of course, be completely innocent, just a horny old man. I know that's more likely. And yet I can't stop thinking about his wife. Nobody has ever even hinted about what happened to her. Mum won't say a word, not even when she's drunk. I know Guy's wife was pregnant around the same time that Mum was pregnant with me, and I know she died when the baby was nearly due. And I know that Guy was so traumatised that Megan is his first proper relationship in the thirty years that have passed. Did he kill her? Did he torment her first, like he is tormenting me? Who knows what else he has done? Whatever it is, he has got away with it.

I walk aimlessly around the apartment, which suddenly

feels like a prison. It's just me and the cello between these walls. I could lose myself in music for a few hours. Then I pick up my mobile and text Megan. I need to see him, to see how he behaves with me. Now that I'm looking, I will be able to work him out.

hey stranger, I write, *where are you? am home alone*.

Within a couple of seconds, just as I am tightening my bow, the phone beeps.

round the corner. lunch, now, mediterranean kitchen. come & join us. m xxx

I was expecting to meet two people, not four. When I see Kate and Ian sitting at the table, with Megan and Guy, I feel a stab of betrayal. Why didn't Meg ask me before? Why didn't Kate? They all knew where to find me. This is one of our favourite restaurants, a matter of yards from our flat. I can't believe they came without me.

'Hello,' I say, staring at Kate and making my surprise obvious. 'How come you're here?'

Ian smiles. 'Meg called us a while ago, asked if we wanted to come along. We were going to ring you, but we were worried about waking you. We all know what jet lag's like.'

I smile back thinly. 'I wouldn't have minded being woken. It would have been more fun waking to a phone call than to an empty flat.'

Kate reaches for my hand. 'Sorry. We were going to go back afterwards to see you. How are you doing?'

Guy has leapt to his feet and found a spare chair, which he carefully places at the end of the table, so I'm sitting between Kate and Ian.

'Evie, lovely girl, you're looking wonderful as ever,' he says, kissing me hard on each cheek. His pores are open, and up close his skin is meaty. He looks supremely pleased with himself as he sits back down and strokes Megan's arm.

'You do, Evie,' she agrees, glancing at me, then looking back to Guy. Her eyes are shining, and her skin is glowing. 'You look great. Not at all jet-lagged.'

'Cheers.'

Ian takes a wine glass from a neighbouring table, fills it with red, and passes it to me.

'So what's new?' I ask breezily. I take a sip, and look round expectantly. A waiter hands me a menu and arranges cutlery in front of me. The atmosphere here is just right for a long lunch. Everything is made from dark wood, and there are blackboards of specials around the room. It's small, but not poky, and we have a prime table in the window.

'Oh, we were just talking about Ron Thomas,' says Kate. 'Guy was telling us what he remembered of him from medical school.'

'We weren't particularly matey,' Guy interjects. He seems, ludicrously, to be attempting to dress younger these days. I can't imagine why: he carried off the Al Pacino look rather well. Today he is wearing a pair of indigo jeans, with a white linen shirt with one too many buttons undone. There is a leather jacket over the back of his chair. I cringe on his behalf. I am used to seeing him dressing his age. I know he used to wear his work shoes at weekends. Now I bet he's hiding a pair of brand-new trainers under the table. We look like a bunch of youngsters being taken on a birthday treat by someone's dad.

'Apparently Ron was the boring swot at college,' Kate

says, with a laugh. 'I suppose that's good. I'd rather entrust my fertility to him than to the class pisshead.'

Guy raises his glass. 'I don't do fertility anyway, my love.'

'So you're back out there in three weeks?' I say, turning to Kate.

'And counting! If this works, wow.'

'Wow,' echoes Megan.

'We'll sign over every penny we ever earn in our lives to Ron if he pulls it off. In fact, I have a feeling we've already done that.'

'You probably have, my dears,' says Guy, with a nod. 'But tell me, I hate to imagine the worst, but I'm intrigued as to what rabbit Ron will pull out of the hat if this doesn't work? What has he said?'

Kate looks at Ian. Ian takes a swig of wine. 'There's no great mystery,' he says. 'He's not going to clone us or anything. He'll just keep selecting the strongest eggs and sperm, keep checking us, Kate particularly, that we're healthy, and keep trying. We've signed up to something where we donate spare embryos to other couples, or for his research, and that way we get a discount.'

Guy shakes his head. 'I hope it works for you two. I hope Ron delivers on his promises. Make sure he explains exactly what he's doing at every stage. He used to be a slippery customer. And he is a well-known advocate of human cloning. Make sure he doesn't get it past you couched in medical euphemisms. "Genetic material exclusively from the healthier partner", that kind of thing.'

'He's said we will end up with a baby. Just like that. He can't say when but he can say that it will happen, even if it ended up as a surrogate baby.'

Meg looks at them with interest. 'Is that legal?'

Kate nods. 'Legal, but probably a nightmare. We'd rather not get into it if we could avoid it. I'd rather adopt than turn to surrogacy. And I don't want to adopt at all.'

I glance at Guy. He is looking very strange. He seems sad, and lost in thought. I realise I barely know him at all.

Someone needs to break the silence. I am opening my mouth to babble about New York when Guy seems to pull himself together.

'Did you see your mail, Evie?' he asks, with his usual bonhomie. 'Megan and I put it in your room for you. You seem remarkably popular.'

I stare. My heart starts beating faster. 'I got it, thanks.'

'It didn't just look like bills either, did it, Meg? You seem to have a correspondent. It's not that pop singer boy, is it?'

'There's been another letter since then,' says Meg, smiling at Guy. I am embarrassed by her devotion to him. She has no idea what she's getting into. Neither do I, of course, but I sense it's not good. I wonder if I could try to tell her to stay away from him. 'I put that in her room for her too,' she says, awaiting her lover's approval.

'You're a devoted flatmate,' he replies, with a smile that turns my stomach.

'Well, it was mainly bills,' I say, too harshly. 'And no, I've dumped the pop singer boy.'

After two large glasses of wine, I get up just after Guy and follow him to the loo. I wait outside the men's until he comes out. He starts, surprised to see me. We are round the corner from our table. No one can see us.

'Hello, Evie,' he says, trying to get past.

'Guy,' I tell him, 'I just want to say, I know.'

He hesitates. 'You know what?'

'*You* know what. What you've just been talking about. I know.'

He looks into the middle distance. The colour has drained from his normally florid face. 'How do you know?' he asks.

'I just do. So don't mess with me, all right?'

'Is this some sort of a threat, Evie?'

I walk away, into the ladies' loo, and shut my eyes. He is hiding something. I knew it.

It is pouring with rain when we leave. We have been there for three hours, and have eaten far too much. When I ordered an extra portion of chips I never expected them to be piled into an enormous wooden bowl, and to represent a meal in themselves. I will have to go to the gym, later, because of them.

'I'm a bit drunk, actually,' I tell Kate, as we shout a final goodbye to the waiter and fall through the door on to the slippery pavement.

'I can see that,' she says with a smile. 'I'm not.'

We follow the others back towards the flat. Even though it's not far, I get soaked through. None of us has an umbrella. I like the way my hair sticks to my head. I can feel water running down my face, and hope my mascara really is waterproof. My thighs are soaked, my jeans unpleasantly heavy.

'How's Jack?' I ask, at once.

Kate looks at me and laughs. 'He's doing fine. Back from Scotland, renting a flat in Camden. He came back rather abruptly for some reason.'

'And Sophia?'

'Around, I think. Why? Are you jealous?'

'Of course not. I left him, didn't I?' I resign myself to being drenched, and slow down.

'Of course you did.'

We take a few steps in silence before I change the subject. 'So you'll be implanted in three weeks?' I ask. 'It's been quicker than that before, when you had IVF here, hasn't it?'

Kate has pulled up the woollen hood of her cardigan, from underneath her coat. 'Yes. Ron's more thorough, I think, with his quality control. Plus we wanted to space out our trips a little. There's no point coming home and then rushing straight back out there. At least this way we minimise our time off work. Christ, Evie. I'd forgotten what this was like. How awful it is.'

'The weather?'

'Not the weather. The treatment, you idiot.' I look at her, and see the strain on her face. She is pale and exhausted. 'I can talk about other things,' she continues, 'but only because I force myself. Like at lunch today. It's always going on, this running commentary at the back of my head. What if it works? What if it doesn't? What if we get a positive pregnancy test and then have a miscarriage? Would that be worse than not getting pregnant at all? Should I eat this steak for the iron or should I be having oily fish for the fatty acids? How soon before I could find out if there was an embryo still in there, or if I'd miscarried them all? Why does a twelve-week scan seem a million years away, when it could be thirteen weeks away? Thirteen weeks is nothing. It's for ever.' She looks at me and shrugs, pained. 'It doesn't stop. I know I've been here before – God knows, you know I've been here before, you've listened to this endlessly – but I'd forgotten. It's probably like labour. You forget how terrible it is. The main thing is the question when? When will I get my child? Why can't it be now? I have a phantom child, you know. The one I would have had if I'd got pregnant the first month we tried. That child would be going to be three in August.'

I have a phantom child, too. My child is fourteen, and the difference is that she really is out there somewhere. Sometimes I wish I knew that for sure. Some children die, after all. Some children get ill, particularly, perhaps, if their birth mothers have tried to abort them. Even in the most respectable homes, some children are abused. I yearn for Elizabeth. I want to protect her from everything.

I touch Kate's arm and we both slow down, letting the others get almost to the front door.

'Kate,' I tell her, 'I'm so sorry for what you're going through. I feel sure that this time you've got all the luck on your side. The chances are it's going to happen for you. You're working with the best, using the best eggs and sperms, put in by the best bloke in the field. You're doing everything you can to get your baby. Stop me if this is a platitude, but being calm about it is really the best way to help it work.'

'Yeah, I know. So then I start eating myself up with guilt about that. If I keep worrying, I'll cause a miscarriage.'

'Kate! You will not!'

'Sorry. You can see how easy I am to live with at the moment. Poor old Ian can't say the right thing. I know you all think we're perfect together, but sometimes I wonder. I can be a bitch from hell to him. He's put up with it so far, because he's a saint, but I do wonder how much longer that can last.'

'He's not a saint,' I tell her firmly. 'He's a father-to-be, and right now his job is to look after you. If it was men who had to get pregnant, he'd be worse than you are. They all would be. Anyway, soon he'll be looking back on this as a time of calm and peace, when you're throwing up all over him every morning.' We are on familiar territory now. Kate recites our usual conversation, with a little relief in her voice.

'When I'm showing him my piles,' she says with a smile.

'When you're swearing at him all through labour. Not to mention when the two of you are trying to persuade three little babies that they do, actually, want to sleep at night. Not just one or two of them, but all three.'

She smiles thinly. 'Thanks, Evie. It's easy to forget the end result in all this. What if we did have three? How would we even hold them all?'

We each step in opposite directions to avoid an enormous puddle in the pavement. I tiptoe on the edge of the kerb, just as a number 27 bus speeds past and covers me in dirty spray.

'Wanker!' I shout after it. A passenger standing at the back, ready to get off, laughs at me, ostentatiously. He is a blur of suit and mouth. I flick him the finger. He vanishes into a haze of rain and spray, and I don't think he saw my elegant riposte.

'I'll come and live with you for a bit,' I offer, wondering if she'll realise that I'm serious. 'Hold a baby. Do a bottle-feed in the night. Push a pushchair.' I wonder how holding a baby would make me feel.

She laughs. 'Evie, you're so sweet. I hope it comes to that, I really do.'

I tuck my arm through hers. 'It will.'

As we turn the corner, dripping wet, towards the apartment block, I try to make myself believe that the spirits of baby Elizabeth and Kate's many unborn children are walking with us, but of course they're not. Both of us are on our own. That is the point.

We arrive at the flat, dripping wet and laughing. I feel childish, like a little girl who has been out jumping puddles. Meg is in the shower, and Guy and Ian are talking in the kitchen.

'Evie!' says Ian, holding out an envelope. 'This was on the mat for you.'

'What is it?' I ask, taking it without thinking.

Guy doesn't look at me. Nor does he say anything.

'Just a letter,' says Ian.

I drop the envelope on the work top and look at the address. This time it just says 'Evie', printed, as ever, on a computer. This has been delivered by hand. I take it into my room and drop it on to my bed. He has been here, while I've been out. He probably watched me going out. He might have followed me to the Mediterranean Kitchen, and then nipped back to the flat, to leave this letter.

Or else he had it in his pocket all the time, and dropped it on to the mat when he deliberately came back before me. It would have been easy to distract Ian and Megan. He is ignoring what I said.

I pick it up to open it. Then I stop myself. For the first time, I don't think I want to know.

On Sunday night, I pick a fight with Megan. I do it deliberately, because I don't want to be her friend any more. I don't want to be anybody's friend. I cannot make myself upset Kate, but I don't need anyone else in my life.

Guy leaves with barely a word to me. From time to time I have caught him looking at me, but he always looks away again as our eyes meet.

'Meg,' I say sharply, after he has gone.

'Mmmm?' she asks, a dreamy smile on her face. We are in the sitting room, leafing through the Sunday papers. Megan looks a little more worldly than she used to. She is dressed in a vest and drawstring trousers, with her bra strap showing, and she keeps smiling to herself. Her rosy cheeks don't look as innocent as they once did.

'How old's your dad?'

She turns a page of the colour supplement. 'Fifty-eight. Why?'

'So Guy's younger than him, at least.'

She frowns at me, but it's a gentle, puzzled frown. Then she stretches her legs out. 'You don't have a problem with that, do you, Evie? You were the one who introduced us.'

'And I wish I hadn't,' I tell her. 'I do have a problem. Guy's fifty-five. He has a past. He's definitely old enough to be your father, and he looks it, too. What is wrong with men of our age?'

'What, like Dan Donovan?'

'Dan's history. And there were twelve years between us.

169

Not twenty-eight. You and Guy look sick together, like he's into kids or something.'

Megan stands up and stares at me. She drops her magazine. 'I thought you were more open-minded than this. Where did this come from? What business is it of yours?'

'It's just what everyone thinks. I've known Guy for ever, and I find your relationship with him disturbing. If he had children, they'd be older than you are. And you're so loud together. I can hear *everything*. I know exactly what you do together. And I find it disgusting.' As I say it, I know I am being unnecessarily cruel and that Megan doesn't deserve it. I don't care. I'm sick of having her as a friend.

'Right, thanks for telling me how you feel,' she says, and leaves the room. I hear her bedroom door slam. Ten minutes later she creeps back into the sitting room to fetch the phone. I don't look at her, and she doesn't look at me.

chapter twelve

Five days later

Until now, I have treated the letters as a mild annoyance. Occasionally they have scared me, but I have almost enjoyed the frisson. I have never, ever imagined that whoever was writing them was really going to come to the flat and attack me.

That was until this morning. I abandoned Meg without a second thought and ran away, because he came to get me. He actually came to get me. I heard him, so I ran as fast as I could.

That's why I'm sitting in Camden, on Jack's sofa. That's why I'm fiddling compulsively with the ring pull of my Coke can. I don't even like Coke. I could do with some Calm Iced Tea.

Jack is sitting next to me, his arm around my shoulders. For once, I don't want to shrug it off. I'm glad Jack still wants to put his arm round my shoulders. I don't want to be married to him, but I do want to be able to run to him when I need to.

'Go with them,' he says firmly. I open my mouth to tell him all the reasons I can't, and he touches my hand. 'Don't say anything. Just do it. You know it's your only option.'

I nod. Then I look at him, at the tender way he's looking at me. It pleases me. 'Come with us?' I ask him, in a small, appealing voice.

Jack laughs, but kindly. 'Evie, I would *love* to. New York, with you and Ian and Kate. It would be great, like old times. A blast. But it wouldn't be right. If there was a chance we were getting back together I'd drop everything, but that's not what you really want, is it?'

'I don't know what I really want.' I lean my head on his shoulder.

He looks to the door, and I know he's wondering whether Sophia will reappear. He seems nervous. She must have her own key.

I stare down at the empty can in my hand. I'm still shaking. This is annoying: I ought to be able to control myself better than this. Although it's good that Jack's seeing me vulnerable, and feeling sorry for me, I would have preferred him to have seen me fake-vulnerable, rather than the real thing.

I bought the Coke this morning because I needed a caffeine fix, and I didn't have time to get a coffee. The newsagent was next to the bus stop. I ran in and ran out and jumped on to the back of the bus that had come and almost gone while I was waiting for my change.

'What number bus is this? Where's it going?' I asked the conductor. I was panting for breath. He looked at me with the long-suffering manner that I imagine a London bus attendant quickly acquires. He was a young man, but he looked careworn.

'It's a twenty-seven,' he said. 'Chalk Farm.' I thought about it. I could go to Chalk Farm, but I didn't know what I would do when I got there. Then I remembered Jack.

'Do you go through Camden Town?'

He looked bored. 'One pound.'

A fake-casual call to Ian revealed Jack's address, and as I waited on the doorstep, glad to be out of the way of the crowds heading to the market, I didn't even consider that he might not have been alone. I assumed that I had already sabotaged his relationship with Sophia.

He opened the door after ten minutes of repeated knocking. He was rubbing his eyes, and wearing nothing but a pair of pants. Even the sight of his old grey pants reassured me.

'Evie?' he asked, peering at me, confused. His face was puffy and sleepy.

'Sorry to wake you,' I said. He looked at me, and I saw his expression change.

'What's wrong?' he asked, warily.

I was about to ask if I could come in when I saw her behind him. She was small, but curvaceous, with thick dark hair and dark brown eyes. She was wearing his old green dressing gown.

'Oh,' I said, looking at her and sizing her up as she did the same to me. A large part of me was pleased to meet her. 'Oh God, sorry, I didn't realise.'

'Evie,' said Jack, clearly hating what he was having to do, 'this is Sophia. Sophia, this is Evie.'

'Hi,' Sophia said, eyeing me warily.

'Hello,' I said back to her, unable to make my voice calm. I heard the catch as I said it and wondered how mad I seemed. I realised that only I could rescue the situation, and I tried to pull myself together.

'Sorry, both of you,' I heard myself say, and I consciously forced a smile. 'I didn't mean to wake you up or to barge in on you like this. I just didn't know where else to go.' At this, I crumpled, and the next thing I felt was Jack's hand on my arm, leading me inside. 'Sorry,' I kept saying. When I was sitting on the sofa, I looked around for Sophia. She wasn't in the room.

'Where's she gone?' I asked Jack, who was standing over me.

'To get dressed,' he said. 'You look like you need coffee and breakfast, and you also need to tell me what's going on.'

'Sorry,' I said, blinking. 'I shouldn't have come. I'm sorry.'

'You're here now. It's OK. Tell me what's happening. Is it those letters again?'

Sophia came back into the room, dressed in red and looking striking.

'I'll be at mine,' she said to Jack, and gave him a kiss on the lips. Then she looked at me, sensibly distrusting my motives. I wanted to suggest that if she didn't want to feel threatened by her boyfriend's wife, she might like to consider finding a boyfriend without one. Instead, I gave her a weak smile. 'Call me,' she added, to Jack.

'Sure,' he told her, and she was off.

'Sorry,' I said again, as the door slammed. Jack relaxed visibly, and took me in his arms.

174

'It's OK,' he said again. He buried his face in my hair and kissed my neck. 'Tell me.'

I pulled away and breathed deeply. I looked around. His flat is the ground floor of a townhouse in a genteel street off the main road.

'Nice place,' I told him. He hasn't made much of an effort with the decor, but I'm sure he will. 'You live here on your own?'

He looked at me. 'Yes. Been here two weeks.'

I sat on the sofa and played with the ring pull of my Coke. 'Sophia doesn't know about. . .?'

He shook his head. 'None of it. I wondered if she suspected, but she didn't say anything. She never asked. What's happened?'

He sat next to me. I drained the rest of the drink, put the can on the table, and told him.

'You have to go with them,' he says, again. 'Put as much distance between you and this nutter as you can. And give me that bloody can. I'll put it in the recycling and make you a coffee. You don't even like Coke.'

I hand it to him. 'I know. Have I screwed things up for you with Sophia? I really am sorry. I've been so confused about us, I thought it was best if I left you alone. I didn't want to mess you around. I didn't even know whether you were still seeing her . . .'

Jack leaves the room. 'Yes, Evie,' he calls back. 'I am still seeing her.'

'That's good.' I'm not sure what else to say. The sight of her in his dressing gown has burned me to the core, and I am pleased to have something normal to worry about. Splitting these two up is a project. It beats worrying about the stalker, who is now a potential intruder. 'I should have gone to Kate,' I tell him, 'but she doesn't need to be worrying about me right now. And I haven't really got anyone else. I've concentrated on work so much for years and years that I haven't really got many good friends. Megan and I aren't speaking. The people I'm on best terms with at the moment are PR people.'

He calls from the kitchen. 'Babe, it's not just that you've been working too hard, is it? You don't honestly work any harder than, say, I do. It's more that you've always cut yourself off.' He appears in the doorway. 'Remember, we were together eight years. I've been thinking about this, about us, a lot. When we were together I was always out with work mates, or other mates, or off on stag weekends or whatever. And you weren't. You'd groan if the phone rang in the evening. You'd put on your charming face when you had to, and chat to people, and you got away with it because there is something captivating about you. Everyone can see that. But you never gave anything away. Even to me, really. That night when we got together, last month. I felt I saw a part of you then that I'd never met before, and we've been married, you know, all this time.' He goes back into the kitchen, then returns with a steaming cup, which he places carefully in front of me. 'Try this. I got a new coffee machine like the ones they have in cafés. Makes a wicked latte.'

I pick it up, but my hand is still shaking, so I put it down again. I push my hair behind my ears. It's lank and greasy. I hope to God there wasn't a photographer waiting for me outside this morning. I'm still wearing track-suit bottoms, a denim jacket, and the T-shirt I wore to bed last night, teamed with a pair of flip-flops which are entirely unsuitable for March. I haven't even got a bra on. If I'd known I was meeting Sophia this morning I would have paused at least to put on a half-decent outfit and to scrape my hair back. No wonder she gave me such a strange look. Still, if she relaxes about me she won't bother to fight me for him. I will have an advantage.

'Have you really been thinking about us?' I haven't the energy to take in what Jack just said. 'You do know me, Jack. Why do you think you don't?'

He smiles. 'I love you, Evie. I can't help myself, but I still don't believe I completely know you. I think you're holding something back. I've always known it, but I've never known what it was.'

I manage to pick up the coffee and take a sip.

'But you love me all the same?' I ask, with my best smile.

'I'm afraid I do.'

'I love you too, Jack.'

'So what shall we do?'

I put the cup down and look away from him. 'I don't know. The last thing I want to do is to mess you around. You mean so much to me. That's why I've kept away. With these letters, and a few other things that are going on, I want us to get back together for the right reasons, not the wrong ones.' I am scarcely aware of how much I am manipulating him. I am too shaky to think about it. It just comes naturally.

He looks at me, hard. 'Is that true, Evie?' I nod. 'What are you going to do now?'

'Invite myself on the New York trip, like you said. Go along for the implantation. Extricate myself from a charity concert in Brighton and an interview on *Woman's Hour*.' I look down at myself. 'Meanwhile, I suppose getting changed would be a good start.'

Jack bites his lip. He looks happy. 'I suppose it would be bad form to offer you Sophia's clothes,' he says. 'Plus you're too tall.' He passes me the phone. 'First things first.'

I sigh, and dial the number of my local police station, which I know by heart. I ask for Eleanor, but she's not there, so I talk to the duty sergeant instead. I stutter out my story again, trying to tell it logically this time.

'So you're saying that you saw him?' he checks.

'No. I didn't say that,' I say as clearly and as patiently as I can. 'I'm saying that I *heard* him. Someone was trying the door to the flat this morning. They rattled it and I'm sure they tried to get a key into the lock.'

'We'll need to come to visit you, if there's been an attempted break-in.'

'You can't do that. I'm not there.' And Megan is, and I don't want her to know about any of this.

'Can you meet us there? We'll need you to make a statement. He didn't succeed in gaining entry?'

'No. I called out, asked who was there. He rattled the door again and then I heard footsteps walking away.'

'And you know it was the writer of the anonymous letters?' He sounds sceptical. I am furious.

'The fact that he left one behind would suggest so, yes,' I say icily.

'Sweetie,' says Jack, 'do you have the letter with you?'

I feel in my pocket. I was so frantic when I left that I can't remember what I did with it.

'No,' I tell him.

'Do you want me to take you home? I'll stay with you. You know you need to be there if the police are coming over. And you need to be able to show them the letter. I'll take you home and sort everything out for you. I won't leave you.'

I look at him. 'Thanks, Jack. It means everything to me. If we go back, I can change into some decent clothes and stop looking deranged.'

'Evie?' he says. 'It takes more than this to make you look deranged. You look wonderful.'

Jack pays the taxi, and holds out an expectant hand for my house keys. I hand them to him, feeling unusually ambivalent. I'm relieved that Jack will look after me, that he still loves me, that the option of Jack is still available to me. Yet I hate the fact that my dependence on him, right now, is genuine. I preferred it when much of my life was a charade, and when I looked after myself and relied on no one.

Does Jack know, I wonder, that I am struggling to hold myself together? Even though he knows what is happening to me, he has no idea how I'm feeling. Perhaps he's right. Perhaps he doesn't know me at all. More and more, my self is bound up with Elizabeth. Jack can never know me unless I tell him. I have no desire whatsoever to tell him.

But I feel terrified about the letters. I am trying to think of anything but the man who is writing them.

'Come on,' he says, passing through the door before me, looking around the hallway, and motioning for me to follow him. He takes my hand, and we walk up the four flights of stairs together. My hand feels small in his. I have missed human contact.

Jack opens the door and goes in first.

'Megan?' he calls. 'Are you there?'

Megan and I have not said a single word to each other in the past week. She doesn't reply now. 'She might be out with Guy,' I say, my voice falling away into nothing as I hear it breaking the silence of the flat. 'Or even in Bristol,' I continue in a whisper. 'I don't know what her plans were.'

Her bedroom door opens. I tense up, certain that it will be Guy.

It's not. Megan looks from one of us to the other, then down at my hand in Jack's. She looks away. She is wearing her pyjamas and dressing gown, but she has clearly been awake for some time. She is pale and unsmiling. Her hair is loose down her back, and she looks like an ill child.

'Meg!' I say, walking quickly to her. I force myself to overcome my pride, because I know I have wronged her, and I want Jack to carry on liking me. 'Are you OK?' I ask her. 'I'm sorry, about everything.'

She pushes me away when I try to touch her. Jack comes closer.

'Megan?' he says. 'Talk to me at least, even if you don't want to speak to Evie.'

She looks from me to Jack, and back to our hands, which are still clasped together. Then she shakes her head abruptly, and turns away. I start to go after her, but she is in the bathroom with the door locked before I have a chance to get close. I tap on it a few times.

'Megan?' I say, desperate for her to talk to me. 'Please,

Meg,' I call. 'What's happened? Please tell me. Has something happened? Has he come back?'

The door flies open, and she is staring at me. 'Has who come back, Evie? Who?'

I look at her. She is distraught and confused. I'm not sure what to say to her. 'I don't know.'

'The guy who wrote *this*, perhaps?' She takes a piece of paper from her dressing gown pocket, and thrusts it towards me. 'Is this who you're talking about?'

I take it. Without looking at it, I nod my head. 'Yes.'

She looks at me levelly, suddenly calm. 'So would you like to enlighten me? What in heaven's name is going on?'

This morning's note wasn't in an envelope. It is just a white piece of A4 paper, folded several times. The message, as usual, is printed from a computer. The grammar has got worse, lately. I know this person can spell, and can string a sentence together, but now he doesn't bother.

evie you slut you whore you bitch. now you know I know where you live. i can get a key. i will come for you next week. be waiting for me. you will love it.

'Is it from one of your lovers?' she asks, looking pointedly at Jack. 'One of the many? A perverted game? That's the best explanation I can think of. The only all right one.' She leaves the alternatives hanging in the air. Then she looks me up and down, noticing my hair, my clothes. I see her expression shifting as curiosity takes hold of her.

I look at Jack.

'Tell her,' says Jack, firmly. 'I'd better make some more coffee. Tell her everything before the police get here.'

'Police?' asks Megan.

'Did Guy not stay last night?' I ask, knowing that she only wears pyjamas when she's alone.

'No,' she says. 'Though I don't see what it is to you.'

'He's always been here on Friday night before.'

'Well this week he's been at a conference in Nottingham.' Her tone is defensive. 'What is going on?' she adds. 'Whatever it is, why didn't you tell me?'

'Come to the sitting room.'

I stare at our plants while I start to explain about the letters. Megan's hostility is almost tangible. I tell her that I have now had twenty-five of them, and that they are all openly threatening. The geraniums need watering. The rubber plant is growing a new leaf. It is half unfurled. Megan and I sit at opposite ends of the sofa. We face inwards, towards each other, and our feet touch where the two cushions meet. While I speak, I can't look at her face. I pushed Megan away and I hate having to let her back in.

'And you went to New York for more than two weeks, and left me here?' she says, some colour returning to her cheeks. I nod and look away from her face. 'Right. Just making sure we've got our facts straight.' Her tone is acidic. 'So I was obediently picking up your poison-pen letters and piling them neatly in your room. OK. Carry on. What *exactly* happened this morning?'

'I woke up early,' I tell her, still avoiding her eyes, 'at about half seven, and I got up to make a cup of tea because all this stuff was going round my head. So I was sitting in the kitchen flicking through your *Vogue* when I heard noises around the door. I thought it was the post, or maybe you or Guy arriving, not that you often come home at eight in the morning.'

'But it wasn't,' she prompts in a high voice, as I tail off.

'No. First someone was rattling the letter box, but nothing was coming through it. Then they were pushing the door. Then I heard him trying to shove something into the lock.'

'And you thought it was me?'

'I hoped it was you, but I kind of knew it wasn't really. You don't do clubbing till the morning. And you don't do arseing around with the front door, either.'

'So what did you do?'

'I checked it was double-locked with the chain on, which it was. So then I said, "Who is it?" really quietly, and then something came through the letterbox and I just heard their footsteps walking away. It sounded as if they were being very quiet, on purpose.'

'You didn't open the door and confront him?'

'Bloody right I didn't.'

We look at each other for a moment.

'And what have the police said?' she asks quietly.

I stare at a photo of a Thai beach. 'The best thing they can get him on is sending obscene materials through the post. I think it's an offence against Her Majesty. Unless he does anything, of course.' She says nothing, and doesn't look at me. I know I have to try to patch things up, much as I don't want to. 'I'm sorry I didn't tell you,' I say, quickly. 'Really sorry. I wanted to, but at first I thought it might be Jack pissing about, and I didn't know you that well at that point and I didn't tell anyone. Then, when I realised it wasn't him, I didn't want to worry you. I wanted to sort it out on my own. This has got nothing to do with you. It's all about me. When I didn't sort it out at all, I didn't know how to explain that all this time I hadn't told you about it. It became harder and harder. Sorry, Megan. I feel terrible about it. I have done for ages.' I swallow hard, and make eye contact. 'It hasn't seemed like a real threat until today. Now it does.'

She looks down. I try to read her expression. 'I wish you'd told me. Does Kate know?'

'No. Just Jack.'

'What are you going to do?'

'Right now? The police are coming. I'll make a statement. They've got all the other letters. Almost all of them.' She looks at me questioningly. 'I threw away the first one, because I thought it was from Jack. In fact I burnt it.'

'I remember that. In my Le Creuset pan?'

'Yes.'

'It's OK, it came off. I did wonder, but I thought divorced people must make grand gestures like that all the time. Burning old love letters and so on.'

We sit in silence for a moment. Fleetingly, I consider adding that my only suspect is her boyfriend. On balance, it's probably best not to mention Guy. *At a conference* could mean anything.

I send mental messages to Jack, begging him to come in with our coffee, but he is clearly giving us more time to talk. He is too considerate. As I start to stand up to seek him out, Megan speaks.

'What are you going to do after that? I mean, we shouldn't stay here, surely?'

I sit back down heavily. 'I don't know,' I tell her. 'We need to talk about this, I guess.' I look into her eyes, properly, for the first time. She is still enormously pretty, but her face looks different. I realise that not only does she no longer like me, but she is also as terrified as I am. 'Neither of us should stay here, under the circumstances. You know that it's not you he's after, just me. But while I'm here neither of us is safe. Even if I wasn't here, he might not know that. I'm sorry I went to New York like that without telling you. So sorry. I'd convinced myself, until this morning, that it was what the police said, just an empty threat, some crazy wanker sitting in their scummy bedroom living in a fantasy world. That was until I heard him trying to get through our front door. I think you should go home, Meg, and I think I'll go too, to my mum's. Let's get out and go to Bristol. Then I'm thinking about going further afield for a while.'

'Good idea.'

'And Meg?'

'Yes?'

I draw a deep breath and make myself say it. 'I'm sorry about what I said about Guy. I was stressed about this and I shouldn't have taken it out on you. It was because you were nearest, and that was the easiest way to lash out. I didn't mean it and it was none of my business. Sorry.'

I wait for an answer, but there is none. I wish I hadn't bothered.

I hear Oliver Sinclair's outraged voice shouting tinnily through the receiver.

'Yes, Daddy,' Megan says patiently. 'We are going to the police. They're coming now.

'Of course you can come and collect us,' she says a moment later. 'See you in a couple of hours.'

While her parents are driving their enormous people carrier to pick us up, the police come and go. Luckily, it's Eleanor, and she confirms everything I've said, and expresses relief that we are leaving for a while.

'Stay away as long as you can,' she advises us, and Megan shoots me a black look.

Mum and Phil would never dream of driving to London to fetch me. They always assume I will turn up by train and taxi. Oliver Sinclair seems fussy to me. He dotes on his little girl. However, if I told Mum about the letters and the intruder, she would probably drop everything too. I imagine that any parent would. I expect that if Elizabeth materialised and needed me, I would rush to her side. In fact, I know that I would be there like a shot.

Jack makes lots more coffee, and rustles up some sandwiches from the random ingredients in the fridge. Megan and I start packing. As I'm cramming my clothes into every bag I can find, she appears in my doorway.

'How long are you packing for?' she asks coldly. 'Do you think I should take things for a few days, or clear my room out?'

I barely look up. 'I don't know,' I say. 'I really don't. Since it's your dad's place, I suppose you can leave stuff here, no matter what.'

She turns round. 'Well, I'm taking all my underwear. I don't want some pervert coming in and thinking he's found your knickers.'

I look at her. She should never have rented the room to me. There were sixty-two other people who wanted it, after all. 'Good point,' I say. 'Are you wishing you'd picked someone else to be your flatmate?'

She maintains eye contact. 'Yes.'

Jack declines to come to Bristol with me, even though I suggest it several times. I would like to cuddle up to him tonight.

'Evie,' he says firmly. 'I'd love to, but I've got things to sort out here. You'll be fine when you're out of London. Take your cello, take your stuff, and go and see your mum. Hang out with Tessa.'

'Things to sort out with Sophia?'

'Yes.'

He takes out his phone, and checks it anxiously. As he starts to type a text message, I interrupt him.

'But what if he's waiting for me there? What if he knows where they live? It wouldn't be hard for him to find out.'

Jack puts his phone away and pulls me towards him. I like the feel of his hand on my waist. 'He won't be there, I promise. He'll think you're still here.'

'He might watch us leave. He could follow us all the way.'

'Even if that did happen, you sleep on the top floor at your parents' place. There are plenty of other people in the house. They've even got a burglar alarm, haven't they? Make sure it's set at night. It's the best place for you to be, babes. Far better than sleeping at mine.'

I look down. 'I know. I've messed your life up enough already. I'll miss you.'

He smiles. 'You haven't messed up anything. I'll be ringing you every morning and every evening to make sure you're OK. Don't worry, Evie. It's not your fault.'

I dread driving home with the Sinclairs, but less than I would dread either staying in the flat by myself or going alone by public transport. Oliver Sinclair is in a strange mood when he arrives. I expected him to be worried and angry. I barely dare to look at him, at first. I have brought a psychopath to his prized London apartment and put his daughter in danger. But he seems almost ebullient.

'Evie!' he exclaims, and kisses me firmly on each cheek. I suddenly realise that he reminds me of Guy. They are even the same age. Oliver may be three years older, but three years is nothing. It is not just their age. It's their mannerisms, too. Megan is, essentially, having sex every weekend with her father. I wonder what Oliver thinks of the relationship. I don't even want to mention Guy in front of him, in case Megan hasn't told him. If he knows about it, he is probably with me on the subject.

Oliver and Jack, together, carry our bags and my cello down to the car. Oliver gets back behind the wheel, and waits for us to say goodbye. Josie sits next to him, and I see her looking at me. She doesn't look friendly. As soon as she catches my eye, she takes a make-up bag out of her handbag, and starts reapplying her foundation with a studiedly casual air.

I feel self-conscious, saying goodbye to Jack with an audience.

'Thank you so much for looking after me,' I tell him quietly, stroking his arm. 'It means everything. There's no one else I could have gone to. You're the best.'

'I'm glad you came to me,' he says warmly, 'and not to that godawful teenager. Or to anyone else.'

I look at him. 'The thing with Dan never really happened,' I say softly, 'and when Megan said I had lots of lovers, it wasn't true. She was just getting at me.'

'You'd better go,' he says. 'Love you.'

'Love you too.'

We gaze at each other. For a moment, I almost believe myself.

'Play the cello!' he adds suddenly.

I smile. 'Of course I will.'

'No, play it properly. Play it like you used to. That'll keep you grounded.'

'Nice boy, your husband,' says Oliver, as he pulls the people carrier authoritatively on to Kensington Church Street. A cycle courier swerves and swears, and Oliver affects not to notice. 'He appears to be very supportive.'

'He is.'

Meg looks at me appraisingly. 'Are you getting back with him? Or are you just trying to mess things up with his new girlfriend?'

Oliver roars with laughter. I try to see Josie's expression, but she is facing forwards and is not participating in the conversation.

'Neither,' I say firmly. 'Some people really do stay friends when they split up. Jack is the first person I go to when something happens. He's my best friend. That's all.'

Josie speaks up. 'Does he realise that you're using him?'

I stare at the back of her head, but she doesn't turn round.

'He was happy to help us out today,' I tell her, 'and he wasn't pretending. He really didn't resent it. Did he, Meg?' I look to her for support. She shrugs.

'Don't really know him,' she says.

* * *

189

Late at night, Mum, Phil and I drink red wine, and once we are certain Tessa is asleep, I tell them the whole story and not the abridged version that I have managed to whisper in instalments through the early evening. They are horrified.

'So it seems as if someone really wants to harm me,' I tell them. I have never spelt it out before. 'All the time they've been writing to me, and they've really meant it.'

'Darling,' says Mum. I know she wants to hug me, and I have purposely sat in a chair, not on the sofa, to stop it happening. I need to be self-reliant. 'Promise me you won't go back.'

'Of course I won't go back. Do you think New York is a good idea?'

'Yes. Get as far away as possible.'

Phil leans forward. 'And make sure you tell Howard everything you've just told us.'

I nod, meekly. 'I texted Kate earlier,' I tell him, 'because I didn't really want to talk to her. I couldn't face explaining all this again. I said I was going to New York at the same time as them. She was pleased. I hope she gets pregnant, I really do. It's about time something good happened. The ad is apparently on all the time now, and the concert at Lincoln Center has been confirmed, so I'll be able to stay out there for weeks and months if necessary.'

I smile my best smile, first at Mum and then at Phil. I hope it takes them in. Inside, I think I must be close to rock bottom. Sometimes I wonder if I might be mad, if I could be writing the letters to myself. I deserve to be hounded. I had a beautiful daughter, but I gave her away.

Elizabeth was mine while she kicked me and rolled around in my womb. She is not mine any more, and she wouldn't know me if she passed me on the street. I would not recognise my own daughter. I am no kind of mother to her. We would be friends now, Elizabeth and me. It should be the most important relationship in my life, and instead I am empty. I have done the worst thing any woman can do, and now I have nothing.

I lie awake for most of the night, convinced someone is about to climb in through my window. I hear his breathing. He never arrives.

chapter thirteen

Two weeks later

'Delighted to meet you,' he says, holding out his hand with a practised smile. 'Ron Thomas.'

'Evie Silverman,' I reply, giving him a fake smile of my own. I dish these out often enough to know one when I see one. Fake smiles have been my sole currency lately, as, more than ever, I have needed to mask everything I am really thinking, everything I am feeling.

This man is just as false as I am.

'Right!' he says, pointing to me, his head on one side. 'The Calm cellist, yes?'

'That sounds about right,' I agree.

'That ad is on *all* the time. You must be stopped in the street every five minutes, aren't you?'

'Not really. I've seen a few people recognise me in Manhattan, but you know what Manhattan's like. People have far too much attitude to say anything.'

'It's a good place to be famous,' he agrees.

I have been in America for three days. Being here was

supposed to make me feel better. Instead, I am lost. I feel as if I have been cast adrift in the world, and it is hard to make sense of anything. The only thing that is keeping me going is company, and my well-honed ability to put on a show. As long as somebody is with me, I can pretend to them that I am all right. I have managed to spend next to no time on my own in the past two weeks.

Although those letters do not reach me out here, I know they are still being written. It makes no difference whether I read them or not. Somebody hates me enough to threaten me. Every day I have a new idea about who it could be. I don't trust anybody at all any more.

At least I have a prestigious concert to worry about in a few weeks. I practise my cello every day, which helps me blank things out for a while. Being an extremely minor celebrity in America also helps. I saw my advert on Howard and Sonia's TV on the night I arrived. It gave me all the adrenalin rush of a live performance, and distracted me wonderfully from the inside of my head. I was critical of my rendition of 'The Swan', my appearance, my slightly wonky bow. I was terrified, even though I knew they would never be allowing it to air unless they were completely happy with it. I've seen it again, twice, since then. I'm getting used to it. It allows me to be Evie Silverman, famous cellist, rather than Evie Silverman, the teenage girl with a secret.

Above all, I must concentrate on my surroundings. Deflecting all talk about myself, on all but the most shallow levels, and surrounding myself with other people is the only way I can preserve the appearance of sanity. This is a disastrous time to crack up, and I cannot allow myself to do it.

Ron Thomas is more or less as I'd expected. He knows about minor celebrity himself, as he appears regularly on television drumming up business for his clinic, and commenting on any fertility-related story in the news. He looks younger than Guy, but I know he's the same age. Without a doubt, he goes to the gym before six thirty every morning, and I'm sure that if you added up the cost of everything he's wearing the total would be more than five thousand pounds. He has a suspicious head of hair: it is too full, and too black. His skin is smooth, and his frameless glasses have 'Armani' written subtly along one arm. Given how much Kate and Ian have already paid him, I'm surprised he's not dressed even more ostentatiously. Given what Guy said, I'm also surprised he's not waited on by an army of Ron Thomas clones, oozing their charm in unison.

His clinic, however, is a lot smarter than I had imagined. I knew it was going to be posh, but I never expected a five-star hotel. We came up a mile-long drive to reach the building, which nestles in landscaped parkland, and I even saw a couple of deer in the distance. I drove the hire car, with Kate next to me, reaching back to clasp Ian's hand. I find driving in America to be something of a compulsion, and insisted that I should be the only named driver when we made the rental. Being in control of a vehicle gives me a responsibility. I know I won't fall to pieces at the wheel. The worst I could do is point the car west and keep going until I hit the Pacific. From one ocean to another: the temptation occasionally feels overwhelming, and I will probably do it one day, when I am least expecting it.

The house is grand and luxurious. It is furnished with plush dark red carpets that cover my ankles. The walls are cream and white, and bear expensive-looking, exquisitely tasteful canvases. Some are traditional landscapes. Others are contemporary and abstract. All of them are perfectly chosen. Black-and-white photographs of smiling babies grace the reception area, and a noticeboard in there is filled with thank-you cards. I looked at a few of them, and they all say, essentially, the same thing. Thank you for bringing our child into the world. This man is, in certain circles, a demigod. I wonder whether Elizabeth's new parents have ever wanted to send a card like that to me.

Ron leads us into a sitting room, which is furnished like an English gentlemen's club, and motions for me to sit in an armchair. I sink down into the cushions.

'Won't be long,' he says, as he leads Kate and Ian away. 'You just make yourself at home. There's coffee and tea over there.' He motions towards a varnished table which bears a coffee machine, a kettle, and tea bags from across the spectrum, as well as a huge plate of Danish pastries. 'Help yourself. Please eat the pastries. We throw away so many of them, because I make my patients follow a strict diet. I'm sure Kate has familiarised you with that.'

Kate winces. 'Evie knows *all* about it. So does everyone else I know.'

'But Evie's not planning assisted reproduction any time soon, is she?' he asks, and I shake my head with a little laugh. 'So you go right ahead. Eat them all, make my day. Now, Mrs Dawson. Let's get you pregnant.'

I sit back in the leather chair, and look around the room. This place is eerily quiet. The only person we have seen has been the frighteningly well-groomed receptionist. She was beginning to page Ron when he turned up, professing to be absolutely delighted to see us. He is American in all but accent. He has certainly come a long way from being the class swot at Bristol University's medical school.

I stand up suddenly. It could be Megan writing to me. The letters started soon after I moved into her flat. I don't know her well enough to know why she could be doing it. Now I have insulted her, God only knows what she might do.

I hate being alone. It makes my mind run wild. I walk to the wide French windows, and look out on to the lawns. They are, of course, immaculate. There is a cedar tree, whose branches make gentle horizontal lines against the pale blue sky. There are immaculate beds of daffodils.

If someone was following me, waiting to get me on my own, he could be behind the tree. He could be behind the door. I have no idea in which room Kate's treatment is taking place, and apart from that the clinic appears to be empty. Quickly, I pour myself a coffee, put an apricot Danish on to a small plate, and head back towards the reception area.

In fact I am certain I am not being stalked by a stranger. I'm certain that it's someone I already know. This doesn't make it any less scary.

The blonde woman looks round, startled. 'Hi there,' she says, when she sees me. 'May I help you?'

'No,' I say, and see confusion passing across her face.

'Didn't Ron show you to the drawing room?' she asks, beginning to stand up.

'No, it's fine. He did. But if you don't mind, I'd rather sit in reception. I'm sorry. I just – it's hard to explain.' I realise how strange I must appear. 'I'd appreciate some company, that's all. I'm not very good at being on my own at the moment.'

She smiles, her professionalism restored. 'Sure. I see you have refreshments. Help yourself to a magazine.'

I pick one up from the top of the pile. It is called *Ceramics Monthly*. That will do.

While I drink and eat, covering the front of my sweater in flaky pastry as I do so, I take sneaky glances at the receptionist. She is older than she initially appears. At first I thought she was twenty-six, but in fact she's more likely to be forty-two. She, like Ron, has had cosmetic surgery. Her hair, like so many American women's hair, is immaculate, and Barbie-blonde. She has it arranged in a chignon. She's wearing a uniform: a dark red jacket with a white blouse. I am certain that, under the desk, she has a short red skirt, perfect legs, and high heels. She's like a flight attendant.

'Nice baby photos,' I say, gesturing to the wall.

She smiles. 'I'm pleased you like them. They went up recently. I wondered whether it could be seen as insensitive by couples who are experiencing troubles, but Ron decided it was inspirational.'

'Are they all babies conceived here?'

'They sure are.'

'Wow. How long have you worked here?' I am desperate to force a proper conversation on this woman.

'Me?' she says. 'Oh, I've been here for four years now. I met Ron through his partner, Anneka. She's one of my best girlfriends. We were at beauty school together. When this post came vacant, Anneka tipped me off.' She smiles, checking whether she's answered my question.

'I think I should go to beauty school myself,' I say, looking down at the crumbs on my black jumper.

'Oh, honey, you are so pretty. Look at you, you're practically a model, and you're on the TV every day. If there was one thing, perhaps I'd get your nails seen to.' She holds out her own nails, which are long red talons. I look down at mine. I file them every few days, and usually paint them with a clear varnish, but that's as far as I go. I don't let my eyebrows out of control for a moment, but nails have never been something I've bothered about. In my line of work, nails are functional.

'The trouble with nails, for me,' I explain, 'is that I have to have them short. Yours are beautiful,' I lie, 'but I just couldn't do that. I wouldn't be able to play.' I make a face that is supposed to be self-deprecating.

'Hmmmm.' She gestures to me to come closer. I walk over to her, and she picks up my hand. 'You see, I hear what you're saying, but, honey, you should still visit a salon. Look at these cuticles. They're ragged. I'm afraid it's the only word that fits. Give one of the girls at my salon five minutes with your hands, and you'll be a new woman. I have the card in my purse. Take it. You should have a pedicure at the same time.'

This woman cannot even see my feet. Yet clearly she knows about the hard skin and the chipped varnish. I usually get a pedicure when spring arrives and the open-toed sandals come out. New York is much sunnier than London was. That day is almost here.

It is relaxing to be making small talk about inconsequential trivia with someone who has never met me before. I need to try to do more of this.

'How long are you with us in New York, Evie?' she asks, and I pull up a chair.

'I don't know,' I say, with a smile. 'My father lives here, you see, and I kind of like it. Of course, everyone loves New York. As long as I have my cello, it doesn't matter that much where I am. I'm going to stay for a few weeks, for sure. I'm playing at Lincoln Center in three weeks. Kate and Ian will be around for a while too, won't they?'

'Sure they will. Ron doesn't advise patients to travel by air in the weeks following implantation.'

'And I have people to see here too. My album is out.'

The receptionist beams. 'Oh, I know! I saw it in the store, and I made sure to buy it because Ron said you were Kate's friend. And here you are! We never thought we would actually meet you. I haven't listened to it yet but I just know I'm going to love it. I don't mind saying, it is a bit *different* for me – I'm normally an R. Kelly kind of girl.'

'Thank you for buying it. That means a lot.' A thrill runs through me. If I can pick up the R. Kelly market, I will have a Malibu beach house next year. But then again, the receptionist only bought mine because she had a connection with me. At least it was in the shop. The store.

The phone rings, and my new friend mouths, 'Excuse me,' and picks it up with the words, 'Aurora speaking?' Then she laughs.

'Yes, Ron, she's right here.' She turns to me. 'They thought they'd lost you! Apparently poor little Ian is worried. I guess he knew you didn't like being alone, honey!'

I stand up. 'Is it done, then?'

'It is. Kate is resting. She will rest here for a couple of days now, as you know. I think she'd like to see you now.'

I replace my copy of *Ceramics Monthly*, having learned nothing whatsoever about its subject, and turn to head back down the corridor. Aurora stops me.

'They'll come for you, honey,' she says. 'You don't know where you're going, do you? And remember! Cuticles!'

I nod, obediently. Cuticles it is.

Kate is lying back in a beautiful double bed, wearing the negligée we picked out yesterday in Bloomingdales. She looks flushed and happy.

Ron and Ian stand back to let me into the room first, and I hurry to her bedside and kiss her.

'Hey!' she says, beaming. 'Whatever happens next, I'm pregnant now!'

'Congratulations!' I say. 'How do you feel?'

'Kate,' says Ron Thomas, sternly, 'you know I don't encourage you to think or talk that way. You're not technically pregnant. A test would come up negative. We don't know whether any of the embryos will implant. If this didn't work – and you know I am highly optimistic that it will, given your age and health – then I would like you to see it as an attempt that was unlucky, and *not* as a miscarriage.'

I look at Kate anxiously, before remembering that she

has suffered far worse knockbacks than this mild telling-off. She smiles at Ron.

'Sorry, sir. But you must admit I am hosting three tiny little babies.'

'Three tiny little embryos.'

'Potential babies.'

'Indeed; they have enormous potential.'

She looks at me, triumphant. 'See?'

I glance around. It's a large room, light and airy. I assume that the door leads to an en suite bathroom. The long windows give a view on to the parkland, with those deer visible among some trees about half a mile away. I give it a quick scan, just in case. There is no evidence of shady characters lurking.

'Nice pad,' I say to Ron.

'I'm pleased you like it,' he replies, courteously.

'I'm quite jealous of Kate, actually, getting to sleep here. It makes me want IVF myself. Does it matter that I'm single?'

He smiles, that fake smile again. 'Not a jot. We have many techniques which could help you. This does make for an expensive hotel, but I'm sure a girl with your earning capacity can afford it.'

I see Kate and Ian exchanging glances. I know they are worried about the fact that they now have no assets whatsoever, and I decide that as soon as Ron has gone I will offer them a further contribution.

Ian looks over to Ron, who is standing with me at the window. For a second I consider Ian as a suspect. Of course it's not him. I smile at my paranoia, and rule it out.

'Ron, did we ever mention our friend Guy to you?' he asks.

'Evie's friend more than ours,' Kate interjects nervously.

Ron looks at me questioningly. 'Guy?' he asks, and I study his face for recognition.

'My flatmate's boyfriend,' I tell him, and wonder whether I see him relax slightly. '"Boyfriend" is really the wrong word,' I add. 'He's a million years older than she is. It's a strange relationship – we fell out because of it. Or rather, because I was ungracious about it. He's a friend of my family's, in Bristol. He knows you from medical school. Guy Chapman.'

All three of us watch his reaction. He is a professional: he regains his cool almost instantaneously, and I wonder whether the others notice the flicker that crosses his face. For a second he looks astonished, and horrified. It is exactly the same reaction that Guy had when I told him Ron's name, but it is covered up even faster.

'Guy Chapman?' he muses. 'You know, I think I do remember him. He wasn't one of my immediate crowd. Liked a drink?'

I nod. 'That'll be him.'

'And you say he's involved with your flatmate? Is she your age? I assume your flatmate is a she?'

Ian laughs, and I smile. 'Oh yes. Megan's younger than I am, actually, but they both seem happy.' I have no desire to start talking about Megan. I haven't even told Kate and Ian, yet, that we've moved out of the flat. Let alone anything else that has gone on.

'Guy had a girlfriend when we were at college,' Ron says, and I notice him watching me intently. 'I assumed they were going to get married. Her name was . . .' He casts around for it, so elaborately that I know he is pretending. 'Marianne! That was it. Guy and Marianne. Lovely girl, Marianne. Do you know what became of her?'

'No idea,' I say. 'But he was married, I know that. His wife died. I don't know her name. My mum knew her.'

Ron shrugs. 'I do hope it wasn't the beautiful Marianne. Would I have known your mother, Evie? What was her maiden name?'

'I doubt it. She never said, and she knows Kate and Ian are having treatment with you. Her name was Anna Shaw.'

He shakes his head. 'You're right, she must have been after my time. What a small world it is, all the same. Bristol. That takes me back.'

He flashes a bright smile at us, and we know that it's time to change the subject.

Ian and I leave Kate to the attentions of the Babylove Clinic, and I drive him into Manhattan. I chat inanely all the way, to keep my mind occupied. I am uncomfortable being alone in a car with any man, so I baffle Ian by telling him about the New York Philharmonic Orchestra and the first rehearsal I'll have with them, in a couple of weeks. I give him far too much detail about anything I can think of.

I make a long detour to ensure that we arrive via the Brooklyn Bridge.

'There it is,' I say happily, gesturing to the island. 'The Manhattan skyline.' The clouds that were hovering lightly earlier have dispersed, and the sky is now pale blue and absolutely clear. For a moment I can barely breathe. This city is magical.

'You sound like a true New Yorker showing the sights to the silly British tourist,' he observes.

'No, just two silly British tourists caring about their first sight of the city. A true New Yorker would be far more insouciant. If you say a word about the twin towers being missing you'll blow our native cover for good.'

'Oh, Evie,' he says, 'you'll be a New Yorker before you know it.'

I look at him sideways, then swiftly readjust my gaze to the road as a taxi approaches from a slip road and blasts a long hoot at me for not getting out of the way. 'What do you mean?' I ask, when I have negotiated the crisis.

'Nice one. Most girls I know would never drive here. Where are you parking?'

I smile. 'At Howard's office. We can ditch the car there and go for a drink. He'll take it home for me tomorrow. But what did you mean? I'm a Londoner.'

'Not a happy one, though.'

'What?' I am startled.

'You seem determined to get away from Jack. Surely you will also want to get away from the city where you lived together? You call it moving on, I know, but it could also be seen as running away.'

'That's not true,' I tell him defensively. 'I'm just sorting my life out.'

'Whatever you call it, Jack's afraid you'll stay here for good. You have it made out here. No one could blame you.'

'What else does Jack say?'

We are heading uptown along Bowery. Abruptly, at the last minute, I turn left along East Houston. I love this part of town, this mix of seedy garages and slightly scary groups of people, with fashionable bars and galleries. 'Howard's office is this way, I'm sure it is,' I say, before Ian has answered me. 'Tell me if you see it.'

Ian grabs the armrest between us as a cyclist with a loud stereo on his handlebars gives me the finger. 'I don't know what it looks like.'

'You're no good then. It's called H and D Telecom.'

'I know about the letters,' Ian says suddenly. I look at him, but he is staring straight ahead. It is strange to see the shadow of Jack on his features. I consider, again, whether Ian could be writing to me. I very much doubt it, but I don't feel that I can rule anyone out.

'Did Jack tell you?' I ask, cautiously.

'He knew he shouldn't, but, well, he did anyway. He started off telling me that Sophia was pissed off with him and he was thinking of finishing with her, and then it all came out.'

'Have you told Kate?'

Finally our gazes meet. I quickly look back to the road.

'No,' he says. 'I thought that was up to you. And she would be upset. She needs to be calm.'

'I know. That's why I didn't want her to know. Any other time and I'd have gone straight to you two, not to Jack.' I pause, and wonder whether what I've just said is true. I'm not sure that it is. 'I'll tell her after it's all cleared up. Perhaps when she's had the twelve-week scan.'

We drive on for a while. I am cruising around randomly, looking at the buildings I pass without seeing them, at the shops and cafés and bars and apartment buildings. I turn left and right as the mood takes me, being careful only to travel the right way down one-way streets. Suddenly, despite my casual attitude to navigation,

Howard's office leaps out at me. 'There it is!' I say, triumphantly, as I see the large H and D looming on the other side of the road, and I pull into the car park. I find Howard's car, park close to it, and leave my key with the receptionist.

We walk through the SoHo streets, enjoying the cool sunshine. Manhattan is buzzing. It is glorious in the sunshine. I appreciate it all on a hypothetical level. I know that it is an exciting, energetic place to be. I can pretend that I am swept up with the excitement. My heart, however, is with my baby and my correspondent.

I'm not sure what to say about the letters, and Ian doesn't seem to be asking any follow-up questions. I know he is thinking of Kate, resting resolutely as she waits for the embryos to embed themselves in the lining of her womb. I consider saying something trite and reassuring – 'It'll work, I know it will', when I know no such thing – but on balance, it's best to leave him to his thoughts.

The pavement teems with people. Besuited workers on their way to meetings charge impatiently past tourists. *Sex and the City* girls scan shop windows and chat on their mobiles. As a six-foot blonde wearing seven-inch heels struts past, I look at my black boots. My feet are sweating in there. They would look and feel wonderful if I was wearing a pair of strappy sandals, which had perfectly painted and shaped nails peeping from the ends. I resolve to go shoe-shopping tomorrow. That is a pleasingly shallow occupation.

The streets are full of yellow taxis and buses and kamikaze cyclists. People hurry past us, clearly on their way to important places. They carry briefcases and handbags, and charge across at 'Don't Walk' signs. It takes me a while to acclimatise to New York, to come to accept that, for instance, it's OK to set off across a road when a 'Don't Walk' sign is flashing, that they give you much more time than you get with a flashing green man at home. It takes me a long time to feel that I'm part of it, rather than an awestruck observer. I can't believe anyone feels that way about London. London sucks you in and offloads part of its misery.

'Look at that,' I say to Ian, pointing to the road. 'Yellow cabs, and steaming manhole covers. Do you think they just lay that on for people like us?' It feels odd to be wandering around with someone. I have so few friends.

'What?' he asks. 'So we can burst into song? "Start spreading the news!" So we get so excited about being in New York that we tell all our friends what a great place it is to be? I don't think this city needs that sort of attention. This is just Manhattan being itself.'

'It's an amazing place.' I look up, at an enormous shiny skyscraper. 'I mean, the buildings. I get quite freaked out by them sometimes. They're so tall. So much is going on above us. God knows what – things I will never understand, like deals and mergers and, I don't know, acquisitions. All those wires buzzing, and phones ringing and emails zinging around the world. And it happens up in the air. Which obviously has a sinister side to it these days.'

Ian looks up too. 'It's all a bit frantic for me. I couldn't handle it here. I love visiting, but London's always going to be home. Crappy as it is, it's where I belong.'

I take my black jumper off, and sling it over my bag.

'Really? You'll stay there for ever? What about when you have kids?'

He shrugs, and again I see Jack's features in his. 'I don't think it's a terrible place for them, whatever anyone says. If we feel it's not ideal, we'll move out to somewhere like St Albans, or Brighton. But you've got the parks, you've got the galleries, and there seems to be a playground on every street corner, or maybe that's just something you notice if you're in our situation. Bright-eyed toddlers shrieking on swings.'

I notice a bar. It looks a little too trendy for us, with me in my jeans, T-shirt and trainers (and none of them my best ones), and Ian looking like a politician on a day off, with a buttoned-up shirt over jeans. But I am desperate for a drink, so I lead him in anyway. We are afforded a mild welcome. I order a large glass of Sauvignon, Ian drinks from a bottle of Miller, and we sit in comfortable padded chairs and look round at the bleached floorboards and the baffling art on the walls.

I smile at Ian. I am beginning to enjoy today's role play. I like being someone who is happy to find herself at a loose end in Manhattan on a sunny afternoon.

'So what are you going to do?' Ian asks, abruptly.

I look at a swirly red and black painting. 'I don't know,' I tell him. 'Today is about Kate and you. Tomorrow I have to play my cello all day. Very soon I am scheduling a state of utter panic about my Lincoln Center concert. In the long term?' I spread my hands. 'That depends on a lot of things.'

'You should stay here,' he says firmly, taking a long swig of beer. I wait for him to elaborate, but he doesn't.

'Right,' I say, and there is a slightly awkward silence. 'You think I should stay out of Jack's way?'

'That's not what I meant at all.'

I look at Ian, and bite my lip. 'I haven't treated him very well.'

Ian smiles. 'Jack's a big boy. He can look after himself. You don't exactly hold a knife to his throat – he'd do anything for you. Sophia knows that. That's why she's mightily pissed off. She told Kate he comes with too much baggage.'

'But he needs to get on with his life,' I protest, over-joyed that, at least, I am succeeding in keeping Jack where I need him. 'He should be with her.'

'He should be with you,' Ian corrects me. I am surprised at his forceful tone. 'I never understood why you two split up. Kate tried to explain, but I don't think she knew either. You had a good time together, didn't you? Jack loves you. You told him you love him. I don't really see what's missing.'

I quell the urge to criticise Jack. Ian is, after all, his cousin.

'It's all been my fault,' I say, as meekly as I can. 'I do love him, but I don't want to mess him around. Things hadn't been working brilliantly for a while, and Jack knows that really. Actually,' I tell him, leaning forward, 'it was Kate that made me realise it. It was the night before that royal birthday performance, and we were talking about the fact that her period had started and she was depressed. I remember her saying to me, "I'm so glad you guys don't want children. If you got pregnant I'd be happy for you, but it would just kill me inside to see you making a child when I couldn't do it." And that made me think. I've always wanted children, really really wanted them, but Jack and I never discussed it. And I realised that the moment had arrived for us to start trying, if we were going to have them. I couldn't imagine the reality of me going home that night, and suggesting to Jack that we should start trying for a baby. It didn't feel right. So of course that makes the whole relationship unravel.'

Ian is shaking his head. 'Call me a witless bloke here, Evie, but if you want kids, why don't you want them with Jack? You two would have beautiful babies. Wouldn't Jack be a great dad?'

'Of course he would. Would I be a great mother? I doubt it.' I stop for a few seconds, and compose myself. For a moment I have an insane urge to confess everything. The moment passes. I drain my wine glass. I am beginning to feel pleasantly fuzzy-headed. I will order another, when the waitress comes back. 'I'm not blaming Jack, Ian. I'm blaming myself. Call it an early midlife crisis, if you like.'

Ian looks at me. 'I don't understand women,' he says. 'I just don't. I'm glad I don't have to go on dates and fathom out people like you.'

I reach out and squeeze his hand. 'You're lucky. You and Kate have everything.'

'Yeah, right,' he says, bitterly. 'Everything apart from the one thing we really want in the world. I think you look at us sometimes and see the perfect relationship, Evie. Jack does too. Things go on behind closed doors that you will never know about. Fertility treatment is hell. It would test the best relationship. Don't think otherwise. If it doesn't work with Ron, we're going to have to think about adoption. And if that happens, it means giving up the thought of our own child. We've held on to the idea of our own baby for all these years, and we don't want to give it up. Kate in particular wants to cherish our child in her body. You know, the little girl who might have Kate's hair and my nose, the boy with his mummy's eyes and his daddy's footballer's legs. Adoption would be fine as a last resort but it would be a different matter entirely. In a way we would have to say goodbye to our own child, even though he or she has never existed, before we could think about giving a home to someone else's.'

I touch his hand again. 'Would you feel strange about taking on someone else's child?' I ask him, suddenly nervous.

'Yes. I would at this precise moment, because my wife's undergone treatment today. Those are our little bundles of cells in there. By the time it comes to adoption, if it does, I think we'll feel grateful for the opportunity, more than anything else. But only once we've accepted that we've done everything we can to try to have our own.'

'Do you think all adoptive parents feel that?'

'Feel what?'

'That taking on someone else's baby is second best. That it's what you do when you've run out of other options.'

Ian puts his bottle down on the table. 'I don't think that, exactly. I think adoption is a very, very frightening prospect, much more so than having your own child, not least because we'd be highly unlikely to be able to adopt a new baby, so from the very beginning we'd be faced with God knows what behavioural problems and traumatic background. But when we're ready for it, I think it's going to be a very positive thing, and I would hope against hope that we'd never, ever make the child think it was second best. And part of me is certain that it will come to that.'

'Really?' Kate has never wanted to speak about the possibility of adoption, and I have been only too happy to go along with that. The subject makes me tremble, but it is fascinating. I motion to the waitress to bring me a new drink. I need it, and another after that.

'Of course. But what I'm saying is, the idea of adoption is something for Kate and me to get our heads round if and when the time comes. People mean well when they say, "Oh well, you can always adopt," but it's not that straightforward. And the idea of starting to try for your own baby is equally mind-fucking. It took us a while to pluck up the courage to do it, and then of course we wished we'd started sooner. And I think that, after you had that chat with Kate, you were probably freaked out at the idea of you and Jack having children, for all the normal reasons. And it sounds to me as though you projected that on to your marriage, and found the whole thing so alarming that you took the easy way out.'

I snort. 'It's hardly been easy.'

'What, prancing about in front of the cameras with a sixteen-year-old hanging off your arm? It must have been hell. The sacrifices we make for our art.'

Instantly, I hate him. 'You have no idea what you're talking about, when it comes to me and Jack,' I tell him, 'and on top of that it really isn't any of your business. You don't know the full story and you probably never will.'

He shrugs. 'Whatever you say, Evie.'

'What do you mean, whatever I say?'

'I mean, I'm trying to be reasonable here.'

'Well, you don't entirely know what you're talking about.'

'You're pissed off with me. Well, maybe I'm pissed off too. Jack's my best mate, as well as my cousin, and I don't like to see my mates or my family being taken for a ride. You're either with him or you're not. It stinks to run to him when you need someone to hold your hand, trashing his relationship in the process, then to run off again once he's stood you back on your feet. You're either with him, or you leave him alone. I think, and Jack thinks, and Kate thinks, that you should be with him. I am trying to help.'

I glare at Ian. This has all gone wrong very quickly. 'I did not run to him to hold his hand. I asked him to come here with us. He said no. And you know it. Plus, what happens in our marriage is up to us. And, frankly, none of your business. I don't interfere in your marriage.'

'Oh, apart from coming along to our fertility treatment.'

'Because Kate asked me to! I had no idea you had a problem with that! God, Ian, do you hate me or something?' I stare at him. He moves up a couple of places on my list of enemies and potential suspects.

He slumps in his chair, all the fight drained away. After a few moments he looks up at me. 'No, I don't,' he admits. 'Sorry, Evie. I don't know what I'm on about. It's a stressful time, you know? Everything's resting on this. I can't bear to go through the agonies of a failed treatment again. I had no problem at all with you coming along today. It's good to have company.'

'Are you sure?'

'Yes. Let me get you another drink. We may as well get drunk. And I know it's none of my business, about you and Jack.'

'Thanks for being so open about adoption. Kate's never wanted to talk about it.'

'I'm afraid that one of our problems is that Kate has a lot more capacity for perseverance at the baby with her hair and my nose than I do. It's been three years and if this doesn't work I'd be ready to call it quits. But she wouldn't, and I know it's her decision. It's her body. Surrogacy's not for us and we both know it, so IVF is our last chance to have a child with any of our genetic material in it.'

I reach out for his hand again. 'I'm sorry, Ian. I really, really hope this is it for you.'

'Thanks.'

'And you're probably right about me and Jack.'

He smiles. 'At the risk of offending you again, I know I am.'

'So what do you reckon about Sophia?'

He hesitates. 'Lovely girl, but I don't think you have to worry about her. She's very independent-minded and she doesn't like being second best. Which, for Jack, she definitely is.'

I am delighted to hear it. 'Let's talk about something else,' I tell him, as our new drinks arrive.

'Hey, Jack said you thought those letters might be from Guy. I've always thought he was an odd one.'

'Why?'

'Everything about him. He's been asking us way too much about Ron Thomas. He wants to know everything:

214

what's the clinic like, is Ron married, what exactly has he said about Guy? He pretends he doesn't know him when he obviously does. What's that all about?'

I lean back and sigh. 'Ian, I have no idea.'

chapter fourteen

The next day

I spend the morning taking my hangover out on my cello. I bash my way through every scale – major, minor and chromatic – and every arpeggio. I work my way through dull studies that I normally ignore in favour of the more interesting pieces from the repertoire. I play notes, mechanically, to improve my technique. I do bowing exercises, and repeat them over and over again. I use the whole bow and half a bow, play staccato and legato, with slurred and detached bowing. I dread to think what it's like for poor Sonia, who is attempting to mark a pile of essays, to have to listen to this turgid rubbish. This is the way I should practise every day. I don't think I could bear to be this aggressive to my poor instrument more than once in a blue moon.

I am sitting on Howard's work chair, in the room I have now almost completely colonised. He doesn't use his study any more. He works, when he has to, at the kitchen table, like a schoolboy doing his homework. Howard's study is now called 'Evie's room'. My clothes hang from shelves in his bookcases, obscuring his library. My toiletries occupy every space on his desk. All his stationery has been shoved into a drawer. I have taken up residence here, but I know I can't stay long.

I am doing this intense practice partly to fill my mind with the mechanics of my trade, but also because when I picked the cello up this morning, I was terrifyingly bad. I was, in fact, atrocious. I didn't practise yesterday, or the day before, and only briefly the day before that. On the day I arrived, I bashed out a quick rendition of 'The Swan', which is taking the place in my repertoire previously occupied by the Bach suite. That was for Sonia's AA friends, who were having a Virgin Mary party.

I have neglected the instrument lately, and that is the one thing I cannot afford to do. If the cello goes, my livelihood goes with it. I am nothing without it. I would have to get a job, and I am not qualified to do anything. I have a first-class music degree from nine years ago. The only thing you can do with that, apart from music, is teach. I would be a diabolical teacher. I know I could never concentrate on my pupils. I would want to show off to them, all the time.

Until the Easter of the final year of my degree, I assumed that teaching was my destiny. I didn't particularly want to do it, but I wanted to keep playing, and couldn't see any other way. About half the people on my course were thinking the same thing. There must be a lot of terrible music teachers about, for this reason, and I would have been one of them. Then something happened that almost made me believe in God. I haven't had a proper job since then.

The last place I worked was at Dorothy Perkins in Broadmead, in the Christmas holidays when I was twenty.

I had already got a place on a PGCE course, so I could become a class music teacher. The final orchestral concert of the academic year was held at the end of the Easter term, so everyone could revise over the summer. I was playing the Dvořák cello concerto. Luckily, my new look was fairly refined by this point. I had slimmed down, settled on a shade of blonde for my hair that looked so good everyone soon forgot it hadn't always been that colour (in those days, it was Clairol Industrial Blonde. Now it is done at a salon), and my wardrobe was cheap, but full of classics. While the others in my music class were wearing droopy skirts or patchwork trousers and over-sized white cotton shirts, I sported wide-legged black trousers and tight sweaters. All my clothes were from Warehouse and Top Shop, but I chose them carefully. My friends stomped around in Doc Martens; I clicked down pavements in high-heeled boots. I was the only person I knew who owned an iron. People thought I was naturally stylish, but I wasn't: it was my disguise. I was a new Evie. The old one had been as badly dressed as everyone else – in fact, she had favoured those faded black skirts which had a little bit of embroidery and tassels around the hem. The Evie who had got pregnant had had a tangle of mousy hair which she rarely remembered to brush, but just scraped back into a ponytail every morning. The new one spent so much time on her appearance that she got up at seven o'clock for a nine-thirty lecture, and spent an hour in the bathroom. New Evie dedicated herself to her cello and her degree. She was polished and friendly, but she never gave anything away. She held herself back, and strangely found herself more popular than she had ever been before. For the first time in my life I heard people talking about me with a degree of awe. I would be amazed to overhear snatches of conversation about myself.

'We're having a party tonight,' I heard one of my classmates tell another, in the cafeteria. 'Evie's coming.'

'Is she?' said the other. 'Fantastic!'

It is strange, my transformation. Not only did I change myself physically, but after Elizabeth, I started practising the cello with a devotion and hunger that was entirely new. My teacher had always told me, and Mum, that I was talented, but I had infuriated her by barely remembering to practise from one week to the next. Suddenly, it was all I wanted to do. I wanted to be brilliant at something, and the cello was it. It is almost as if I knew that those two things – makeover and music – would give me a unique career.

Mum and Phil were pleased by my transformation. They thought it was a sign that I was growing up, putting 'it' behind me, and finding my feet as an adult. In fact, I was putting on a huge act, and nobody ever realised it. Nobody noticed that I was colder and harder than I had been before, because no one in my life except my family had known me before. The only person who came close was Kate. Kate had met me at my lowest ebb, without ever knowing what I was low about. She was taken aback when we met up in Bristol in the university holidays and, each time, I was more of a little adult than the last. As we sat in the cheap pubs near Mum and Phil's house, she occasionally tried to ask me why.

'Your hair looks great,' she would say, uncertainly, as we drank cider and tore bags of crisps down the middle to share. I knew at once that she wanted to ask me what I was up to, but didn't know how to phrase it.

'Thanks,' I'd say with a grin, tossing it back in a manner that I had practised endlessly in the bathroom mirror.

'You must spend loads of time on your make-up?'

'Not really. It doesn't take five minutes – a little bit of foundation, a quick dab of mascara, smudge of eyeliner, bit of lipstick.'

'Mmm. Is everyone like that in London?'

I saw my escape clause. I was uncomfortable talking about my transformation, because Kate was the only person I was still in touch with from my olden days. I would sometimes wonder if I should sacrifice that friendship to make reinvention complete, but happily I could never bring myself to do it.

'Yes,' I said firmly. Kate was studying English at Exeter, and was still a devotee of floaty skirts and clumpy boots. As the years passed, however, she caught me up, and now we like exactly the same clothes. We're the same size, too. We swap, sometimes. It makes me feel good, to have a friend to share clothes with. I am well aware of the fact that she is the only friend I have.

By the time the Easter of the third year came round, Jack and I were engaged. I was deliriously happy – nobody would have wanted to marry the old Evie – and proud that I had created a future for myself. Jack was going to marry me, to take care of me, to pledge himself to me for the rest of my life. All the girls at Goldsmiths fancied Jack, and all the boys fancied me, but he had pursued me single-mindedly from the day we first met, in the first term of our first year. As a couple, we were glamorous and fêted. I took cello lessons at the Royal Academy, and Jack used an easel and a palette, and let his hair flop into his face.

Thus I was walking on air at the Easter concert. For the first half, which consisted of Shostakovich's Fifth Symphony, I had worn a black skirt and white blouse like all the other girls in the orchestra. In the interval I changed into the dress that Mum had bought me for my concerto. It was sleeveless and fitted, just a sheath that clung to my body. It was made from crimson velvet, and came down below my knees. When I stood up, it looked like the world's most impractical cello-playing dress. Thanks to the slit up the back, however, I could just about manage it. I wore it with sheer stockings, a gorgeous pair of high red shoes, and no underwear whatsoever. My hair, after much consideration, was newly coloured, blow dried into a glimmering bob and I wore lipstick the exact same colour as the dress. If I hadn't made an effort that night, I might be a cello teacher in Kingston-upon-Thames by now, trying to persuade my pupils to practise their scales, and entering people for exams they didn't want to take.

She waited for me after the concert. I thought she was somebody's mother wanting to congratulate me, so I paused with a polite, dismissive smile already on my lips.

'Evie Silverman?' she said. She was small and friendly, wearing a businesslike blue suit and a white blouse. Her hair was dark brown, short and practical, and she was about forty-five.

'Yes!' I replied warmly, unleashing my smile.

She put out her hand. 'My name's Barbara Hall. I'm with ABC Music's classical division. Could you spare me a few moments?'

Barbara had come to the concert because her goddaughter played the flute in our orchestra. She explained that ABC were looking for a Nigel Kennedy, for a classical musician who would have what she called 'crossover appeal'. She said she loved my look as well as my talent, and invited me to come to her office and meet some people. For a while I thought she was joking, but I went along with it, and went home that night with her card in my pocket and an appointment for two thirty the following afternoon.

Things moved quickly. I was sized up, evaluated, recommended an agent. He negotiated a contract, and by the time I graduated, I was signed up. I recorded some favourite tunes from the repertoire, nice, easy themes from adverts and love songs that everyone would know, and the publicity department organised a blitz when it came out. I went on *Richard and Judy*, back in the days when they broadcast in the mornings, from Liverpool. I was interviewed on what felt like every local radio station in the country, and spoke to local papers in Bristol and London. I was even mentioned in magazines like *Marie Claire* – magazines I actually read. Magazines that I fervently hoped Louise still read.

Jack was as excited as I was, to begin with. He found my success inspirational, and assumed that if his fiancée could do it, then he could too. The idea of success lost all its unattainability to him. It began to seem normal, or even inevitable. He started touting his paintings around, with a new ambition. He walked around London, took his portfolio on buses between Jay Jopling and Maureen Paley, confident that it was just a matter of time before a dealer took him on. He started going back to college to hound his tutors for their contacts. They were, by all accounts, a little taken aback by his late-onset determination to become a Young British Artist.

Even Jack knew, secretly, that he was chasing the wrong dream. I was as desperate for him to succeed as he was. My new career was frightening, and I wanted my life partner to experience the same rush, to discover what sudden recognition felt like, to appreciate how vulnerable and dependent it makes you, and how you can keep the vulnerability under control by developing a hard exterior.

He tried for a year. After university we moved into a little house together, in Bow, for six hundred pounds a month. We had a big bedroom, which doubled up as my music room, and a smaller one which was Jack's studio. He stretched canvases, set them on easels, mixed his oils, then stared at them. Sometimes he painted abstracts, other times still lives or, occasionally, portraits of me or of our friends. His figurative work was very good – he had a distinct style, and people liked it – but he wasn't content to be a conventional painter. He had to be at the cutting edge, and so he pressed ahead with abstract work.

'It's no good,' he would say, when we convened downstairs for coffee, or for wine at the end of the day. 'Abstract canvases have been done to death. After Robert Ryman's white paintings, where can you go? Everything I do is derivative. Even if I think of a new idea myself, it turns out that someone's been there before.' He looked at me, pleading for an answer. I always offered the same advice. It was never what he wanted to hear.

'You're fantastic at people,' I'd tell him. 'Set yourself up as a portrait painter. We know enough potential clients to get you started, and the more you do it, the more work you'll get. You can do it at the upper end of the market. You can make fantastic money, and work on whatever else you want to do in your spare time. You could do one of me for my next CD, maybe.'

He would shake his head. 'No, Evie, I want to be something special. Not just another jobbing painter. I might as well set up as an interior decorator.'

He frustrated me, and he frustrated himself. A year later, after we were married, he applied for a job as an IT technician for an insurance company. The post came with training, and he talked his way into it, despite his fine art degree. At first he was doing it to save up enough money to devote himself to his art for a year. Then we stopped talking about his painting. That was when our relationship stopped being idyllic, and crashed down to earth. Jack resented me for being successful, and I resented him for giving in and taking the most boring job in the world. I knew he had only done it to spite himself, but he grew into his new role, and before long he had become an IT consultant. I heard him, once, saying to one of his colleagues, 'You know what, mate, I used to be an artist!'

'You stupid twat,' said the man, laughing at him. Jack joined in.

'I know,' he chuckled.

I hated him for that.

The new, improved Evie Silverman, by contrast, went from strength to strength. When I was eighteen, I had decided not to be a musician, and had applied to universities rather than music colleges. Yet I found myself doing it anyway. I was paranoid about my ability. Lots of people in the classical music world hated me, and still do, in the same way they hated Nigel Kennedy or anyone else who has been promoted on image rather than ability. I started getting up earlier and earlier in the mornings, so I could practise for an hour before having a shower, styling my hair, dressing and doing my make-up, and still be ready to start the day at nine. Usually, starting the day simply meant going straight back to the cello. As far as I was concerned, I was less talented than I had any right to be, and so I needed to put in the hours to avoid being found out. Jack resented this. He hated waking at six to find me slinking out from under the duvet and creeping downstairs with my cello. He reasoned that he was out from eight till six thirty anyway, so I had plenty of time to practise without letting it intrude on our few hours together. I knew he was right, but I woke up every morning catching my breath in panic about the fact that I was being promoted as a great talent, when I was actually just adequate. I knew that, unless I was obsessive about it, I would be finished almost before I had started.

My talent has not expanded in the intervening years, yet I have, recently, let my diligence slip. If it comes apart, I have nothing to fall back on. I wouldn't mind letting it go if my career was coming to a natural end, but it isn't. By all accounts, I am selling well over here. Ron is right: my advert is on all the time. This is the worst moment for me to fall apart. Whatever else is happening, I can't be unmasked as a crap musician. I know it will happen, but it mustn't happen yet.

So I sit in my father's study, and work on my technique. Slowly my dexterity comes back. I move on to pieces. My next engagement, the Lincoln Center concert, the scariest thing yet, is in three weeks' time. Much depends upon it. I will be playing with a stunning orchestra, and, as so often happens, I will be playing the Elgar. Everyone wants to hear it, but what they really want is Jacqueline du Pré's interpretation. Often, I do my best to give it to them. I am a musical tart. I play to the lowest common denominator. I am popular with readers of the *Daily Mail*, and less so with anyone who knows anything about classical music.

When I feel more confident, I begin to tackle the Elgar. Every time I'm not happy with something, I stop and iron it out. I am more patient than I have been for years. By the time I reach the end of the first movement, and am reasonably happy with what I have achieved, I discover that it is nearly two o'clock. I have been playing for six hours. I smile at myself in the mirror. Six hours, and very few ugly thoughts. Evie Silverman isn't washed up yet, after all.

I run downstairs, hungry, thirsty, and happier than I have been for a long time. Sonia comes out of the sitting room, and meets me in the hall.

'Hello there!' she says, laughing. 'What a treat! Evie, I

have had the most wonderful morning, grading papers to the sounds of your angelic playing. People pay good money for this!'

I smile back. It feels strange to be genuine, for once. 'I didn't disturb you too much?'

'Oh, not at all! I wish you'd live with us for ever. My pupils will be pleased with their grades tomorrow, I'm in such a good humour.'

'Thanks, Sonia. I lost track of the time completely.'

'Wonderful, just wonderful. Let's get you some lunch, shall we?'

I feel comfortable and safe with Sonia. I know for certain that she is on my side, so I do everything I can to cultivate her friendship. We sit outside, in their small garden, and I tilt my head back to catch the spring sun on my face. Sonia has made us huge sandwiches, with mozzarella, tomatoes, arugula and sweet peppers. It turns out that she made them at half past twelve, and has been waiting for me to emerge before she tackled hers. I am rarely fed. I desperately want my stepmother to adore and protect me for ever, but I cannot tell her that. She thinks I am sane.

'This is gorgeous,' I tell her, taking a huge bite from my sandwich and feeling the mayonnaise running down my chin.

'Glad you like it,' she says. 'Now, Lincoln Center. I'm afraid you will have one or two supporters there. That's all right, isn't it? Every time Howard or I tell a friend about it, they immediately get themselves a ticket. Plus my school and our AA friends have both made block bookings. I'd be surprised if there were any tickets left. But the last thing we want to do is to embarrass you.

I've been telling my pupils about my talented, beautiful stepdaughter until they beg me to get back to the lesson.'

I laugh. 'Please, Sonia. Please fill the hall with people who are going to clap. I'm scared shitless.'

'What do you plan to wear?'

I lean back and smile slightly. 'Now, that is the best question you could possibly have asked. I haven't got anything glamorous enough with me. Will you come shopping?'

'Will this afternoon do? I'm not in school today and I've finished my papers. Let's do it. What's your budget?'

I shrug. 'For something like this, there is no budget. Whatever makes me look good. I've got money in the bank. I don't mind going wild if that's what it's going to take.'

'Fifth Avenue. We'll start there and head on up to the Upper East. This is a treat. Colour? Design?'

I stretch my legs out and finish my sandwich. 'It has to be a dress, obviously, and with a long skirt that will fit round a cello. And yet I'd prefer it if it didn't look like an item from Barbie's wardrobe. I have racks of Barbie dresses at home. You wouldn't believe some of them. Frills and flounces seem to be de rigueur in my profession.'

Sonia wags her finger at me. 'Barbie is *so* out. Sleek and slinky, perhaps?'

I nod. 'Classic. No satin. No Barbie. No bridesmaids.'

'You got it.'

Four hours later, we are riding home on the F train, with tired feet, caffeine vertigo, and the satisfaction of a job well done. A bag containing my dress is reverently draped across my knee. The dress is long and plain. It reaches the floor, and is cut classically in a way that makes me look both skinny and curvy. As a result of American portions, I am definitely leaning more towards the curvy end of this scale at the moment, and vow to eat nothing but fruit and vegetables, and to drink nothing but juice and water, for the next three weeks. The dress is a deep purple that is almost black, and has a matching pair of shoes that I will practise walking in until the concert. It makes me look serious, and yet, the shop assistant and Sonia promised, also sexy. It has no overtones of weddings or plastic dolls.

'Honey,' says Sonia, as we walk home, up the hill, past the small but pretty houses. 'You are going to be gorgeous. Please don't worry about your concert. And you will stay with us as long as you like?'

'Really?'

'Sure. People say to me, "Oh my God, do you not have issues with your stepdaughter living with you?" and I tell them, "Actually, no." And since you're beautiful and talented and successful I'm not quite sure why I don't! You just know that you're welcome.'

I squeeze her arm. 'You like me because you know that an insecure little girl is hiding behind the façade. You like me because you know one of my secrets.'

She laughs. 'One of them? I hope you don't have too many others in that vein!'

While I am boiling the water for a cup of tea, Sonia listens to the messages on the answer machine. 'Evie!' she calls. 'I don't believe this! Three messages, and they're all for you!'

The first message is from Ian.

'Hey,' he says. 'Hope we're all right from last night. No hard feelings, yeah? Kate's leaving the clinic tomorrow. Just wondering if you wanted to come with me to pick her up? In fact, I should rephrase that. Hoping we can use your car to go and pick her up. Call me at the hotel. Cheers.'

I nod. I'll fit my new practising and fitness regimes around that trip.

The second, gratifyingly, comes from Jack.

'Hello, Howard and Sonia,' he says politely. 'It's Jack, calling for Evie. Just wondering how you are and if everything's OK. Call me or drop me an email if you like. Bye.'

I want to run upstairs and email him at once. I only feel secure if I know that Jack, my reserve team, is in place.

My final message, unexpectedly, is from Megan. My heart sinks as she begins to speak.

'Hello!' she says, sounding slightly uncomfortable speaking to a stranger's answer machine. 'This is a message for Evie Silverman. If this is the wrong number, I'm sorry, please ignore me. It's Megan. I'm still in Bristol and I've decided to leave my job for now. It's time to move on. And I hope you don't mind, but Guy found me a return to New York for a hundred and fifty pounds on the internet. Is that OK? I thought I might come out for a week or so. Only I've never been there and I'd like to see you. And we've got some things to talk about. Call me back if you can, or else email me, OK? Thanks. Bye.'

Sonia is looking back at me with raised eyebrows. I haven't told her or Howard about the letters, though from the way they are treating me I suspect that Mum mentioned them on the phone before I came. All Sonia knows is that I used to live with Megan, that I upset her by being rude about Guy, and that our flatshare arrangement was abruptly terminated.

'Is this welcome?' she asks tentatively.

No! I want to say. No, it most certainly is not. I am sick of Megan. She doesn't like me and she is the last person I want trailing around New York in my wake.

'I'm not sure,' I say instead, heading back to the kitchen to make our tea. 'Last time I checked, Megan didn't like me much. She was glad to see me go and she regretted ever inviting me to move in with her. She said so. I'm not sure why she feels the need to leap on a plane and follow me out here. I'm not sure how that makes me feel.'

'She didn't mention when she was arriving.'

'Or where she was planning to stay.'

'She can stay with us, if you'd like her to. Or not, if you wouldn't.'

I look at Sonia. Having Megan about would, I suppose, provide me with another distraction. It wouldn't make me happy, but neither does anything else. 'Are you sure?' I ask her. 'It's been just you and Howard for years, and suddenly here I am moving into Howard's study, and then my flatmate turns up too. It's only a little house, I know that. Why don't I book her a room in Kate and Ian's hotel?'

'This is a three-bedroom house, and it's been a long time since it's been used as such. If she's going to be here a week, and if you plan to spend time with her, she must stay with us.'

231

Sonia knows about the letters. She wants me to have company. I take the milk from the fridge and pour it into our cups.

'If you're positive.' I hand her a mug. She takes it.

'I'm positive.'

chapter fifteen

Late March

I feel nervous on Meg's behalf, because the afternoon she lands is the first stormy day since I arrived in New York. I drive to JFK through torrential rain, hoping my car will not be struck by lightning, and wondering whether the rubber tyres will really stop me being electrocuted if it is. The sky is black, and I hope her flight is delayed, for her sake. I imagine Meg's plane skidding on the runway, and smashing into another one, and bursting into sky-high flames.

In my head I replay the conversation I had with Jack at lunchtime. We spoke for over an hour. It was a comfortable conversation which reassured me that we do have things to talk about. We can be easy with each other. Things do not have to be dramatic. If I crack up any further, I can go back to him. I don't want to have to do that, but I know that he will be there if it becomes necessary. I trust Jack.

I didn't let him know what I was thinking. I just chatted

to him, and he chatted back to me, and I think we were both happy.

Jack said he misses me and that, though he is still with Sophia, his heart is not in the relationship.

'You should get out then,' I told him, grinning to myself. 'It's not fair on Sophia.'

'Do you think so?'

'You know I'm right.'

He paused. 'Yes, I suppose I do.'

I suppose I am using him, but I don't care. I have to look after myself right now. There is no alternative. Nothing else matters.

Meg saunters into the arrivals lounge thirty minutes late, and not noticeably injured or traumatised.

'Megan!' I call, causing the fat woman in front of me to turn round and look at me.

'Hey!' she says. 'I've seen you on TV!'

Out comes my one-hundred-watt smile. 'You probably have,' I tell her, 'but only on an ad.'

'*Only* an ad!' She laughs. 'Well, it sure is great to meet you.'

'I'm Evie,' I tell her, prolonging the moment.

'You're British! I'm Ray.'

'It's a pleasure to meet you, Ray,' I tell her, as Britishly as I can.

'And you! You have a nice day, now!'

By now Meg is by my side, and I turn to kiss her cheek. I study her face and try to work out why she is here. I trust no one.

She looks exhausted. Her hair is scraped back from her face, the ponytail down her back makes her look far too young, and she's wearing no make-up. She has lost weight, too. Her cheekbones jut out and cast shadows over her hollow face.

'How are you?' I ask lightly. 'How was the flight? I was thinking of you. What a storm! It must have been horrible.'

She looks surprised. 'Oh, that,' she says. 'Little bit bumpy. Nothing too bad. I always look at the flight attendants, and if they don't sit down and strap themselves in I know it's nothing to worry about. We did take a few attempts to land, though.' She looks at my face, and away. 'How are we getting back to your dad's place? Are you sure that it's all right for me to stay?'

'Yes. I've got the car.'

'You drive? Everyone can drive except me. I think I missed my window by not bothering when I was seventeen.'

I take one of her bags. 'Oh yes. I am driving like a regular New Yorker these days, as Ian will testify. I scared him rigid the other day,' I babble. 'His fingernails were practically bleeding from hanging on so tight. I hope the rain's let up a bit. I was crawling all the way here.' When I pause to glance at her, she looks away from me, her face tightly shut. Fine, I want to tell her. You wanted to come. I never invited you. I bite it back.

It is still raining, but the thunder and lightning are more distant. I concentrate on the road, and try to work out why Megan is here. She is clearly still furious with me. This should make for an interesting week. She sits in silence while I negotiate the wet roads and the evening traffic. I try to blame her unresponsiveness on exhaustion, but nobody invites herself to stay with a friend, then clams up and refuses to speak to them. I ask more about the flight, but she answers with monosyllables.

'Why are you here when you still hate me?' I ask, not looking at her, but indicating carefully and moving into the lane on my left.

'What do you mean?' she asks, blankly.

'I mean exactly what I said. Words of one syllable. Not difficult to understand.'

I feel her looking at me, but keep my eyes on the road. 'Guy said I needed a break,' she says uncertainly.

'You can't stay with me if you don't even want to speak to me.' I realise how churlish I sound, and try to be more reasonable. 'Howard and Sonia are looking forward to meeting you,' I add, more pleasantly, 'and I thought we could be friends again now.' I didn't really. I don't need a friend. 'But you are clearly . . .' I search for a word, and something Sonia says comes to mind. '*Not OK* right now.'

'You sound American! Americans say "not OK " like that.'

'It's a funny figure of speech, isn't it? So bland. I hadn't noticed that I'd picked it up. I've been hanging out with Sonia. She's lovely.'

Megan's voice is taut. 'You're right, I am *not OK*, but it's not about you, if you can imagine such a thing. Things haven't been great at Mum and Dad's, to be honest.'

I look at her for a moment, to check she's not crying. She is close to it. 'No?' I ask. The last thing I need is Megan landing herself on me with family problems. I came here to escape from things like that, to sort myself out.

'No. It's complicated.' We sit in silence for a while. I

suppose her parents hate me for bringing a pervert to their daughter's door.

'Sod it,' she says suddenly. 'It's not complicated at all. It couldn't be simpler. Dad hits Mum. He beats her up. Quite often.'

I am surprised. 'Does he?'

'I think he's always done it.' She stops and I hear her take a few deep breaths. 'I know he's been doing it at least since I was eleven. That was when I became aware of it. But it's worse now.'

'Does he do it in front of you?'

'Not exactly. He does it when I can hear. Something will go wrong, something absolutely tiny and utterly insignificant, and if I'm not in the room, he'll start shouting at her. Or even if I am in the room. Then I walk out because I can't bear it, and Mum'll call after me to stay because she knows he won't actually do it if I'm there. She sounds so desperate, she begs me to stay, but I go. I can't do anything else. I know it sounds awful, but I can't get involved or the whole family would fall apart. And next time I see her, she'll have some insulting, crap story about tripping over a stool, or walking into a door because she hadn't realised it was shut. I try to confront her, but I see it in her eyes. She's pleading with me not to talk about it. She puts up with it. She is a stupid fucking bitch. And she thinks I am too, if she reckons I'll believe her lies.'

For Megan to swear, I know it must be bad. 'What about your dad?'

'I'd like to think he wasn't my dad, to be honest. I'm going to start calling him Oliver, like you do with your dad.'

237

'For a very different reason.'

'For a very different reason. You do it because you're friends. I'm going to do it because I hate him.'

I reach out and touch her left hand with my right hand. 'I'm so sorry, Meg,' I tell her. 'Stay as long as you like.'

She pulls herself together to meet Howard and Sonia. Megan has a glass of the wine I have bought specially for the occasion. Howard gallantly uncorks it for us, and we both drink quickly and accept refills. Meg assures them, too, that, actually, the flight was fine, that she hadn't realised how severe the storm was until she had landed.

I try to read Howard and Sonia's impressions of this wan, unhappy girl who has turned up on their doorstep, but they are impossible to interpret. Perhaps they are like me: perhaps they present false faces to the world. I know both of them have been through hell, and they never show any scars. So they must be covering them. They both happily describe themselves as 'recovering alcoholics', but never talk about what their respective lives were like, back then. I have no idea how Howard used to behave when he was with Mum. Is it possible, I wonder, to keep alcoholism under control, to function as a loving husband and father while dependent on drink? Is that dependence a gradual process, or is there a day when you go from liking a drink to being a booze-fuelled monster? I can't picture my calm, sane father in a whisky-driven rage. If there is such a thing as a rational, highly functioning alcoholic, then Howard must have been it.

I wonder whether he started off like me. More and more, when I feel stressed, I reach for a bottle. I am aware of what I am doing, but I cannot tackle it yet. I need my crutch.

Megan goes to bed early, and I take my cello as far away from her tiny room as possible, and do more terrified practice. Lincoln Center audiences must be among the most discerning in the world, and they will come ready to sneer at me for the fact that I am only known as the Ad Girl. I am uncomfortably aware that I can't cruise through any more, that no one makes it in America without a reason. Nobody gets there by being mediocre. I don't want America at my feet, exactly. I just don't want to let people down. I need to keep my face in the public eye, because I need to keep up the pretence that I am glamorous and successful and in some way enviable.

Alexis has been calling. He wants to take me out to dinner again. I am back on the publicity wheel. At least my days will be full now. They will be packed. He even offered to rent me an apartment while I'm working towards the concert. If it's a reasonable size, Kate, Ian and, if she's still here, even Megan can come to stay with me. I will cram my flat with friends.

I go to bed pleased with my progress. I am, currently, still playing it like a substandard Jacqueline du Pré, but I'm starting to add some of my own touches. All I ask is that I don't embarrass myself and Alexis. Day and night, I imagine my disgrace. I picture expensively dressed women standing up in their seats and swishing out of the auditorium in disgust, their men following apologetically behind them. I imagine myself making the final flourish, playing the emphatic final chord of the concerto, and a deafening, crushing silence. Sometimes, in my dreams, I look out and see the audience asleep. Every single one of them, even my friends and my father.

It is pitch black when I wake with a start. My body goes into panic mode instantly. A floorboard creaks, and, as my bedroom door is opened silently, a little light from the street outside seeps into the room. I hear breathing. The intruder stands on the threshold, looking at me.

I am sweating and shaking. I have never known how I would react to something like this. I try to breathe silently. I try to think of a weapon. There is a telephone on the desk, but I wouldn't get to it in time. My best weapon is my voice.

I fill my head all day long with anything I can think of to avoid having to think about the realities of a stalker. Now there is someone in my bedroom. I have to face it.

I reach out a trembling hand, and switch on the desk light which is on the floor, by my head. Then I spin round, ready to scream.

'Megan,' I say, too loudly. My heart is beating so fast, so strongly, that it must be audible to her. 'Meg,' I say. 'You scared me.'

'Sorry,' she says, mildly, and sits down on the edge of my mattress.

She looks like a Victorian ghost, in a long white nightie. Her hair is tucked behind her ears, and falls over her shoulders.

I check the clock on the desk.

'It's half past four,' I tell her angrily. 'What's wrong?'

'Sorry. I didn't want to wake you. But I couldn't sleep.'

'Fair enough,' I say harshly. 'You can't sleep – why should I?' She smiles, missing my sarcasm.

'I've tried reading a book,' she says, 'but I can't get into it.'

Reluctantly, I move up, and she sits beside me and pulls the duvet over her legs.

'So what's wrong?' I decide to be brusque about it. 'Jet lag or parents?'

She lies down. Her feet touch mine, deep under the covers.

'Both,' she says, putting her head on the pillow. She has more colour in her cheeks now, and she looks me in the eye as she speaks. 'Parents, mainly. All those years I ignored it, just pretended it wasn't happening and got on with my life. But I've always known he was doing it. I wish I could still pretend. Your mum and Phil seemed so normal at Christmas. I wish they were my parents. And your dad and Sonia.'

'None of them has had an easy ride.' I sigh. I do feel bad for Megan over this, so I start trying to say the right things. 'Do you think we need to encourage your mum to get out? She could go to a refuge or something. I'm sure there are places like that in Bristol.'

'There are. I found the details of Women's Aid, who have a helpline, and left them out for Mummy, where Daddy wouldn't see them. Oliver. Where Oliver wouldn't see them. But she didn't do anything, and when I asked her, she told me she'd thrown them away and I shouldn't interfere.' Meg sniffs. 'I shouldn't have deserted her this time, but what can I do?'

'Keep on at her, I guess.' I want to switch off the light, but I know that if I did I would fall asleep. 'Make sure she knows there are options when she feels ready to take them.'

'It's not just Mum and Oliver either,' she continues, as

I shut my eyes and lean my head back. 'It's Guy as well.'

'Right,' I say, in what I hope is the voice of someone who is too tired for any further discussion. I do not want to talk about Guy. In my heart, I know my letters are not from him, that his secret is something entirely different. I cannot really believe he would harm me. That is why he is my favourite potential correspondent. He is the safe option.

Megan's words come out in a rush. 'He was so flipping keen for me to come out here,' she says. 'He found the flight, paid for it as a present, made me ring you, got it all sorted. He put me on the plane as soon as I could pack my bag. And I don't know why. When he told me he'd found a cheap flight to New York, I was over the moon. Because I thought he meant for us both to go, together. We've been a bit weird with each other lately, since you and I fell out. In fact he was sending me away. That's how it feels. He kept encouraging me to get in touch with you. He said you needed me and I had to put aside our differences and be your friend. He has no right to tell me how to be with my friends.'

'He knows about the letters, then?'

'Of course.'

'Megan, can I tell you something? You might not like it.'

'That's never stopped you before.'

'I do wonder why you're here, but since you are, here goes. I thought Guy might be writing those letters. Don't interrupt. So when we were at the Mediterranean Kitchen, I told him that I *knew*. I didn't say what I knew. I was testing him a bit. He went white and asked if I was threatening him.'

She is quiet for half a minute. I wait for her to speak. 'Oh,' she says, eventually.

'It doesn't necessarily mean he is writing the letters, but he's hiding something.'

'Oh heavens.' She tuts. 'I never thought you might think he was writing to you. But since you mention weird letters, he has given me something to post, Evie, and I have no idea why that is. A letter to a woman. Someone he knows here. He said it would be cheaper to post it from New York. I mean, for one thing it's a matter of pennies, and for another. . . He wouldn't tell me anything about this woman. He pretended it was something to do with work, but if it was, work would pay for the stamp. And now you think he's been writing to you. It almost makes sense. Except it's Guy and he wouldn't do that.'

'Ian doesn't trust him either.'

'Will you come with me tomorrow,' she says, 'to see this woman? We can take her the letter and see who she is. Ms King. That's what it says on the front of the envelope.'

'Of course. It would be good to do something. We should open it first.'

'No, we should let her open it.'

'Meg,' I say, 'has Guy ever said anything to you about his wife?'

She props herself up on the pillow. 'Marianne? Not really. That's something that freaks me out. He told me about a month ago that I was his first real relationship for thirty years. Now I'm sorry, but that's scary.'

'He has had girlfriends in that time, but not very many, and they've never lasted. So her name was Marianne?' I shiver at the confirmation. The beautiful girl from medical school is dead.

'He mentioned her, and he said that she'd died while she was pregnant. When I asked what had happened, he clammed up completely. He kept shaking his head. In the end he said it could have been avoided and that he blamed himself. Then he changed the subject and that was it.'

I try to focus my sleepy brain on this information. Even though it's scant, it's more than my mother has ever told me.

It is a perfect spring day, like an exceptional English summer. The sky is pale blue, and we wear T-shirts and sandals. I am being resolutely upbeat. It is good to be doing something. Megan and I are unlikely partners, but we are united in wanting to discover what Guy is up to.

Ms King, it seems, lives in a stunning apartment block on Central Park West. I am adamant that we should not deliver the letter without opening it first. Megan insists that we should hand it over, wait for her to read it, then recruit this woman to our small detective team. I give in.

'I bet she's got huge windows and a view of lovely grass and trees,' I say wistfully, as we wait for the doorman to call her for us. I'm not sure what my apartment, courtesy of Alexis, will be like, but I am willing to bet that Ms King and I will not be neighbours.

'Yeah,' says Megan grumpily. 'You can have a view of trees and grass in Somerset and it doesn't cost you two million dollars.' She is suffering far worse than I am today. I don't think she went back to sleep at all last night.

'Who the hell is this woman?' I wonder again. 'He didn't say anything?'

'Not a thing,' Meg confirms. 'I should have made him tell me, but I had too much else going on to think about it.'

'Yes you should,' I say, cross with her, and uneasy. 'You should have refused to take the letter without him telling you who she was. You're his girlfriend. You're allowed to make demands like that. It's very trusting of him to assume that you won't read it.'

'Not really. Guy knows me well enough to know that I wouldn't.'

The doorman, who is red-faced and middle-aged, puts the receiver down.

'She's not answering, ladies,' he tells us.

I am relieved. 'Great. Let's go for coffee and open the bloody thing.'

The lift door opens, and a woman steps out. She is tall and skinny and beautiful. Her hair is blonder than mine, and she is wearing a simple, deadly-expensive trouser suit.

'Oh, Miss King,' the doorman says, in greeting. 'These young ladies are asking for you.'

'Yes?' she asks, turning to us with an impatient half-smile. 'May I help you?'

I'm glad I dressed up for this meeting. I look at Megan, who is white and exhausted, with black bags under her eyes.

'We're friends of Guy Chapman's,' I say. Ms King looks blank. I look at Megan again, expecting her to take over, but she is still not prepared to speak.

'He told Megan he knew you,' I continue, cursing Meg

for making me do her dirty work. 'He's from England. He asked us to post this to you, but we were passing, so we thought we would drop it off.' I am smiling my polished smile. Megan holds out the white envelope, and Ms King takes it without looking at it. She is staring at me, instead.

'Forget this Chapman joker,' she says suddenly. 'I know *you*, don't I? Where have we met?'

I giggle slightly. 'On an advert for Calm Iced Tea, probably,' I tell her. She still looks blank. 'I play the cello? All the traffic stops?'

She points at me. 'I've got you! Well, well. Look, girls, I have to go to work now and I have to confess I'm a little baffled by this' – she glances at it – 'this communiqué from Britain. If I didn't have to leave I'd invite you to coffee and we could work out who he was, this man friend of yours. But thank you for the delivery. It's always a pleasure to meet a musician. I'll read it in the cab. Whatever it is.'

And she sweeps away, tucking the letter into her bag. Megan and I look at each other, and raise our eyebrows.

'We should have opened it,' she says. 'I really don't trust him now.'

I glare at her.

We go straight to the coffee shop on Lincoln Circle, to meet Kate and Ian. Kate has finished her bed rest, and is now embarked on an intensive programme of not lifting anything or straining herself in any way, and spurning all the gorgeous food around her. She turns down coffee for a cup of ''erbal' tea, and ignores our variations on eggs and potatoes in favour of no breakfast at all.

'I had a fruit salad earlier,' she says happily, nibbling on a corner of dry toast from Ian's plate. 'From the deli. And a smoothie. I have been going wild for fresh fruit. I need some oily fish later.'

Megan smiles at her. 'You're going to be the most fantastic pregnant woman. Your baby will come out doing yoga chants and it'll be one of those kids who don't like chocolate.'

Ian laughs. 'Not if she breast-feeds.'

'Which I will!' Kate interjects hastily.

'Because,' he continues, 'the moment she's given birth, Kate will be scoffing chocolate and sweets and cake like there's no tomorrow. They will flow through the milk and straight into the child. The milk'll be so chocolatey it'll come out brown.'

I watch them exchange a glance, full of the future. There is a tenderness in the look that I barely remember between me and Jack. I think we had it, once. I suspect he might still look at me like that if I would only let him. Jack and I, though, have never been through an ordeal together. I shut him out of the big trauma of my life. No one sitting around this table has any idea who I really am.

Again, I consider my reserve course of action. I could go back to Jack, and tell him everything. If he loves me like he says he does, like Ian says he does, then he would accept it. The idea of a world where baby Elizabeth is not a shameful secret makes me giddy.

I stare out of the window, watching a teenage girl walking past. She has brown hair, tied back, and clear skin. She's slightly shorter than me, and she looks a bit like Britney Spears. Her legs are perfect under a short denim skirt. She could be Elizabeth. So could any of her friends.

I hope this works for Kate. At least if she has a baby,

the balance will be restored. If she has one, there is a chance that maybe, one day, I can tell her about mine. We are all assuming that their fertility troubles are over now, but there is no guarantee, none whatsoever. This is only IVF, and they've had it before. A fifteen-year-old gets pregnant by mistake every single day. People with strong relationships, with comfortable homes and good jobs, people who will love and protect their child, are tested to the limits. It will have to work for them soon.

I force myself to stop examining the teenagers, and tune back into the conversation.

'She was so glam,' Megan is saying. She looks stressed. 'Really, not someone you'd expect to be Guy's friend at all. Plus she didn't know him.'

Ian frowns. 'She didn't *know* him?'

'She couldn't think who he was. But she took the letter off us because she recognised Evie off the advert.'

'Right.' Ian is trying to catch my eye, but I refuse to look at him. I don't want to think about what Megan and I have just done. I went against my better judgement every step of the way. Instead, I turn away from his puzzled glance and pat Kate's tummy. I know lots of pregnant women don't like people doing this, but I also know that Kate will appreciate it. She has been longing to have something pattable in there.

'Three little babies, hey?' I say.

'Embryos,' she corrects me. 'They become foetuses at twelve weeks and babies at twenty-eight weeks. Currently they are about three weeks. Not many people even know they have a fertilised embryo at three weeks. I won't believe it till I miss a period.'

'Three tiny embryos,' I say. 'Wow.'

'I'm trying so hard not to worry,' she says, 'because it can't do them any good. But it's impossible to think about anything else. You know?'

I remember the day I was forced to face my own pregnancy, after twenty-nine weeks of wilful ignorance. Elizabeth had graduated from embryo to foetus and on to babyhood before I acknowledged her. I will never forget my four months in New York, waiting for her, losing her, and trying to see a way forward without her.

'I know,' I tell her.

'I wish I could forget. But when you've been thinking about something for so long, you just can't.'

'Mmmm.'

Ian claps his hands. 'Babies are banned. We're going to talk about Meg and Evie instead. Evie's concert. Meg's holiday. Shall we go up the Empire State Building?' He catches Kate's eye. 'It is *perfectly* safe for a woman in your condition,' he adds, forestalling her protest. 'Eat up, everyone,' he orders. 'We're tourists, and we've got work to do.'

The queue isn't as long as I expected. Last time I came here I was sixteen, and it went all the way round the room and out of the door before doubling back on itself. This time we only have to wait ten minutes.

Last time I was wobbly and faint and my abdomen was still aching. My baby had been cut out of me and taken away four weeks before, and I was killing time until I was allowed to fly again. I found myself free from the shame of pointed fingers and whispered comments, real or imagined. No one knew I had a daughter. Nobody knew that my slightly saggy stomach wasn't always like that. Howard took me out sightseeing against my wishes, and in the end I was glad he had. Whatever else happened, I had seen the view from the Empire State Building and the World Trade Center, Manhattan and the Boroughs spread out dizzyingly and exhilaratingly below me. I had been inside the Statue of Liberty and across to Staten Island on the ferry. Taylor, who was five, was impressed with all the souvenirs I brought back for him. Nobody else thought to ask.

We go up in a lift, swap to a different one, and go up again. Kate, Ian and Megan stand together, looking downtown, to the skyscrapers and the Harbour. I walk away, slowly. They don't notice. I stand on my own, looking north to the park, and watch the cars navigating the city, streaming towards me or away from me, obeying the one-way system. I can make out the tiny shapes of pedestrians. The wind plays with my hair as I stare down. One of those people could be Elizabeth. The chances are that I can see where she lives from here. This is the closest I have felt to her for years.

chapter sixteen

April

Aurora is at her desk, but she looks subdued.

'Hi!' I say, beaming at her, fully expecting to be greeted effusively. She looks up and seems to force a small smile.

'Hi there,' she says, without feeling. Her hair has been pulled into a ponytail without being styled at all, and her make-up is cursory.

'Aurora,' I say to her, 'are you all right?'

She looks at me, and behind me, at Kate, Ian and Megan. 'Yes, sure. I'm just a little off colour today,' she says, smiling at everyone. 'I'll page Ron for you now. Take a seat.'

Kate and Ian don't seem to have noticed anything, since their attention is focused squarely on the blood test they are about to have, and its instant result. Megan hasn't met Aurora before, so she doesn't see the transformation.

'She was completely different last time,' I mutter to her quietly. 'She was really funny.'

Meg shrugs. 'Even Americans have off days. Even they

must have times when being nice and polite and friendly to absolutely everybody gets too much.'

'I suppose.'

I look down at my nails. They are perfect. The girls at Aurora's salon were horrified at the state of them, and soaked them, prodded the cuticles painfully back into place with a pointed stick, smeared them with lotion, put my hands into vibrating warm mittens, filed the nails cleanly (expressing sorrow on my behalf that I could neither grow them nor have false ones attached) and painted them an understated pale pink. I have been using hand cream every day since, and I can't stop looking at my beautiful new nails. These are someone else's fingers. However badly I play next week – next week! – at least no one will be criticising my hands.

While we wait, I kick my shoes off, and straighten my legs. The girls were astonished at the hard skin on my feet, and spent forty minutes fighting it with several different pumice stones. My feet got the moisturiser treatment, as well as the hot vibrating socks. My toenails are neat and tidy, and they are a bright fuchsia pink. I feel polished and buffed. I have a hair appointment for tomorrow, too, with Sonia's hairdresser. All this self-tweaking feels like a displacement activity. There is far too much going on for me to think about, and I am happier contemplating my own feet.

'Mr and Mrs Dawson!'

Ron's voice is hearty, and I glance up, pleased to be seeing him again. When I look at him, however, I see that he too has changed. He has lost weight around his face, and his eyes are ringed with black. Although he's dressed as well as ever, he is slightly hunched. He catches my eye and smiles weakly, before leading Kate and Ian out of the reception area.

'You know where to find the refreshments, Evie,' he says over his shoulder, and walks away without waiting for a reply.

Megan and I sit in the plush reception for a minute or so.

'Did he say refreshments?' Megan asks after a while.

'Mmmm,' I tell her. 'Tell you what, why don't you go through – they've got papers in there, too – and I'll come in a minute.' I incline my head towards Aurora. 'It's down the corridor, the big room at the end on the left. Follow the smell of coffee. You'll find it.'

Meg smiles. She has cheered up enormously in the ten days she's been in New York. 'I certainly will,' she agrees.

As soon as she has gone, I sit in the chair nearest Aurora.

'What's happened?' I ask her.

She looks up and meets my eyes. 'Ron didn't want either of us to say. He doesn't want to upset Kate. He takes such care of his patients.' I see tears in her eyes, and hand her a paper tissue from the box on her desk. She takes it. 'Thank you. When he's got a lady at a delicate stage like that, he won't allow *anything* to upset her.'

My mind is racing through possibilities. Ron or Aurora has cancer. They have been having an affair and have just been found out by Ron's girlfriend. The clinic is bankrupt. The needles there are infected with hepatitis C.

'Tell me,' I say, as purposefully as I can manage. I want her to feel she doesn't have the option of arguing. 'Tell me and I promise I won't tell Kate. I'll only tell her if she isn't pregnant. I can keep secrets, you know.'

'I believe you. I'm actually surprised you haven't heard already. I'm afraid it's worrying news. It's Anneka. Remember I told you about her? She went missing.'

'Missing?' I try to let this sink in. 'Ron's girlfriend has disappeared, and he's carrying on without even telling his patients?'

She nods.

'Why?'

'We each have our special way of coping. This is Ron's way. He carries on. We have no idea whether she has gone away of her own accord, or whether something terrible has happened. She took nothing with her. It does not look good, I'm afraid, Evie. Ron wants, more than ever, to bring new life into the world. I pray to God that Kate has good news. There's more depending on that than she will ever realise.'

'How long has she been missing?'

Aurora shakes her head. 'A few days now. Over a week . . .' She tails off. I put a hand on her shoulder, then pull my chair right up next to hers, and put my arms around her. She smells of Jennifer Lopez's perfume. 'She was my best friend,' she adds.

'She still is,' I tell her. 'You shouldn't be at work. You should be at home.'

She shrugs. 'If she wanted to call me, she would call me here. Do I really want to sit in my apartment watching Ricki Lake and looking through our high-school yearbook and calling the police again? And if Ron's here, how does it look if I stay away? He needs support.'

'Christ. What a nightmare.' My words sound lame, and I look around the room, casting about for something else to say. 'Does this sort of thing happen often?'

'Not really. Not without a clue. No one has come forward with any leads at all. That makes us fear the worst. Ron wouldn't say anything to you or to your friends, but I think he is falling to pieces.'

'Had they been together long?'

'Seven years. Anneka is devoted to Ron. They were great together. She is a wonderful human being, and he would do anything for her. Just the way he would look at her . . .' She stops for a moment, breathes deeply, and carries on. 'You know, Ron was married twice before, but he always said that meeting her was like coming home. It was the first time he knew how beautiful a relationship could be.'

'Has he got any children?' It had never occurred to me before to wonder about the fertility of the fertility guru. I wonder whether anything in his own experience is propelling him to provide babies for others.

'He has a son from his first marriage, Troy. Troy's seventeen now. He's something of a wayward child.' Aurora smiles. 'It's his age. He's a wonderful boy really. He is a great comfort to his father in this dark time. Anneka and Ron had just started trying for a baby together, you see. I didn't know.'

I hug her again, and wonder what to say. Every phrase that comes to mind sounds trite and insincere, but I suppose that to utter a cliché is better than to utter nothing.

'That is absolutely terrible,' I tell her. 'I'm so, so sorry.' I almost say that it's a blessing that she wasn't actually pregnant, because at least Ron didn't lose his baby too, but I stop myself. He lost his potential baby at the same time as he lost his potential baby's mother.

We sit in silence for a while, my hand over her shoulder. When the phone rings, it shatters the silence and startles both of us.

'My Lord,' says Aurora, a hand to her chest. 'Evie, I am so sorry. I hardly know you and here you are comforting me like an angel.' She snatches up the receiver and speaks urgently. 'Good morning, the Babylove Clinic, this is Aurora speaking, may I help you?'

While she talks, I stand up, and notice Megan standing in the doorway looking concerned. With a glance back at Aurora, who smiles and waves me away, I follow Meg back to the drawing room, and accept the large milky coffee that she hands me. Then I pile three pastries on to a plate. For the moment I don't care about my figure, the gym, or the Lincoln Center. I need a sugar rush.

'Bloody hell,' I tell her. 'Sorry to swear, but Christ.'

She laughs nervously. 'I have nothing against swearing, remember? It doesn't offend me. It offends me more that I'm still controlled by the evil nuns. What is it?'

I tell her everything Aurora told me.

'Ron's dealing with this,' I finish, 'by getting completely involved in his work. So let's just hope that when they come back, all three of them have got smiles on their faces.'

We sit and eat and drink and look out of the window. This place is lovely, but it suddenly seems soulless. It is a pretend stately home, a fake English manor house. The aristocratic façade hides the laboratories where sperm are chosen under microscopes, and mixed with eggs in test tubes, or on petri dishes, or wherever test-tube babies are actually created. This place is at the cutting edge of science, yet it goes to great lengths to hide that fact.

'What do you think of the place?' I ask Meg, for something to say. I gesture around the room, taking in the French windows, which are open today, and lead out to the grass and the cedar tree.

'I adore it,' she says fervently. 'It is utterly glorious. When I'm rich and famous my hideaway will be exactly like this.'

I look at her. 'Really?'

'Yes. I want a big secluded place in the middle of the country, maybe not in America, though. Although, in fact, America is as good a place as any. I always thought I'd create my ideal hideout in Nepal, before, up in the mountains. But I would stand out there so much. I hate that expat thing, the fact that even as a backpacker with three pounds a day I was richer than the vast majority of people in the countries I visited. So building myself a mansion in a developing country might be a bit rude and I don't think I'd be able to live with myself. At least everyone else would be loaded around here. So yes, here will do me fine.'

'Meg, are you serious? You want to hide away from the rest of the world? From what?'

She laughs, with a hint of bitterness. 'Well, right now, obviously, from Mummy and Oliver. But from London, from that stalker who's after you, from crowds and people and jobs that I hate. From weird boyfriends who I don't trust any more, and the glamorous women they write to. All I need is unlimited cash, and I'd get myself a great camera, lots of books, lots of classical music, a couple of friends around from time to time. I swear, I'd be a pig in clover.'

'Truly?'

She stands up and walks to the French windows. 'Of

course. Wouldn't you? Isn't that what everyone wants – an escape? I like my own company and I know I could cope with it. All I need to do is to win the lottery, and that's not going to happen.'

'You never know,' I remind her. 'Someone has to win it.'

'Well it won't be me, because I never buy a ticket.'

'Good point. Me neither. You know, *not* everyone has that fantasy. I don't. I'd hate to be stuck out in a faux-genteel place like this on my own.'

She turns and looks at me with interest.

'So what's your ideal life?'

I think about it, edit out the one thing that would make me complete. I am almost tempted to tell her about Elizabeth, and I would do if it wasn't for Guy. She might go home and fall in love with him again, and sooner or later it would slip out.

'A supportive network of people,' I say finally. 'I haven't really analysed it before, but it's very important to me to have friends and family around who I can trust. No secrets. I suppose I'd like to live in the countryside somewhere, like this, near a big city, but I'd like the place to be full of people who love me. I know it's asking a lot. It sounds like some ridiculous utopian community, doesn't it?'

Megan laughs. 'Evie, hello? Surely everyone does love you?'

'What? Of course they don't. If everyone loved me I'd be happy and secure and, well, I certainly wouldn't have a stalker rattling the door, wanting to rape me. I wouldn't pick fights with friends for the hell of it.'

'Yeah, but the stalker is someone who doesn't know you. I can't believe what you're saying. Ever since the day you came to look round the flat I've envied you. You turn up with two lovely friends. You've got a fantastic family, and you get on not only with both parents, but also with your stepfather and your stepmother and your stepbrother. That has to be unique. Your ex-husband would do anything for you. You sell bucketloads of records because you're so gorgeous and talented, and you're about to play the most prestigious venue in America. And you say that all you want is to be loved? What more is there?'

My baby, I want to say. My baby is what I want. That is why I crave love. I don't tell her. I just shrug and join her at the window.

'All I'm saying,' I say, as lightly as I can, 'is that I am not cut out to be alone.'

'Fair enough.'

There is a light tap on the door, and we both look round.

I can't stop myself gasping loudly at the sight of them. I hadn't realised, until this second, how much Kate's baby means to me, as well as to the rest of them. I want a baby in my life. It is not going to be my own just yet.

My legs go weak, and I grip the window frame to keep myself upright. Ron, Ian and Kate are standing there. I scan their faces.

I can tell the result from their eyes, and draw another sharp breath. Then I ask anyway. 'Well?'

I haven't seen Kate grinning like this for years. She runs towards me and throws her arms around me. 'January the seventh. Keep it free. It's the day my babies are due.'

Ian hugs Megan, and I look over Kate's shoulder, as her tears wet my shirt, at Ron. He is smiling indulgently, and

I am as glad for him as I am for them. I see him looking at me, see him registering that I know. He holds a hand up, to say 'not now'. I nod.

'Kate,' I tell her, 'congratulations. You're going to be the best mother in the world. And this baby, these babies – do you know how many there are?'

She shakes her head.

'Not yet,' says Ian. 'But Ron's going to do an early scan when we get to seven weeks, and then we'll find out, and after that we're going to fly home.'

'Once we've seen a heartbeat, or heartbeats,' Ron says drily, 'my work is done. I will be happy to hand over to the National Health Service, although I would be happier still, of course, if all four of you, plus the embryos, would stay with us here in New York. I will miss seeing the pregnancy progressing. With my local patients, I like to deliver the babies myself.'

Kate and Ian look at each other. 'Could we have them here?' Ian asks.

Ron shrugs. 'It could be done, I'm sure. It would cost more money, but on the plus side your babies could have US passports. That is certainly not a decision you need to make now.'

Ron's pager goes off. He picks it up and reads the display.

'Ah,' he says. 'My next patients are in reception. Do stay here as long as you wish. Please, please, eat the food.' He glances at the plate. 'I see you girls have made good headway. And, Evie, I shall be coming backstage for an autograph next week. I'm bringing my son with me. I imagine that he will be most taken with you. To tell you the truth, he already is. I even caught him with a bottle of that iced tea the other day.'

I laugh. 'Really? I didn't think anyone actually drank it.'

Ian frowns at me. 'Evie, you can't be like that about it. That drink pays your rent and buys your clothes. It's arrogant to sneer at the people who buy it.'

I smile. 'Oooh. Sorry. You're right.' But I am stung. I feel as if Ian is always criticising me.

Ron turns and looks behind him. Aurora is leading a couple into the room, and I quickly collect our cups and plates into a neat pile. Ron introduces Kate and Ian – 'who,' he says proudly, 'have just had some extremely successful treatment, some very good news' – to Koreena and Daniel, 'who are just embarking on the same process'. I am certain he would have avoided the introduction if the IVF hadn't worked. Koreena and Daniel are older than we are, and are dressed extremely expensively in shades of beige and brown. Their outfits may coordinate, but I notice in passing that their perfumes clash. His aftershave overpowers her scent, which in itself is not subtle.

'Good luck,' I wish them, as I leave the room.

'Yes,' says Kate, who is glowing. 'I really hope it works for you. I'm sure it will. Ron is the greatest. Take care.'

'Thank you, and congratulations,' says Koreena, in a husky voice. 'We hope to follow in your footsteps.' As we follow Aurora to reception, I hear Koreena saying loudly, 'But they are so young! Was IVF really necessary, Ron?'

I hug Aurora on the way out, and settle Kate in the back of the car like an invalid. Ian climbs in next to her and holds her hand.

'No mad driving,' he tells me sternly. 'Baby on board.'

'I will do thirty all the way,' I promise.

'Can we stop at a drugstore?' Kate asks breathlessly. 'I need to buy a couple of pregnancy tests, just to confirm it.'

As I drive, I half listen to the excited baby talk in the back. Kate has never been pregnant before, has never had a positive test, has never been through this euphoria. She and Ian talk incessantly about names and numbers and the chances of their coming back here to have the baby, or babies, with Ron. This is clearly a ridiculous idea, but I don't tell them so. As soon as they get back to London, they'll realise.

Megan joins in with them when she gets the chance, commenting favourably on their choices of names, and agreeing with them that they should assume that only one embryo has implanted so that they won't be disappointed at the scan if there's only one heartbeat. I drive slower than normal, determined not to upset anyone by being reckless. As I do so, I almost slip into a trance.

I try not to think about Ron's girlfriend. I don't know her, and there's nothing I can do. I suppose I'll send Ron a card to let him know that I'm thinking of him, but it ends there. I can't bear to tell Kate or Ian at the moment. They are too happy. They would be horrified if they knew that Ron's life partner (or at least, I think cynically, the latest in a string of life partners) had vanished and he hadn't even mentioned it to them; that he was putting their happiness before his grief.

I like Ron. Guy doesn't, and in a way that endears Ron to me further. I cannot shake off the feeling that both of them are somehow caught up in the letters which, presumably, are still piling up for me on a doormat somewhere. Ron may be extremely rich, and he might have charged Kate and Ian £10,000 for a procedure that would have cost them a couple of thousand at home, but he seems to me like a good man. Obviously, in an ideal world, he would be doing the procedure for a little more than what it cost him, but life isn't like that, and at least they have their tiny embryos.

Suddenly I realise that I want to talk to Ron. I want to tell him about Elizabeth. He works in a related area. He might know someone who might remember me, the awkward British teenager who had the Caesarean then went away. If they didn't remember me – and they wouldn't, really, not after all this time – then maybe they could look me up.

I am frantic with the urgency of my need. I have to know what sort of a home she went to. Who her new parents were, and whether they were New Yorkers. When I saw Koreena and Daniel, the first feeling I had was that they were the sort of people who might have taken my baby. Obviously they haven't – they are too young, they are having fertility treatment – but they are as I imagine her parents to be: New Yorkers through and through. I try to picture my little girl now.

I think about her all the time. I project her on to every teenager I pass on the streets. One of them might have been her. I could have brushed past her on Fifth Avenue, stood pressed up against her on the subway, queued behind her in Starbucks, and I would never have known. This is driving me crazy, and I can't bear to wait till she's eighteen, and then to start waiting for her to contact me. I need to know that she's all right now.

I succeeded in shutting her out for fourteen years. It was Louise who made me do it. As soon as she spread my news around the school, I realised that I'd lost my best friend as well as my baby, and the best friend part of the equation was easier to assimilate. I threw all my energies into hating Louise, and assured Mum that I wasn't missing Elizabeth at all. It was strange, because, before that, I had liked her slightly too much. She had always been the more popular of the two of us, though neither of us was particularly sought after, and she knew that I looked slightly better for hanging around with her. I was useless, as a teenager. From the age of eleven onwards I was paralysed with shyness, and could hardly bear to speak to anyone at all. I hated the way I looked, hated my height and the brace on my teeth, and I hunched my shoulders and looked at the ground and did my best to pretend I was somewhere else, or someone else. In photos, my pain shines out of me. I was awkward and miserable, the definitive inept teenager. Being good at music did not make me cool either: at my particular school, girls who did music lessons were sad. I knew I was destined to be a loser all my life. Louise rescued me, somewhat, and she knew that this meant I owed her.

I sigh. I was unlucky. I was emphatically not the sort of teenager who gets pregnant. If you'd asked anyone at school to list our class in order of the likelihood of under-age sex, my name would have appeared close to the bottom, if not at the very base of the list. It wasn't meant to happen. It shouldn't have happened.

I did it to impress Louise, because she dared me. She set it up, agreed with Mark that he would 'do it' with me, and sent me to him, taunting me that I was too scared. I was too scared, but I was even more scared of having no friends at all, so I gritted my teeth, kept as many of my clothes on as I could, and went through with it. As Mark pushed into me, I thought he was going to kill me. I vowed never to do it again in my whole life. I knew about condoms, of course, but I could not say a single word to him, on any subject, so I told myself he had probably taken care of that side of things. I had not been watching his actions very closely.

Mark was spotty. He was scrawny and white with thick, greasy hair. Nonetheless, he was sought after, and I was, as Louise always reminded me, lucky that he had wanted anything to do with me.

I tried to speak to Louise a couple of times, after she betrayed me, but she wouldn't let me say anything. I wasn't very good at being assertive. I waited for her after school, walked alongside her and said, 'Louise? Why did you tell them?' I can picture myself now, desperate, in spite of everything, to have my only friend back. I had no self-esteem, no pride. If Louise had made an excuse about how they had tricked her into telling them, I would have made myself believe her, and I would happily have taken my place back by her side.

'Because you deserved it,' she said sharply. 'Go away, Evie. I'm not your friend any more, all right?'

Looking back, I am incensed. Incensed at what she did to me, and incensed at the way she spoke to me then. I hate the way she implied that it was my fault that she'd betrayed me. When I'd first told her I was pregnant, in a phone call on the day my mother rumbled me, she'd been falling over herself to be nice to me. She had come straight over to the house after school, and put her arm around me and promised me that everything was going to be all right and that she would keep it secret.

'It's Mark's?' she asked, knowing that it could not possibly be anyone else's. I nodded mutely. 'Are you going to tell him?'

I shook my head. 'It's not his fault,' I said bravely.

She told me that she would be there for me, that this was what friends were for. I can picture her now, too clearly, sitting there in her school uniform. Her black fringe fell into her eyes, and she sat very close to me. Her young body was spiky and angular. Mum brought us tea and chocolate biscuits, and Louise put her hand on my stomach. After a few minutes the baby stuck out a limb.

Louise leapt back. 'Oh my God! Your baby kicked me!'

I smiled. 'I know.' I had been ignoring these movements for weeks, pretending to myself that I had indigestion, that my bowels were acting strangely, that my period was about to start (though that was a line of thought I did not pursue). Even when I could clearly see the outline of a little hand or foot sticking out of my belly, I pretended nothing was happening. I was waiting for someone else to see, and to take control. It was nice to be able to talk to Louise about it, fleetingly.

'That is the sweetest thing,' she said, smiling. 'Wow. Your baby kicked me. Do you think it knows my voice?'

'Probably.'

'You're definitely doing the best thing,' she said solemnly. 'I mean, growing up in America, that is the best gift you can give your little child. Evie, you're going to have an American kid! You and Mark!'

'But I'll never know him. Or her.'

'But you'll know he's happy.'

I thought I was lucky to have such a good friend. It didn't matter that I didn't really have any others: she was all I needed.

In a sense, everything I have done since then has been to show Louise that she was wrong about me. People think boys are the mean ones, but there was not a single girl in my year, or in the entire school, who expressed any sympathy towards me, or performed even the tiniest act of kindness. They gossiped incessantly, and called me names. They looked at me slyly and looked away when I caught their eyes. I hate every single one of them, and I always will.

I denied it. I said I'd been ill, and Mum told the headmistress, who made sure that everyone was told that I'd had glandular fever. Our teacher announced to the class that she was disappointed by the malicious gossip that certain people had been spreading – I watched her look at Louise at that point, and watched Louise gazing innocently back – and finished by saying, 'I want to make it clear to everyone that Evie Silverman has been ill with glandular fever, and does not deserve to be the subject of these absurd rumours.' I kept my eyes fixed on Louise, who no longer sat at the desk next to mine, and watched her catching people's eyes, shaking her head, and pulling her jumper out to form a big belly. I saw Mrs Gibbs watching her too. She turned her eyes to me and they were full of impotent sympathy.

I find it strange to remember that even then, I was Evie Silverman. I am proud to have reclaimed the name. At school, those two words conveyed everything that was dorkish and forgettable, until the gossip began. Then my name became synonymous with scandal and huge cock-ups, with undertones of 'but who would want to do it to *her*?' and the whispered reply, 'Mark Parker.' I thought I would forever be tarnished by my name. I even considered changing it and starting again as someone else. For a while I had an alter ego called Roxy Fontaine. I almost went to sixth-form college under her auspices, but Mum stopped me at the last minute, when she caught me filling in a form, and I'm glad she did.

Now Evie Silverman summons up glamour and talent and mainstream success, from the outside at least. I did start again, but I did it as a better version of myself, one that was not going to be prone to cock-ups like the previous model. Part of me lives in constant fear that the real Evie is lurking inside, ready to come out one day. There is a dork inside me, and not many people know that. That's why I'm so happy to have had my nails done: they keep Teenage Evie at bay.

I hope Elizabeth hasn't inherited my teenage ineptitude. I hope she is popular, pretty, and thoughtful. I hope she would be kind to a girl out of her depth in a terrible situation. I hope I meet her.

I park in a horrendously expensive car park in central Manhattan, and hand my keys to a young man who pops his gum at me.

'Shuts at seven,' he says. 'Penalty for overnight stay.'

'That's fine,' I tell him haughtily. I turn to the others. 'Shall we go for a drink?'

To my surprise, Kate and Ian decline, and say they're going back to the hotel for a rest. Megan practically runs away from me, announcing over her shoulder that she wants to go to MoMA. I would go with her, but she clearly doesn't want me to. Ian suggests we all meet again by the boating lake in Central Park in two hours. Suddenly, I am alone. I put my car keys in my pocket, and look around. I'm a couple of blocks from Fifth Avenue, so I decide to go shopping.

I stayed away from FAO Schwarz when I was here fifteen years ago, because I hated the idea of seeing anything that made me think of babies and children. I couldn't bear to see them streaming in there, with their parents and their nannies. I hated the queues and the men in toy costumes policing the revolving door. I hated everything about it. This time, I go in.

It is a noisy shop. The same tune plays over and over again, and after five minutes I find myself singing 'Welcome to our world of toys' in time with the clock, without even knowing what I am doing. I consider buying something for Kate's baby or babies, but it's too soon, and it would be madness if I started a collection of dolls or books for Elizabeth. Instead, I watch the children, relieved that nobody here is old enough to be my daughter. I bet she has been here. This is the one place in New York that I can be absolutely certain she has visited. In a way, this knowledge makes me feel closer to her. I am clutching at straws.

The little girls are expensively dressed, with glossy hair and shiny shoes. The younger ones hold hands with their mothers. I try to picture my little girl holding hands with her adopted mother, choosing an elaborate doll that her birth mother, at that point a music student, could not have afforded to buy her. They bustle around, picking up toys. I ride up in a lift shaped like a transformer robot, and stumble into the Barbie department. These dolls look like me on performance night, so I shudder and leave.

I head straight over the road to the Plaza. The doorman smiles and calls me ma'am, and I head busily for a corner of the bar and order a vodka martini. Then I sit back. It is quiet in here, and it smells expensive. Nobody takes much notice of me. I smile around, and pick up a newspaper that someone has left nearby. My martini disappears surprisingly quickly.

I check the listings for my concert. Sure enough, it is there. I am second on the bill (of two), behind a famous and brilliant pianist who is also a publicity junkie. I am described as 'British cellist from TV'. This in itself is enough to make me order a second drink. I will have to leave the car overnight, after all, and go home on the train.

Then I notice another listing. It is for tomorrow night, and it is a very small entry.

Dan Donovan, it reads. *Two nights only. British singing sensation.*

He is playing at a small club in SoHo. I smile at that. We are all desperately trying to break America, and it would seem that I am doing rather better than my erstwhile lover. I will not go along to gloat, although it is tempting.

I sit on a bench by the boating lake, and wonder where the others have got to. I'm looking around, but although there are plenty of people here, none of them are my friends. It is beginning to get cold. I do up my cardigan and wish I had brought a jacket. The weather is changing. Clouds are rapidly filling the sky, and my feet are suddenly numb with cold in my new sandals. The stubble is standing up on my legs. I wish I had worn jeans, rather than a skirt with bare legs. I was too excited by the reappearance of spring to consider that it might be temporary.

I begin to curse them. I am waiting, on my own, in the cold, and it's just about to rain. This is not fair.

He sits next to me. I don't look round, at first.

'Hi, Evie,' he says softly.

I look up, expecting Ian.

'Jack?' I stare at him, frowning. It can't really be Jack.

'Hello.'

'What are you doing here?' I still don't believe it's him. Jack is in Camden.

'I've come to see you, sweetheart. I've come to sort things out, once and for all.'

'Sort things out?' I am beginning to dread what is coming. 'Did Kate and Ian set me up?'

'Of course they did. Brilliant news, isn't it, about the pregnancy?'

'Yes.' I am distracted. 'Fantastic. But you came all this way to see me? Not to find out about the pregnancy?'

'Of course. We've been messing around for too long.' I look into his face. It is open, and he is beaming. Jack really believes he has come to reclaim me. 'I love you,' he says happily. 'And you love me. You said so. Ian said you do. Everyone knows it. You've been confused, I've been confused, you messed around with that boy, I ran

271

headlong into a rebound relationship. None of that matters. I want you to come back with me, Evie, and I want us to start again. As if we'd just met. I want us to get a new house, maybe out of London, and have babies. We can renew our marriage vows, invite all our friends back again. We can make this into the best thing that ever happened to us.'

A couple of drops of rain land on my face, and I shiver. 'You came all the way over here for me?'

'I'd have gone to Timbuktu for you. I've been looking at places for us to live. I've brought some details for you. We could have a cottage in the country, and I could easily make it into London for work, or I might even give up my job. Perhaps even try some portrait painting.'

'Are you serious?'

He is looking at me. I can see how scared he is. I have been married to Jack for over eight years, and I have never known him to make a gesture that is anything like this. Jack likes an easy life. I assumed I could drop him and that he would move on. He did move on. I dragged him back to me because I wanted to be sure I didn't need him before I let him go. This is my fault.

I stand up. He stares at me for a while, then stands up too. I walk to stand under a tree, to shelter from the rain.

'What do you say?' he asks, his voice cracking.

'I've got a concert next week,' I tell him. 'I have to stay here.'

He laughs. 'Oh, I know that. I'll be in the front row. Well, the sixth row. It was the best I could do. I got my ticket weeks ago. I wouldn't dream of not supporting you. It's a wonderful opportunity.'

'Yes it is.' I am sad and heavy with guilt. A small part of me wants to agree to all Jack's suggestions, to force myself to go back to the marriage, to tell him all about Elizabeth, and to see what happens. In a way, I love him. If we had no secrets, I could have some more babies.

I try to make myself smile and nod and say what he wants me to say. But I can't.

'Jack,' I tell him gently, 'I'm sorry, but I don't think I can do it.'

He stares at me. 'What do you mean?'

'I do love you, but I can't go back to you. I wish I could, but I can't. Go back to Sophia, Jack. You're much better off with her.'

'Evie?'

I walk away from him, through the rain, and I don't look back.

chapter seventeen

The following afternoon

Ron offers to fit me in for an hour between appointments, and I make the familiar drive to the clinic. It takes over an hour, and I try to make my mind blank all the way. Jack started to follow me across the park, but I didn't slow down, or look back, and by the time I reached the zoo he had gone. I can't believe he misjudged me so badly. I can't believe I allowed it to happen. I knew exactly what I was doing. I was using him. I was using him because that's the kind of thing I do.

Yesterday was when my marriage really ended. I haven't heard anything from Kate or Ian since, and though Megan turned up early in the evening, at Howard's, I hid from her, using my cello as an alibi.

I try to forget Jack and to panic about the concert instead. It is six days away. I played for hours last night, and for three hours this morning, waking the house up as I did so.

I don't want to do it. I'm not good enough. The old

274

Evie, the one who was never good enough for anyone, is threatening to break out of her coffin and perform this concert herself. That would be a disaster. The posture would be atrocious, the intonation random, the concerto barely audible above the orchestra. I have humiliated my husband, and I'm going to be a disaster on Thursday.

Ron, at least, is glad to see me. Aurora smiles warmly as she begins to page him. He forestalls her by appearing in the doorway.

'Evie,' he says, and his voice is full of emotion. 'Come along, we'll go to my living room.'

'Thanks,' I say, and smile back at Aurora as we leave the reception area. She gives me a little wave. She looks better than yesterday: she has applied her old mask of make-up, and her hair is coiffed almost as professionally as it used to be.

Ron leads me upstairs, and I peep into rooms as we pass them. I see several bedrooms, like the one where Kate rested after her implantation. They are all impeccable, like bedrooms in the Waldorf Astoria, and I know they each have a bathroom of a level of luxuriousness to which I would never think of aspiring in my daily life. Some doors remain shut, and I wonder how many patients are reclining behind them, praying for the fertilised egg to like its new home, to decide to stay there and grow for nine months. Others must be waiting for the unpleasant-sounding 'transvaginal ultrasound' which Kate had for her egg removal. There must be hundreds of procedures carried out here of which I know nothing. There are doors, slightly ajar, revealing slices of consultation rooms which

275

look like cosy sitting rooms, yet which somehow retain an air of reassuring professionalism. We pass men and women, some in clinical white coats, others dressed as maids and clearly servicing the rooms as they would in a hotel. Ron greets each of them with a nod and a clipped 'good afternoon'.

His living room is surprisingly small, and is lit by a full-length window. It is more functional than the rest of the clinic: the furniture is plain, not pretentious, and there is a small television in the corner. Nothing is varnished, and the walls are plain white, unadorned by any sort of art or any photos of babies. He offers me the small blue sofa, and I kick my shoes off and tuck my feet up, taking the opportunity to admire my pink toenails and their viciously tamed cuticles.

I decide to speak first.

'I'm so sorry, Ron, about Anneka,' I say quickly. 'Is there any news?' He looks at me, opens his mouth, closes it again, and sits down.

'Thank you, Evie,' he says in the end. 'I appreciate that. No. No news. It is beginning to seem to me, and I hate to say this, that it is now just a matter of time before they find . . . well, before they find a body. Anneka's body.'

'I can't imagine how it must be for you.'

'No,' he agrees. 'I could never have imagined this myself.'

I can't think what else to say on the subject, so wait for him to speak. In the end he stands up, leaves the room, and comes back in with a tray of coffee. There is also a card, still in its cellophane wrapper, and a pen on the tray.

'Milk?' he asks, and I nod. 'Sugar?' he continues, and I

shake my head. He hands me the cup, and I take a sip.

'It's great coming here,' I tell him. 'You know you get good coffee.' In fact, the coffee is mediocre and tastes as if it has been standing in the machine all day, but I needed something to say.

'We do our best,' he says, then sips his own. 'Evie, you are being too kind. This is not good coffee.'

'It's coffee.'

'True.' He pushes the card and pen towards me. 'Will you do me a favour?' he asks wanly. 'Write this card? We need some new ones on reception and none of my babies are due for the next couple of months.'

'You want me to write it?'

'Dear Ron, How can we thank you for the joy you have brought into our lives? Baby Blah Blah was born yesterday morning, etc, and you can make up a name. And the baby's name too. This demonstrates how much I trust you, Evie. It shows you what kind of man I really am.'

I look at him and can't help laughing. 'You cynical git! How many of those cards on reception are fake?'

He shrugs a shoulder. 'One third? One third to one half.'

'OK.' As I write the card, I cannot stop myself putting the name Elizabeth. My baby never had a middle name, so I make one up. She becomes Elizabeth Miranda. Before I sign it, I look up and ask, 'Can it be from lesbians?'

'Sure.'

I write their names with a flourish, 'Roxy and Tallulah Fontaine'.

'Roxy and Tallulah Fontaine?' Ron asks sceptically, perusing my handiwork. 'They're married? Are they from Vermont?'

'Tallulah took Roxy's surname because it was so much more fabulous than her own. Which was Snodgrass.'

He smiles. 'Fair enough.'

I wait, then decide to launch into it. 'Ron,' I tell him, 'I need your advice. I've never told anyone about this. I hope you don't mind.'

I tell him the whole story, beginning a month after conception and ending at the present day. When I finish, Ron nods his head. He's looking thoughtful.

'And you're hoping I could help you find out what became of her?'

'Yes. I'm sorry, it's probably a really insensitive thing for me to do, offloading on you at a time like this.' I look at him, but he shakes his head.

'You have no idea what a favour you've just done me,' he says. He looks exhausted, but there is the beginning of a sparkle in his eyes. 'You've given me a project. Aurora thinks I'm screwy, but I have to keep myself busy to make it through the days. I'm busy looking for Anneka, but now I have to accept that there's only so much I can do. For the first week I had a full-time job convincing the police that she wasn't at the bottom of my lake, cut into pieces.' I wince. He ignores me. 'Kate's result was good, but this is better. Everything is a drop in the ocean . . . I know it's a difficult thing for you, Evie. I do know a couple of people who might be able to help.' He pauses. 'So you had her at St Vincent's. I was affiliated there myself for a while, but that would have been after your time. I'll make a couple of calls. First of all, though, we should discuss what you're going to do. You do know you don't have the right to contact your daughter? Until she's eighteen, and then only if she wants contact with you. You can fill in a form and add yourself to the Adoption Registry so she can find you if she wants.'

'I know. Can I do anything except wait?'

He looks at me, and smiles, a genuine smile. 'Officially, no, but actually, Evie, yes. I'll do my best to help you. I can't make any promises, but I'll call in a couple of favours and see if I can't find you a lead. As long as you promise me – I know how emotional these matters are, and I know how much you must have invested in her – so promise me that you're not going to turn up at her house and make a scene. If you do, and if it comes back to me, I'll be deeply, deeply in the shit. OK?'

I smile at him and swallow the small amount of luke-warm coffee that remains in my cup. 'Of course. I don't know what I will do, but I won't turn up and introduce myself. I think . . .' I pause and wonder whether this is true. As far as I can tell, it is. 'I think just to know who she is and where she lives and that she's OK should be enough for me. I'd love to meet her, but only when she's ready. She might not even know she was adopted.'

'Indeed, although her parents should have been told it was far better for the child to know something like that from the very beginning.'

'I think I'd feel much calmer if I knew what her name was and whether or not I'm really likely to be seeing her every five minutes on the streets of Manhattan. I mean, she might live in California, mightn't she?'

'She might, but the chances are she was adopted on the East Coast. There's no saying where the family might have gone from there.'

279

'Since I've been back in New York, I haven't been able to stop thinking about her. It is such a relief to talk about her to you. None of my friends know. I used to push her from my mind quite effectively, but now I can't. I'm even wondering if there's any chance of her being in the audience at my concert next week.'

Ron nods. 'Unlikely, you do realise that. Highly unlikely.'

'I know.'

'And you might find that knowing about her makes you even more desperate to meet her.'

'I don't think it will. I think I have pretty good self-control, normally, and I know I'll be able to hold off for three more years. I might tell a few more people, though.'

'You said you haven't told anybody at all?'

'Not even my husband. We're separated, as I might have mentioned, but we've been married for eight years and I never told him. He's just turned up in New York thinking that I was ready to go back to him. I've screwed him over completely, but that's not the point. He thinks my Caesarean scar is from appendicitis.'

'Clearly not a medical man. So Kate and Ian and the waif-like Megan are all in the dark?'

'I couldn't bring myself to tell Kate when she was having such a hard time with infertility. It seemed like the ultimate slap in the face. But if this pregnancy goes well . . .'

'You know, I have every confidence. Kate hasn't been pregnant before, and that actually stands her in pretty good stead. Her body doesn't have a history of rejecting foetuses. Of course it's impossible to know, because she hasn't got a history of nurturing them either.'

'Fingers crossed.'

'Indeed. You and I have each got more invested in this than Kate can possibly realise.'

I look him in the eye. He seems more relaxed than earlier. 'Shall I tell her about Anneka?' I ask, carefully.

Ron exhales loudly and leans back in his chair. 'It's in the paper, so I'm quite surprised she hasn't seen it already. You know, "TV doc's partner feared dead". All that. But no. I'd appreciate it if you wouldn't. Not yet. Perhaps we'll say something when she reaches her second trimester. Maybe we'll wait until her baby is born. I have always made a point of not allowing my personal circumstances, whatever they may be, to affect my work, and I think it would be highly unprofessional if I let this awful matter upset Kate. She's at a delicate stage and I want her to be happy. It's good that someone can be happy.'

'OK. I told Megan, though.'

'I saw that in her face. Am I right in thinking that that slip of a girl is Guy Chapman's girlfriend?' He is smiling now, but it is a tense smile. Ron looks wary.

'Yes, kind of. Possibly his ex-girlfriend, though I'm not sure if Guy knows that yet.'

'Bloody hell. How on earth did he manage to attract a girl like that? I mean, the man's my age, and as I recall he was a hell of a drinker.'

'He certainly is. He's nowhere near as dapper as you are, Ron.'

Ron gapes at me, then chuckles. 'Dapper?' he echoes. 'I'm dapper?' He looks at me, leans forward, and laughs loudly, seeming to find this genuinely funny. 'Well, thank you very much, Evie. Dapper is what you call an old man who wears a suit to buy his morning bagel, and polishes his shoes every night. What about sexy? Or handsome, or at least fit?'

'Well, obviously you're all those things, certainly to a higher degree than Guy has ever been.'

'Thank you. That's all I ask. So what does she see in him?'

I feel relieved to be able to talk to someone. 'She has a few hang-ups, I suppose. She has a complicated relationship with her father, that's certainly something that's come out since she's been here.' Megan's mother rang Howard and Sonia's house when we were all in Manhattan yesterday. No one was in, and she left a short, desperate message. When Meg called back, worried sick, she got Oliver. He told her not to be stupid, that everything was fine and she was imagining it. 'He hits her mother,' I tell Ron. 'Yesterday she packed up and tried to leave, and Oliver caught her. Meg managed to speak to her in the end, but only by telling her dad she was going to call the police if he didn't prove to her that her mum was still alive.'

'The poor girl.'

'So her dad lets her mother speak to her for a few minutes, then snatches the phone and tells Meg to keep out of it. She was devastated when she hung up. Now she doesn't know what to do.'

'Has she called anyone? Do they have friends who Megan could alert, who might be able to step in and take her mother to people who would help her? Can't Guy do something? I might be able to mobilise someone in Bristol if you need me to.'

I shrug. 'My mum would help if it came to it, but I don't

want to get anyone to swing into action without Megan agreeing. She was considering going home, but she's angry with her mother too, for putting up with it for all those years. She despises her, in a way, for cocking up her escape attempt. But at least she's trying now. That's a big step forward. I hope Meg will come to realise that. She's been very harsh to her mother. I think that's the only way she's been able to cope.'

Ron stands up and walks to the window. 'Guy, then, is the nice older man she'd like her father to be?'

'Except that she has sex with him.'

He turns round and smiles at me. 'With that exception, yes.'

I decide to ask him. 'Ron, what happened between you and Guy?'

He looks back out of the window. 'What happened?'

'I know something happened. Guy goes all strange whenever you're mentioned. Why?'

'He hasn't said anything? I thought he couldn't have. None of you would have been so normal with me if he had.'

'Is it to do with Marianne?'

Ron stares at the glass for a while, then turns back to me. He looks at his watch. I am shocked to realise that I have been with him for more than an hour. I leave the question hanging for a few seconds, then cave in.

'Sorry,' I tell him. 'You must have patients waiting.'

He relaxes visibly, and comes to kiss me on the cheek. 'Time flies in good company. Thank you for coming to see me, Evie. This past hour has been a breath of fresh air. It's refreshing to think about something other than my own troubles, and I'll let you know as soon as I have any news for you. For the record, any little girl would be proud to have you as her mother.'

My eyes fill with tears. 'Thank you.' Nobody has ever said anything like that to me before. It is, without a doubt, the biggest compliment I have ever received.

chapter eighteen

A week later

I sit in my dressing room and look at my dress on its hanger. At least I don't have to worry about that. It is perfect, and because I paid so much money for it I know that it will stay perfect. It is not the sort of dress which suddenly changes as you allow yourself to doubt it. It is bigger and better than I am and it has an arrogant aura which I love.

The shoes are equally wonderful. They are strappy and high and purple, and I have practised walking in them so I can be fairly sure that, barring a disaster, I won't fall flat on my face or, worse, flat on my cello.

I wish someone was here with me. I didn't ask Kate or Howard to come backstage beforehand, because I thought I should be warming up and trying to meditate, as I usually do. This time, though, I am terrified. I wonder whether Jack is out there, or whether he's gone home. Someone to talk to would calm me down, I think. Still, I haven't got a phone in here, and I'm not going in search of a payphone. I will get through this.

My good-luck cards are standing on the dressing table. There are six of them, from the family in Bristol, Howard and Sonia, Kate and Ian, Meg, Ron and Aurora, and Alexis and everyone at the label. I read them again. I have to do well tonight. All these people are rooting for me. A couple of people are probably willing me to fail too.

I look at the cello, standing up in its open case. I try to think of it as a part of myself. The cello and I are one, and we will play this Elgar together. I have practised like a real musician since I've been here, and I know that technically I can do it. It's the interpretation I'm worried about. Rehearsals with the orchestra have been fine, but I know that I'm not brilliant. This orchestra – the New York Philharmonic – are the best, and they are used to playing with the best. I am unable to look at the cello section, because I'm sure they must all be sneering at me, knowing that any one of them could do better.

I know I will not be sending people away amazed at my prowess and my musicianship. Being not bad, within the parameters of acceptability to this audience and this orchestra, is all I ask of myself. I just hope that the posters with my image on them attract a dilettante audience, who will be easily pleased, like the people who used to go to see Nigel Kennedy playing the *Four Seasons*.

The first half of the concert is in full flow. I can hear it through the intercom, but then I stand up and turn the volume down. A young man is playing a Mozart piano concerto, quite brilliantly. He is a native New Yorker, a couple of years older than me, and he sells CDs by the truckload. He is on home turf and everyone adores him.

This audience has, almost to a man or a woman, come to see him, rather than me.

I take the cello out and warm up some more. First I make sure it's still in tune, then I tackle some scales and arpeggios. I play the first few minutes of the concerto, and then stop. I try part of the second movement, and realise that nothing I do now will make any difference. It's like cramming for an exam at the doorway of the exam-ination hall. If I can't do it now I'll never do it. I lay the instrument carefully on its side, loosen the bow and place it on top, and try to think of nothing.

The auditorium is silent. The final chord hangs in the air. I know where I am, but the whole of the performance has been so hyperreal that it is more like a dream than reality. The orchestra behind me is different from the way it was in rehearsals. It is a part of my performance. I am barely aware at all of the first violins, only a foot or two behind me and to my right. The bright lights, which have always, in past performances, filled me with adrenalin, now seem natural and unremarkable. I don't care how I look, whether I'm making a comical face. I don't even care if my knickers are showing. This is how it is supposed to be. I have never played like this before.

I keep my bow on the strings long after the chord has died away. The orchestra is also keeping its position, until the conductor ends the performance with a jerk of his baton. Suddenly, I am smiling so broadly that my face hurts. I have done it; and I did fine. I have never played this well in public. This is the peak of my career, and I am amazed at myself. I pulled it off. Even if I never play again, I have now had a career that makes me proud.

No one in the orchestra, no discerning and knowledgeable member of the audience, will go home thinking they have witnessed the birth of a new legend, but I acquitted myself well, and that is far more than I dared to hope for. I have done more than not disgracing myself. The auditorium is enormous, and every seat is filled. I try to discern the faces, try to look for teenage girls, but the people merge together in the darkness. I count back to the sixth row to see if Jack is there, but I can't make anyone out. I stand up and smile, and give a little bow, and smile again. I direct applause behind me, to the orchestra, and hold hands with the conductor as we take a bow together. Luckily, my breasts stay within the dress. He kisses me on each cheek, holds me by the upper arms and looks at me, and tells me, 'You were beautiful, Evie.' He gestures to the leader of the orchestra, who tries to take my other hand before he notices that it is holding my cello. I accept the most spectacularly tasteful bouquet I have seen in my life. It matches my dress, and I think these are orchids. All the time, they keep clapping, and I keep smiling. I'm almost crying. I have validated myself as a musician at last. I breathe deeply and tell myself to remember this moment. There are not many of these to a lifetime.

People are waiting in the wings to congratulate me, and I smile gratefully at the members of the orchestra, and murmur my thanks. I don't stop to talk to anyone, and they let me through in respectful silence. When I reach my dressing room, I close the door behind me and stand there for a moment. I hug the cello to me before putting it gently back in its case. We did it together after all. I have never felt a sense of achievement like this, and I vow to keep practising at the same level from now on, so I can make something of myself.

I sit down and pour a glass of water. Immediately there is a gentle tap on the door.

'Come in!' I call, hoping for Kate.

Alexis puts his head into the room. 'Evie Silverman!' he says, beaming. 'I knew you were good, girl, but I had no idea you would be *stunning*! You are a star. Everyone is talking about you. New York is at your feet.'

I smile at his hyperbole. I could not stop smiling if I tried. 'Thanks, Alexis. I can offer you a celebratory glass of water, and that's it.' I hope he isn't looking at the bin. If he does, he will see three empty crisp packets. I have not exactly adhered to his beloved Atkins diet: the only times I have boycotted carbohydrates have been when I've been with him, and even then I normally come away so hungry that I buy a sandwich on the way home. Yet I like him to think that I am his soulmate in my devotion to the process of ketosis.

'We'll solve that!' he announces, and nips out of the door, to return immediately with an ice bucket containing a bottle of champagne, and four glasses in the other hand.

I am amazed. 'Alexis! But you don't drink!' I love the way I am feeling. Nothing can penetrate this shell of euphoria. A small voice tells me to be careful: the last time I felt like this, I left Jack, and the trouble began.

'I drink occasionally,' he corrects me. 'I prefer to do it in extreme moderation. This is an occasion.'

I laugh with delight. 'Extreme moderation? That sums

you up perfectly, Alexis.' As he is so pleased with me, I add, 'My next album doesn't really have to have a pop backing, does it?'

'We'll talk about that another day.'

While he pops the cork and fills two glasses with frothy bubbles, I look at myself in the mirror. I am successful. I am somebody, even if it doesn't last. I have never, in my adult life, felt as secure as this. I know it's dangerous to rely on the approval of others for one's own self-esteem, but tonight I am happy to do it. They loved me. They loved me not because they saw me in a magazine or read an insincere interview in a newspaper, but because I did what I am paid to do, and I did it well.

My cheeks are pink, my eyes wide, and I look unspeakably happy. I watch myself for a few moments. A few strands of my hair have escaped from the tight bob that Sonia's hairdresser sprayed into place this afternoon, and they curl gently around my face. The dress's strapless top is ridiculously flattering, and my collarbone and shoulders jut delicately above it. I try to pinpoint what it is about me that is different tonight, and just as I am deciding that, for the first time in years, I am not wearing any sort of a mask, there is another knock on the door.

Alexis jumps to his feet and opens it. Kate, Ian and Megan pile into the room, closely followed by Howard and Sonia.

'Wow,' I say, looking at them. 'Everyone's here.'

Kate rushes up and hugs me. 'You were fantastic,' she laughs. 'I've never heard you play like that. Well done.' She has dressed up in a short pink dress, and she looks as excited as I am.

'I've never heard me play like that either,' I admit. 'Thanks.

Have a drink.' She shakes her head. 'Oh,' I remember. 'Sorry. Hope there hasn't been too much excitement for the baby.'

'Nope.' She shakes her head. 'He's going to have to get used to hearing Auntie Evie's music.'

Ian is introducing Alexis to Howard and Sonia. My dressing room is small, and it is extremely crowded, but I like that and I hope no one suggests moving the party elsewhere. I am walking on air. The chatter is loud, and the bottle of champagne lasts no time at all. I look at Megan, who seems radiant.

Alexis claps his hands. 'OK, ladies and gentlemen. Might I make a suggestion? I know there are a lot of people out there waiting to meet our dear Evie. I propose we leave her to change and sort herself out, while we reconvene in the bar and then on to Café Des Artistes, just over on West Sixty-seventh.'

He looks to me, and I smile and nod. At Alexis's suggestion, I brought a short purple dress from Calvin Klein with me for this express purpose, despite the fact that I was utterly unable to imagine a time when the concert might be over. When I did think about it, I could only think about slinking away to JFK and waiting for the next flight home. Megan and I bought the dress yesterday. We made sure it was the same colour as the concert dress so I didn't have to buy new shoes to go with it.

They file out slowly. Howard doubles back from the door and gives me a second huge hug.

'I'm very proud of my little girl,' he tells me, his words muffled against my hair. 'I'm calling your mother right now.'

'Thanks, Howard,' I tell him. 'Knowing there were so many friends out there made it happen.'

He kisses me on the cheek – a scratchy, beardy kiss – and leaves the room. I move the ice bucket, which is already half water, half ice, from my chair, and sit down. There is so much to do, and already I am exhausted. I force myself to be sensible for a moment and make a mental list, because I know that, otherwise, Alexis will come back in an hour and find me sitting right here. Sort out hair, tone down make-up, change into new dress, put shoes back on, pack up bag and cello, and take everything to the bar. It's manageable.

I have just got myself into my new dress, and am admiring its sleek contours, when there is another knock on the door. It is a gentle, female knock. It cannot be Jack. I am thrilled at the idea that Kate or Megan has doubled back to help me. Apart from anything else, I need to ask them whether he's here.

'Hi!' I call.

The handle twists, the door opens, and a woman stands hesitantly on the threshold. I look at her, surprised that she is neither of the people I was expecting. I don't know this woman. She has shoulder-length black hair, expensively cut, and is wearing an immaculate grey trouser suit with high-heeled boots. Her body is slender and toned, the body of someone who exercises with a personal trainer every day, even on Sundays. She is perfectly made-up and manicured, a Manhattan career woman in every respect, until she opens her mouth.

'Hello, Evie,' she says, and her smile is sudden and familiar. 'Long time no see.'

I grip the back of the chair and look down at my white fingernails.

'Louise?' I ask. The word is barely audible.

'I hoped you'd remember me. Congratulations on your performance. It was stunning.'

'Thanks.'

I meet her eyes, and, unable to read them, look away again. Even though she has come to me at the most triumphant moment of my life to date, I am instantly feeling awkward, inferior, embarrassed. For the past eight years I have hoped that Louise has been watching, and today she was. I should be happy that she witnessed my triumph. But for all these years I have also been hoping that she's a miserable failure. She is clearly not, in material terms at least.

'When I saw your name on the programme I had to come along,' she adds, looking around the room. 'I'm a member of My Lincoln Center, you see, so I get the programmes emailed to me in advance. Your name jumped off the screen.'

'You live in New York?' All this time I have been looking for my daughter, when the person who was coming to my concert was Louise.

'Yes, I've been here for years now. I was headhunted from London about six years back. And once you get here, believe me, it's hard to get away. I wouldn't want to.'

'No, it's a good place to be.'

'It's been a long time, Evie. I've seen you on telly a thousand times. How are you getting on?'

'Fine, thanks.'

'Are you heading for the bar? I saw your friends leaving the room about ten minutes ago.'

'You've been watching?'

'I wanted to say hello, but I didn't want to intrude while you had guests.'

'Oh. Right.'

I pack up all my things. I don't want Louise to see anything personal. I start to take down the good-luck cards from the dressing table. As my hand moves towards them, Louise picks one up and looks at it.

' "All our love and thoughts from Mum, Phil, Taylor and Tessa"!' she exclaims. 'How are your mum and Phil? And Taylor too, he was only about five last time I saw him. What is he now, eighteen or something? Who's Tessa?'

I see her looking at me, intrigued. She thinks, I realise, that Tessa is my daughter, that I reversed the adoption and took her home.

'Mum and Phil had a baby when I was eighteen,' I tell her coldly, taking the card from her and putting it in my bag. 'She's twelve now.' I say it firmly, and leave her to do the maths, but I'm sure she won't believe me. She will be wondering, now, whether Tessa is actually nearly fifteen. Whether she is Elizabeth. 'Taylor's twenty,' I add. 'He's all grown up.'

I pick up my bag and sling my cello over my back, hang the dress in its cover over the crook of my elbow, and motion to Louise to open the door.

'Let me take something,' she offers, reaching for my bag. I keep tight hold of it.

'No,' I say. 'I'm balanced like this, and I'm used to lugging a cello around.' I don't want her touching any more of my things.

We walk down corridors side by side. I am amazed by

the strength of my hatred. She has been nothing but bland in the past five minutes, but I detest her. I feel physically ill at breathing the same air as her, and her presence at my concert has deflated the achievement in retrospect. If I'd known she was there at the time, I would probably have gone to pieces.

Ron, Howard and Sonia know what she did to me. Nobody else has the slightest idea. I don't want to introduce her to Kate or Megan. She could tell them, and I know she would. Louise is my nemesis, and she has found me. There is no way I'm allowing her to accompany me to the bar.

chapter nineteen

Late April

Nobody could call this apartment grand. If I were a pop star, if I sold millions of records, if I was as successful as Dan is optimistically attempting to be, then I might have got a Central Park palace. As a humble classical musician I am allocated a studio in Turtle Bay, which is a district I had never heard of, a few blocks south of the Upper East Side, not far from Howard's old place. At first the area is full of pregnancy memories, but I push them aside and begin to enjoy myself.

The whole apartment is the size of our living room in Notting Hill. Meg and I share a double sofa bed, which in the day, through necessity, is a sofa. It is the one piece of comfortable furniture in the flat. We have a smeared window which overlooks the street, but as we're on the fifth floor we can't see it, and a rickety door on to the fire escape. This is where we sit on warm evenings. Other than that, our home contains a galley kitchen, comprising two cupboards, two gas rings and a couple of electric sockets, and a bathroom with a shower, a loo, and a tiny window which opens into a dark space punctuated only by other people's bathroom windows. It is minuscule, a negligible piece of Manhattan real estate, and I adore it. For the first time, I can really pretend I live here.

I like having Megan around too, in a funny kind of way. She keeps me from my terrors. I could never have moved in here without Megan as a flatmate. I realise, now, that I am a long way from being ready to live on my own. When one of us wakes up in the morning, the other is bound to join her, because it's impossible to be quiet. I have tried, almost every morning since we moved in, to creep out of bed, to tiptoe to the bathroom, putting a pan of water on a gas ring on the way, and to have a quiet shower, but it never works. If I don't swear at the eccentric gas ignition, I flush the toilet, and once that happens, the noisy plumbing begins its screeching and wailing for the day, a situation which is exacerbated by my subsequent use of the shower. When I step back into the main room, Megan is either sitting up in bed rubbing her eyes, or at the stove, making us cups of weak tea. The teabags here are different from the ones at home, and we have failed to make our tea anything other than watery.

I don't mind having her around. In fact, for the first time, I find I quite like her. I liked living with her in London, but I know that was only because she was awestruck by me and the sort of life she thought I led. We weren't friends: I was basking in her adoration. Now Megan knows me a bit better, and she realises that I am selfish and unkind and that my image is built on lies.

This seems to be a better basis for friendship. I don't understand it, but she doesn't seem to mind seeing all my flaws.

Megan hasn't judged me over my treatment of Jack. Kate and Ian were bitterly disappointed in me, and Ian has not said a single word to me since the rainy afternoon in the park. I can see our friendship slipping away. I will be distraught to lose Kate, but Jack is their relative, and he has been wronged, so I suppose it is logical that their allegiance is with him. It makes me feel empty; and it makes me determined to build a real friendship with Meg. I am coming perilously close to having no friends at all.

I worry that I will never form a meaningful relationship with anyone. I worry about Elizabeth. Meg worries about her parents, she worries about Guy, and she worries about my stalker. I have put the letters from my mind, for now. I worry more about whatever Guy is up to. We are a pair of neurotics, and we need each other.

She talks about her parents more each day.

'I used to be able to block it out,' she says, out of the blue, one morning. 'Then I couldn't any more. It is a huge denial. Looking back, I can't believe I managed, for about fifteen years, to pretend it wasn't happening. Home, you know? One minute it's all calm and normal and slightly boring, and then suddenly everything blows up. When the only home you have becomes violent and loud and absolutely petrifying, where do you go?'

'You get out,' I tell her, 'and you get your mum out too.'

'That's why I went travelling as soon as I could. But when you're eleven?'

I don't know what to say to her. 'No child should have to experience that,' I tell her, lamely.

'I know. But it happens all the time, even in "respectable" homes. I have to get Mum out of there. Do you think your mum and Phil would help?'

I sigh. 'Meg, I'm so glad you've asked. Of course. I'll call Mum and explain the situation.'

She smiles at me, and I return the smile. It feels good, and unusual, to be genuinely trying to help someone. I am not used to having no ulterior motives.

'You know when you worked in banking?' I ask her when she emerges from the shower, wrapped in my white towel, with her hair casting drips over the thin beige carpet.

'I do,' she confirms.

'What did you actually do? I never even asked you about it because I couldn't imagine I'd understand a word of it.'

'I quite enjoyed it, actually. In a funny kind of way. I prefer not working, like everyone, but there's something quite reassuring about dressing up in a suit and wearing proper shoes and going to work. I used to like myself as a worker. I didn't do anything high-powered. Talked to people on the phone, mainly, about money. Did things on my computer. You'd definitely have understood it.' I hand her a cup of tea. Megan has always liked it weak, so she drinks it gratefully. 'I used to do the filing half the time. I'm not exactly trained in finance.'

'But isn't that incredibly different from taking photos in Cambodia? Weren't you frustrated?'

She sits down on the bed. 'Not really. I don't think you have to be doing the thing you love best all the time. I don't think to do that does most people any good. It's different for you because you've made a career out of it, and it works for you, but I would hate the pressure. If I was out on assignment taking photos of something I'd been ordered to photograph, I wouldn't be enjoying myself. It's because you've never had a job, isn't it? That's why you don't get it.'

I consider this. 'Of course it is. Maybe I should get a job, just for the experience. Work in a bar or a hotel or something. I know my musical career isn't going to last for ever. But I couldn't possibly do anything else. No one would employ me.'

'They would.'

'Not to do anything halfway interesting.'

'You'd be fine.'

I think about it for a bit. I can't imagine that I would be fine. Everyone else seems to manage it, but I can't picture myself working for someone else, nine to five. I like being the centre of attention too much. I like organising my days to suit myself. I am profoundly self-obsessed; and I would be a dreadful employee.

'Evie?' says Megan, towelling her wet hair dry. 'I hope you don't mind, but I think I've got to go.'

'Oh?' I say, absently. 'Go where?'

'Home.'

I sit up. 'Really? When? Why?'

She strokes my arm. 'This has been exactly what I needed to do,' she says, 'and I really appreciate you taking me in like you have. But being away from home has made me realise that I have to go back. I stayed around to see your concert, but now there's too much going on at home for me to carry on swanning around New York pretending I live here. It's lovely of you to share your bed with me, but I know it's an imposition.'

I begin to panic. 'You're not imposing!' I tell her angrily. 'You're allowed to stay ninety days! And you haven't even been here a month.'

'I know, but I've got to go and sort my mum out. Haven't I?'

'My mum's a deputy head. She's brilliant at sorting things out.'

'I know. But Mum needs me as well. When she was most scared, she called me. I was the person she thought of and I haven't been there for her.' She pushes her hair back from her face. 'Christ. I can't tell you how odd it is to be talking like this about my own mother. She's supposed to take care of me, but I suppose she has done, as far as she could. I'm grown up now, and much as I would love her to be someone who would be a rock for me for ever, life's not always like that. She needs a rock of her own, and I'm going to go back to Somerset and I'm going to be it.'

'What about your dad?'

'What about him? I suppose ideally I'd get him to leave, but he won't, I know he won't. I can't see him leaving his beloved country manor and losing face with his friends. So I guess I'll get Mum to somewhere safe, maybe with your mum's help, and we'll leave him to stew. Then I suppose I'll go back to London. Not to Bedford Gardens, though. If I had enough money saved up I'd go travelling.' She breaks off and looks at me, a smile spreading across her face. 'Why don't we, Evie? We can both save some money and go off, have six months or a year away from it all.' She raises her eyebrows. 'That's what modern women are supposed to do when they see off their husbands, I believe.'

I try to imagine myself travelling. 'I can't,' I tell her. 'I couldn't take a break like that and hold on to my career. It would be disastrous. I'd have to come back and retrain as a primary school teacher or something.'

'That wouldn't be so terrible.'

I shudder. 'It would for me. You'd be better off taking your mum. When are you going?'

'Guy booked my return flight for about two weeks' time – I can't believe I let him be so bossy – but I've decided to change it. I'll see what's available.' She looks at me, big-eyed and more like a china doll than ever. 'Do you mind if I ring him? I'll pay for the call.'

I gesture to the phone. 'Go right ahead. Why don't I go down and get our breakfast, so you can have some privacy?'

I dress quickly in jeans and a pink top, and run my fingers through my hair. The deli is on the corner, and we always have the same in the morning. Two large skinny lattes, one cinnamon and raisin bagel, toasted, with butter and jelly, one banana muffin, and two random pieces of fruit. Plus a newspaper. It is all efficiently packed into a brown paper bag. I loiter a little before going back in the clanking lift up to our tiny home. I want Megan to have the chance for a proper conversation. I am nervous on her behalf, and on mine.

I don't want to live on my own. I'm not used to it, and I'm not brave enough. I would much rather be in Howard's study, or in a hotel where I could lift the phone and summon instant help if I needed to.

As usual, I scan the paper for news of Anneka. Sometimes there is a brief paragraph, essentially saying that nothing has changed. Today there is nothing.

I sit on our front step in the sunshine for a few minutes. A few neighbours smile as they pass me, so I can't look too much like a vagrant. A small headline jumps out at me. *Brit singer extends tour*, it reads. Next to it is an extremely smudged photograph of Dan. Dan Donovan, I read, has played to packed audiences. His song is in the *Billboard* top ten. He is about to start touring the States. I smile to myself. It is early days, but my eager young lover might be doing it after all. He must be in this city, and for a moment I consider seeking him out. His success would reflect well on me, and mine might even help him a little. On the other hand, I would only cramp his style.

Two teenage girls pass by on the other side of the street. One is popping gum. Both are wearing tight trousers and brightly coloured T-shirts. One girl is clearly not my Elizabeth, as she is black, but the other could be her. Her hair is highlighted, and she's a bit shorter than I am. She's pretty and confident. I would be proud to get to know her.

They notice me watching them and nudge each other and laugh. I'm too far away to hear what they say, and I stand up and go slowly into my building.

Megan is doing the washing-up when I get in.

'That was quick,' I say, trying to judge her mood.

'I know.' She doesn't look particularly happy.

'How was Guy?'

She rinses a cup. 'He was all right. I don't know.' She sighs and reaches for the brown bag. 'I thought I was

303

finishing with him but he didn't seem to get it. He wasn't really interested. He was just distracted. How does he expect me to be his girlfriend when he never rings me and when the way he talks to me makes me feel like I'm his secretary? He can't even let me finish with him properly, because he doesn't care enough.'

'How did you leave it?'

'Well, I suggested to him that I'm just another of the women he's used for a brief fling. He didn't disagree. One more on top of thirty years' worth. I'm not sure why I was with him in the first place, except that physically . . .' She looks at me and laughs. 'You don't want to know about that. He didn't really want me to come back. He was more interested in asking me to pass on a card or something to Ron. Because of his girlfriend being missing. I just don't know how to read him. I mean, if he wants to send Ron a card, why doesn't he just post it to him? Like with that woman?'

I can't think of an answer, so I take my bagel instead, and put my coffee down on the arm of the sofa, now restored to its primary function.

'I said that, actually,' she continues, 'and he said he didn't have his address. How lame is that? A surgeon can't find the address of a clinic? It's on the internet. He knows it's called Babylove because we laughed about it. And you know what else? I keep thinking about that woman. I mean, who was she? What was Guy doing?' I nod. This is something I have been trying to forget, without success. 'And since it's Saturday, and since she was pleased to see you, would you come with me to go and see her again? I'd love to know what he sent her.'

I swallow my mouthful. 'Sure. Why not? I'd like to know too. But, Meg?' She looks at me, eyebrows raised. 'You have got to do the talking this time. And you have to be prepared for it to have been something really bad.'

The doorman remembers us and greets us solemnly.

'We've come to see Ms King again,' Megan tells him with a smile. 'She's not expecting us, but could you just see if she's in?'

He stares at her. 'You've come to see Ms King?'

'Yes, like we did last time.'

He looks from Megan to me, and back again. 'You haven't heard the news?'

I speak first, but I already know what he is going to say. I think I've known it all along. I just haven't allowed myself to think it through. 'What news?' I ask him.

'Ms King disappeared over four weeks ago. She has not been heard from. I assumed that as friends of hers you would have been informed. In fact, people have been trying to track you down.'

Megan's mouth is gaping. 'She's missing?'

'Anneka King,' I tell him urgently. 'Her name is Anneka, isn't it?'

The doorman looks surprised. 'Why, yes. Of course.'

Megan and I exchange fearful glances.

'And how's her partner?' Meg asks him. 'Ron?'

'Ron is doing everything he can,' the man says sadly. 'At first people were thinking he had something to do with it, but nobody says that now. He's actually in the building right now. Would you like me to tell him you're here?'

Megan begins to shake her head, but I say firmly, 'Yes please.'

He is astonished to see us. The lift goes directly into the apartment, and as its doors open I see Ron standing, arms folded, waiting.

'Evie Silverman,' he says, 'and Megan. To what do I owe this highly unexpected pleasure?'

I have never seen Ron looking like this before. He's wearing faded jeans and a washed-out blue shirt which doesn't seem to bear any designer insignia. His face is drawn and he looks desperately worried.

'You won't believe it,' I tell him. 'It's so weird. But we don't want to intrude.'

I look around the apartment. It's beautiful, with light flooding in from the huge windows which overlook the park. Every surface is white, and the furniture is perfectly selected and immaculately clean. I would never be able to keep an apartment this white. There are piles of clothes on the chairs, and I can see a couple of bags full of them.

'Why don't you go to the coffee shop?' he says, after a while. 'I'll take a break in a moment. One block south, and one west, on the corner of Broadway. It's Annie's favourite. She'll find me there if she needs me. I'll see you in there.'

While we wait for him, sitting at a booth indoors and wondering whether to order another breakfast to justify our presence, we try to piece together what has happened.

'Four weeks ago,' says Megan, frowning. 'That must have been only a couple of days after we saw her.'

'Do you think Ron would have any idea what Guy said in the letter? She can't have said anything to him, because he would have mentioned it to me, for sure. We talked about Guy last time. And he didn't say anything.'

She shrugs. 'We can ask him. But I doubt it.'

'How the hell did Guy know her?'

'She didn't know him, did she? When I asked him who she was he just said she was a friend of a friend. He was no way going to tell me what was in the letter. I knew we should have opened it.'

'Meg, you wouldn't *let* me open it! And you told him that Ron's girlfriend was missing, and he didn't say anything about her being his Ms King?'

'No. He sounded mildly surprised, that's all. God, Evie, what has Guy done?'

When he joins us, Ron looks slightly better.

'There's no point,' he says, as he sits down next to me. 'The police have been over it all a thousand times, but I can't stop myself looking through her things, hoping to find something they've missed. Thank you for rescuing me for a while.'

'Sorry to have interrupted,' I tell him.

'That's fine. I'm baffled, but it's fine. I was going to call you today, Evie, anyway, so you've pre-empted me.'

Even though Megan's here, I can't stop myself. 'Have you got any news?'

He smiles. 'Nothing concrete yet, but I'm confident that we will get something.'

'What?' asks Megan. 'What's going on?'

'Nothing,' I tell her. 'I'll tell you later.'

'You're not having IVF as well?' she asks suspiciously. Ron and I both laugh.

'No,' I tell her. 'I believe a partner is usually necessary for that process.'

'Not necessarily, the way Ron does it,' she says quickly. 'Not according to Guy.'

Ron stares at her. 'What does Guy say?'

She looks away. 'Nothing really. Sorry.'

'That's right.' I remember now. 'Guy did say something, didn't he? I'd forgotten that. He had some half-arsed theory that you were offering to clone Kate or Ian.' I look at Ron, smiling. I want to make him smile. He doesn't, so I carry on talking. 'Anyway, look at Roxy and Tallulah Fontaine. They did all right, didn't they? A bouncing baby girl.'

'Guy Chapman said I was cloning?' he asks. His face is grim.

'He was just talking crap,' I assure him, wishing that Megan had kept quiet. 'He was a bit drunk. He didn't mean it.'

'Didn't he? What else did he say?'

'Absolutely nothing,' I say firmly.

'Megan?'

'Nothing. Just what Evie said. It was to do with using genetic material from the stronger partner or something.'

Ron shakes his head and looks at nothing, across Megan's shoulder. 'He should keep quiet.'

We tell him about the letter we delivered to Anneka four weeks ago. Ron is amazed.

'You've known all along!' he says a few times. 'I wish you'd made the connection. This is the only lead we've got. The doorman said two girls came to see her, but no one has had any idea of who they were. It was you!'

'She didn't know him,' I tell him.

'Of course she didn't,' he says. 'Why would she? I don't talk to her about long-lapsed acquaintances from medical school. He sent her a letter? A letter or a package?'

'Just a letter.'

'And you have no idea what was in it?'

'No.'

'Yet you happily carried it through Customs? Even after anthrax, ricin, and all the publicity?'

Megan nods, looking slightly ashamed.

'What did you say when they asked if you were carry-ing anything for anyone else?'

'I said I wasn't.'

'Right.' Ron shakes his head. 'Guy Chapman. The last bloody thing I need.'

When we get home, there is a big brown envelope wait-ing for me. I am almost nervous to open it, but it's just from Alexis.

Beautiful Evie, says his note. *Enclosed some fan mail. Congratulations. Speak soon, A.*

There are eight letters enclosed. I skim-read them. Alexis has sent batches like this before, and each letter has been so charming and appreciative that I half suspect him of writing them himself, Ron-style. As I've sat down to compose my exquisitely polite replies, I have wondered how many cranky ones he's thrown away.

A woman in Detroit is uplifted by my recording of the Bach solo suites, my signature tune if I have such a thing. A retired gentleman in Illinois thanks me for my appearance on his favourite commercial, and details the considerable trouble to which he has gone to find out my name and how to contact me. He respectfully requests a signed photo. A fifteen-year-old girl – my heart beats a little faster – whose name is Morgan, wants to be a cellist herself, and asks for my advice. She came to my concert and lives in New York. I study Morgan's letter carefully. It could be her. She could be my girl, drawn to me for reasons she doesn't understand. Her interest in the cello could be genetic. Except that it isn't her, because Elizabeth is fourteen, not fifteen. But she'll be fifteen in June, so perhaps she is exaggerating to make herself feel more grown up. I might invite Morgan to meet me for coffee, just in case.

The next envelope I pick up hasn't been opened. It looks as if it's been included by mistake. I open it with my mind on Morgan, but when I see the familiar font, I suddenly fear I am going to be sick.

you think youv got away but you will never get away, it says. *I know where to find you and find you I will, no need to worry about that. see you soon, love from me your friend.*

I lean back and take deep breaths.

He knows I'm in New York. Of course he does. It cannot have been difficult to find that out. The fact that he wrote to the record company, not to this apartment, or to Howard and Sonia's house, provides a modicum of comfort. But he is still out there. He is still coming after me. I have not escaped at all. I am still being hunted.

'Meg,' I say quietly, holding it out. I don't meet her eyes.

'Yuh-huh?' she asks brightly, and comes over and takes it from me. I watch her face as she reads it.

'Oh,' she says. 'This is a nuisance.'

I snort. 'You could say that.'

'But he doesn't know where you live.'

'He will.'

I call Alexis. I am dreading asking him about the letter, because I don't want to know how many he has hidden from me.

He is panting when he answers his mobile, but is as impeccably polite as ever.

'Evie!' he exclaims. 'This is a pleasure.'

'Sorry to bother you on a Saturday,' I say politely. 'Is it inconvenient?'

'Oh, don't worry about that for a minute,' he assures me. 'Although I might call you back in a half-hour. You've caught me rebounding.'

'Doing what?'

'Rebounding. It's an exercise class. Using trampolines. Evie, I can't tell you the buzz.'

'You're in a trampolining class?'

'I slipped out of the room to take the call. Don't worry, I'm not rebounding as we speak. Is something troubling you, Evie?'

'God, sorry,' I tell him, then force myself to articulate it. 'There was a nasty letter in with the ones you sent me.'

He is silent for a moment. 'Was it a letter typed on a computer, with no name to it?'

'How many others have you seen?'

I can almost hear his thought processes, as he wonders whether to be honest or whether to protect me.

'A few,' he confesses eventually. 'I was going to tell you but I thought they were cranky and harmless. Though I could of course be wrong.'

'You could. I've had these at home. The police have got them. The guy who's writing them tried to break into my apartment in London while Megan and I were there. I can't believe he's got to me here. Have they all been posted internationally?'

'I think so.'

'So at least he hasn't literally followed me. That's good.' I don't tell him about my most secret fear: that I might have been writing them to myself; that I might be completely mad. This letter was posted from London, ten days ago, so I did not write it.

'Would you like to involve the New York police?' Alexis is asking.

I think about it. 'Not really. Not right now. I'll let you know. Did you throw all the others away?'

'I'm afraid we did. We discussed it in the office, and that was the general agreement.'

I hang up the phone, imagining Alexis, in his Lycra, going back into a roomful of similarly earnest New Yorkers, to jump on a trampoline and partake of what I imagine to be the latest fitness fad. Perhaps I should have asked him how rebounding differs from the trampolining we used to do in the gym at school, but he might have taken any question as a sign of interest, and forced me to go with him.

'Today is going great, isn't it?' I ask Megan. She takes the phone, and dials purposefully. I look at her, eyebrows raised, and she smiles a steely smile at me.

'Guy?' she says. 'It's me again. I have no idea what's going on but I wish you'd been upfront with me about Anneka. I know who she is now, and I don't know what you're doing. If you know where she is . . .' She stops to listen, and tries to interrupt a few times. 'But,' she says. 'No, but . . .' Eventually she raises her voice. 'You do know what I'm talking about,' she says angrily, 'because you do know that she was Ron's girlfriend, and when I told you she was missing you never said she was the same *friend* of yours that we gave that letter to. . . Yes, *gave*, not posted. Anyway, what I'm ringing for is to say that we're finished. Over. No arguments. That is what I was trying to say this morning.' She stops, and listens to him, rolling her eyes to the ceiling. 'Guy, you *don't* love me. No I don't. I don't. I might have done, I'm not sure, but I don't now. Fine, do what you like, I don't care, it's up to you.'

She hangs up and smiles at me. 'That's got rid of him. He wasn't happy. This is such a relief, I don't know why I didn't flipping well do it properly sooner.'

I grin back at her. 'One good thing to happen today. Well done.' I look at the letters in my hands. 'It's got a bit claustrophobic in here. Want to go out?'

She nods. As I'm putting my fan mail away, and tucking my hate mail into a drawer in case it's needed in the future, I notice a small card I haven't read yet. It is not in an envelope, so I know it's been vetted.

Dear Evie, *it says, in neat handwriting*. It was so lovely to hear you play last Thursday, and to see you afterwards. I'm sorry if I surprised you a little by turning up like that. I would like to renew our acquaintance if you are willing, and perhaps to talk about what happened to us all those years ago. My contact details are below. I hope to hear from you.

With all good wishes,

Louise Parker

I make a face and throw it into the bin. Megan fishes it out, curious.

'What's wrong with this?' she asks, skimming it. 'I thought she was your friend? This is nice, very polite. Don't you want to see her? Aren't you curious?'

'No I'm not.'

'And this is because you had some bust-up when you were fifteen?'

I tried to explain my intense reaction to seeing Louise the other week, but because I couldn't add any details, no one was impressed. Everybody except Howard and Sonia and Ron thought I was being petty.

'She really, really screwed me,' I say firmly. 'I hated her and I still do. Nothing on earth would induce me to start being matey with her now.'

'But she might be cool,' Megan complains. 'And she could show us round town and introduce us to her friends. She might know some nice single blokes. One last night of fun before I go home . . .'

I look at her suspiciously. 'You only like crumbly old men.'

'I'm thinking it's time to try something new,' she says with a wink. 'I mean, there are a lot of men out there, and younger ones might not have quite so much baggage.'

I shake my head and put my shoes on. 'Come on,' I tell her abruptly, walking to the door and holding it open.

'Walk in the park. Gorgeous weather, nice cold drink, blow away the cobwebs and we can both enjoy being single without chasing every young man in Manhattan.'

She bounds after me like a puppy. 'Sounds OK to me.'

chapter twenty

Two days later

Alexis doesn't make me go trampolining, but he does take me to his gym. I pant and puff, go red in the face, and try to look calm. When I look around, I see bodies. I don't look at the people, just at their bodies. I am feeling fiercely inadequate, though people seem to be ignoring me. I keep thumping on, on the treadmill, not increasing or decreasing my speed, and trying to look less exhausted than I feel. I want to look as cool as everyone else does. There is a woman, two treadmills down, who is filing her nails as she runs. I can't take my eyes off her, in the mirror. She is wearing purple Lycra hotpants and a tiny tube top which displays her iron stomach. Her frame is minuscule.

This is hell. The room is air-conditioned, but I'm sweating far too much. I have never been fond of gyms, and at home have easily kept my figure by eating healthily most of the time and walking everywhere I can. Now I have discovered, thanks to Alexis, that because I'm going to go on television, I need to make myself 'Hollywood slender'.

'I know,' he told me, 'that you already do Atkins, and believe me, Evie, that is wonderful. I would be seriously worried if you didn't follow a reputable nutritional regime. But I think we could add some tone to the package. I'm thinking Jennifer Aniston. Snare yourself a Brad.'

The next day he delivered me a guest pass to his gym. Not only that, but he brought me here, personally, and introduced me to the receptionists and a couple of personal trainers. He is currently on a rowing machine, behind me and to my right, keeping a close eye on my blotchy thighs. Every time I look at him in the mirror, he gives me a wave and mouths, 'You're doing great!'

I had to buy myself some work-out clothes, so I'm dressed in a pair of three-quarter-length Lycra cycling pants and the loosest T-shirt I could find in the sports shop. It is black, so at least the sweat patches are camou-flaged, and it says 'Baby' across the breasts. I thought it was cute, until I had the horrible realisation that it is prob-ably a maternity top. New York women wear these over their bumps, when they go to pregnancy aerobics or maternity pilates. That would explain its bagginess.

If Alexis wasn't in the room, I would leave, shower, have a large breakfast, and call him later to tell him what a great work-out I'd had. Because he's here, I have to carry on for as long as he does, and I fear it's going to be closer to two hours than one.

I try to forget that I'm running, in a crowded room full of semi-naked people. I let my mind drift back to Ron. He wants to see me later today, and I can't wait to hear what he's going to say. I don't dare hope, so I wonder if it could be to do with Guy. Megan arrived in Bristol yesterday, went straight to Guy's house, and found that he was out. The police want to speak to him, Ron has tried to call him, but he too seems to have vanished.

We gave Anneka a letter from Guy, without knowing what was in it. She immediately disappeared. Whatever was in the envelope must have, somehow, made her leave. It could have contributed to her death. I don't know what it could have been or how it could have worked, but it is possible. Ron mentioned anthrax and ricin: that is what got me thinking. The news is always full of poison gases and dirty bombs. Guy is a medical man. He would have access to hospital chemicals. I wish I had any sort of science background so I would be able to speculate a little better. The fact that he too has disappeared is more incriminating than anything else.

What Guy might have written to Anneka is a mystery. I am seeing Ron later. I intend to make him tell me everything he knows about Marianne, and why Mum and Phil went so strange when I mentioned Ron's name. Megan and I are caught up in something we don't understand at all.

I am lost without her. Kate and Ian are leaving next week, after their scan. Perhaps it has been too easy, living here in a free apartment, with my closest friends around me. Life does not carry on like that, and the day is almost here when I will have to make a few decisions.

My career is going well. My marriage is over. Those are the only definite things in my life. I have nowhere to live, few friends, a stalker who I never shook off after all, and a phantom daughter. And I am directly responsible for whatever has happened to Anneka.

I am supposed to be going on television next week. All my friends will be gone, and I'll be in my apartment on my own. I am so convinced that the stalker, whether he's Guy or the old *Sun*-reading pervert, might track me down that I am considering moving back into Howard's study, or going home altogether. After the rash of TV appearances Alexis has conjured up for me, I will have to go back. New York is a wonderful place to be, but even Manhattan doesn't contain enough magic for me right now.

At least Kate and Ian are doing well. Ian is treating Kate like a delicate china vase, and she's not straining herself by doing anything whatsoever, as far as I can tell. Whenever I meet them, they turn up by taxi. I always want to suggest, as gently as I can, that there is no need for her to act like an invalid, but I know how much depends upon this pregnancy being successful.

My attempts to lose myself in thought are unsuccessful. I think I prefer exercise to thinking. At least if you're puffing, red-faced, on a treadmill, you are doing something. It is possible to forget everything else and concentrate on the embarrassment and the agony. These are comfortingly shallow preoccupations. I will exercise more. I begin to see why people do it.

I hate the music. It's too loud, too relentless. I know someone, somewhere, is trying to motivate me with these interminable garagey thuds, but I can't bear it. If I had a set of headphones, I would wear them just to block out the sound. I wouldn't tune into 'cardio-theater' at all, unless it has a classical channel.

The garage track finishes, and to my surprise a familiar voice comes over the sound system. Dan's sole hit – 'If You Want Me' – has been remixed to a dance beat, and I laugh as I run. If they are playing him in the gyms of Manhattan, he must be doing something right. I catch Alexis's eye in the mirror, point to the speaker, then mouth the words, 'I know him.' He raises his eyebrows and motions me to stop running.

'Did you say you know Dan Donovan?' he asks, standing next to my treadmill.

'Dan and I had a brief fling,' I tell him.

'Please, Evie,' he interrupts. 'A romance, not a fling.'

'OK. We had a romance around Christmas last year. It had a lot of coverage in the British media. It fizzled out very quickly, though, mainly because he's younger than my little brother, and his management didn't approve. They thought I was way too old and experienced for him.'

'Of course they did. A married woman such as yourself is not the right demographic. I presume they want to keep him single for the target audience?'

'Quite. Anyway, it was never exactly serious.'

'But he's doing very well here. You must have heard this song everywhere? We can use your connection, Evie. Could you be seen with him in New York? It would do you the world of good.'

I sigh. 'Really? He's quite hard work, conversationally. Very young.'

'Your point being? You'll need to seek him out yourself, because his people here will have exactly the same issues with you as his people in London did. Captivate him, Evie. Take him out. Show him off. It sells.'

I row five miles upstream and strain my arms. Then I cycle for twenty minutes and flick through a copy of *Vogue*, which doesn't mention me at all. I would never normally expect to find my name in a random copy of an expensive magazine, but Alexis has raised my expectations, to the point where I feel I should see myself everywhere. I almost think they owe it to me now.

Finally, we do some free weights together. Alexis grabs some unfeasibly large dumb-bells and does some rapid tricep curls. I copy him with the smallest weights on the stand, and still struggle when I reach five repetitions. I hate weights, and I think I would prefer to be rebounding. I don't share this thought with Alexis. If I did, I know what would happen.

Is this, I wonder, my future? Will I find it slightly easier next time I come here, and easier still the time after that? Will my daily routine soon incorporate an early gym visit in place of my early cello practice? Am I going to stay here and become an honorary New Yorker, like Louise?

I shower with relief, and change, and dry my hair and redo my make-up. My body is aching, but pleasantly, and I am finally experiencing a little of the serotonin buzz that Alexis promised me. It does not compensate for the trials of organised exercise, and I can't get over the strangeness of working out in a windowless room with fifty other people, all pedalling or running furiously and getting nowhere. Still, I will come again, because Alexis will force me. I will go out on a date with Dan again, also because Alexis will force me. It is almost pleasant to have someone else to make my decisions for me.

* * *

'Thanks for coming before Kate and Ian,' says Ron, smiling and handing me the inevitable cup of coffee. 'I wanted to see you and I know they want you around for the scan.'

'It's a pleasure,' I tell him warmly. 'Any news on Anneka?'

'No. No sign of Guy yet either. He's not making things any better for himself. Anyway, have a seat.'

I can't hold off any longer. 'Have you got anything for me?'

Ron laughs. He is making more eye contact than usual, and I hope that is a good sign. 'I can't blame you for being keen. At least sit down first.'

We are in his sitting room, again. I notice a framed photo of Anneka on the mantle.

'Nice photo,' I tell him. 'Was it there before?'

He looks at it. 'No. If things had turned out differently I would have papered the room with photos of Annie and our baby when the time came. I was holding out for that. Who knows? There might even have been wedding photographs too.'

'Maybe there still will be, one day.'

'Maybe.'

'How are you doing?'

He puts his head on one side. 'I'm getting by, thanks. Now let's talk about you.' He smiles broadly, and it looks genuine. 'More to the point, let's talk about Miss Darcey D'Angelo, your fabulously named daughter.'

I gasp. 'Darcey D'Angelo? Baby Elizabeth?'

He nods, and takes a slip of paper from his pocket and hands it to me. I unfold it. I stand up, unable to keep still, and he does too.

'Darcey D'Angelo,' I read, 'daughter of Frank and Carla

D'Angelo.' There is an address in Stowe, Vermont. 'She's in Vermont?' I add. 'How far is that?'

'That's their last known address. She may not be there now. It's quite a schlep away. Maybe two hundred miles north of Boston.' He looks at me. '*Not* that you're going to go and find her.'

'Of course I'm not. Do you know anything else about her?'

'Evie, I'm nervous at having done this much. It's illegal. You mustn't go and find her.' He says the words sternly, but his eyes are kind, and I know he knows I have to see her. He wouldn't have given me her address otherwise.

I pocket the piece of paper. 'Thanks, Ron. You're fantastic.' I look at him. 'Really.'

He puts a hand on my waist. 'No, Evie, thank you. It's been good to be able to help you with this, and I appreciate your friendship. It's funny how few friends I actually appear to have.'

'I don't believe you.'

'It's true. Life is full of people, but when something like this happens, you see what you really mean to them. I don't blame them for doubting me, but it makes me sad. I mean, I would doubt me too.'

'You mean people think you've done something to Anneka?'

'It's the obvious explanation, isn't it? She vanishes without trace, and I'm the boyfriend. The police seem satisfied that I didn't do anything, but Annie's friends are less logical, and like I said, I don't blame them.'

'Aurora trusts you.'

'Aurora knows me.'

'Well I don't doubt you. I'd trust you completely, Ron, *even though* I know about your fake cards.'

His hand is still on my waist. I realise that it's there for a reason. When I look at him, I see he's gazing at me intensely. I decide that I don't mind. It is probably high time I kissed someone, and I would rather it was Ron than Dan.

He puts his other hand on my waist, and pulls me towards him.

'Evie,' he says, looking hard into my eyes.

'Ron,' I say lightly. I try to glance away, but then I look back at him. Ron is well preserved and I like the smile lines around his eyes and mouth. He is a fantastically unlikely partner for me. He doesn't stop staring. I wait for him to kiss me, but he drops his hands.

'Sorry,' he says. I am a little disappointed. I'm more disappointed than I should be, considering that he's fifty-five and a shady character.

'Sorry for what?' I ask, a little tersely.

'Sorry for this.' He gestures to the room at large. 'Sorry for grabbing you. I'm far too old for you, and as you yourself said, the best that can be said of me is that I'm dapper.'

'That's not true,' I tell him. 'Actually, I didn't mind at all.'

He raises an eyebrow. 'Really?'

'Yes. Although I know I'm just a distraction, because your head is full of Anneka. Obviously this is not the moment for anything serious. And that's all right by me. We both need a distraction.'

He is perfectly good-looking in his way. He's fit and he's kind and he likes me. He is enormously rich. He knows my secret and he hasn't judged me. I will be grateful to

324

him for ever for finding my baby. Besides which, I am not exactly inundated with offers.

'Maybe we could have a drink sometime?' he asks, hesitantly.

I smile at him, hoping that my face doesn't show how odd, yet welcome, this sudden change in our circumstances feels.

We are interrupted, happily, by Aurora, paging Ron to let him know that 'the Dawsons' have arrived. Kate and Ian now have their own rental car, having spent a small fortune on taxis in the city, so I have been spared the need for awkward explanations regarding my own appointment with Ron. Ron snaps back into professional mode and I can see the relief on his face as we revert to our normal roles.

'Wait in here if you like,' he says, halfway out of the door. 'I'll call you on that phone once we've scanned her. There's nothing quite like seeing the heartbeat. I won't even ask Kate if she'd consider inviting you in, since at this stage it has to be a vaginal scan.'

I laugh. 'Fair enough. Definitely one for gynaecologists and other halves only.'

When he's gone, I stand at the window and look out at the grounds. In the near distance I see a woman sitting on a bench under a tree. From here, I can't see her expression.

I take the piece of paper out of my pocket, and read it again. She was Elizabeth Silverman for five minutes, and now she is Darcey D'Angelo. The name makes her sound dark and glamorous, but she can't really be black-haired and dark-eyed. She has no Italian ancestry. She must be fair. Perhaps she is the only pale member of a Mediterranean family: the blonde sheep of the family.

Vermont is north of Boston, and Boston is miles north of here. I'm going to have to fly. I have to see her. Nothing could stop me now.

I am consumed by her. She is my baby, my little girl, and I have a chance to meet her. I love Ron, because he did this for me.

When the door opens, twenty minutes later, I jump. I have been in a daze, thinking only of my little girl. I wasn't expecting him to come back. I thought he was going to phone.

I barely look at him.

'Hello,' I say. I am in my own world. I'm imagining my future relationship with Elizabeth. I could get used to calling her Darcey. I'm sure I could.

'Evie,' he says. 'Can you come to see Kate and Ian, please?' He sounds far more formal than he did half an hour ago, when he almost kissed me. I look at him, puzzled.

'What's happened?' I ask him. He is completely in his professional mode.

'I have to tell you that the news isn't good,' he says quietly, looking me in the eye, then looking away. 'We were unable to detect a heartbeat.'

'Could you have missed it?'

'No. I'm afraid this is what we call a missed miscarriage. Which means the embryos have died, but Kate hasn't miscarried them. She will need a D and C to remove the material from her womb, to prevent the possibility of infection.'

I stop listening when he says 'the embryos have died'. This is not possible. It cannot be happening to them. We walk together, slowly, to Kate's room. I hesitate outside the door. Then I push it gently, and go in.

chapter twenty-one

The following afternoon

It's not hard to get a number for the D'Angelos, since I have their address. I hold my breath and press the buttons. It is extraordinary that a random sequence of numbers can take me directly to my daughter. The phone rings three times and then a woman answers it.

'Hello?' she says. I attempt an instant analysis of her voice. She sounds distracted, but essentially well disposed towards anyone calling her house. She is probably in her forties.

'Hello,' I say, my voice wavering as I try to decide whether to be British or American. It comes out exactly like a British woman trying an inept American accent. I plump for American. 'Is Darcey available, please?'

She laughs. 'I'm sorry. Darcey has a busy social calendar. You might catch her after nine this evening. Who may I say called?'

I have no idea. 'Roxy,' I say, on the spur of the moment. 'But I'll try her again later. Thank you very much.'

'Will she know what it is regarding?' Mrs D'Angelo is curious, and I don't blame her.

'No. It's to do with school. Nothing to worry about. Thanks.'

I hang up before she can say anything else. I lean back on the sofa and try to regulate my breathing. Then I realise she could have got my number and called me back. I stare at the phone, and for every second that it doesn't ring, I try to relax. She sounded busy. She won't be brooding on the strange woman, allegedly from the school, who rang for her daughter. If it was a man who had called, that might be alarming. Darcey must have female callers all the time. I might even have sounded young.

I try to imagine my little girl and her busy social calendar. I can't do it. The only way for me to get a picture of her in my head is to go there and see her.

I look at my watch. It's two in the afternoon. Darcey must be at school right now, unless it's the holidays, which it almost certainly isn't.

The buzzer rings, and although I'm not expecting anyone – although I cleared this afternoon especially for Darcey – I rush to the door.

'Hello?' I say breathlessly. I half hope it's going to be Ron. We both need the distraction.

'Evie.' It's Kate. I buzz her in without a word.

I stand in the doorway and watch her coming out of the lift. She looks the same as she did yesterday. You'd never know that anything had changed. Then I see her face.

'How are you doing?' I ask her, as gently as I can.

Her face is contorted. 'Crap.' She pushes me away as I try to reach for her. It is impossible to comfort someone at a time like this. I know that anything I say will be wrong. She sits down on my sofa, picking up Ron's note of Darcey's details and balancing it on the arm of the sofa without looking at it.

'Tea?' I say hopefully. 'Coffee? Alcohol?'

She nods. I try to examine her face, to see whether she's been crying, but there is nothing there but bitterness. Previously, when fertility treatment hasn't worked, she has been in floods of tears and I have comforted her with platitudes like 'your time will come', or 'it will happen, I promise', or 'you'll be a wonderful mother'. Before, she has nodded weakly and agreed not to give up. Today, she would clearly be enraged by such clichés.

'Was that a nod to alcohol?' I ask her.

'Why not? Nothing to lose. Lost it all already.'

'Kate,' I say, 'I'm so, so sorry.'

She waves my words away. 'I know. Everyone's sorry. I've been speaking to my family and I've had it with the platitudes. Everyone says it'll work next time and that it's nature's way and all that. No one has the faintest idea how it feels.'

'I know. And I would never say that I know how it feels.'

'You want to know how it feels, though? It feels like God has just told me to fuck off. It feels like I am the hugest, most enormous failure ever to have walked this earth. What can everyone else do that I can't? For thousands of years, the women in my family have had babies. Every single woman ancestor of mine, from my mother to my grandmother to some girl in a cave wearing a mammoth skin, they've all been able to do it, and I have a direct line back to all of them. And now I can't carry it on. And that's it:

no more family. Ian and I can't even make a baby. And when Ron made some for us, and put them in the exact place where they needed to stay for nine months, my body can't even look after them.' She is staring straight ahead, and her tone is flat. 'He told Ian he was implanting some of our embryos in someone else. We said he could, ages ago. It got us cheaper treatment. But I bet she manages to carry them. Not only can I not have my own baby, but someone else can. I'm not a real woman, Evie. I can't function.'

'Of course you're a real woman. Didn't you tell me that one in six couples has fertility problems? You would never look at them and say that they're not real women, and the men aren't real men. You wouldn't say that about Ian, either.'

'I know. It's personal. I had my babies inside me, and I was so certain that that was it. I actually let myself believe that we'd done it, and that now I would nurture them for eight more months and we'd be a family. I always thought that if I could only get pregnant, I could do it. I didn't mind if it was three babies or two or one, but I was so certain that it was going to work. I bought myself maternity clothes the other day. And while I was buying them, all three babies were dead inside me.' She laughs bitterly. I open the fridge and take out two beers. Kate takes hers and twists the top off.

'And the worst thing,' she continues, in expressionless tones, after a long gulp from the bottle, 'is the anger. I'm furious that we can't do it. We'd be good parents and now we're not getting a chance. We're broke now, because of Ron, but we'd be able to provide for a family. We'd give them a fantastic home. I'd stay at home with them and

331

they would have all the stimulation, everything a child could want. And yet I'm not able to do that. And at the same time you see teenagers with great big pregnant bellies, and you know it's happened by accident, and that just makes me mad. And the thought of someone else having our actual genetic babies . . .'

Even now her voice is flat. I've never seen Kate like this. She has always managed to be optimistic, or to pretend to be optimistic, before, and now she has lost all hope. I remember my conversation with Ian in the bar, and try to approach the subject gently.

'I know it's very different from having your own baby, but have you thought about adoption?'

She takes a huge swig from her bottle. 'Yeah,' she says harshly. 'Adoption. Of course. Everyone says that. Never mind, dear, there's always adoption. Ian's all for it. I'm not ready. We're going to have another IVF cycle with Ron first. Not that I can find it in myself to be excited about it this time round. I think I'd like to give it a break. Maybe six months. Only I'm thirty-one and every day that goes past decreases my chances. So we'll probably just take two or three months off and then start again with the bloody injections. It's a joy, Evie, it really is. You should try it sometime.'

'No thanks.'

'You're right, you'll just get pregnant at the drop of a hat. Please don't, though. Not yet.'

I go to the window and adjust the curtain. 'OK,' I say and hope she leaves the subject alone. When I look round, Kate has picked up the piece of paper.

'Is this Ron's writing?' she asks. 'Who's Darcey D'Angelo? A porn star?'

'No,' I say, too quickly. 'A kid he knows.' I think on my feet. 'A girl who plays the cello. He wanted me to maybe give her some advice. I might go up to Vermont and do a workshop at her school.' This, I realise, is a brilliant idea. I will get Alexis to arrange something. It'll be easy to find out where her school is. Of course, she is unlikely actually to play the cello, but I might meet her. She might have music lessons of some sort, though I won't mind if she doesn't. 'Good for my image, apparently, to be seen encouraging kids. Particularly if it makes its way into a press release. Apparently it's also good for my image to be seen with Dan again. So I'm supposed to be ambushing him at his hotel.'

'Right.' She drops the paper, no longer interested. 'Nice for Jack to see all that phoney crap in the papers again.'

Kate is a different person this afternoon, and I struggle to know how to handle her. We drink two beers each, and then I suggest an outing.

'Where?' she asks dully.

'I don't know. The park?'

She shakes her head. 'Let's just stay here. Sometimes it's better to hide.'

'Does Ian know you're here?'

'He knows I went out.'

'Do you want to ring him? He's probably worried.'

'Let him worry. He'd be better off without me anyway. There's nothing wrong with him. It's all me. He could have children of his own if he was with someone healthy.'

'Kate! You are *not* unhealthy. Let me ring him, please?'

'If he was that worried he'd have rung you. You know this is the first place he would try.'

Immediately the buzzer goes again. We look at each other, and Kate returns my smile thinly as I get up and pick up the handset.

'Hello?' I say, fully expecting Ian.

'Evie!' says Ron, faintly. 'Is this a good moment?'

'Come on up,' I tell him.

'Ron,' I tell Kate. She pulls her legs up and buries her face in her knees.

'Ron?' she asks. 'What the fuck is he doing here? You're not shagging him too, are you?'

'No I'm not,' I tell her.

'Do you want me to leave?'

'No.' In fact, I do, but I can't tell her that, not today. 'I'll get rid of him as quick as I can.'

He is surprised to see Kate, and they greet each other nervously. Kate gets up and announces that she's going to the deli to get some food for us. She insists it's what she wants to do, so I give her my keys.

'You haven't run away to Vermont then,' Ron says with a small smile, as soon as the door closes behind her. He sits next to me on the sofa and moves his leg slightly so our knees are touching. I don't pull away.

'It seems not.'

'When are you going?'

'This is where I'm supposed to say "I'm not", isn't it?'

'Humour me.'

'I'm not.'

'Good. Evie, the police have found Annie's car.'

I sit up, then slump back down because I liked the touch of his leg on mine. 'Found it? Where?'

'In New Jersey. And in it they found the letter from Guy.'

'Which said?'

'He says a lot of things, Evie.'

'Enough to make Annie walk out on her whole life?'

Ron sighs. 'It appears so. It's all happened very suddenly. Aurora discovered that her passport's gone. She never uses it from one year to the next, and Annie knew that. This morning Aurora went to look for it to check it was valid, because she was planning a holiday in the Caribbean. And instead of the passport, she found a note from Annie, saying she'd received some information about me, and that she needed some time alone to think about it, and that no one should worry about her.'

'Now she tells us! Has she gone abroad?'

'They're working on that as we speak.'

'What did Guy tell her?'

'That I'm the Antichrist. That I'm a Dr Frankenstein character who wants to create armies of clones. That I experiment on those closest to me and that . . .' He stops.

'That what?'

'I think you might have felt this, a little, over your baby. Though you have nothing to be ashamed of. You know the slightly sick feeling when you know there's something in your past that you don't want anyone to know, and you are absolutely certain that everybody will find out one day?'

'And every time you think about it you feel sick and you try to convince yourself it won't happen?'

'Guy's never said anything about this to you?'

'He implied that you have some dodgy practices, and I ignored him, assumed he was jealous. But it was clear there was something else going on. What, Ron? What is it between you and Guy?'

'I suppose I'd better tell you. It's very hard for me to speak about this.'

He pauses, then launches into his story. I sit down on the floor and lean back against the wall. 'Thirty-one years ago, Guy and I were obsessed with reproductive technology. We were the most focused, the brightest in our class, and that was the area that obsessed us both. We knew there was going to be a test-tube baby and a huge future for the manipulation of human reproduction. Whatever either of us has told you, we were the best of friends. We were partners. We shared a flat in Bristol, and we were going to be at the vanguard, together. Guy and Marianne were solid as a rock – I was very envious of them. I wanted that for myself. So, one day Guy told me that Marianne was pregnant. It wasn't planned, but they were over the moon, planning the wedding and so on. Sure enough, they were married in a trice, because that's what you did back then, you sorted it out before she was showing. He moved out of our cosy little flatshare and they set up home together. I do remember your mother, Evie, from that time. Anna Shaw, she was a lovely girl. Stunning. I may well have propositioned her and suffered a rebuff myself.'

'She was married to my dad and about to have me, surely?'

'Hence the rebuff, I imagine. Or maybe she simply found me repulsive. It took more than that to deter me at that point in my life. I remember her legs. She wore tiny little minidresses—'

'Ron! Shut up!'

'Sorry. It's not healthy to fancy both mother and daughter, is it?' I smile to myself. This is the first time he has actually said that he fancies me, and even though I can see the fling I had envisaged receding over the horizon, I am glad to be flattered. 'So. We carried on with our researches. I'd go to their house to eat a couple of times a week, and I'd bring different girls with me, almost for Marianne's approval. All I wanted in the world was a set-up like theirs. I wanted Guy and me to make a test-tube baby, and I wanted a beautiful pregnant wife.

'So of course it all went wrong. One night we were late at the lab, and then we went for a drink. Marianne was thirty-five weeks, so Guy wasn't going to stay out late, but one drink led to another and we were still there and it was nearly midnight. I dropped Guy home, because drink-driving wasn't such a big deal back then. I was blind drunk. What we didn't know was that Marianne had gone into labour early, and that she'd been waiting for us to come back. For Guy to come back. As soon as she saw the car from the window she came running out across the road to get to us. I never even saw her. Or I did. But it was too late.'

He stops talking. I try to prompt him. 'Did you hit her?'

He gives a little sound which is almost a laugh. 'Of course I did, Evie. You know I did. I ran her right over. Too drunk to stop. I went right over her and the baby.'

'Fuck. Ron.'

He looks me in the eye. 'So as you can appreciate, Guy has some fairly strong opinions about me.'

'What about the police? How come you didn't go to prison?'

'I got off by saying it was a medical emergency and we were about to take her to hospital. A tragic accident. Guy backed me up. He wasn't pressing charges. He didn't care about anything. He'd have said anything.'

'Was the baby a boy or a girl?'

'Boy. Guy didn't want to give him a name, but he did in the end because people kept saying it would help him. He called him Angus. It didn't help him, though.'

'He's never come close to getting over it.'

'I know. And he told the whole story to Annie in this letter.'

I look into his eyes. 'Ron.'

He strokes my hair. 'Bad tactics of me to spill it out to you.'

'He will never forgive you.'

'He wouldn't let me go to the funerals. We finished our training together and never really spoke again. I came over here as soon as I could, to get away from all the memories and all the guilt, and I've stayed here ever since. But I've never forgotten Marianne and the baby. Every life I bring into the world now is some kind of atonement.'

'Right.' I can't help feeling cynical about this. If he was trying to atone, he wouldn't be charging quite so much money. He would be working with pregnant women in the slums of India. 'So now what?'

He sounds uncertain. 'How do you feel about what I've told you?'

'I think it was a mistake that you've paid for. And I think it could just as easily have been Guy as you. He knows it was his fault too. He was happy for you to drive him home like that. You were in it together. So he has to demonise you.'

'I did it, Evie. I was at the wheel. I was so drunk I could hardly see.'

'What did the police say about his letter to Annie?'

'I told them it wasn't true. They weren't that interested in something that happened thousands of miles away, thousands of years ago. They're interested in finding Anneka now. As am I. I'm sure she's alive.'

A key turns in the lock, and Kate appears with a brown paper bag.

'What?' she says at once, looking from me to Ron and back again.

'Evie can tell you when I've gone,' Ron says quickly. 'Bye, Evie.' He stands up and kisses Kate on each cheek. She pulls away from him. 'Bye, Kate,' he says. 'I really am so sorry that it hasn't worked this time. You know where to find me when you're ready to try again.'

He leaves. Kate frowns at me. She is pale, her face still set angrily. I wonder whether she's miles away in her own painful world.

'What was that?' she demands.

'It was Ron,' I tell her, 'explaining what happened with him and Guy, and Marianne. Years ago, before we were even born.'

'Are you going to tell me?'

'Have you got me a muffin?'

She dumps the bag on my lap and sits down. 'Double chocolate. Come on then. Distract me.'

chapter twenty-two

Friday

Elizabeth lives in a wooden house, on a hillside, not far from the residence of, of all people, the von Trapp family, from *The Sound of Music*. The house is not huge, but is beautiful. It is painted white, and has a manicured lawn and a spectacular view of mountains. It is shaped a little like a chalet. I'm not surprised the von Trapps like it here. It is a little piece of Austria in New England. The air is fresh, there is a breeze, and I am so relieved that my daughter has grown up here, in the safest and most wholesome place I have ever been, that I can't stop smiling.

I am also unable to stop shaking. I am overwhelmed by a mass of contradictory emotions. I love my baby. I hate myself for giving her up. I'm terrified of seeing her, terrified of not seeing her. I am jealous of Frank and Carla D'Angelo. I am empty. Since they took her away and refused to give her back even for five more minutes, I have not felt her loss this keenly.

I take her photo from my purse and look at it. This is

something I have stopped myself doing for years. I have barely ever looked at the little pink face, the eyes, nose, mouth and ears that were made inside my body. In the photo, Elizabeth is wrapped in a blanket. She is asleep. She is perfect.

In being here, I am absconding from *The Late Show with David Letterman* and from a party where I was supposed to reintroduce myself to Dan. I couldn't care less. Alexis must be furious with me: I informed him that I was going away for a few days by leaving a message on his work voicemail in the middle of the night. I had too much else to think about: I could not bear to speak to him. This morning I left far too early for the airport, just to avoid taking his call when he got my message.

The only person I wanted to come with me was Ron. Now that we know each other's secrets, we belong together. I wanted to ask him more about Guy, to try to work out, with him, why Guy has been writing to me. If he has. His letter to Anneka was completely different from the letter I expected him to have written her. Ron, however, refused to leave the city. He wants to be there when they find Anneka and bring her back. He is obsessed with resolving his story as I am with my own.

I haven't brought my cello with me. I should be playing it every day, but I'm only going to be here for a short time, and I don't want to annoy the people in the Stowe Inn by playing it in my hotel room. I can't draw attention to myself in any way.

I get out of the car, and open a can of Calm Iced Tea, lemon flavour. I am developing something of a taste for it. I'm parked at the end of the D'Angelos' drive. There

341

is nowhere to hide – no handy café over the road, no other houses around, and not even a hedge to screen me from view, and I'm not sure how I'm going to watch the house without everyone in the house looking out of the windows and watching me right back. It might be better if I sat in my hire car.

It's hard not to be conspicuous when you're looking at a house which is surrounded by fields. If Elizabeth lived in the middle of Stowe, I would be fine. It is a picture-perfect town, with white wooden houses, like this one, a wooden church, and countless little cafés and bars and restaurants. A harmless-looking woman like me could browse in a book-shop for hours while keeping an eye on the house over the road, and no one would suspect a thing. That's how it would happen if I was in a film. Here, I have no cover.

I walk down the road a little way, and sit on the grass. Then I stand up and fetch my paper from the car. I sit back down and fold back the *New York Times*, narrowly avoiding scattering it across the countryside when a gust of wind attempts to seize it. If anyone asks what I'm doing here, I'll think of something.

Half an hour passes. Five cars have gone by, each of them slowing next to me as the drivers look with concerned faces, wind down their windows and ask if I'm all right. My iced tea is finished, and no one has come or gone from the D'Angelo house. If I had a pretext for going to visit, I would stride up the drive. Perhaps I could pretend my car has broken down. I'm sure they would help me, particularly if they recognised me from the advert. If I knew how to, I could remove or break a comp-onent from the engine, but that would be beyond me.

I put the bonnet up anyway. Then I put it back down again. I don't want to draw attention to myself, and if I'm sitting here with the bonnet up, I am almost asking for help. I'll feel stupid if someone stops to help me and the car starts first time.

Where is Elizabeth Silverman? Where is Darcey D'Angelo? I look at my watch. It is half past four. School must have finished by now, but she hasn't come home. I'm not even supposed to talk to her, but my heart is in my mouth. Every time I look at her house, I am petrified, but I know I can't pull myself away now. This is where my baby lives, and I'm not leaving until I see her.

I think about Kate, and wonder how she is. She scared me, the other day, and I haven't seen her since. Neither of them has returned my calls to the hotel. I called Megan this morning, from the airport, but although I know she's staying with her parents in Somerset, her mother said she was out and that I should try again later. I wanted to ask Josie what she was going to do, where she was going to go, but I knew she would hate it if I did. I should ask Mum whether she's been to see them. If I had a cellphone, I could call her from here. It would be a good way of filling the time. But I haven't, and I don't think I could keep my location from her either. I don't want to tell her about this until something has happened.

This is terrible. I can't spend the day loitering outside someone's house. I jump to my feet and, without allowing myself to stop to think, stride up the drive. The lawn on either side of the drive is well kept, with a bench under a tree, rose bushes around the edges, and a wrought-iron table and chairs on a terrace next to the house. This is an idyllic house. If it didn't say D'Angelo on the mail box, I would think that Ron sent me here just to cheer me up and shut me up. If I hadn't already called the house looking for Darcey, I wouldn't believe she actually lived here, and until I see her, I won't believe she is my daughter.

Two cars are parked to the side of the house. I ring the bell, and hear feet approaching inside. I can't turn and run, much as I want to.

The red door swings open, and a girl stands in the doorway.

'Hi?' she says, looking at me with a question.

I look at her. This is not my daughter. This girl is only about eight, and she has frizzy black hair. She looks like a D'Angelo should look.

'Hi there,' I say, and hope something good is about to come from my subconscious. 'I'm sorry to bother you. Are your parents in?'

She grins. 'Sure.' Then she turns and calls, 'Mom! Someone for you!'

Her mother approaches. She is like she sounded on the phone. She is in her forties, and dark, petite and pretty, with huge black eyes. The girl looks like her natural daughter.

'Hello,' she says, assessing me quickly and finding me no threat. 'Do come in. May we help you?'

I step into the house. The hall is carpeted and an immaculate vase of roses stands on a windowsill. I bet all the beds here have hand-stitched quilts on them. 'Thank you,' I say as graciously as I can. 'I'm so sorry to bother you. I'm on holiday here – well, I'm working in New York, playing the cello, but I'm here in Stowe taking a short break on my own. This is going to sound so stupid, but I'm a huge fan of *The Sound of Music* and I've managed to drive around in circles for the past forty minutes looking for the Trapp Family Lodge. Could you point me in the right direction?'

Mrs D'Angelo laughs. 'Honey, you could barely be closer! Of course we can show you the way. You go back along this road until you reach a fork, then take a left, and head up. It's pretty steep, but it's not far.'

I beam at her. 'Thank you so much. I have a shocking sense of direction.'

The little girl is looking at me curiously. 'Are you American?' she asks suspiciously.

'No,' I tell her kindly. This is my opportunity to get a conversation going. 'I'm British.'

'Do you speak French?' she asks, looking at me with saucer eyes.

'I do, up to a point,' I reply. I look at her mother, who is smiling indulgently at her younger daughter.

'Say something in French then,' demands the girl.

'OK,' I tell her. '*Bonjour, jeune fille. Où se trouve la banque, s'il vous plaît?*'

'*Wow*,' she breathes, gazing at me. 'That's clever. Did you learn English at school?'

'Ellie, sweetie,' interjects her mother, laughing. 'British people speak English, just like we do.'

'Nearly like you do,' I interject. 'I'm actually from England.'

'And England is where English comes from,' says her mother.

'Why do we speak English?' asks Ellie. 'Why don't we speak American?'

Her mother looks at me and laughs again. 'Do you want to tell her about the colonial days, or shall I?'

I jump in. I have to be as outgoing as I can, so she will invite me to stay for a drink and to meet the other daughter. 'America used to be the home of the . . .' I stop myself saying 'Red Indians' just in time, 'Native Americans. Then some white people came, mainly from England, on boats, and decided they wanted to live here too. So they did. Which wasn't so great for the Native Americans.' I look to Mrs D'Angelo. 'Does that cover it, in a nutshell, do you think?'

She laughs. She is, potentially, my friend. 'I would say that will do for now. I'm sorry to be rude, but have we met you before?'

Bingo. This is exactly what I needed to happen. That's why I threw my cello into the conversation early on. 'I don't think we've met, but . . .' I pause, mainly to show likeable modesty, but also to calm my nerves, 'I'm in an advert which seems to be on TV quite a lot at the moment. It's for Calm Iced Tea.'

Ellie jumps up and down. 'And you play music! And all the cars stop! I *love* that ad!'

I smile at her. 'I'm pleased to hear it.'

Mrs D'Angelo grins. 'I know the one. Fancy you turning up here in Stowe, and at our house. May I offer you a drink? Coffee or something cold?'

I relax slightly. I have tricked my way in. 'A fruit juice would be wonderful,' I tell her, with my very best professional smile.

We sit in the spacious pine kitchen, which is immaculate. I don't feel up to small talk, so I launch straight in with a question. I'm glad my life has involved so much insincerity. It allows me to mask my precarious emotional state, and to pretend to be breezy and casual; the charming stranger.

'Do you have any other children?' I say, hoping I'm not trembling.

'Yes,' she says. 'Oh, yes. Ellie is our youngest. She has an older brother, Mitchell, and a sister, Darcey. We always intended to have two, and then she came along, a miracle baby.'

'Miracle?'

'Very much so. The older two are adopted. We'd been told our chances of a child of our own were a million to one, for various reasons. We were getting along fine as a family of four, when suddenly, hey, I'm pregnant.' She shrugs. 'Just one of those things that come along when you're not looking for them.'

I look at Ellie. She doesn't seem to be traumatised at that description of herself. In fact, she's making a phone call.

'Darcey,' I hear her say. 'You have to come home now. There's a lady here from TV! She says she's British, and she speaks French, but she comes from England.'

'Would you mind?' asks her mother. 'Darcey would love to meet you. She'll be home in ten minutes. Could you stay to say hello to her?'

I don't have to force this smile. 'I'd be delighted. I'm Evie, by the way.'

She smiles and holds out a hand. 'Carla.'

The moment I set eyes on her, I know I have found my baby. She is as tall as I am, far taller than Carla, and she has my hair. She actually has it my length. We both sport a bob cut just above the shoulders, but she doesn't dye hers. I expect she will, but now she is mousy brown, like I was when I had her. She is fair-skinned and pink-cheeked, and she has hazel eyes. She's wearing expensive jeans and a tight blue T-shirt which shows off my old skinny figure. I can't stop looking at her. I must have turned deep, hot red, from my head to the soles of my feet. Darcey is Elizabeth, and both of them are beautiful. I knew my baby would grow up like this. Her skin isn't teenage and spotty, but clear and creamy. I never suffered from adolescent pimples either. She gets that from me. Not from Frank or Carla, not from Mark, but from me. And she seems to have an aura of confidence that passed me by entirely until I was nineteen. That probably does come from Carla.

I know I'm pink in the face, and I'm breathless. I know I have to appear normal. One day, I don't know when, but one day, I will need to reveal myself to her. I don't want her to look back on me now, and to resent anything, or to see me as a liar or a con artist.

'Hi,' I tell her, standing up and shaking her hand.

'This is Evie,' says Ellie, importantly. 'Evie advertises Calm Iced Tea.'

Darcey rolls her eyes. 'Yeah,' she says. 'I know.' Her handshake is firm. Her hands are a good size, like mine. She could be a cellist. She has wide pads on her finger-tips, and she could easily stretch to reach extensions. Her nails, however, are long and shapely and painted pale pink. 'Nice to meet you,' she tells me, slightly shyly.

'Nice to meet you too,' I reply, though nice is not, perhaps, the best word for it. I am getting from one minute to the next on automatic pilot. If I stopped to think about what was happening, I would grab this poor girl, clutch her tight, and cry all over her. I would beg her to come to England with me. Instead I say, formally, 'I'm sorry to impose myself on your family like this. I just stopped to ask for directions.'

'We wouldn't let her leave,' says Carla with a laugh. Darcey goes to the enormous stainless-steel fridge and pours herself a huge glass of lemonade. She holds the bottle out towards me, and raises her eyebrows.

'Sure,' I tell her. Elizabeth wants to give me something. I want to give her everything. 'Why not?' I hold my glass out, and will my hand not to shake. 'Thanks,' I add, and take a long swig of it. Then I sit back down, as my knees are trembling.

'Darcey?' I ask. 'Do you go to school locally? Only my record company suggested that I could do some musical workshops in schools, and I'd much rather do that in Stowe than in New York. It's lovely to be out of the city.'

Her eyes light up. 'Sure! I go to Stowe High School. They'd love to have you in. Will you still be here Monday? I can introduce you to my teacher.'

'I was going to fly back to New York on Tuesday, so yes. That would be great. Thank you. If they are interested, I'll maybe come back a week later or something. I don't even have my cello with me for this trip.'

'Evie has come to see the Trapp Family Lodge,' says Carla. Darcey is uninterested.

'Right. We've never had anyone from TV at school before.'

'I'm not really *from* TV. It's only an advert.'

349

Darcey shrugs. 'Right. TV is TV.' She stands up and smiles broadly, a smile I will treasure. I wish I could think of an excuse to take her photograph. 'I have to go now. Great to meet you. See you again.'

'Of course. Great to meet you too, Darcey.'

I watch my daughter slouch out of the kitchen. I am proud of every aspect of her, whether or not I have the right to be. Ellie follows her. I stay for another drink with Carla. There are a few things I need to ask her.

'I hope you don't mind me asking,' I say tentatively, once the girls are out of range, 'but my closest friend has just had some bad luck with fertility treatment. They've been trying for three years. She finally became pregnant through IVF here in the States, but then she lost the babies quite early on. They're thinking of adoption now. I'm interested in how that was for you, if you don't mind me asking about it. Sorry to be so personal.'

Carla laughs. 'As you've seen, it's a topic we discuss freely in this house. We were very lucky, you know. We took Darcey as a newborn baby – her mother was very young and had known through the pregnancy that she was giving the child up straight away. That was a kind of dream adoption. When you take them from that age, it really is almost as if you've given birth to them. We were so lucky. Everyone wanted Darcey. She was called baby Lizzie then. I'd forgotten that. It was what the nurses called her – I guess it was the name her mother gave her.' She shakes her head, as if to rouse herself from a daydream. 'Mitchell we found two years later. He was older – eighteen months – and that was much harder, but we got through the settlement process and he's done very well. It means there's only six months between them in age, and you should see people trying to puzzle that one out. They're often mistaken for twins. For your friend, though, I think you need to be prepared to take an older child. There are going to be issues, it's completely inevitable. However easily they settle, that child is going to throw out at you that you're not their real mother, and that's always going to hurt.'

I look at her. I've never thought about Elizabeth's adoptive parents, other than as an inconvenient barrier between me and her, or, at best, as the inevitable custodians who took care of her while I couldn't. Carla is a lovely woman, and Elizabeth – Darcey – seems like a well-balanced and happy girl. How differently would she have turned out if she had stayed with me? How different would my life have been? I cannot imagine. All I want is for my baby to be happy. I feel overwhelmingly grateful to Carla, though the gratitude is almost drowned out by the fierce envy.

'Do yours really say that? That you're not their mother?'

She shrugs. 'Sure they do. It's a gift to a teenager, particularly to a teenage girl. Darcey's nearly fifteen now, and she knows how to get to me. I usually stay calm, though. I tell her, "to all intents and purposes I am your mother." I would never remind her that her real mother didn't want her, but she knows it as well as I do.'

I am stung. 'I'm sure it wasn't really that simple, though. I mean, Darcey's a beautiful girl. If, like you say, her mother was young, it must have been a terrible wrench for her.'

'Oh,' says Carla, 'I know that. I am supremely grateful to her for starting off my family. I've often wondered about

351

getting in touch with her, and with Mitchell's mother, to tell them about the kids and to thank them, but I know it's Darcey and Mitch's decision really, and that it's not my place to interfere.'

'Really? Do you know anything about their mothers? Their birth mothers?'

Carla puts her mug down. 'I met Mitch's birth mom. She was mixed up with drugs, and he'd been taken from her as a baby and kept in care, and I met her when she finally agreed to put him up for adoption. She was in a state. Trying to get clean, and handing over her baby permanently. I can't blame her. I've often wondered whether she's cleaned herself up over the years. I hope so, and I hope if Mitch decides to get in touch with the Adoption Registry when he's eighteen that she will be able to see him.'

'How about Darcey's?'

I put my hands on my lap. I don't want to betray my nerves. I don't think Carla has noticed anything strange about my questions yet. She shakes her head.

'You know, I know next to nothing about that girl. Darcey was born at St Vincent's Hospital in New York, and I don't even know what her mother's name was. I assume the hospital has a record, but to be honest with you, Evie, at the time I kept expecting her to change her mind and take my baby away before I'd even got her, before she'd become my baby. As it was, she was able to make a clean break. No one thought it would do her any good to meet us, though I think today they would probably encourage it.

'I don't think the girl was much older than Darcey is now. Frank used to remind me constantly that, even when we went to the hospital to collect her, there was no guarantee that she wasn't going to look at her baby and change her mind. It was an emotional time. We had all the paraphernalia, far more stuff than we actually needed, everything for a girl and everything for a boy too, and we knew there was at least a fifty-fifty chance that we wouldn't even get the baby.'

'That must have been hard.'

'Hard for everyone. I don't judge either of their mothers, you know. I'm just grateful for the chance they gave me to nurture their babies. But, Evie, I am so sorry. Here I am spilling it all out to you when all you did was tell me about your friend and ask my advice about adoption.'

'Not at all,' I tell her quickly. 'It's so interesting to talk to you about this, and I appreciate your being so open with me.'

'We're open about everything. For your friend, I would suggest beginning the process as early as she can. Is she planning to adopt here or in Britain?'

'In Britain, I think. But she hasn't even got that far yet. She's still determined to carry on having fertility treatment. She's feeling very bleak at the moment. Her husband is interested in adoption, but Kate doesn't feel ready for it yet. Ian was talking about the feeling that they have to grieve for the natural child they'll never have before they start the adoption process.' I am babbling, relieved to talk about something objective for a few seconds.

'Never say never! Look at Ellie. But seriously, I agree with him. It's important to accept that your role is to give a home to someone else's child, and it's impossible not to wonder about their genetic heritage, whether they look

353

like their mother or father, and so on. Frank had to prod me to make that decision too. If your friends are ever coming to Vermont, or if they'd like to come with you if you come back next week to go to Darcey's school, we would love to invite all of you to dinner here and talk to them about it.'

'That's so kind of you. Thank you.'

'Not at all. You seem like an old friend already.'

The phone rings. Carla excuses herself and picks it up. It sounds as though she is talking to Frank. I put my head in my hands and force myself to take deep, calming breaths. I have to leave, right now, or I will give it all away.

The next day, Saturday, I spend alone. I haven't done this for a long time, and from the moment I wake up, in my insanely comfortable double bed with its patchwork quilt, I am surprised by the feeling of calm that has descended on me. I expected to be a wreck today. Perhaps I could stay in Stowe for ever. That would solve everything. The phantom letter-writer might track me down eventually, but it would take him a while. I would be far away from Ron and Anneka and Guy and Louise. Kate would know where to find me if she needed me. Above all, I would be near my daughter. I should start thinking of her as Darcey. I am glad, however, that Carla remembers she was originally Elizabeth. I hope she has told Darcey. Although I wouldn't have chosen it, Darcey is her name and it could be an awful lot worse. I wish they had called her Ellie, though. Ellie could be short for Elizabeth. That would have been perfect.

I feel as if I'm skipping school, though what I have actually done is far worse. I have skipped the Letterman show, and tonight I will skip my rendezvous with Dan. I eat breakfast on my own, with a book propped against my coffee cup. The waitress is friendly, and tells me to find her if I need anything at all, and apart from that I speak to no one all morning. I don't want to speak. I want to think. I spend the morning walking along a trail that takes me beside a river and across fields. I'd like to come here in winter, when the snow is on the ground and the town is full of skiers. Perhaps I will. I try to remember every word Darcey said, every expression that crossed her face, every move she made.

By mid afternoon, the work-related guilt is beginning to catch up with me, and I find a payphone and buy a phonecard. I postpone calling Alexis, and talk to Howard instead. He wants to know all about Darcey, and I describe our encounter in the smallest detail. It feels good to talk about it, and I know Howard is one of the few people who would not be bored by a loving description of a teenager taking lemonade out of the fridge.

'Be careful,' he reminds me. 'She'll find out you're her mother one day. Everything you say now, she'll be looking back on. Don't you think you should stay away, now that you know she's all right?'

'I know I should. I know exactly what you're saying. But I don't know if I can. I am actually here, now, in baby Elizabeth's home town. It's going to be hard to tear myself away from that. Nothing I've said to them has been a lie, or hardly anything. I suppose I pretended to be a rabid *Sound of Music* fan. But otherwise it's been omission rather than lying.'

'You're being disingenuous, Evie, and you know it. How

will Darcey see it when she looks back on it? You've walked up to her front door and into her life without telling her who you are. It's dangerous. Get out now.'

'I'll think about it.'

Howard sighs. 'Something else for you to think about. Alexis is not happy. You know you were supposed to be on Letterman last night. He's furious. He's called several times for you. You have a lot of bridges to rebuild there, honey. You didn't even tell him.'

'I left a voicemail message on Thursday night.'

'Yes, at his work. He said he finds that offensive. The least you could have done was told him in person, he says. He feels he's been made to look stupid – he went to great lengths to get you on to that show and now the producers are going to laugh next time he offers anyone. He takes it as a personal insult from you to him, sweetie. Really, give him a call.'

My happy life in Stowe comes crashing down. 'Sorry, Howard. I should have called his cellphone.'

'You should have done the show.'

'I know. Did you watch it? Did they get someone?'

'No, didn't watch it, but I'm sure they got by. They have dealt with worse than an AWOL cellist in their time, no doubt. And I'm sure you won't be asked back.'

'Oh well.'

'He said he's had lots of letters for you. He's been shielding you from them, but he was so mad yesterday morning that he told me.'

'Told you what?'

'The nasty ones. They are arriving every day, sweetie, more or less. And they're posted in Manhattan.'

I close my eyes and lean on the side of the phone booth. 'Wonderful.'

My correspondent is really not going to disappear from my orbit. He is after me and he has taken a huge step closer. Either the police must get him, or he will get me.

Despite my father's advice and my own better judgement, I go to school with Darcey on Monday. I haven't called Alexis, haven't called Kate or Ron, and haven't summoned the mental energy to do anything more than read, sleep and walk. The countryside here is beautiful: open and dramatic. Before my date with Darcey's teacher, I drive to the Trapp Family Lodge, which is now a hotel and timeshare apartment complex, and buy music, mugs and blueberry pancake mix. They seem like good, random gifts. It must swiftly become hellish for the women who work in the shop to have to listen to the music from the film, on a loop, every day.

'So this is where they came when they escaped from the Nazis?' I ask, mainly because I want to check that my voice still works.

'That's right!' says the woman. 'Although real life was different from the film. Very different. But this is where they ended up. Maria loved it here.'

'Maria von Trapp!' I am impressed, despite myself. 'Is she still around?'

'No, she died a few years back. It's her son who's in charge now, Johannes. He's the only child she and Captain von Trapp had together.'

It's sunny, and I have attempted, using the few clothes I have brought with me, to make myself look sober yet glamorous. Darcey will have told everyone that I'm 'from

TV', and I need to look the part. I am wearing Armani jeans, a tight red T-shirt and red strappy sandals. My hair is loose, and it's held back from my face by sunglasses on my head. I'm wearing enough make-up to make me look good, but, I hope, not so much that I look ridiculous. Normally I only make these calculations when I'm making a public appearance. This is more frightening than Lincoln Center ever was. It is my most important public engagement ever.

It is lunchtime. I park opposite the school and walk purposefully through the yard, ignoring the few kids who notice me. I have never been anywhere near an American school before, and even though I am nearly thirty-one, I am intimidated. I have watched too many films and TV series to be able to take this venue at face value. I know that you need a hall pass to be out of a classroom during lessons, that you need a date for the prom, that the children form cliques of popular blonde girls with shiny hair, and that everyone who's not popular is a geek. I would have been a geek. Now, on the surface, I am a popular blonde girl with shiny hair. My inner geek quails as I walk through an open metal door and into a wide hallway which is lined, as I knew it would be, with lockers.

Darcey meets me in the hall as we arranged.

'Hey!' she says, with a smile. She looks lovely in a short blue skirt and white top. Younger, and more innocent. She reminds me, on the surface, of myself at her age, and I ache for my lost innocence. To see Darcey, just a little older than she is now, sporting a huge pregnant belly would be heartbreaking. I know that, when I tell her the truth one day, she will ask about her father. I will gloss over the unpleasant banality of her conception. For her sake, I will try to make it sound like love, or, at least, friendship.

'Hello, Darcey,' I say, and I lean forward to kiss her cheek. I hope I will get away with this by being European. She smells of perfume and moisturiser and deodorant. She is clearly extremely clean, and she doesn't appear to mind being kissed. I have kissed my daughter.

'Cool. Mrs Mosse is waiting for us. She thinks it's a great idea for you to come in. So does, like, everyone else.'

'Great!'

We walk side by side. The hall is bustling with children, many of whom stop and stare as I pass. Word has clearly spread. Darcey swings her hips as she walks. She is, I realise, proud of me. She is proud to be in the company of someone who is recognisable from TV. I wonder whether she would be proud if she knew I was her 'birth mom'. I don't think she would be distraught. I could tell her. I could tell her right now.

Mrs Mosse, who is fat, blonde and friendly, is delighted to meet me, and Darcey looks from me to her, and back again, and beams. We arrange that I will come in, with my cello, next week. When I get back to New York, I tell her, I will check my schedule with Alexis, and liaise with Mrs Mosse over a day to return to Stowe. I omit the fact that Alexis is no longer speaking to me, that he has the power to end my career in the States.

'Evie's going to stay with us when she comes back,' Darcey says. 'Aren't you?'

'Am I?' I ask her, surprised. Alarm bells ring. *Bad idea*, says my inner Howard.

'Yeah, Mom said. If you want.'

'Thank you very much.'

'I have to give you our number so you can call to fix it.'

'OK.'

I already have their number, and I know it by heart.

'Wonderful, Evie,' says Mrs Mosse, with a wide smile. 'We look forward to seeing you next week. With your cello. We have a few very talented musicians in the school who will be delighted to meet you.'

'I look forward to it.' I turn to Darcey. 'Am I allowed to take you out for some lunch, Darcey, or do you have to stay in school?'

My daughter looks at Mrs Mosse hopefully.

'I'm sorry,' Mrs Mosse says firmly. 'Darcey has to stay here. Perhaps you two can get together next week.'

I smile at both of them. 'Of course we can,' I say, as calmly as I can.

chapter twenty-three

Tuesday

As I let myself into my apartment, I wonder whether I used to feel like this when I'd been away from London. I don't think I did. I used to like returning to the chaotic grey streets, because they signified home. London itself did not excite me. Manhattan is exciting me. I tell myself sternly that if I lived here it would soon become mundane, but I don't really believe it. It has taken me five and a half hours to get here from my daughter's town. That is manageable. If I lived here, I could see her regularly. She could come to stay with me. Every teenage girl would love to visit Manhattan. Every teenage girl except the one I used to be. My daughter, I am sure, will not make the same mistakes I made. Yet I cannot think of her existence as a mistake: my mistake is all in the way I have handled myself since she was born. I did not need to keep her secret. I am proud. I want to talk about Darcey, and nothing else. I love her.

I love everything, at this moment, even though a part

of my brain is aware of the fact that my life is falling apart around me. I loved the cab ride from the airport. I loved emerging from the tunnel a few blocks from my home. I love the way the sun makes all of Manhattan look like a film set. I love the fact that, for now, I have a home here. I can stay here on my own for a while. I know I can.

It won't be for long, anyway. The flat is messy and comfortable, and full of my things, and the answerphone is flashing ominously. I put my bags down, say hello to my cello, which is standing, forlorn and neglected, in a corner, and press the play button.

'Evie. Alexis. Call me.' There are several more in this vein. He will make me move out of here now and go home, and I don't blame him.

'Hi, Evie, it's Megan. Just wanted to let you know that Mummy and I are staying with your mum and Phil for a while. You might know that already. Give us a call.'

'Hello, Evie, are you there? It's me.' It's Kate. 'Pick up if you're there . . . OK, you're not there. You said something about Vermont but I didn't know if you meant it. We're giving up for a while and going home. Flying on Thursday. Hope you get this before then. I'll try Howard and Sonia's.'

'Evie? Ron. I'm home. I know where you are, young lady. I'd like to speak to you when you're back. Tell me you haven't had me struck off?'

'Darling, it's me. We're all missing you. Please call us. We're taking in Megan and Josie for a while. Love to speak to you. Bye.'

Finally, honeyed tones which I immediately recognise

leave a message. 'Hello, Evie. This is Louise Parker. Alexis gave me your number. He said if I tracked you down please could I get you to ring him. I wondered if you'd got my note? It would be good to see you. I feel I have a lot to say. Please call me. Thank you.'

He gave my number to Louise! The bastard. He must be furious with me. I pick up the receiver, stretch the cord as far as it will go, and lie on the sofa to start returning calls. I know which one has to come first.

I'm hoping for voicemail, but I get the real thing.

'Alexis?' I say nervously. 'It's me. Evie.'

I apologise profusely, without telling Alexis why I had to go to Vermont. He is not interested in me any more, and tells me to move out of the flat by the end of the week. He is cold and offhand, and is obviously in the process of dropping me as quickly as he took me on.

'I thought I could rely on you,' he says, several times. 'And I was wrong. That's OK. Now we know where we stand. I'm afraid we have no future together, Evie. We will honour your contract but all promotional work is off, as far as I'm concerned.' Somehow, I don't care enough. This should be devastating, but it's not. I suspect this fact means my solo career is as good as over. 'And Dan Donovan has been out and about with a very young girlfriend,' he adds, 'so I think you've missed the boat there also.' This, at least, is a relief.

I return everyone else's call except Louise's. If she's waiting for me to forgive her, she will be waiting for ever. Talking to my friends restores me somewhat. When Mum asks me when I'm coming home, I find myself saying, 'Very soon.' Of course I'm going home soon. The dream of living here for ever was just that: a dream. It will never happen.

I don't tell Mum about Darcey. I'll save it for when I see her.

I arrange to meet Ron for dinner, to update him and to let him update me. After I hang up, I go outside and empty the mailbox. There is a large brown envelope for me, from Alexis. I know what it will contain.

I don't even open them. I throw six white envelopes under the bed and try not to imagine what is in them. I don't want to know what he has planned for me. I don't want to know what names he is calling me this week. He knows so much about me, and I know nothing about him.

Then I get my cello out, and spend the rest of the afternoon playing. Even this lacks some lustre today. I can't use music to switch my mind off. I think about the almighty cock-up I have made with my career, and wonder whether it has been worth it. Of course it has. Now that I have Darcey, my career is secondary. It no longer validates me. I run through my repertoire without any joy or soul. It is mechanical, but at least I'm playing. I am keeping my options ajar.

At seven, I dress in a short skirt and a sparkly top, with a pair of shoes in which I can barely walk, and tidy the flat just in case I end up bringing Ron back. He might be persuadable. On the other hand, he is probably waiting for Anneka to come back. I hope I can overcome his scruples. It would be better to bring him to my grotty little apartment than to go back to his, because if we were here, neither of us would worry about Anneka reappearing and catching us. I fully intend to do my best to seduce him tonight. I need to get drunk, and I need to have sex. It is a liberating thought. Ron is not my soulmate, and will never be my 'boyfriend', but he is a very unlikely good friend. I can allow myself some fun, if he can.

As I leave the building, the early evening sun is making everything golden. The steps of the building opposite are honey-coloured. The sky is deep blue. There is still a chill in the air, but summer is nearly here. This spring has been perfect.

I'm not sure whether I have come a long way, or no distance at all, since the summer when I stayed here, gave birth to my daughter and bade her farewell all in one traumatic episode. I am beginning to think that I am, finally, getting somewhere. I might be able to sort my life out now, to look out for a new partner, to have no secrets, and to downgrade the career that was all about my looks when it should have been about talent. I am finally nearly ready to fit into my rightful place in the world.

I am smiling in anticipation of my first vodka-based cocktail when someone walks purposefully towards me. I don't look at them, because my mind is elsewhere.

'Evie,' she says firmly. She grabs my forearm. I don't need to look at her to see who it is.

'Hello, Louise,' I say. This is not entirely a surprise. She looks stressed. She's wearing a lightweight black suit with a short skirt and a fitted jacket. I keep walking.

'You got my message?' she asks, walking alongside me. 'And my card?'

'Yes,' I reply, without looking at her.

'Why didn't you call?'

I still don't look round. 'Because,' I say, 'I didn't want

365

to. I didn't see any point in our becoming friends now, and to be honest I'm surprised that you want that. You made it very clear fifteen years ago how you felt about me and I don't think anything that's happened will change that.'

She walks companionably next to me. 'But I wanted to apologise. At least let me do that.'

I still don't look at her. 'OK, you've apologised. Thank you. Fine. It's all forgotten. Now let's get on with our lives.'

'We were such good friends.'

'No we weren't.'

'You know we were. For years.'

'Good friends don't ruin each other's lives.'

Her voice is soft and persuasive. 'You've done fine. Look at you. You're nothing like you used to be. You're a huge success. You're on an advert. I know I did a terrible thing, and I'm sure it did ruin your life for a year or so, but you have more than bounced back. At least come for a drink with me and let me talk to you. Please.' I look at her. She looks back at me with big, soft eyes. 'We have all done stupid things, especially as teenagers. We have all been cruel. We all have regrets.'

I see a trace of my old friend, the old Louise, in her face, hear her in her voice. Perhaps I have wanted to be friends with her again for all these years. Maybe that is why she has been on my mind so much.

'I'm meeting someone in twenty minutes,' I say brusquely. 'Have you got a phone you can lend me? I'll put him off for half an hour.' She hands me a tiny mobile, and I call Ron. 'Right,' I tell her, handing it back and already regretting what I am doing, but knowing I need to get her out of my life, or into it. I can't have her hanging around on the periphery any more. 'Thirty minutes.'

We go to the nearest bar, which happens to be an Irish pub. I have a vodka and tonic, and Louise drinks a glass of sauvignon.

'So?' I say, as coolly as I can. 'What can I do for you?'

She smiles eagerly. 'You can say you forgive me.'

This troubles me. 'Why?' I demand. I notice men at nearby tables turning to look at us, and lower my voice. 'Why do you want me to forgive you now? I would love to forgive you for spreading the gossip about me, Louise, but I don't think I can. You were the only friend I had and you ruined it for me. I have hated you ever since. You have no idea how what you did has affected me.'

She stays calm. 'Evie, teenage girls do stupid things. I was stupid, I know. I'm not making excuses. I wanted to be friends with all the popular girls, and I still am friends with some of them. I didn't realise quite what I was doing. What gets me is the fact that you are clearly more than fine. My telling the others didn't do any lasting damage. So what's the problem?'

'Who are you in touch with?' I ask her.

She begins counting on her fingers. 'Katya. Sarah B. Sarah H. Jess. They're all in London except Jess. Jess is in Hong Kong. Katya's got a little girl. Sarah B is pregnant.'

I cut her off. 'So it's been worth it. You traded me in for them, and you've got some lasting friendships out of it.'

'That's not the way it is.'

'That's the way it looks,' I tell her. I am stung by the

names of the popular girls. I hate all of them. I don't want to know what they're doing. 'And I don't want to sound sorry for myself, but there *was* lasting damage, and that's just a fact. Going through a pregnancy like that and then finding yourself without a single friend is not something you get over. I'm not saying any more. Louise, please accept that I have the right not to want to be friends with you.' I knock back my drink, and stand up. I do not want to give in to Louise and agree to be friends again. A small part of me does, but I am resisting.

'Don't you want to know anything about what I've done since school?' she asks plaintively.

'If you'd been tending to the orphaned children of Sierra Leone I might be impressed with you. Making a vast amount of money in Manhattan doesn't really cut it for me, I'm afraid.'

'I'm not working at the moment. I'm getting divorced.'

'Oh, right. Still doesn't do it for me. I'm getting divorced too.'

'I know. From Jack.'

'You read the magazines.'

'If I see your name, then yes, I do. I know about Dan, too. You should have stuck with him – he's doing great.'

'Please give up, Louise. This isn't going to happen the way you want it to.'

'Am I embarrassing you?'

I look at her. I have to be hard. I cannot let her back into my life. 'Yes.'

She puts her drink down, and her expression hardens. 'Good,' she says, in a completely different tone. 'You know, Evie, I can think of many people who would be interested to hear about your illegitimate child. I've kept your secret for a long time now.'

'Someone told the *Sun*, but they couldn't find any proof.'

'I know, that was Katya. Katya is my best friend. We only did it to scare you. Otherwise we would have told them where she was born – St Vincent's, wasn't it? – and they would have found themselves with a story on their hands.'

I stare at her. 'Are you threatening me?'

She laughs. It is an unpleasant sound. 'No! Of course not. Just trying to get your attention.'

I put my head in my hands. 'You haven't changed. You're as vindictive as ever. I can't believe I thought you genuinely wanted to apologise. The least you can do is buy me another drink.' She smiles serenely and stands up to go to the bar. 'Double!' I call at her back, and she gives me a thumbs-up without turning round.

'I don't understand what you want,' I tell her, when we're settled back with our drinks. 'You are saying you'll make the story public, complete with hospital details, unless . . .? What? Money?'

She smiles. Her sweet smile is beginning to make me murderous. I can still discern the vicious teenager behind it. In the years since I have seen her, Louise has learned to mask her inner bitch, but it is still there.

Even then, she would never choose a confrontation. She likes to pretend that everyone is best friends, all the time. She does her dirty work with a smiling face.

'Of course I don't want your money,' she assures me with a tinkling laugh. 'I have money of my own. I had the forethought to marry a rich man. I have lovely apartments here and in London. You should come over sometime.'

'So, what?'

'I want you to admit that everything that happened was your own fault. Not mine. That's all. It is easily done.'

'What do you mean?'

'You see yourself as the innocent victim. You still do, I can see that. Remember, Evie, that I know something most people don't know. I know who the father is.'

I look at her, baffled. 'So? He's not exactly Prince William, or Elvis Presley. I don't think News International would stop the presses for Mark Parker.'

'You don't know what happened, do you?'

She wants me to ask what she means, so I don't. 'Did you ever tell him?' I ask her.

'Oh yes, I told him. He didn't believe me.'

I look at the next table, where four men in badly fitting suits are drinking pints of Guinness. One of them catches my eye and leers. I look away.

'I was fifteen,' I tell her. 'I was under the age of consent. It was statutory rape.'

'But it wasn't actual rape, was it? I was in the next room. I didn't hear you screaming. You were up for it. You knew exactly what you were doing.'

'I was terrified. I hated it. I wanted you to think I was cool, that was all. I was a silly little girl.'

'You made my brother take your virginity because I dared you to. How pathetic is that? You had his baby and you gave it away without even telling him. It wasn't just your baby that you got rid of. It was my niece. Remember? So, you clearly don't know what happened to my brother.'

'Of course I don't. I don't exactly have fond memories.'

'He killed himself.'

I look at her closely. I think she would say anything to get to me. She is playing mind games.

'Right,' I say, suspiciously.

'You don't believe me. He's dead. He hung himself last year. It wasn't a cry for help. He took an overdose and then hung himself, just to be sure. He'd been there for days when I found him.'

'Is that true?'

Her face is pinched and pale. 'Yes, it's true.' She takes a piece of paper from her handbag, and passes it across the table to me. 'I thought you might not believe me.'

I unfold it. It is a yellow cutting from the *Bristol Evening Post*. *Bedminster man found dead*, reads the headline. His name is there. Mark Parker, 32, was found dead in his flat in Bedminster after family became worried and broke into his home. The dead man was found by his sister, Louise, 29.

This shocks me, and scares me. I don't know what she is planning. My voice falters. 'I'm really sorry,' I tell her, trying to maintain eye contact, 'but it wasn't connected with me, was it? I hadn't seen him for fourteen years.' I look at her face. 'But I am sorry,' I repeat. 'I really am. It must be devastating for you and your family.'

'Uh-huh.'

'And in what sense is this my doing?'

She looks away. 'Mark was lonely. He had no one. If he'd had a child, he would never have done it. He needed responsibilities. He needed someone in his life. When you gave away that baby, you killed him.'

371

I wish I had a phone. I would text Ron secretly under the table, and get him to come here, now.

'That's not fair, Louise,' I tell her as calmly as I can. I am casting around for a way out of the bar. If I ran, she would probably catch me. I'd have to take my shoes off first, or I'd trip up. I slip them off under the table, just in case. 'I couldn't even face the fact that I was pregnant until my mum noticed,' I remind her. 'I was very, very young and naive. I had no idea what to do. Yes, if I'd been, say, twenty, or twenty-two, and your brother had got me pregnant, of course I would have involved him in the decision. But I was fifteen. Fifteen! And it was too late for an abortion. At least Mark's daughter, your niece, does exist, somewhere in the world. Is that some sort of comfort?'

Louise snorts. 'You can cut that crap.'

'Meaning?'

'Does the name Tessa mean anything to you? My mother said years ago that your mum and Phil had a little girl. I knew straight away what you'd done. You hadn't had her adopted at all. You'd changed your mind and got her back, and you hadn't told Mark or me. Then I saw her name on that card.' She stares at me, challenging. I sigh.

'I knew at the concert that that was what you thought. It isn't true, Louise. Tessa's twelve, and she really is Mum's and Phil's. It's easy enough to prove that if that's what you want.'

'Right.'

'Really.'

'I know you're lying.'

'I know I'm not.'

'It's a bit of a coincidence, isn't it? You go away to America to have a baby, Mark's baby, and give her up, and then the next thing we know, a baby girl has suddenly appeared at your parents' house.'

'Three years later. People have babies, Louise. It wasn't that rare, last time I checked.'

'I don't believe you.'

'I don't care.'

'As I said before, I can make you care.'

I stand up. 'Right. I've had enough of this. I was on my way out when you accosted me. Now I'm going to the loo.'

'The loo! That's very quaint. They must love you out here. It's called the bathroom, honey. The restroom.'

I look back at her as I walk away. My shoes are still under the table, and I've got my handbag with me, in case I decide to run away. Luckily there is a payphone next to the toilet door, round the corner from our table. I pump it full of quarters and dial Ron's cellphone, whose number, thank God, is written in my diary.

'It's me,' I tell him breathlessly. 'I'm with Louise. Yes, that girl. She's scaring me. Will you come and find us? We're at O'Flanagan's Bar on First near Sixty-fifth. Come now. Please. Sorry to do this to you. Thanks. Quick as you can.'

I go to the loo, while I'm here, and buy two large vodka and tonics on my way back to the table. I will stick it out, and wait for Ron.

'So?' I say, looking at Louise as calmly as I can. 'Where were we? I think you were in the process of blackmailing me.'

'Oh, Evie, I would never blackmail you,' she gushes. 'Don't be ridiculous. All I want is justice.'

'Meaning?'

'Meaning that Tessa belongs to my family as much as she does to yours. We want her. We want access to her, and we want her surname changed to Parker. It's only fair. She's all that's left of Mark.'

'Tessa is *not Mark's child*!' I tell her, too loudly. The men at the next table go quiet, and I lower my voice again. 'She is not my child. We can do a DNA test if you like, to prove it. I don't dispute that Mark was the father of my daughter, but that baby was adopted, here in New York. You have to believe me.'

'It seems to me that you are a popular girl. Last time I was in Britain I couldn't help noticing you in the papers every day wittering on about your marriage. The British tabloids are quite something, don't you think? I could help them out with a few facts.'

'Cheers, Louise. Why were we ever friends?'

She takes a delicate sip and puts her drink down. 'Why? Because you were a total loser, weren't you? No one else would be your friend and you clung on to me like a pathetic little kid. I took pity on you. I even introduced you to my brother. Got you some bedroom action. Helped you lose that geeky "virgin" label.'

'You're saying Mark committed suicide because of me. That isn't true. He didn't even believe you about the baby.'

'Don't flatter yourself. He wasn't depressed because he was cut up about a godawful random shag he had when he was seventeen. Christ, no. He was depressed about a lot of other things, and he was lonely. If he had known about Tessa, who was living *three miles away from him* at the time, he would have had something to live for.'

I look around, hoping to see Ron. Then I look back at Louise, at her controlled features, at the pain she is projecting on to me. I must keep her away from Darcey at all costs.

'Louise,' I say, trying to mollify her for now. 'I'm so sorry about Mark. I had no idea. I can see how painful this is for you, and I'd like to help in any way I can. But I can assure you that Tessa is not Mark's daughter. Tessa is my half-sister, and she's completely innocent. Please leave her out of it.'

Louise smiles. Nothing makes her lose her temper. 'Of course she's innocent. I don't want to harm her, or corrupt her, or anything like that. We like Tessa. That's why we want to see more of her.'

'She's nothing to do with you.'

'You know she is. It's a bit old-fashioned, isn't it, giving your child to your parents to pass off as their own?'

I look closely at her. 'Is there anything I could say that would make you change your mind? Suppose your assumption was incorrect? What would make you accept that?'

She shrugs. 'I would like a DNA test, actually. I want to see it on paper that that girl is my niece. Just to stop you pretending.'

'Then we'll fix one up. I'll explain all this to Mum and Phil and they'll find a way of making it OK for Tess. All right? I'm going back to Britain soon anyway.'

She opens her mouth to make yet another calm, vicious reply. I look round, and, to my intense relief, I see Ron striding towards our table. He looks tense.

375

'Ron!' I say, with the first genuine smile of the evening.

'Hello, Evie,' he says, charmingly, and kisses me on the cheek. 'Fancy seeing you here.' He looks questioningly at Louise.

'This is Louise,' I tell him. She is furious at the interruption, but she doesn't say so. 'You didn't quite meet at Lincoln Center.'

'No,' says Louise, smiling. 'I was sent away before I could tell Evie's friends about her scurrilous past.'

'Well, it's a pleasure to meet you now,' says Ron, unruffled. She takes his extended hand reluctantly. I move over and make room for him at the table. Ron goes to the bar to buy drinks.

'Is that your lover?' Louise hisses, as soon as he's out of earshot. 'Bit old for you, darling. From one extreme to the other.'

'No,' I tell her. 'He's a friend. He lives round here too. I've been to this bar with him before.' In fact, his city apartment is on the other side of the park, but I am keen to present this meeting as coincidence.

'Does he know about your past?'

'None of your business.'

She laughs. 'He doesn't, does he? Would he be interested to find out, do you think?'

'Fuck off, Louise.'

Louise looks up as Ron sets three drinks down on the table and takes the chair next to mine. She smiles at him and twirls a strand of hair around her finger.

'Sorry to interrupt you, ladies,' he says, looking at me with concern.

'No, not at all,' I say quickly. He has bought himself a

pint of Guinness. 'Louise was just accusing me of killing her brother.'

He frowns. 'I'm sorry?'

Louise is taken aback, but only momentarily. Between us, we tell him the story. He looks from me to Louise, and back again. I let Louise tell him her version, and just interject 'which isn't true' from time to time.

When she finishes, the silence lasts about ten seconds.

'Louise,' says Ron, eventually. She fiddles with an earring and looks down at the table, then back at Ron. She is flirting with him. He puts a reassuring hand on my knee, under the table.

'Mmm?' she purrs, her voice lower than usual.

'It seems to me that you've been writing some letters to Evie, haven't you?'

She doesn't give anything away, though her voice returns to its normal pitch. 'What do you mean?' she asks Ron, levelly. 'I sent her a card but she didn't bother to acknowledge it.' I reach down and clasp Ron's hand with mine.

'That is not what I meant, Louise. You've been writing her letters from London and you've been sending them to her here as well. Haven't you?'

She laughs slightly. Her eyes are bright. 'No. Why, is someone else after you?'

'Many of them,' Ron adds.

'My God!' I exclaim: 'You have!'

Louise looks defiant. 'I don't know what you're on about.'

'You've written me about fifty letters! You pretended to be a bloke and said you were going to rape me! Did you even come to the flat in London and try to get in?'

She looks away from us both, towards the men on the next table. 'I wasn't trying to get in,' she says blankly. 'I was trying to scare you. It worked. You came flying all the way over here, you were so terrified. Poor little Evie. Always the innocent victim. Luckily I have an apartment here, so it was easy for me to follow you. Very considerate of you.'

Ron leans forward and stares at her. 'Louise. You have obviously been through a hard time. I'm enormously sorry about your brother. I really can understand some of what you've been through. I think it would help you to talk to someone. I can refer you, if you like. I can also prescribe something to make you feel less depressed. Why don't we, we three, find a way through this together?'

She stares at him, and for a moment I think she's going to agree. Then her face hardens.

'I don't need help. I should have made it public years ago. I don't know what stopped me.'

I can't help myself. 'A last remaining shred of common decency?'

'Right. You would know all about that.'

She stands up, puts her jacket back on, and picks up her handbag.

'I've had enough. All I wanted was to ask you for access to Tessa, and you're not interested. So I'll leave.'

'I've said we can do a DNA test.'

'Yes, we'd better do that. To make it all stand up.'

She turns and leaves. I begin to stand up to go after her, but Ron restrains me with a hand on my arm. He pushes me firmly back into my seat.

'Pointless,' he says. 'Chances are she won't do anything. She's probably trying to scare you. But we're going to have to wait and see.'

chapter twenty-four

Wednesday

It is with some relief that I call Mrs Mosse and tell her that, due to a change in my schedule, I am flying back to Europe on Saturday and will not be able to give that workshop after all. I cannot risk leading Louise to Darcey. It's much better that I stay away. She is disappointed, but repeatedly emphasises that she fully understands, and appreciates my letting her know. I promise that I will come back when I can, and I will. I will not go anywhere near Stowe, however, until Louise has been sorted out, one way or another. I will write to Carla and confess my identity as soon as I get home.

Kate and Ian fly home, dispirited, two days before I do. I see them before they leave, but all of us are distracted in our own ways, and I can't even think about telling them about Louise. This is not the moment to mention, in the background to another story, that I have a daughter.

I don't speak to Alexis again, though I hope he will forgive me. I hope Mary O'Rourke overrules whatever he says about me, and at least keeps me on with the label. My career means little to me right now. I would like to live a quiet life, at home (or in Vermont), and ditch the mini-stardom. It would be nice, however, to sell the odd record in America. Perhaps I will look into joining a chamber ensemble, or getting orchestral work. I could even exploit the other facet of my career, and get myself on to a celebrity reality TV programme. The thought makes me shudder. I don't think I want to be a celebrity any more.

On the morning before I leave, Ron and I ride the Staten Island ferry in the sunshine. It is warm and windy, and the sky over Manhattan is blue, with a few wisps of cloud. We stand on the deck and lean on the railings, and watch the skyline receding.

'I've loved it here,' I tell him, 'despite everything.'

He puts an arm over my shoulder. 'I know. And now it's time for you to go home, isn't it?'

'This could become my home.'

'Maybe it will. You've got a lot to sort out.'

'And so have you.'

He turns his head towards me. Our faces are almost touching. 'She rang me,' he says.

I lean my head on his shoulder, and look up at him. 'Anneka? She rang you?'

'This morning.'

I pull away slightly. 'Why didn't you say? That's fantastic news. Is she all right?'

'Yes, I think so. She didn't talk for long. She was pretty wary of me. It turns out that the morning you gave her that letter, she had just discovered that she was pregnant. Our first month of trying! Because of all the problems I

381

see at the clinic, it never occurred to me that it would happen so quickly for us. She was, of course, intrigued by the letter hand-delivered by a girl from an advert. She called Guy as soon as she read it, and he told her everything.

'She believed him. And she was shocked because she thought we'd been honest with each other, and I'd never hinted that anything like that had happened. She didn't know what else I was covering up, and with Guy telling her that I was the lowest of human scum, and a cloner to boot, she panicked about having my child, was convinced I would bring her and the infant to a nasty end, and decided to take a trip.'

'On her own?'

'Guy wanted to fly her to England, but thankfully England has never appealed to her, and she turned him down. Instead – you'll love this – she went to Florida. Where she has been sunning herself and, it seems, suffering from some fairly shocking morning sickness for the past few weeks.'

'But the police were looking for her.'

'And it's very easy not to be found. She used Aurora's passport as airline ID – they look similar enough to get away with it. All anyone ever sees is the golden thatch. Then she paid cash for the hotel. And she stayed on the beach wondering what to do.'

'Poor Anneka.' Poor me, is what I'm thinking. I have missed my chance for a fling. All I wanted was a bit of fun and now he is going to be a father and he won't be able to do anything with me. I am still horribly selfish. 'So,' I say, pulling myself together. 'Did she come to a decision?'

'I think she's decided to talk to me at least. To give me

a chance.' He puts an arm back over my shoulder, and pulls me towards him. 'It's been a strange time, Evie. I'm at a crossroads now. I would have quite a decision on my hands, if it wasn't for the baby. The baby has decided it for me. But you know, I was enjoying being with you. I thought Anneka had left me, full stop, and I was beginning to look forward to new possibilities. Which I realise sounds grotesque, after all these weeks of imagining her body being dragged from the Hudson.'

'Really?' I can't help smiling. Ron and I would never end up together in the long term. It would have been a good boost for both of us. 'I'm kicking myself now for not having my wicked way with you while I could. But you belong with Annie and your baby.'

'Of course I do. I find it hard to believe, though, that a girl as wonderful as you would have been interested in having any sort of way with me. You have your pick of the bunch, surely?'

'I couldn't have got through any of this without you. You found Darcey for me. And you sussed Louise out just in time.'

'Both done out of friendship.'

'You've been a great friend to me.'

'And,' he says, 'there's no reason to stop being friends.'

The wind blows my hair around my face. I know we won't stay in touch. I will never be friends with Ron and Anneka and their baby.

'Look,' says Ron, and points to the other side of the boat. We are coming in to Staten Island.

'Do we get off?' I ask him. 'Or do we just turn round and go straight back?'

'If you wanted, we could go to the zoo and the Botanical Garden. If you really want. The Island is widely regarded as a dump. In fact, literally. Much of New York's waste ends up here.'

I look back across the harbour. 'We should probably go straight back. Get a drink. Then I've got a plane to catch.'

chapter twenty-five

Sunday

I am expecting a subdued homecoming. I plan to head straight to Bristol to warn Mum and Phil about Louise. They will know what to do. I've brought all her letters back with me, so I have the proof, at least, that they exist. I have no proof at all that she wrote them, except for Ron's testimony. Ron says I should have taped her talking about them, but I couldn't have done, because I had no idea. I am beginning to feel relieved that, however poisonous she is, at least those threats were empty. She was only trying to frighten me. There was no deranged *Sun* reader after all, and Guy was never out to get me.

I'm surprised at how happy I am when the plane lands, and the tentative sunshine of Heathrow filters through the clouds. I have ignored my fellow passengers, and watched a film and dozed all the way home. It's easier to sleep in business class. Now I have to sort some things out.

The last thing I expect, as I push my baggage through Customs and out into the stifling atmosphere of the arrivals hall, is to hear someone male calling my name. It startles me, and I look round, smiling, wondering if it could possibly be Phil, if he could be here with Mum to meet me.

One moment, I am weighing up the relative merits of the National Express bus versus the rail-air link to Reading station, and the next I am besieged.

'Evie!' calls a second voice. I am confused. A man in front of me lifts a camera – several people lift cameras – and flashes go off all around. The family that walked through Customs in front of me turn and stare, clearly trying to work out who I am.

'Evie?' shouts a harassed-looking woman. 'Evie, do you have any comment to make on these allegations?'

I recognise the woman. She is one of the *Sun*'s show-biz reporters. She is blonde and tanned and much younger than I am. I stop next to her.

'What allegations?' I ask slowly. People crowd around.

'You've not seen the stories?' she asks, excitedly, and pushes a paper towards me. I glance at the front page. *Evie stole my dead brother's baby.* I have the presence of mind to realise that I don't want to be photographed reading it, so I fold the front page inwards and tuck it behind my handbag, in the top of the trolley. I carry on walking. They turn and follow me, holding cameras up and yelling questions. I glance into WHSmith as I pass, and see my name and face on, it seems, every front page. I can't go and buy them. I wish I had my mobile with me, but there seemed no point in taking it to America when it wouldn't have worked there. I can't stop at a payphone. I can't get on the bus either.

I think of myself dozing in business class while all this was going on. The secret of a lifetime has come out, and I was completely oblivious. Then I remember Kate. Everyone knows my secret now. Kate must see this as an enormous betrayal.

They swarm around me as I stride as confidently as I can towards the taxi rank. A driver takes in my predicament, winks at me, and gets out to open the door for me, insisting that I jump the queue. He loads my bags and my cello in next to me.

'Evie!' they shout. 'Have you had a breakdown? What happened with Letterman? Are you being dropped by your label?'

The driver, who has a chubby, kind face, slams my door, then gets behind the wheel. He turns round and laughs.

'Christ Almighty!' he says, cheerfully. 'What a shower. Where to?'

'Um.' I try to think. 'Would you take me to Bristol? I don't care what it costs, but could I put it on a credit card?'

'Of course, love. Two per cent extra.'

I lean back and exhale. 'That's fine. They're going to follow us, I'm afraid.'

'They can try. They won't be parked at the cab rank so they'll have lost us already.' He looks in his mirror. 'No, you're right, I tell a lie.'

I turn to look through the back window. Four cabs are pulling away, directly behind us. The travellers in the taxi queue look bewildered (foreign) and irritated (British). They have just had their cabs stolen by tabloid journalists.

I read the *Sun*, and wonder how much Louise was paid for her twisted concoction of half-truths. She has told them everything she told me. I remember how calm she was. She must have been extremely plausible. At least they haven't mentioned Tessa by name. Every word of Louise's accusations has been legally approved, and it is carefully framed so that the central charge is not quite made. Mum and Phil's house must have been surrounded for hours.

The driver, who is called Frank, tells me what he has heard about my story.

'You're supposed to have seduced her brother then had the baby adopted without telling him,' he informs me jovially. 'Then he committed suicide because he didn't have access to his kid.'

I stare at him in the mirror. 'Did anyone say how old I was when this happened?'

'No, I don't think so. Couple of years ago, was it?'

'I was fifteen! The bitch. She's twisted this to fit the tabloid agenda. I was below the age of consent!'

'Nah, haven't heard that, love. You might like to get that straight as soon as you can. And what about your husband?'

'Jack?' I haven't thought about him for days. 'What about him?'

'It said on the radio that he's getting married again. But his bird seems to have had a nice chat to one of your favourite papers about you. Said you were a nightmare, always ringing him up and making him come rushing over to see you. Said he even left her to go to America for you, and when he got there you told him to piss off.'

I slump in my seat. 'Was her name Sophia?'

'That's the one.'

'Great.'

'Sorry. Don't mean to be a downer on you. I think we've shaken one of them off, if that makes you feel any better.'

I look out of the window at the M4. Cars are streaming towards the West Country. The land round here is flat and dull. The sunshine is watery. I can't wait to get to Clifton. To get home.

'Frank?' I ask, after five miles have passed. 'If I gave you some money, would you let me use your phone?'

He passes it through the screen without turning round. 'It's pay-as-you-go. Just give me whatever you use. Help yourself.'

We pull up outside the house. Frank and I have prepared my exit, and Mum should be standing on the other side of the front door, ready to let me in.

He screeches to an abrupt halt. 'Go!' he cries.

I open the door and run up the garden path, holding only my handbag. The door opens and I rush in. Taylor slams it behind me, and Mum takes me by the hand and leads me into the kitchen. The shutters at the dining room window are closed, and even the kitchen blind is down. I have never seen it down in my life.

'Sit down,' she orders. I obey.

'Where's Tess?' I ask her.

'Staying with her friend Ally. We're hoping that they won't go after her on her own, and so far it seems to be working.'

'Does she have any idea what this is about?'

Mum sits next to me. 'Does anyone? You tell me.'

I play for time. 'Where are Megan and Josie?'

'Gone out the back way for provisions.'

'Over the wall?'

'They were giggling like schoolgirls. Good to see someone happy.'

Frank and Taylor come in, with my bags and cello.

'Here you are, love,' Frank says, cheerily. 'Back up the M4, then, for me. If you give me your credit card I'll call it through from here, if I can.'

I hand it to him. I don't even ask how much I owe him. He rings his office and they take the payment. I don't have any sterling, so I give him a hundred-dollar bill, an absurd tip, and four pound coins from the side pocket of my handbag to cover my use of his mobile. He gives me a pat on the back and wishes me well.

As the door opens to let him out, I hear a small commotion outside. I wonder if Frank is being offered money to talk about me.

'They'll get bored,' I say hopefully.

'Not until you set them straight.'

I put my head on my arms on the table. 'I know.' I look up. 'Mum,' I tell her. 'It's been Louise, all along.'

Together we formulate a strategy. I am going to have to speak to a friendly journalist and put the truth across. They are desperate to get to me – notes come through the door all day long – but I don't want to invite somebody in from the doorstep. The only person I can think of to talk to is Jane from the *Mail*. The *Mail*, however, bought Sophia's story, so I am loath to speak to them.

'Have you talked to Jack yet?' Mum asks, at one point.

'No.' I remember the rain on my face, the hairs on my legs standing up from the cold. I remember the excitement on Jack's face as he told me about the new life he had planned for us. I remember how easily I crushed him. I remember walking away, and hearing him running behind me, then stopping. I can't blame him for going straight back to Sophia. I imagine she will treat him properly. She will be a far better wife than I ever was.

I dial his mobile number. He answers on the fourth ring.

'Anna? Phil?' he asks warily.

''Fraid not,' I tell him.

'Just a second.' I hear rustling, a door closing. 'That's better. Evie? What the fuck is going on? Who's Louise Parker, and what the hell is she talking about?'

'She's talking a load of crap.'

'Because I may be unobservant sometimes, I may be a complete mug, but I think I might have noticed if you'd had this girl's brother's baby while we were married.'

'You never noticed a thing, did you? So gullible. Of course that's crap. It's a very long story, but it turns out that she was the one who wrote me all those letters.'

'Are you going to sue her arse off?'

'I doubt it. I'll tell you the whole story. It'll surprise you, I'm afraid.' I pause. 'How's Sexy Sophia?' I use her tabloid moniker. 'I hear congratulations are in order.'

He sighs. 'Yes. She's fine. I told her not to go to the papers, but she's kind of angry with you on my behalf.'

'I don't blame her.'

'And she wanted to raise her profile. It was a good opportunity for her.' He sounds weary. I pity Jack, caught between two ambitious women.

'Right. I'm sorry about Central Park, Jack. I was a bitch. All along, really. I know it and I'm sorry and . . .' I draw a deep breath and force myself to be nice. 'I hope you and Sophia will be very happy together.'

He is brusque. 'Thanks.'

'I suppose we're getting divorced, then, if you're getting married?'

He sounds embarrassed. He even gives a little cough before he answers. 'You know this is not what I would ever have chosen, but yes, it's clear that our relationship has no future, so we'd better get divorced. I know where I am with Sophia. My solicitor says it's best if you divorce me for adultery. Then everything can happen within months. Is that OK?'

I'm divorcing him for adultery. That doesn't sound in the least bit fair.

'It's sad, Jack. It's very, very sad. I'm sorry I instigated it. God.' I am surprised at how desolate I feel. I know this is inevitable, and yet I am not prepared for it. 'We were happy, weren't we?'

'You tell me. I thought we were happy. Why, Evie? Why did you walk away from me like that? I was . . .' His voice tails off. 'Gutted, I suppose you could say.'

'You're much better off this way.'

'I know. I think I'm someone who's only really happy in a stable relationship.'

'I think you are too. Good luck.'

'Whatever. So it was a woman writing to you all along. Not an old pervert in a dirty mac. She's an old school friend, is that right?'

'She's an old school enemy. Jack, I'm afraid I'm going to have to tell you something. I never told you this for the whole of our marriage.'

'We're still married.'

'I've never told anyone except the people who knew about it at the time.' And Ron Thomas, I add mentally. 'But unfortunately I now have to tell the press before they crucify me still further.'

I tell him about Elizabeth, but I leave out everything about her becoming Darcey. I am dying to finish the story, to tell him that I met her a week ago, and I wouldn't hesitate to fill him in on everything, but for the fact that he would tell Sophia and she would tell the press. He is shocked that I had so huge a secret. By the time I finish, he is definitely feeling better about forcing the divorce upon me.

'And Jack?' I say, before hanging up.

'Mmm?'

'Tell your fiancée that it would have been more dignified to maintain a wall of silence.'

'Yeah. I know. She's just got a part in *The Bill* so she thought it would be good.'

I laugh. 'Sophia's in *The Bill*? Are you a serial minor-celeb monogamist?'

He hangs up on me, and I don't blame him.

The moment the phone is back on its cradle, I burst into tears. Mum looks as if she's about to ask me what's wrong, but wisely thinks better of it, and hugs me instead.

'You can't let it all catch up with you now,' she warns. 'You need to sort this out so at least they know to leave Tessa out of it.'

I sniff and nod. 'Mum, there's something else. The most amazing thing. I met her.'

'You met . . .'

'She's called Darcey now. She looks like me. She's my baby and I met her.'

Mum smiles, but warily. 'How did you . . .? But never mind that now. Does it make you feel better?'

I wipe my eyes on the proffered handkerchief. 'So much better. Better for seeing her, and, now, very, very glad that she has no idea who I am. She has a lovely life. It's amazing. I would have chosen that family for her, out of everybody in America. I'm going to write to her mother and tell her who I am, once all this has died down.' I look at Mum, still teary. 'When I saw her I thought I was going to die. I've never had to control myself like that. But now I feel OK. She's better off there than she is here right now. If she does want to contact me when she's older, at least her mother will know where to find me.'

It is an effort to say all this, because in spite of everything I wish Darcey was with me now. I would give anything to have her by my side.

'Brave girl,' says Mum, stroking my arm.

We are interrupted by a frantic banging on the back door. Taylor lopes past us and stations himself firmly in the doorway before he opens it. Megan and Josie rush in, laughing. I don't think I've seen Josie smile before. She has always been tense. Now she looks relaxed.

Megan stands still when she sees me. 'Evie!' she screams, holding her arms wide. 'You're back! Welcome to the madhouse.' She turns to Mum. 'No offence. It's not the house that's mad, you know that.'

Megan looks lovely. Her hair is pulled back into a

ponytail, and she's dressed casually, without make-up. She looks happier than I have ever seen her before.

'Of course I do,' Mum assures her. 'You both seem a little hyper. Were you chased?'

'Not by the press. Some woman saw us climbing over the back wall and started yelling.'

Josie joins in. 'We should have stopped to explain to her, but we were halfway over by then, so we just laughed and carried on. I imagine she's called the police.'

I smile, and Josie smiles back, briefly, before looking away. She seems uncomfortable with me, as ever. Last time we met she was with an abusive husband, living the life of a well-to-do Somerset woman, and I was fleeing Louise's letters. Both of us were terrified, in different ways. Now she is my mother's lodger, and I have the press encamped outside.

'Nice to see you, Josie,' I tell her.

She smiles shyly, and perhaps slightly mockingly. 'You too.'

I ask Taylor to call the *Daily Mail*, and I grit my teeth and prepare myself to sell out. I'll give the money to charity. He manages to tempt Jane to the phone, eventually, by saying, mysteriously, 'someone she really, really wants to talk to' every time he is asked who is calling, and by refusing to leave a message. I knew she wouldn't resist it if he said that enough times.

'That Jane, then?' he says eventually, and my heart starts pounding. 'Would you like to speak to Evie?'

He nods and holds out the phone to me.

I draw a deep breath and screw my eyes tight shut.

'Jane?' I say, in my professional, fake voice. 'I don't suppose you'd be interested in an interview?'

I know, by now, that I hold all the cards, that she wants what I have more than I want to give it to her, so I make her come to Bristol to see me. She is sugary and sympathetic and tries to entice me to London by offering lunch at the Savoy, 'or anywhere else you'd really, really love to go. *Sketch?* Really, Evie, you name it.' I nearly laugh as I explain to her that I am not in the mood to relish the sampling of new gastronomic delights. She must think I am terribly shallow if she calculated that glitzy restaurants were the way to get me to agree to save her the drive.

'Come to my mum's house,' I instruct her firmly. 'I'll give you the address.'

'No need,' she assures me breezily. 'Got it. Thank you, Evie. You are doing the right thing.'

I'm doing the only thing I can think of. I take her to the upstairs sitting room, and sit her down with a glass of wine and a plate of biscuits. I carefully drink a cup of peppermint tea, because I cannot afford to misplace a single word. Jane has clearly come straight from the office without having time to preen herself. Her hair is less helmet-like than before, and she has obviously applied a new coat of fuchsia lipstick hurriedly, probably just before getting out of her car, because when she drinks her wine, she leaves imprints of the creases of her lips around the glass. I wonder whether to tell her she has lipstick on her teeth. She is wearing a pair of wide black trousers and a grey top, and I know that if she'd had time to go home and change, she would have dressed up. I think she looks nicer like this, apart from the stray lipstick.

'So, Evie,' she says softly, as she places her tape recorder on the coffee table and turns it on. 'You're used to these, I know. This must be a terribly hard time for you and I do sympathise with what you're going through.'

She looks at me with a half-smile, her mouth turned down at the corners so I know she's not actively happy about my situation. She is, though. She has got the exclusive interview, and she can barely contain her joy.

'Thank you,' I say, hating her and myself.

'This is a wonderful opportunity for you to put your own side of what happened. Shall we go back to the question of the unwanted baby?'

I surprise myself with the vehemence of my reaction. 'She's not unwanted!' I say sharply. 'I would never want her to think that I didn't love her or that I haven't thought about her. I was fifteen, Jane. It's hard to make those decisions when you're fifteen.'

She is surprised. 'You were fifteen?'

'I know. Louise kept that a little bit hazy, didn't she?'

'I believe she said you were eighteen. How long have you known Louise?'

I describe what really happened. Although I leave out everything about Ron and about finding Darcey, I tell her all about going to America to give birth, about Louise letting the whole school know what had happened, and about the fact that I'd never told Mark that he had become a father.

'I thought Louise might tell him,' I explain. 'Which would have been fine. I didn't exactly have an ongoing relationship with him. To be honest, I couldn't even look him in the eye. I never told my family who the father was because he wasn't a part of my life. And,' I remember, 'because I didn't want to get him into trouble.'

'You were below the age of consent,' she says thoughtfully.

'I was. And he was seventeen, I think, at the time.'

'So you were shielding him.'

I nod, emphatically. 'Yes.'

'Evie, this is great. It must be horrendous for you to have to relive it now.'

I shake my head. 'I've always been reliving it. A child, you know, Jane, is not something you can forget about. I hope I might meet her when she's old enough to trace me. I've already filled out a form for the New York Adoption Registry, but I can't actually register there until she's eighteen. I plan to do it on her birthday. That way, as soon as she wants to look for me, she'll be able to find me.' I don't mention any of the real story. 'I hope that she'll understand why I did what I did. I would love to become a part of her life.' I blink back tears. For once, I am not being fake.

Jane nods approvingly. Everything I am saying fits in with her paper's conservative ethos. This story is a gift to her. 'So the speculation that Tessa is your daughter . . . ?' she asks. 'You understand, I just have to clarify that point, in your own words.'

'Of course. That is not speculation, it is a lie spread by Louise. You can work out the dates. Tessa's too young.' I take a piece of paper from the arm of my chair and pass it to her. 'Here's her birth certificate. It's got my mum's name on it, and Phil's, because they are her parents. If you really want to, I'm sure that, if I ask her to talk to you, the headmistress of my old school will confirm when it was that I went to America. She knew about it.'

'Thanks, Evie. I would like to speak to her, because the more people we bring in to back you up, the less it looks like your word against Louise's, and the more it becomes a case of setting the record straight.'

'Right,' I agree. 'Fine. Now, there's something else that we haven't covered yet. Louise has been writing letters to me. I've got some of the recent ones here, and I'll be taking them all to the police when you've seen them. You can copy them if you'd like to. I can run them off for you on the fax machine here.'

I sit back and watch Jane's face light up as she reads them. This is it. This is the last time I do something like this. From now on, I withdraw from the public eye. I have finished with insincerity.

epilogue

October

The heat of the day is fading, as we reconvene on the beach for early evening beers. I'm still wearing my bikini and sarong from the day's sunbathing, but Kate and Megan have changed into proper clothes. Ian is in long shorts and a T-shirt. Kate, Ian and I are just golden enough to feel we are properly on holiday now. We have relaxed. Megan has been travelling for two months, to date, and was tanned and laid-back long before she came to southern Thailand to meet us. In fact, I think coming to meet us made her a little uncomfortable, reminded her of things she had managed to forget, but she has settled down with us now.

We move a little way away from the bar, and sit down on the sand, the four of us. Then we stare out to sea. There is a soft breeze that blows sand on to us, but it's gentle, not harsh like it was yesterday.

'I haven't been on holiday since I left university,' I realise. 'This is the first time I've been anywhere, except

Stowe, without my cello. It even came on honeymoon with us.'

Kate laughs. 'Can the rest of them manage without you for these two weeks? Won't you go back and be crap?'

'No, I won't go back and be crap,' I tell her indignantly. 'Well, I probably will, but I'll get back on form. I've barely joined the quartet officially anyway. We haven't got a concert till the beginning of December.'

'Isn't it odd for you,' asks Megan, 'to be playing the fourth part, after all those years of being the star?'

I lie back and let the sand go in my hair. 'It's bliss,' I tell her, looking happily at the blue sky. 'I'm not interested in stardom any more. I was trying to prove myself all those years. I knew I wasn't a natural. Playing with the quartet is an enormous release. Nobody is pressurising me to make a pop record, which is what I was supposed to be doing next. I'm actually only realising now how unhappy I was before. Working with other people makes it different. You know, I have to turn up on time, work for the same hours as they do, all of that. It's a bit more like having a proper job.'

'And yet,' Ian reminds me, 'it's not like having a proper job at all.'

'Of course it's not. You wouldn't catch the string quartet giving me two weeks off to come to Thailand and adopt a baby.'

'They would,' he objects.

'Well yes,' I agree, 'they would, but they wouldn't pay me for it. Your work are amazing.'

Kate stretches out her brown legs. 'Our companies have been great. We had all that time off when we went to

America. And there's going to be some toing and froing in the coming months, I guess. We've been very lucky that they've put up with it. I'll give up work altogether once we've got him home.'

Megan puts her glass down. 'He is absolutely *adorable*, you know.'

Kate laughs. 'Preaching to the converted.'

'Are you going to give him a new name?'

This is Kate's favourite topic. 'We were completely set on Alfie,' she says seriously, 'until we saw him again today, weren't we?'

Ian nods. 'But the name he's got kind of suits him, don't you think? Chet. It's very him. So we might keep that.'

'Chet,' I tell them, 'is gorgeous. And it's his name. You have to keep it. Will you use Alfie as a middle name?'

'Probably not,' says Kate. 'I don't think Chet Alfie Dawson sounds right. We might go for something with a bit more substance. Chet Dawson sounds great, though, don't you think? I can see him as a musician.'

'I'll teach him the cello,' I volunteer immediately. Chet is nearly a year old, a tiny little boy with huge brown eyes and an infectious giggle. The adoption is all but finalised now, and bringing him into the UK looks like being the longest piece of bureaucracy in the process. Kate and Ian will be parents in the foreseeable future. For the first time, we can say that with certainty.

'How about you?' Ian asks, looking at me curiously. 'Us going on about adoption all the time doesn't upset you, does it? I've got no idea if it's one of those things we should be super-sensitive about or not.'

'Not,' I tell him firmly. 'Definitely not. I'm fine. Now

that I know that Darcey's happy and healthy and secure, and since Carla keeps me vaguely up to date with the occasional email, I don't have a problem at all. Of course I can't stop imagining how our lives would have been if I'd kept her, but I don't necessarily think things would have turned out for the best if I had. God only knows what Louise would have done. Kidnapped her, probably. So all in all, she's best off where she is.'

I sit up, and look at them. They are all watching me with concerned expressions.

'I know,' I tell them. 'I don't necessarily mean that completely, but in my head I know it's right. Can you see me with a fifteen-year-old daughter?'

'You'd be mistaken for sisters the whole time,' Ian points out.

'You will be,' Kate says firmly, 'when she's eighteen and you start seeing each other regularly. People will be amazed that you're her mother.'

'I'm amazed that I'm her mother. She will be, too.'

Megan sips her drink. She is halfway down her glass, while the rest of us have almost finished. 'At least you'll be safe from Louise now,' she says confidently. 'If she comes anywhere near you, you can get the police to cart her off.'

'I hope so. I know there's a restraining order, but I have no idea how effective it's actually going to be. She's sneaky.'

'Sneaky,' Ian agrees, 'but she's also on bail. And she knows that Tessa really isn't Darcey, so she probably hasn't got that impetus any more.'

'Of course she hasn't,' says Kate, firmly. She sits up.

'Look, Evie,' she says. 'There's something I want to tell you. We haven't been sure whether to say anything or not, but what the hell.'

'Mmm?' I'm not concentrating. I'm watching some distant swimmers in the warm shallow water, and contemplating one more dip before dinner.

'I always knew you had a baby.'

I smile, not believing her. 'What do you mean?'

'I mean, I lived in Bristol. I knew people at your school. Before I'd even met you I'd been told that a girl was coming to college who'd had a baby the year before. At first I waited for you to tell me, then I realised you weren't going to, and before long it didn't matter any more.'

I stare at her. I know that I have to explain. 'I wanted to tell you,' I say quietly. 'But I didn't tell anyone. I don't know why it was such a shameful secret, because it seems completely natural to talk about it now. Darcey's a part of me, and I'm proud of her.'

Ian butts in. 'I can see you don't really want to share something like that with people who are going through fertility troubles.'

'It just got worse and worse. When you had your miscarriage I thought I'd never be able to tell you.' I look at Ian. 'So you knew too?'

'Of course Kate told me. We thought Jack knew. It took a while before I twigged that he didn't. I could so easily have said something, but luckily I hadn't.'

I stare at Kate again. 'You've known about Darcey ever since you met me?'

She laughs and drains her drink. ''Fraid so. But how could you think I wouldn't want to be your friend because of that? Even when we were at our lowest, with the miscarriage, I never blamed you. You hardly did it to spite me, did you? I just felt, sometimes, that everywhere we went we were surrounded by the ghosts of absent children. You didn't have your baby any more than I had mine, and I knew how hard that was. I did wish, sometimes, that you had felt able to talk about it.'

I look at her. She wouldn't have been able to say any of that a couple of months ago.

'And now you've got one,' I tell her.

'I will do. And you will have your daughter.'

Megan looks at her watch. 'Right,' she says, putting her glass in the sand with an inch of beer still in the bottom. 'I'm off. Meeting Jonas at seven. See you later.'

Jonas is Meg's current backpacker boyfriend. Since she discovered the joys of the younger man, Meg has become more outgoing, far more confident, and happier than I ever imagined her. Guy is still in Bristol, but she hasn't seen him since we got back from America, despite his weak suggestion that they try to 'patch things up'. I have avoided him, when I've been staying with Mum and Phil, but I've been spending most of my time in London, where, suddenly, I feel at home again. Louise is out of my life for ever, and there never was a shadowy man waiting to rape me. I don't feel threatened any more. I have rented my own flat and I am happy there. It is strange to be living without my barriers, to be presenting my real face to the world, but I am getting used to it.

Although I will earn a lot less now that I'm a string quartet player and occasional solo artist, I have enough in the bank to put a substantial deposit on a flat, and when we get back I'm going to start looking in earnest. Howard and Sonia are coming over to visit at Christmas, and Carla has promised to send Darcey to see me, if she wants to come, as soon as she is eighteen.

I put down my bottle. 'Right,' I announce to Kate and Ian. 'I don't know about you guys, but I can't think of a nicer way to celebrate than by getting drunk.'

I see them looking at each other, just a little bit uneasily.

If you have enjoyed Atlantic Shift, you may enjoy the following titles also available from your bookshop or *direct from the publisher*.

FREE P&P AND UK DELIVERY
(Overseas and Ireland £3.50 per book)

Cuban Heels	Emily Barr	£6.99
Baggage	Emily Barr	£6.99
Backpack	Emily Barr	£7.99
A Married Man	Catherine Alliott	£6.99
Olivia's Luck	Catherine Alliott	£6.99
Dancing in a Distant Place	Isla Dewar	£7.99
The Woman Who Painted Her Dreams	Isla Dewar	£7.99
Play It Again?	Julie Highmore	£6.99
Pure Fiction	Julie Highmore	£6.99
Azur Like It	Wendy Holden	£6.99
Fame Fatale	Wendy Holden	£6.99
The Distance Between Us	Maggie O'Farrell	£7.99
My Lover's Lover	Maggie O'Farrell	£7.99

TO ORDER SIMPLY CALL THIS NUMBER

01235 400 414

or visit our website: www.madaboutbooks.com

Prices and availability subject to change without notice.